İSKENDER P

İskender Pala was born in Uşak ir dergraduate degree from the facı University in 1979. He received ... Divan Literature from the same university in 1983. His short stories, essays, academic papers and newspaper columns have inspired his readers to see Divan literature in a new light; his Ottoman Literature seminars are widely attended. İskender Pala is revered for his love of Divan poetry. He is the recipient of the Turkish Writer's Association Prize (1989), The Turkish Language Foundation AKDTYK prize (1990) and the Turkish Writer's Association Essay Prize (1996). He was given the title 'The People's Poet' by popular vote in Uşak. His books *Death in Babylon, Love in Istanbul*; *Katre-i Matem* and *The King and the Sultan, Od and Mihmandar* have won numerous literary awards and enjoy a wide readership. Honoring his success, The Turkish Patent Institute has registered İskender Pala as a brand name. He was granted the 2013 Presidential Culture and Arts Grand Award in literature. İskender Pala is married with three children and teaches at Kültür University.

www.iskenderpala.com

RUTH WHITEHOUSE

Ruth Whitehouse was a professional violinist before completing a PhD in Modern Turkish Literature at the School of Oriental and African Studies in London. She participated in the Cunda International Workshop for Translators of Turkish Literature in Turkey (2009-2012) and the Royal Court International Residency for Emerging Playwrights in London (2010). Her published translations include: *Ali and Ramazan* by Perihan Mağden (Amazon Crossings, 2012), *The Last Tram* by Nedim Gürsel (Comma Press, 2011), *Hotel Bosphorus and Bakhsheesh* by Esmahan Akyol (Bitter Lemon Press, 2011 and 2012 respectively) and a number of short stories in different anthologies.

Publication No. 437
The Complete Works of İskender Pala 64

Tulip Of İstanbul
Original Title: Katre-i Matem
İskender Pala

Translated by Ruth Whitehouse

Cover Design by Utku Lomlu
Page Layout by M. Atahan Sıralar

1. Edition: October 2014
ISBN: 978-605-5107-81-9
Certificate No: 10905

KAPI PUBLICATIONS
Ticarethane Sokak No: 15 Cağaloğlu/ISTANBUL
Tel: +90 (212) 513 34 20-21 Fax: +90 (212) 512 33 76
e-mail: bilgi@kapiyayinlari.com
www.kapiyayinlari.com

Printed by Melisa Matbaacılık
Certificate No: 12088
Çiftehavuzlar Yolu Acar Sanayi Sitesi No: 8
Tel: +90 (0212) 674 97 23 Fax: +90 (0212) 674 97 29
KAPI is a trademark of the ALFA Publishing Group.

TULIP OF İSTANBUL

İskender Pala

Translated from the Turkish by Ruth Whitehouse

kapı

PREFACE

Within a few moments of seeing the sign about an "Auction of Stamp Collections and Old Books" outside Istanbul's Marmara Hotel, I was following the arrow into the hotel conference room. It was unusual for me to act so decisively, especially since I had neither seen the catalogue nor made a reservation to attend the auction. The simple reason was that I was extremely cold and thought a glass of hot tea might warm me up. There was also the possibility that I would see some familiar faces and be able to do a bit of networking.

For years, I had been holding public seminars under the heading "Divan Poetry Hour" at six o'clock every Wednesday evening. That particular day, the discussion had strayed somewhat from poetry and I found myself having to discuss the idea that those who dismiss the importance of anything, in reality consider everything to be important. I had been wandering around Beyoğlu on my own, pondering the questions that had arisen during the seminar, with a blizzard raging around me and a biting wind whistling past my ears and stinging my eyes.

The auction room was bustling with people, many of them well-known collectors. After a few friendly greetings, I went to look at the books on sale. About half of them were hand-written works, so I asked for a catalogue to see if any might be useful for my work. The auction started and I prayed that none of the important volumes would be sold. The very idea of a hand-written book being sold to a bidder who could not read Ottoman Turkish distressed me as much as the thought of a beautiful courtesan being delivered into the hands of an uncouth stranger. No sooner had I started looking at the catalogue than I heard the auctioneer call out, "In batch twenty-eight, we present a wonderful collection of poetry!" Of course, at such auctions the word 'wonderful' tends to lose all value; nevertheless I headed towards the man at the lectern, senses fully alert, my ears intent on what he was about to say and my eyes fixed on the hand-written volume he was holding. The auctioneer launched into promoting the book, which he was obviously determined to sell.

"This book contains excerpts from Genceli Nizami's *Hüsrev and Şirin*, Fuzuli of Baghdad's *Leyla and Majnun*, and Yazıcıoğlu Mehmed's famous *Muhammediye*. In addition, it has the whole of Hamdullah Hamdi's *Treatise on Physiognomy*, the best poems from the *Divan of Yunus the Mystic* and famous quotes from the ballads of Karacaoğlan and Gevheri".

That was enough to whet my appetite. The book he was holding not only contained *mesnevi* and *divan* selections written for the pleasure of aristocrats, but also an Anatolian doctrine entitled *Muhammediye*, some fine examples of Yunus's mystical poetry and also rural folk poetry. It was an extraordinary anthology and I was curious to find out more about the person who had compiled it and why. According to the auctioneer, the book also contained excerpts from *Revelations of the Bards*, *The Manual of Islamic Faith, Worship and Ethics*, and various letters and stories from Veysi's *Collected Papers*. My interest was now uncontrollable. Fortunately, the other bidders were mainly interested in the appearance and condition of covers and any miniatures that the books contained rather than their literary content. This particular book contained no miniatures and its cover, though both marbled and gilded, was torn and creased. Even I had to admit that the book did not look to be worth much, which was perhaps why, after my third bid, I became its proud owner.

It was dark and still snowing but the wind had eased when I left the hotel an hour later. Having surrendered to a personal passion, I could not wait to get home and, once on the ferry to Scutari, I started leafing excitedly through the pages. I remember clearly how romantic and beautiful the Bosphorus looked that night with the snow falling simultaneously over Europe and Asia. To me, the cultural treasure in my hands was equally beautiful. I opened the book at random on a page with a humorous and somewhat lewd tale by Mehmet Gazali and was unable to contain my laughter. I noticed some heads turn to look at me. The people around me looked exhausted, with no thought but to reach home as soon as possible. They probably felt sorry for me and found it strange to see my interest in the book, in the dim light of that rolling boat on such a wintry night. Perhaps some of them saw the Arabic script and silently rebuked me, thinking, "How can that man laugh while reading the Koran? God forgive him!"

When I reached home, I ignored the howling wind and the snow beating on the window and impatiently searched each chapter heading for a clue as to who had compiled such a rich corpus of works. Each of the fifteen- to twenty-page *Mesneve* excerpts and the Yunus poems had been beautifully calligraphed by the same scribe, but with many errors. The prose sections seemed to have been written by the book's original owner. What sort of person would he or she have been? There were also footnotes, barely legible, in the corners of some pages in the same handwriting. The exquisite cover was falling to bits and the rosette embossed on the front was defaced and in need of repair.

But I digress...

The last and longest section of my book consisted of the story I am about to relate to you. The title immediately caught my interest. It was *One Murder, Sixty-six Questions* and was written in red ink with intricately decorated titles. I poured myself some tea and started reading. Within minutes, I was transported into another world.

In what seemed no time at all, I found that it was morning and I was shivering with cold. I was only half way through, yet my mind was completely caught up with intrigues, murders and tulip colours. I had, of course, already decided to publish the story.

Despite extensive research, I was unable to find another copy of the story in any library. All my efforts to discover who had written it reached a dead end. Although there is a personal note in the prologue, it does not reveal the author's identity. By the time I had read to the end, I could understand why. In fact, unlike most Ottoman works, this book contained not a single reference to the author, calligraphist, binder, painter, dedicatee or publisher. Maybe, one day the annals of history will reveal to us who they were. Undoubtedly, researchers will come across the name of the author and perhaps even find another copy of the tale I am about to relate to you and say that a part of Ottoman history needs to be re-written. However, until that time, it is I who will be telling you this story and you will regard me as its author.

I have lived a happy and fortunate life, filled with love and affection, poetry, roses and hyacinths, so it was not a little disturbing for me when transcribing this book into Latin script suddenly to encounter sickening crimes by merciless gangs, tyrannical plunderers and revolutionary mobs. I have to confess that the lines which gave me most pleasure during this work were in the postscripts about love that appeared at the end of some chapters. These postscripts add to the main story by providing a flavour of the deep passions that prevailed in those days. The illustrations that appear in this publication are photographic reproductions of Orientalist gravures.

The first paragraph of the story is repeated in a later chapter of the book. These lines were left incomplete in the original, which suggests to me that the author began the story at another point and then changed his mind. I have remained faithful to the author's original text, so you will find that some chapters are very short while others are quite long.

Needless to say, I have updated the language of the Tulip Period in which this tale was originally written.

And now, it is time to leave you alone to read the story.

PROLOGUE

As I dip my pen into the inkwell – two weeks after the October revolution which was marked by Sultan Ahmet III being deposed and his son-in-law Grand Vizier İbrahim Pasha of Nevşehir being slain – I am undecided as to whether or not I should write about the events to which I have been witness. I feel an obligation to write about certain matters, but the idea of possibly committing the treasonous crime of disclosing state secrets weighs heavily on my conscience. I might also be accused of interfering with perceived views on the tulip, that sacred flower of the East, and cause offence to the horticultural community. However, it would be an injustice to history and to the city of Istanbul if nobody were ever to tell the story of Prince Ahmet and the dastardly deeds of the insurrectionists, or describe the supreme elegance of this heavenly city and the tulips of Sadabat. I therefore find myself compelled to undertake this challenging task.

I shall attempt to contain everything that happened within sixty-six chapters. As I am sure you know, the word *lale,* meaning tulip, represents the number sixty-six in the ancient *abjad* writing system. I have no doubt that I will be risking not only my reputation but also my personal safety by revealing the tragic events that took place in Istanbul, our beautiful city, which rests so gracefully on two continents in the embrace of two seas. However, the truth must not remain concealed. It is one of God's mysteries that everything is revealed in time, as a poet once said. What is the point of writing the truth if it is never read?

But I might yet tear this up and throw it away!

Who am I?

That is of no consequence.

PART 1

EXPOSITION: ONE MURDER AND SIXTY-SIX QUESTIONS

(October 1729)

This story has two heroes, as is the convention.

QUESTION 1
IS THERE NO LIMIT TO SELF SACRIFICE?

"Children of Layhar! This is your home. Yours, not mine. You are all brothers. Those with two parents have been known to cut each other's throats, but the children of Layhar, who know neither father nor mother, see themselves as one and the same. The pain of a needle piercing the flesh of one is felt by his brother as if it were his own. Those who don this robe regard each other as equal in life until death. It is union within a duality. He is your right hand, you are his left. Two sides of one. One body, two heads. You watch out and care for each other all your life. Here, there is no 'mine' and no 'yours'. If there is little, it is made to go far; if there is plenty, it nourishes you all. There is one pot that feeds all, by the grace of God!"

This was the twinning ceremony for two new arrivals at the Gedikpaşa Hamam stokehouse. Two youths, one a fourteen-year-old and the other about ten years older, were standing in the flickering light of a three-armed candelabrum, waiting to be twinned as brothers. Chef, who looked after everything at the stokehouse, brought in the Layhar robe with its two collars and two sleeves. The Foreman then gently stripped the two recruits naked and dressed them in the robe, using the right sleeve for one and the left sleeve for the other so that they appeared as a single figure with two heads and two hands. The clothes they had been wearing on arrival were immediately sent off to be sold at the flea market and any proceeds handed to the Foreman. Stokehouse Baba then turned towards the furnace and recited a prayer, to which the youths, who only knew the Fatiha, the first verse of the Koran, responded, "Amen". This was followed by a feast consisting of pilaf and halva which had been made with ingredients collected from the market by the two brothers now wearing the robe. For three days, dressed only in dirty, ragged undergarments, they had been sent out by Stokehouse Baba to beg with sacks on their backs.

"Feel no shame. Don't be put off if you are thrown out of shops," Stokehouse Baba had said, "Try to avoid getting beaten up but don't be afraid to answer back. If they don't give you what you ask, then ask again. If they still give you nothing, keep asking. Wherever you are, whatever time of day and whatever is happening, just keep asking. Whinge, plead, hang around those shops like flies and don't give up. If anyone gives you grief, play dirty. Go and pester the customers. If they look disgusted, pester them more."

The banquet that day was lavish and the other stokers were rejoicing in the belief that these new 'gentlemen' would be beneficial to the stokehouse, or at any rate lighten their workload and therefore give them more time for pleasure. The new brothers had now been stripped of the Layhar robe and were serving the others semi-naked. Whenever anyone yelled out, "I'm parched, brother!" they would pour him wine from an ice-cold pitcher and serve him with pilaf and halva. "To Sultan Layhar!" they all cried, and drank the 'rooster's blood' as confirmation of their covenant.

"Nobody ever refuses to obey an order here," warned Stokehouse Baba. "Even were we to carve your flesh for *meze* to accompany our wine or for preparing kebabs, you would submit and say nothing. Agreed?"

"Yes, Baba, of course, Baba!"

QUESTION 2
HOW DO YOU FEEL WHEN YOU LOSE WHAT YOU HAVE JUST FOUND?

The scent of philadelphus and sweet basil permeated the mild evening breeze as the couple embraced in their marital bliss. The young man trembled as his beloved's ringlets touched his cheek for the first time.

"Do you see that light?" he asked.

"You mean the light that never goes out?"

"Yes, I do! Just as you remain alight in my heart."

"Will I be a light in your heart for ever?" she asked, her eyes welling up with tears.

The maiden trembled as her beloved's hand touched hers for the first time.

"Do you like tulips?" she asked.

"You mean tulips that are the colour of your cheeks?"

"No, I mean tulips that are the colour of my love: purple tulips!"

With delicate fingers, she placed a tulip bulb into the hands of the young man. It was a twin bulb, like two bodies embracing.

A tear rolled down her cheek.

At that moment, she was totally unaware of being drawn away by the full moon and tides. How could she have known?

She was like a secret treasure trove of pearls. When people spoke of beautiful nymphs in Paradise, they might have been describing her, with her black eyebrows, dark eyes fringed with long eyelashes, pure white skin, tall slender figure and swan-like neck, the braided hair that tumbled down her back, and her gentle demeanour.

She wept with happiness as she nestled in the arms of the young man, who embraced her even more tightly as he answered her question. In the distance, the sound of owls could be heard and heavenly lights lit up the night sky.

All night, the young man gazed into her face with an ardour that belied the coolness of autumn, sometimes marvelling at the grace in her eyes, sometimes weeping at the innocence of her cheeks.

"Nakşıgül, my treasure," he murmured. "Nakşıgül, you are my fate and my fortune. Nakşıgül, you are all I ever dreamt of, Nakşıgül..."

On that blissful night, he envisaged only happiness ahead. He barely slept a wink, but spent the night planting little kisses on her head, inhaling the scent of her tresses and exploring every part of her face with his fingers.

"You are the love of my life, my princess with rosebud lips and rose-tinted cheeks," he whispered to her, wondering with each passing minute whether he deserved such bliss.

The two enraptured lovers whispered these unfamiliar nuptial words to each other and, as their words turned into a spiritual embrace, their bodies also became united. When sleep came, it was an integration of two souls, rather than a satisfaction of physical desire.

Finally, as night was turning into dawn, they closed their eyes and lay cradled in each other's arms, now tired from love and tears.

When Falco awoke, he felt himself linger in that state between sleep and wakefulness, his lips still bearing a smile of rapture and his eyes an expression of deep, delirious love. He inhaled the scent of Nakşıgül's hair as she lay in his arms and, drawing back a stray lock, started whispering words of love in her ear. They had embarked on that night together, become united and fallen asleep together and now he was ready to start their first day of marital life together.

"Nakşıgül. My princess! My darling, my only Nakşıgül!"

Nakşıgül was in a deep sleep and did not wake up. Falco stroked her face with his hand. He lifted her hair and kissed her forehead. But still she did not wake up. Then he noticed that her face was icy cold. He wanted to take her by the shoulders to wake her. Suddenly, he sensed a void beneath the quilt, as if the woman he loved was no longer there in his arms and their marriage had all been a dream. He flung back the quilt.

"Nakşigüüüüüül!"

QUESTION 3
DOES LOVE HOVER BETWEEN LUNACY AND ECSTASY?

"Yeye! I paid ten gold pieces for olive oil in the market yesterday. The trader gave me ten bottles filled to the brim, ten half-full bottles and, since he didn't have change, ten empty bottles. When I returned home, I wanted to share out the oil equally between my three wives. But there were no scales or measures and I couldn't gauge it by hand so, not knowing how to do it fairly, I gave up."

"Fill five of the ten half-full bottles from the other five," said Yusuf, "and give each woman five full bottles and five empty ones, doctor."

"You're a genius, Yeye! That's why I like you so much. You're not only smart, you're polite and considerate! Now, listen to that dulcimer and tell me which mode it's tuned to. Is it the *Zirgüle* mode, or the *Acemaşiran*?"

"Is it not the *Şehnaz* mode, doctor?"

"Forget about Şehnaz for one moment Yeye! Pay attention to me."

"I haven't paid attention to anything for years, ever since I encountered my beloved Şehnaz. She's the reason I'm unable to concentrate."

"Can we just talk about modes for one moment?"

"I still feel the intoxication of that day when my veins were inflamed on hearing each prelude modulate into the *Şehnaz* mode. I don't want to talk about it, I need to see her."

"Look, Yeye, don't upset me. Pull yourself together and talk to me. You might even find a way through this. Listen to that tamboura. Which mode is it in?"

"It's the Şehnaz mode, doctor! Take me to Şehnaz!"

"Very well, if you're going to be stubborn, let's talk about Şehnaz. That day when you were sitting with Şehnaz under the tree, why didn't you protect her from the snake that fell into her lap?"

"My craving to gaze at Şehnaz was such that I didn't even see the snake."

"Were you trying to appear like some sort of hero to her?"

"Even if I was, the snake had got the measure of me, doctor."

"That's as maybe, but Şehnaz was struck dumb with fear by the incident!"

"Şehnaz came to me last night in my dream and we talked. She wasn't dumb then."

"Ha ha! So, what did she say?"

"She said, 'My Yusuf'."

"What else?"

"She repeated, 'My Yusuf'."

"What else?"

"She said, 'My Yusuf' yet again."

"And what did you do?"

"I said, 'My Şehnaz'."

"What else?"

"I repeated 'My Şehnaz'."

"Yeye! Have you ever told us the actual truth about Şehnaz?"

"I'd like to say yes, but I'm afraid of telling a lie!"

"You mean you've been lying?"

"Any mention of Şehnaz makes me confused. I cannot tell what is true and what is false."

Yusuf was tired of hearing the same stupid questions every day. There had been a daughter named Şehnaz at the house where he was raised. Yusuf had been smitten by her and knew he would love her for ever. However, a year ago, he had been the cause of her being struck dumb and, as a consequence, was confined to the woodshed for several months. Not only that, he was forbidden from seeing Şehnaz, which for him was torture. Then, in addition to this, he learned that his mother, who was a servant at the house, had suddenly died. He began ranting and raving, as if the walls of woodshed were caving in on him. Anyone who heard him believed he had become completely deranged. In the end, Şehnaz was taken away from the house, which meant he no longer had any reason to remain there and his insanity turned to aggression. Eventually, four burly men were brought in to restrain him and take him off to Haseki Insane Asylum.

Yusuf thought he had been sent there on the orders of Şehnaz's father, Veyis Ağa, who had been raising Yusuf as a protégé, but had rejected him when he discovered that the boy was in love with his daughter. Before long, Yusuf was accused of stealing gold which was later found in his room. When Yusuf denied the crime, he was accused of lying and word had gone out that he harboured dishonourable intentions towards Şehnaz. However, that had been done to cover up an incident one summer evening, when a wealthy and important visitor to the house made an improper advance towards Yusuf, who had retaliated by threatening him with a breadknife. When it came to choosing between the wealthy guest and Yusuf, Veyis Ağa had sided with the guest, satisfied that by sending Yusuf away he was getting rid of a penniless suitor who had stolen his daughter's heart.

Yusuf was chained up in isolation for his first few weeks at the asylum, after which he was unchained and put into a locked cell. Then the cell was unlocked and he was allowed to mingle with other patients. This asylum had been treating social outcasts given to melancholia and romantic fantasies for nearly two hundred years. Almost everyone there had the same problem: lovesickness.

On the whole, the doctors were well-meaning, but they were genuinely puzzled as to the nature of Yusuf's condition. One day he convinced them that his faculties were intact, the next that he that he should be confined to his cell. They had never before encountered a patient who actually accepted that he was ill, nor had they figured out that Yusuf behaved like a sick man only if he chose to, with the result that he was subjected to numerous interrogations by the doctors in their search for a diagnosis.

At fourteen, Yusuf was the youngest patient in the asylum, yet he amazed everyone with his clever mind. He told the other patients romantic tales from the books he had read, restored hearts that were grief-stricken by love and was always the first to solve any conundrum, riddle or puzzle that involved numbers or words. His affliction appeared to stem from too much wisdom, rather than too little.

Once he was allowed out of his cell, Yusuf became acquainted with the layout of Haseki Asylum. It consisted of eight cells that opened on to a flower garden with a pool. There was also a small domed courtyard with a special fountain that could be finely calibrated. This courtyard was used for dispensing curative treatments, including herbal root syrups and tablets made from minerals and seeds, counselling and listening to stories and legends. Three of the cells were used for the pharmacy, observation room and music room, and the patients were housed in the other five cells, which were graded according to different levels of insanity. Treatment in each cell took between a fortnight and a month, at the end of which the patient was transferred to another cell. For instance, a patient deemed liable to self-harm would be put into the first cell and bound with chains. Once he showed signs of responding positively, he would be moved to a locked cell without chains. The next stage was a cell where the door was kept closed but not locked. After that, depending on the patient's progress, he would be transferred to the chess cell and, finally, to the conversation cell.

There were daily musical interludes at forenoon, late afternoon and two hours after sunset. Every morning the fountain would discharge a single jet of water, in the afternoon three jets and in the evening two, and the sound of the water would mingle with the music beneath the dome. The idea was based on the teachings of a ninth-century music therapist called Farabi, who claimed that patients could benefit from the curative effects of particular modes according to the season of the year. It was now September, so the musicians were extemporizing in the autumn style. In the mornings, patients listened to cheerful music in the *Rast* mode or more tender music in the *Kuçek* mode. In the afternoons, the music was in the fortifying *Saba* mode or sleep-inducing *Zirgüle* mode, and in the evenings the sensual *Ruhavi* or humbling *Hicaz* modes. The jets of water from the fountain increased or decreased in strength according to the mode, thus purportedly magnifying the curative properties of the sounds echoing beneath the dome and into the cells. The famous Islamic philosopher İbn-i Sina also claimed that one way of treating those afflicted with melancholia or love-sickness was to make them listen to music. Yusuf loved music, especially the *Ruhavi* mode which reminded him of Şehnaz and of reading tales of love with his mother on winter evenings. One such story was ***The Dervish's Tale*** about a dervish who lost his heart to a maiden with cheeks as white as camphor, braids as black as musk and lips as sweet as sugar.

When Yusuf was first brought to the asylum, he did not utter a word to anyone for three whole days. A patient who had completed his treatment in the fifth cell visited Yusuf a few times and, after eventually finding out his name, started calling him Yearning Yusuf, because of his lovesick state of mind. Within a month, the other patients were addressing him as Yearning Yusuf too. In the end, the records clerk started abbreviating this nickname to YY in his notes and pronouncing it as Yeye.

Postscript: The Dervish's Tale

There once was a maiden so beautiful that all those who saw her instantly fell madly in love with her. Her cheeks were white as camphor, her hair black as musk and her lips sweeter than honey. One day, a dervish passed by as she wandered in the garden. He was holding half a loaf of bread which a baker had given him out of pity. He dropped the bread when he saw her radiant face. The maiden smiled at his predicament and walked on, but her smile had stolen a part of his soul. The dervish remained there for seven years, pining and weeping as he walked round and round the garden walls, unable to leave the place she inhabited. His poverty disturbed the girl's family and they decided to have him quietly removed one night. The kind-hearted maiden secretly summoned the penniless dervish, saying, "You must leave. Do not wait at my door for something you can never attain. They are planning to get rid of you. Wait no longer. Go!"

On hearing this, the dervish was reduced to tears and, for the first time, opened his heart to her, saying, "Let the lives of a thousand lovers be sacrificed. My life ended the moment I saw you. Do you think I would leave you now for the sake of a mere life? But I am curious. I know you have no feelings for me, so why did you smile?"

"Oh foolish dervish," said the maiden. "Poor wretch, do you never look at yourself? You have a face that makes people smile. No one looking at you can help but smile."

"Love is everything to the lover, if not to the beloved," replied the dervish. "If, my beauteous one, I had the strength to be offended by what you say, I would resent these emotions. But no power can change my love for you."

The dervish remained there another seven nights, after which he was never seen again.

QUESTION 4
YOUR EXCELLENCY! ARE YOU AS CLEVER AS THEY SAY?

Viewed between the minarets of the Sultan Ahmet Mosque, Grand Vizier İbrahim Pasha's palace had aroused the envy of many an Ottoman ruler, with its oriel windows and panoramic views of the Marmara Sea and the Princes' Islands. In front of it stood the Egyptian obelisk, the Serpentine column and the remains of the Roman hippodrome, their rich pasts consigned to history.

Two centuries earlier, when returning home accompanied by oxen laden with statues brought all the way from Vienna, Belgrade and Budapest, Süleyman the Magnificent and his favourite vizier İbrahim Pasha of Parga, known as Pargalı İbrahim Pasha, had never tired of pausing to look with pleasure and amazement at this palace with its decorative lattice work and windows. The wide space in front of it held memories of the whole of Byzantine history and was a place where people from all over Istanbul came to meet and be entertained. Pargalı İbrahim Pasha would look down with lascivious eyes through the latticed windows, seeking out yet another beauty to add colour to his life. The rooms overlooking the square were divided between his concubines and wives according to their level of importance and seniority. In those days, each concubine was assigned a particular duty at the palace, but they spent most of their time squabbling and hatching intrigues to gain the attention of their master. Most of the concubines at that time were Caucasian beauties who would arrive with a bloom in their faces like that of spring flowers. However, the pasha would lose interest in them once their beauty had faded and they turned into middle-aged women. There was, after all, always a younger model from Venice or Rome who made sure she had a pitcher of the pasha's favourite wine hidden in her room, or a beauty from Wallachia who spent her time writing vacuous poems to her pasha. As for the wives, there was constant rivalry between them, each striving to appear the most beautiful and lavishly adorned. Any money they received from the pasha was spent on jewels, silken dresses, perfumes and their exquisitely coiffed hair, but it was the wives who had borne sons who had the most authority. For years, Pargalı İbrahim Pasha's first and fattest wife maintained a feud with his second wife, who wandered haughtily through the palace in a cloud of magnolia essence, and his concubines would play these two ladies off against each other in the hope of financial reward.

Two centuries later, when İbrahim Pasha of Nevşehir became son-in-law to Sultan Ahmet III by marrying his thirteen-year-old daughter Fatma Sultan, he claimed to have divorced his other wives and to be employing concubines for palace duties only. However, none were sent away and they sometimes appeared beside him when he was entertaining at the palace, providing juicy gossip if ever İbrahim Pasha was seen to leave at the end of an evening in the company of an old favourite.

İbrahim Pasha was an intelligent and capable Grand Vizier. His administrative expertise was considered second to none in the world of politics. Since the Treaty of Passarowitz in 1718, the empire had enjoyed a period of peace during which he had singlehandedly overseen Ottoman policy. He had an agreeable personality, a good mind and a refined appreciation of poetry and literature, while the dark circles beneath his eyes, the hollow cheeks and greying hair were considered becoming for a man of his age. He was a patron for many artists and poets, whom he was known to reward with gifts when he read their poems. However, despite his calm and sympathetic exterior, people kept a safe distance whenever he displayed the slightest hint of anger. He knew how to handle foreigners and, in 1718, after the Austro-Turkish War, he announced to the great powers that the Ottoman state would live in peace with its neighbours. Meanwhile, at home, he initiated policies aimed at regaining the former glory and honour of the Ottomans. He considered peace with Russia to be essential, but also formed alliances with European countries. While inciting Austria to oppose Russia and Poland, he simultaneously used Hungarian Prince Rákóczi to initiate friendly relations with Russia. Although all this was at the behest of the Sultan, İbrahim Pasha acted with superb intelligence, discernment and political acumen and, three years previously, had sent Ottoman ambassadors to Europe for the first time to deal with the machinations of the Christian world. One of these ambassadors was Mehmet Çelebi Efendi, who wrote a book about his experiences in Paris.

There was also an artistic side to İbrahim Pasha, or rather a side that appreciated art and entertainment. He had considerable skill in amusing and distracting the public. Just as no expense was spared when it came to the honour and reputation of the state, he went to similar lengths when it came to entertainment.

Another of his quirks was his penchant for solving riddles and problems. Privately, he was always pleased to be presented with an intricate problem and was renowned for his ability to find just solutions to complex conundrums. With a single move he could avert the most difficult political deadlock. It was noted that he would approach problems with an eagerness that might be expected from an adolescent or an overgrown child whose beard had sprouted prematurely.

However, Grand Vizier İbrahim Pasha also had an unsavoury trait, which was his unscrupulous behaviour towards the janissaries. For instance, there was an occasion when, on hearing of the death of two destitute janissaries, he had a special inventory made so that their salaries remained at the treasury, thus saving seven million *kuruş*. Needless to say, the janissary commanders were deeply displeased, because his actions had interfered with their own plans. For months, this and what the Grand Vizier might resort to next were major topics of conversation in coffee houses and tea gardens. Discontented janissaries of every rank would boast of plans to cut the Grand Vizier down to size and call for the incarceration of his scorpions.

That day, the late summer sun set with an air of despondency, covering the city with a shadow of melancholy before disappearing behind the glorious domes of Istanbul. Something seemed to be troubling İbrahim Pasha. He did not even touch the specially prepared prawns or the wine from Marseilles, but made do with a little buffalo cream spread on a piece of toast. As he watched the silhouette of the city become submerged in darkness, he tried to shake off his anxieties and think of good days ahead. After a while, he took a favourite volume of history from the bookcase, genuflected and started reading at his desk. Then, he decided he should write a new ode to win back the heart of his wife, Fatma Sultan. He needed to make up for a mistake he had made a few days earlier.

"How could I be such an idiot? Why do I court a concubine, whom I do not love, in order to arouse jealousy in the woman I do love?" he kept saying to himself. Then the following couplet came to mind.

The strings of a heart when touched but once
If broken, a thousand repairs will not mend

As he repeated these lines, he felt a strange tingling in his soul, as if he were in a bad dream from which he did not have the energy to wake up, and saw a vision of a hefty janissary with a bushy moustache mocking him with dark threatening eyes. Just then, there was a knock at the door and shadowy figure entered carrying a basket. However, İbrahim Pasha was in another world and paid no attention to what his manservant was saying.

"Your Honour!" said the manservant. "A janissary commander sent me to deliver these and say, 'We kiss the hand of the Grand Vizier!' I told him, 'His Excellency will never accept these, but the commander insisted, saying, 'It's important. His

Excellency has requested these. Take them to him at once.' So here I am. Should I have done as he commanded?"

With these words, the manservant held out the basket, but İbrahim Pasha, who was still thinking about poetry and that bushy moustache, dismissed him with a wave of his hand and turned back to his book by the Ottoman historian Naima Tarihi. Opening the section on the martyrdom of Murat I at Kosovo, he read for a long while, which calmed him down yet brought tears to his eyes. He pulled the inkpot and some paper towards himself, but his mind went blank. After a bit of fidgeting and a lot of heavy sighing, he forced himself to start writing. With much crossing out and rewriting, he produced a few couplets similar in style to that of the poet Nedim. Finally, he tidied up his writing desk and stood up. That was when he noticed the basket in the doorway. It was covered with a cloth with a sealed letter on top. He picked up the letter and read, "Honourable Grand Vizier! Let's see if you are as clever as they say! Open the basket. Taste our early crop of fruit and nuts and find the connection."

İbrahim Pasha used the tip of a willow paper knife to cautiously cut through the stitches on the cloth. As expected, the basket was filled with an elaborate arrangement of almonds and walnuts, dried grapes and figs, pistachios and hazelnuts. He was about to take a handful, when his fingers touched something else, something that felt like a moist piece of meat. Turning the basket upside down, he froze with terror at the sight of a freshly severed woman's head rolling across the carpet, its plaits trailing behind.

QUESTION 5
WHY WAS PEARL VILLA SOLD?

It was the middle of the night and Falco was weeping deliriously and calling out Nakşıgül's name. For almost fifteen hours, he had been locked in a damp basement cell at Eyüp Prison, with his legs fastened in stocks from his ankles to his knees. There were five sets of holes, two of which were occupied by other exhausted prisoners. They were all hungry and thirsty but nobody brought them water, or even thought to ask if they wanted any. It seemed like a terrible dream to Falco, who found his mind numbing and memories fading as time passed. He wanted to weep all the time, but when he did so the other two prisoners started cursing and telling him to keep quiet. Fortunately for him, they had been put at opposite ends of the stocks, because one of them was tiny in stature and the other was large. Like Falco, they were there because they had denied the charges made against them. These enormous stocks were famous in Istanbul for their effectiveness as an instrument of torture. The contraption consisted of a log five metres long and seventy centimetres in diameter. It was split in two from end to end, with five pairs of holes big enough to take the legs of prisoners. When Falco was first taken there, a prison orderly had opened the stocks next to the guards' entrance, measured his calves and fastened him into the third set of holes. His legs, now clasped in these holes from kneecap to anklebone, had begun to swell and his calves were throbbing with pain. In addition, any action such as lying down, sitting up, eating, sleeping, urinating, or even the slightest movement was felt by the other prisoners into the stocks and would set them off wailing. Falco knew that there was an even worse set of stocks at Galata. In fact, everyone in Istanbul knew that once put into the Galata stocks, you were unlikely to come out alive and that the few survivors lived out the rest of their days in abject misery. It was said that the Galata stocks were designed to hold not just the ankles but the whole body like a press and were called the bandit's vice. Legendary tales circulated about people locked into those stocks preferring to die rather than confess, or confessing to crimes they had not committed.

But Falco was not thinking about any of this. He was crying uncontrollably, not because of what had happened to him, but because he had lost Nakşıgül. The more he tried to stop, the more his tears flowed, and when he cried he remembered Nakşıgül and so the cycle started all over again. He could not believe that this could happen after just one night of happiness. What he had experienced would make anyone to lose his mind. He was not capable of thinking clearly, but merely reacting to his dire situation.

The door opened and two guards entered.

"Well, my good man, the time has come," mocked one of them as they handcuffed Falco's hands, released his legs from the stocks and raised him up by the arms. The pain spread through his whole body as his legs took his weight, making it torture to walk. Falco was taken to the interrogation room on the top floor, where he saw the Prison Custodian, Nakşıgül's father Aslan Ağa and her mother, the nanny, the butler, the concubine on duty that evening and other members of the household, such as the groom, footman, stable boy and assistant cook. The Prison Custodian was a huge janissary with a bushy moustache, whose colossal size instilled fear into anyone who encountered him. He had requested permission to interrogate the defendant in person and had arranged for two equally burly men to be present – a guard and a recorder for taking minutes. There was a howl of anger when Falco entered, still in a state of distress.

"Bastard! Cur! You vile piece of lowlife! Is this how you repay goodness, you son of a bitch?" yelled Nakşıgül's mother, lunging towards him.

The guard restrained the woman, but then Nakşıgül's father started.

"Tear him to pieces, the bastard!" he bellowed. "Rip out his flesh. Cut him into a thousand pieces and throw them to the dogs. Do to him what he did to my daughter."

"Quiiiiet!" growled the Prison Custodian.

A tense silence filled the room. Everyone sat down, cowering like slaves who had been whipped into order. The Prison Custodian glared at Falco and beckoned him to step forward. Falco summoned up all his courage and obeyed, walking with difficulty but in a respectful manner.

"What is your name, son?" asked the Prison Custodian.

"Falco, sir. Falco."

"Very well, Falco, my boy, I trust that your heart is as clean as your face. Stop crying now and tell us what happened. Start from the beginning."

"I went to sleep and I woke up. That's all I can tell you. You tell me what happened. I need to know."

At this, the other people in the room raised their voices in protest.

"Son of a bitch. Ungrateful wretch."

"An eye for an eye, a tooth for a tooth!"

The Prison Custodian made a signal to the recorder, who ordered everyone to be quiet.

"Son, my time is precious. Don't annoy me. Stop this snivelling and tell me why you did it!" said the Prison Custodian.

"Sir, I swear, in the name of God that I didn't do anything. All my friends know that I would never do a thing like that."

"You mean your friends at the tavern?"

"I have no other friends, sir."

"I heard that you met the victim three weeks ago."

"Yes, sir. I was returning home from Fener and Nakşıgül was walking in front of me. I had no idea who she was. Then suddenly, two hooligans started pestering her with lewd comments. I intervened on religious and moral grounds, but the moment I saw her face, a spark ignited in me and a fiery passion was born in my heart that increased minute by minute. My hands trembled and I couldn't raise my eyes to look at her. Can a person gaze at the radiance of the sun, sir? I was dazzled. Call it light, call it fire – it was like the sun. It burned and consumed me. It was everything I had ever yearned for."

"Look here, my boy! I'm getting cross! Never mind the fairy tale, we need the truth. We don't want all these embellishments. Just tell us what happened. But whatever you do, don't cry!"

"I followed her home. I had no one who could approach the family on my behalf, but God was on my side and sent her nanny out to me."

"Curse that day!" snarled the nanny.

The Prison Custodian shook his head from side to side and stretched his neck, as if he was having difficulty containing his irritation. He looked at Falco and signalled for him to continue.

"I spent three days writing two letters to my angel, the girl of my dreams and I received a reply addressed to 'My charming, handsome prince'. We fell in love and I had no option but to request the help of her nanny again. She informed my esteemed parents-in-law of my situation and I was invited to their house in Yenibahçe one evening. I took presents for everyone, including silks, velvets, rosaries and embroidered handkerchiefs. My father-in-law seemed well-disposed towards me and that evening we settled on a day for the wedding."

"Is that any way to arrange a wedding for the most beautiful girl in the world? If these people treated you so well, why did you show such ingratitude?"

Falco started crying again.

"Your Excellency, I'm not ungrateful, really I'm not. I loved Nakşıgül," he continued, speaking with difficulty. "To be honest, it did occur to me that there might be something wrong with their daughter for them to be giving her away so willingly. But her

beauty mesmerized me and I convinced myself that I would take her even if she had some flaw or defect. If you love someone, you take her for better or worse, do you not? Later, I felt ashamed when I realised that those thoughts were groundless. In any case, nobody in my life had ever laid claim to honour or esteem. My father-in-law is a good man. And I'm not saying that just because he is here in this room. He treated me like a son. When I asked permission to take my bride to live at Pearl Villa, he insisted that we should all live together as a family at his villa in Yenibahçe and that he would treat me like a son. I hadn't experienced the warmth of family life since my dear mother died, so I welcomed the chance of creating a nest of happiness within a family of such worthy people. From that day on, I forsook the tavern and lost interest in my old friends. I had never known fatherly love, but I had now gained a father. My mother was dead, and now I had a mother once again. Furthermore, it was what my beloved Nakşıgül wanted. We were all going to live together for ever."

"Enouuugh!" interrupted the Prison Custodian, his manner turning from benign to threatening. "You clearly have no intention of telling me what happened. In which case, I will ask questions. Let's start with Pearl Villa in Ayvansaray. That's the villa in which you grew up. Correct?"

"Yes, sir. I lived there until I was fifteen with my dear mother, İtir Banu. When she passed away a few years ago, loneliness took hold of me and I became unhappy there. I fell into temptation and started frequenting the quayside taverns at Fener and the gardens on the seafront. I made many friends in nearby villages, such as Cibali, Sütlüce and Eyüp, and we spent the summers promenading at Sadabat and the winters conversing at the villa. We discussed wine, love, beauty and much more.

But within three years I had spent everything. Nothing lasts for ever."

"So what about the pearls you gave to Nakşıgül as a wedding gift?"

"They were given to me by my mother at a time when I least expected it. If I was naughty, she used to say jokingly, 'When I'm gone, you'll have to get by on your own, so make sure you keep these hooks – they were made in England!' A few months ago, I found that everything I owned was gone, all the cash and what was left of my inheritance. My friends and I had grown accustomed to the good life but, as I said, nothing goes on for ever. I had to think long and hard about what to do next, because my situation had become untenable. Anyway, I decided to have one last fling at the villa with my friends and then sign up with a caravan and go to Mecca or Europe. I used my last cents to buy in provisions and invited everyone, even some gypsy acquaintances. But that night, my friends, the musicians and the gypsies all went off to Yeniçeri to comb the taverns, coffee houses and stalls looking for liquor and other pleasure-inducing substances and they didn't return. At that time, the villa was infested with vermin so I filled three sacks with the provisions and hung them up on my dear mother's English hooks so that the rats wouldn't get at them. As I was hanging up the third one, the hook came loose and the sack fell to the floor, leaving a crimson silk bag hanging from the ceiling. I stood on a stool and cut it down with a knife. Inside, I found thirty pearls and a short note which said, 'Falco, my son, this is your rightful inheritance from your father. God bless you!' When I showed one of them to a dealer, he offered me sixty gold pieces."

"Sixty gold pieces each?"

"Yes, sixty gold pieces. I gave all the pearls to my Nakşıgül."

"Were there exactly thirty of them?"

"Yes. I gave all thirty to Nakşıgül as my wedding gift to her."

"Tell me about your father."

"I never knew my father. My mother did not talk about him except to say that she never remarried after his death. When I was little, İshak Efendi, son of Sheikh ul-Islam İsmail, took care of me. It's thanks to him that I received my education. But he never spoke about my father either, and I did not have the courage to ask. On one occasion, İshak Efendi told me that he was dead, but nothing more. Nobody ever told me who he was or what he did. I knew that my mother loved him greatly and, not wishing to open old wounds or make her feel ashamed of her love, I didn't pester her about him. In truth, I was worried that I might be a child of sin, a reality I would have found unbearable. It was better not to know who my father was. You have to understand that."

"Of course. And what about the gold in the bridal chamber?"

"Ah, that. When Aslan Ağa said we should live at his villa in Yenibahçe, he told me to sell Pearl Villa. We were going to set up a partnership with an entrepreneur friend of his and start trading in silk. On the eve of the wedding, the villa was put up for sale. A broker came and bought it at the bargain price of eight hundred gold pieces. It should have gone for one thousand five hundred, but I accepted the eight hundred and gave the money to my father-in-law."

"Never!" interrupted Aslan Ağa angrily. "The bastard's not only lying, he's implicating me!"

The Prison Custodian silenced him with a firm signal and continued his questioning.

"So that was the gold in the bridal room. Very well, let's leave that for the time being and move on to the morning after the wedding. I inspected the room myself and there were traces of blood all over the walls and ceiling. How did you manage so much violence in one night?"

"I didn't do anything, sir!"

"Hmm! Perhaps you feel inhibited in front of the family and find it difficult to explain. You said you can read and write, so perhaps the best thing would be for you to confess in writing. Do you agree?"

The Prison Custodian made everyone leave the room, which they did with much protesting and cursing. He unfastened Falco's handcuffs, placed some paper and writing implements before him and signalled to the guards to leave the room.

"Well now, Falco my boy. When I come back in half an hour, I want to know everything. Otherwise, I'll throw you into Galata Prison myself and you'll find out what torture is really like!"

Falco heard the sound of the key turning in the lock and realized that he was in a desperate situation. His crying abated and he started to think calmly. An inkpot, a pen and paper – what was he going to write? As he reached for a piece of paper, he noticed that he was holding a tulip bulb. He remembered that on the morning after the wedding, when he was attempting the ghastly task of gathering up the body parts strewn around the room with the gold pieces, he had found this tulip bulb in Nakşıgül's tightly clenched left hand that had been severed at the wrist. It was half of the twin bulb from the wedding night. At the time, it had not occurred to him to look for the other half among the scattered gold and blood-soaked sheets. All he was could think about then was the blood splattered all over the walls and ceiling.

QUESTION 6
IS IT ALWAYS TO DO WITH LOVE?

Yeye knew he had to formulate a good plan for his future. While helping mental patients at the asylum, he monitored their behaviour and learned how to display symptoms of insanity in front of the doctors. He put this unusual acting talent to use when the doctors questioned him about Şehnaz.

He knew he could not stay at the asylum indefinitely. Others knew that too, especially Şehnaz's father, who undoubtedly wanted him kept there for as long as possible. Yeye knew that if he were 'cured' and released, her father would find out and seek ways of making things even worse for him, so he had to formulate a watertight plan to ensure that he left no trace behind when he left the asylum. But where could he go to be sure of this? Nowhere in Istanbul was beyond the reach of Şehnaz's father. In the meantime, he had to maintain his role as a madman in the hope that, if he convinced everyone that he was truly mad, they might eventually stop checking up on him.

One morning, the asylum supervisor announced that Yeye had been summoned by the new head doctor, who had just arrived from the renowned Gevher Nesibe Asylum in Kayseri. Yeye was not at all pleased because it meant more questions and poisonous potions and he would have to put on another convincing display of insanity.

"Are you going? Or shall I take you?" barked the supervisor. Whenever the patients heard him say that, they would immediately shut themselves away in their cells to avoid being frogmarched by the supervisor with his customary cuffs and slaps to the head.

Yeye decided to refuse to order to go to the chief doctor's room and put up with the beating in order to maintain his appearance of insanity.

"The chief doctor can go to Hell!" shouted Yeye. Then, seeing an elderly flautist who happened to be passing, he recited in jeering tones a poem containing musical references that included the name Şehnaz:

"Longing to pass from Esfahan through Muhayyer and Buselik
I remain here with Şehnaz feeling utterly lovesick"[1]

Yeye's nose was still bleeding from the supervisor's slick elbow work when he was escorted into the room in which two men in sable coats were seated. Seeing the state of his face, one

1 Meaning: I want the music to start in Esfahan mode and modulate through Muhayyer and Buselik modes, but I start in Şehnaz mode and, despite my best efforts, am unable to modulate into any other.

of the men chided the supervisor, saying that such beatings were forbidden at the asylum. Though somewhat unnerved by this, Yeye was pleased when this agreeable-looking person, presumably the head doctor, dismissed the supervisor from the room. Whenever a doctor treated a patient well at the asylum, he inevitably had an ulterior motive and it meant that the interrogation would probably start in a paternal fashion and gradually become increasingly violent. The head doctor told Yeye to sit down and turned to his junior colleague sitting next to him.

"Firstly, young man, we have to instruct all patients, doctors and orderlies that on no account must patients be treated badly. We have no facilities here for treating physical injuries and anyone with such ailments needs to be in a hospital rather than an asylum."

"Do you mean it's all a question of achieving emotional and mental balance?" asked the young colleague.

"Indeed, it is. And it always concerns love, when emotions flow too strongly in one direction. The treatment of mental illness involves certain calming measures. Just as a groom strokes the flank of a horse to calm it down, so we must help our patients here by soothing their minds. It is a contradiction for any institution called an asylum to resort to degrading measures like bastinado and chains."

"I totally agree, sir. Our elders introduced the principle of chaining up patients in asylums so that they would not harm themselves, but we've developed the practice of beating patients with those very chains in order to bring them to their senses."

"Very true. And unfortunately, we're having difficulty changing this practice."

Yeye listened intently to their conversation and decided that either these two men were playing some sort of game to soften him up, or that this doctor was indeed a good man who had been sent to there to put an end to the increasing levels of violence.

"Do we have anyone here so insane that he should be kept in chains?" asked the younger man.

"Yes, there are three such patients. But in my opinion, no patient should be kept in chains, because love is something that affects everybody to some degree. Some people devote a part of their mind, some half their mind and some their whole mind to love. We label them slightly mad, half-mad or totally mad accordingly. Yet it might not be a case of losing one's mind, but a loss of will-power. In such situations, the emotions come to the fore and dominate the mind."

"How do you mean? Are you saying that emotions replace reason and dominate the thinking process?"

"You could put it that way. In fact, the mind is the most wonderful and simple faculty granted to mankind. People think we are directed by the mind whereas, in reality, the mind is driven by a combination of positive and negative currents: the heart and the flesh. If our mind puts the heart first, then we act according to our temperament. If we put the flesh first, it produces deviancy. Mankind has been given willpower in order to establish a balance between these states."

"But sir is there not a contradiction in what you say? For men who follow their heart are labelled insane and kept in asylums, are they not?"

"Very true! Such men do indeed pay more attention to their hearts than their minds, which can make them unbalanced. Of course the heart is more important than the mind, because

the ultimate attainable point of the mind is actually within the heart. The world is full of people who want to 'follow their heart', because the heart is compassionate and, unlike the flesh, does not lead mankind astray. People who give free rein to their hearts are able to progress at a galloping pace, because they escape the limitations of their minds."

"You mean, sir, that we are chaining up all these people because they have been saved from reason?"

"Oh no. There is a dimensional difference here. It's like the mystery of attaining divine love. Think of the Sufi master Hallac-ı Mansur, or Rabia and her concept of divine love."

"But sir, we're in Haseki Sultan Asylum, not the Baghdad Islamic Centre. We have no mystics here, just local girls and youths."

"What I mean is that emotional unbalance can affect all types of people."

"But, sir. In a moment you'll be telling me these lunatics are saints!"

"No, I wouldn't go that far, but let me say this: when they lose their reason, God no longer holds them responsible."

"As far as I'm concerned, madness is madness."

"In that case, young man, according to you Hallac-ı Mansur was mad, wasn't he?"

"No, but one can't deny that madness is a sickness."

"I believe that, as long as it is regarded as a sickness, I shall be unable to treat the poor creatures here. If it were a normal sickness, all the unhinged people who fill our dormitories would be in hospitals. Yet the Ottoman Empire has established separate asylums for them. Doctors and scholars have not regarded them as sick since the days of Bukrat, Eflatun-ı İhahi and İbni Sina. In my view, it is cruel to label people as insane if they get into this state because of love. It's wrong to call them insane, because insanity means the mind is inconsistent, unbalanced, or unable to function. Like everything else, we measure insanity through inconsistencies. Thus, an insane person is a person without reason. But who can say which madman has no reason? Who is qualified to say that Leyla's Majnun lost his reason?"

"But sir, you can't say that nobody is mad."

"Very true. However, Majnun had the ability to reason. He just devoted it all to Leyla. And most of our patients are like that. Their mental faculties are working but they lock themselves on to a single target and, because they are so wrapped up in their loved ones, they react to nothing else. It's as if their beloved is a sun and they are trapped in the sunlight. Just as it's impossible to escape the sun, so is it impossible to block it out. That's why it is said that people weep when they look at the sun. Is it a question of will if someone weeps when they look at the sun? Who can look at the sun without weeping? It doesn't mean that they have lost their reason, but that their reason is being diverted in the wrong direction. That is something which cannot be rectified with violence and chains, but must be treated by soothing their minds and stroking their backs."

"Well, sir, I applaud you. You almost managed to convince me that Majnun was a man of reason."

"If he had been crazy, do you think so many intelligent men would have sat around discussing him for hundreds of years?"

"Maybe you're right."

"Remember how the poet said, 'Everything in life is love / Science is just commotion'?"

"Yes, it was Fuzuli!"

❦ ❦ ❦

While the doctors were talking, Yeye was remembering the tale of ***The Man Who Wept When He Looked at the Sun***. It was a happy story of a mystic who finds his true love. Yeye thought he would rather die than lose his desire to embrace his sun.

"Dear God, grant me that bliss!" he prayed silently, just like the mystic in the story.

Yeye liked the head doctor's ideas as much as he liked the doctor himself, but he could not assume that the feeling was mutual. He had to be careful, which was why he decided to intensify his symptoms.

"Yusuf, listen to this," said the head doctor in a compassionate tone. "A man has two wives, one occupies the room on his right and the other occupies the room on his left. He vows, 'I will not go to my wife on the right or to my wife one on the left today, nor will I stay in my room. Yet, I will not actually leave the house!' What is the solution to this?"

The head doctor wanted the patient to think hard about this question and then talk through his thinking process, so that he could start analysing Yusuf's personality and establish a doctor-patient relationship. He really wanted the patient to preoccupy himself with this question until their next session together. However, Yeye responded immediately.

"If he exchanged the room of the wife on the right with the room of the wife on the left, he would be next to the one he wanted,"

"What? Oh, idiot boy. We have a lot of work to do on you!"

Postscript: The man who wept when he looked at the sun

Once there was a so beautiful that she broke people's hearts. Her beauty was such that any rose who saw her face turned green with envy. When springtime came, she went out for a walk and sat down in the shade. Light illuminated every aspect of her. Can the clouds ever eclipse the sun? She was like the sun.

A mystic rode past and saw this sun which was clear of any cloud. Captivated by the light, his rapture reduced him to tears. He ignored everyone's counsel and sought to achieve his heart's desire. One day, they met again when she was out walking. This time it was pouring with rain. By coincidence, they both took shelter in the same tent and covered themselves with a dry kilim. Everyone was crying out, "Please God, stop the rain!" But the couple were saying, "Please God, may your merciful rain continue!"

The mystic went even further and prayed, "Please God, may your merciful rain continue, because the time has come for me to swim to my ship. If this rain continues until the day of judgement, it will be a joyful time. Please God, grant me that bliss!"

QUESTION 7
CAN A SINGLE MOMENT LAST A HUNDRED YEARS?

"Your Majesty, with your gracious permission, I wish to discuss a private matter that will take no more than a moment of your time," said Supreme Judge İshak. A chill fell over the assembly. Confidential conversations were not desirable in the Domed Stateroom, because they were a worrying distraction to the viziers.

Sultan Ahmet III finally gave an elegant signal with the fingers of his right hand, dismissing all the assembled viziers, sheikhs, naval commanders and pashas. The Sultan was an avaricious, miserly man who disliked war because of the huge expenses that had to be paid out of the state treasury. In this respect he was unlike his ancestors. The viziers knew this and always approached him with money or generous bribes if they wanted him to do anything on their behalf. Grand Vizier İbrahim Pasha, who had been a childhood friend of the Sultan and was now his son-in-law, was the only person to ignore the Sultan's parsimony. In fact, İbrahim Pasha was perversely lavish in the way he spent the savings accumulated by the Sultan, and even made a point of handing out spending money to the Sultan's sons.

Once the viziers had left the room, the Sultan walked slowly towards his throne and sat down. He made another signal ordering all the guards, except for two deaf mutes, to leave the room. It was common for the Sultan to be approached on matters that were claimed to be important and urgent yet could almost invariably be resolved with gold. He pondered on the amount that might be on offer as he beckoned the judge towards him. How could he know that Judge İshak was the bearer of bad news? Or that this bad news had been troubling Judge İshak for some time and he needed to get it off his chest?

"Is everything well, sir?" asked the Sultan in a tremulous voice, his suspicions aroused.

Judge İshak cringed before the Sultan, his head bowed low, not knowing where to begin. This was unusual for him, as someone who regularly attended the Sultan's poetry evenings and halva parties, the festivities at Çırağan Palace and the gatherings on the promenades at Sadabat and Göksu. Normally, he never hesitated to speak his mind, recite poetry or join in the singing. However, he was finding it extremely difficult being alone with the Sultan in the hallowed confines of the Domed Stateroom for the purpose of delivering confidential information that involved state security.

"As Your Majesty knows," he began in a whisper, "six months after your brother Sultan Mustafa II was deposed, he died of bladder inflammation brought on by depression. It is common knowledge that he had five sons and that these princes are happily living out their lives at your expense, safe under the protection of your government. In fact, your brother…"

The Sultan interrupted Judge İshak with a signal to stop. Any sentence beginning with 'In fact…,' signalled trouble. The Sultan stood motionless for a moment, one single moment that felt like a hundred years of turmoil, as if he was waiting for the heat of a knife wound to pass. His mind clouded, his hands trembled and he felt an urge to strangle the man in front of him. However, he merely raised his head and signalled for Judge İshak to continue.

"Your Illustrious Highness! You will remember that auspicious summer day in 1703, when pall-bearers carried the coffin of your brother Sultan Mustafa to the palace boathouse, from where it was taken by royal barge to Eminönü where your father is entombed and finally to the mausoleum of forty-four chambers donated by Sultan Turhan. Among the tearful palace contingent was a junior doctor, who remained by the side of your dear brother's coffin as it left the royal boathouse. No one noticed that he was in fact one of your brother's concubines, because of the mourning veil that covered her fair face. Not a single person at the funeral ceremony knew the significance of the tears shed by that 'doctor'. It later transpired that this had all been planned by Numan Pasha, eldest son of Fazil Mustafa Pasha of the Köprülü dynasty, a former vizier and chief of the palace guards. You may remember that your brother had so much trust in Numan Pasha that he allowed him to marry his daughter. You may also remember that, with your gracious authority, he managed all your brother's affairs after his dethronement."

The Sultan twirled his wrist as if to indicate, "Never mind all that. Hurry up and get to the point!"

"When the mounted guards joined the cortege at Eminönü, even they were unaware that this silently weeping young doctor was one of the late Sultan's favourite concubines, whom he had taken into his private rooms to care for him during his illness. Numan Pasha claimed that your brother talked endlessly about the tenderness bestowed on him by this concubine and, even though the sultan was almost forty, there was obviously deep affection between them. However, if all they did was pour out their hearts to each other in the private, it is unlikely that your brother would have given orders personally for her to be paid handsomely and cared for after his death. As his confidant, Numan Pasha showed the former sultan great compassion and respect during the last days of his life and told no one about this passion for a concubine. Anyway, once the concubine had left the barge, she mingled into the crowd, sadly taking her first steps towards life outside the palace with nothing more than an enfranchisement document instructing her never to return to the palace and a secret in her belly that was already showing signs of containing the fruit of a joyous and secret love."

The Sultan, who was looking calmer now, rose to his feet and went to a window overlooking the Bosphorus. In truth, a volcano was seething inside him. Mustafa's princes were kept under his control in a safe place, yet this judge was suggesting that another prince existed outside the palace and was completely beyond his control. This was something he could not bear to contemplate. With a frozen stare, he gazed across at the Scutari shore, wishing that Judge İshak would stop talking.

"The concubine's name was İtir Banu," said Judge İshak, clearing his throat. "Numan Pasha gave orders for her to be settled in a house near Ayvansaray, with two servants to see to her needs. When she recovered from her morning sickness, Numan Pasha visited her and warned that, for her own safety, she should tell no one about her secret. And so, Your Majesty, to cut things short, the concubine had the joy of bearing a son, a joy your brother was unable to share. She named the child Ahmet. Meanwhile, Numan Pasha, as a true member of the Köprülü lineage, remained loyal to the memory of Sultan Mustafa. He kept his visits to the house secret and sent nurses and a companion to ensure that the mother was comfortable during the pregnancy and birth. Before his death in Crete ten years ago, in the year of the Passarowitz Peace Treaty, Numan Pasha entrusted the care of the child to my father İsmail Efendi, who was a professor at the time, and handed him a sealed letter to be given to İtir Banu when her son reached puberty. However, Your Majesty dismissed my dear father from his duties and exiled him to Sinop that year, so he was unable to make enquiries about the circumstances of the woman and child who had been put under his trusteeship. Nevertheless, he protected his charge as requested by his old friend Numan Pasha and ensured that they wanted for nothing, even going so far as to have the child educated by tutors in the exact sciences, as well as Arabic, Persian and poetry. My brothers and I knew nothing of this. Three years ago, when my father entrusted me with this charge, I thought that the guardianship of İtir Banu and her son, who was by then an adolescent, was connected with one of my father's charities. That is until last night, when I found some notes relating to conversations between my father and İtir Banu. My father used to read a lot of Baki's poetry. Unable to sleep, I took a book from the shelf to amuse myself and chanced upon Baki's *Divan* in which I found some sheets of paper covered with notes in my father's handwriting. Among them was a note stating that Numan Pasha had given my father a letter and asked for it to be handed to İtir Banu on the child's fifteenth birthday."

The Sultan was looking perturbed again and clearly needed to sit down. Judge İshak rushed to fill the narghile and used a pair of silver tongs to light it with an ember from the grate. After a few puffs, the Sultan waved his hand signalling him to continue.

"And so, one afternoon, my father went İtir Banu's house to deliver the letter," said Judge İshak. "She appeared unusually flustered as she waited for my father to break open the seal, quite unlike her normal calm and dignified self, as if someone for whom she had been waiting many years had just entered the room. 'I could tell her heart was racing despite the heavy robe she was wearing,' wrote my father. He broke the seal on the letter and was about to start reading but, seeing its content, could not get the words out. My father's words are still etched on my mind: 'Had İtir Banu seen my face at that moment, she would have understood everything. In my agitation, I rose and made an excuse saying that I could not decipher the writing which had been exposed to damp and that I would get a calligraphist to read it some other time. Then I rushed out of the room.'"

"Your Majesty," continued Judge İshak sadly, "I think İtir Banu understood everything when my father was unable to read her that letter. Finally, after what seemed an eternity to him, she thanked him and he left. I think, having kept this knowledge to herself for so long, she was just glad that someone knew the true identity of Ahmet, someone who would not harm him. But, I don't think she wanted Ahmet to find out. At least, that is what I inferred, given that she never once alluded to that letter and henceforth showed enormous gratitude towards our family. In short, the concubine had given birth to a prince. However, she was not an ambitious mother who wanted her son to be a sultan, but an ordinary mother who merely wanted her son to have a good life. That was why she never told her son this secret."

The Sultan listened to Judge İshak with a show of great patience, successfully concealing his agitation, anger and astonishment with bitter smiles and an occasional sympathetic glance. He now rose, and with some irritation, took the slim case containing the imperial decree from Judge İshak.

"Is the concubine still living?" asked the Sultan, after a few moments.

"No, Your Majesty. She died three years ago..."

"Does the child know anything about this?" interrupted the Sultan, indicating that he wanted brief answers.

"No, Your Majesty! But..."

"In that case, does anyone know about this apart from you?"

"No, Your Majesty, I..."

"Is it possible that the boy will find out?"

"No, Your Majesty!"

"Is he married?"

"No, Your Majesty!"

"Do you think he should be disposed of?"

"No, Your Majesty!"

"So you don't think he's likely to cause any mischief?"

"No, Your Majesty!"

"I repeat, do you think he is likely to cause any mischief?"

"No, Your Majesty!"

"Are you absolutely sure about that, İshak Efendi?"

"Yes, Your Majesty!"

The Sultan barked out these questions like orders and Judge İshak answered them earnestly, almost as if making a pledge, because once the talking was over, responsibility for dealing with Prince Ahmet would rest on Judge İshak's shoulders. The Sultan's last question had made him tremble, because he realised that his head would be the first to roll if Prince Ahmet ever found out his true identity and chose to claim his title. What if he were to ask for a share of the sultanate's coffers? Or gather men around him and start a rebellion? Or even, in those unsettled times, merely spread rumours about such activities?

"In that case, bring me back news as soon as possible," said the Sultan, sounding unconvinced.

When the Sultan was finally alone, he read Numan Pasha's letter and tore it up angrily. The letter was as follows:

"To İtir Banu, from a loyal servant of the Sultan:

Greetings to Ahmet, Prince of the Ottoman Empire,

I hereby declare that:

I met your father, our late Sultan, when we were both young and played together in the palace gardens. He was an uncommonly fortunate man to have met you, my dear lady. That was manifestly clear because, after meeting you, his face continually beamed with joy. Would that he had found you when he was still in good health.

My Sultan has decreed that:

After being discharged from service, you should remain away from Istanbul for nine months, during which time you will be un-

der constant supervision. You shall not be allowed to marry nor shall any man be allowed to approach you. The Sultan's wish is that you should have the child, whether it is a son or daughter. Otherwise, at the end of nine months, you shall be cast out. If you are not cast out, your child is to receive a legacy from the great Ottoman dynasty and you are both to be protected for the remainder of your lives. In addition, since the marriage was not formally recognized, you are to be granted a share of the Sultan's personal treasury. The task of protecting you both, whether openly or in secret, is hereby assigned to the Köprülü family and its descendants.

I, Numan Pasha, declare that:

I am grateful to have lived long enough to have seen Prince Ahmet. I hereby give this letter to Sheikh İsmail Efendi who will read out the conditions to you when the time comes. What you now know should be known by no one else other than God, and you must live out your hopes and dreams accordingly. May God protect you and keep you in his grace.

These lines were written as the will and testament of Sultan Mustafa and should be read and implemented accordingly.

A humble servant of destiny,
Protector of the Sultanate and of the Sultan
Numan Köprülüzade."

QUESTION 8
DOES THIS ROBE BELONG TO YOUR WIFE?

As always since İbrahim Pasha had attained the position of Grand Vizier, he was served a cup of coffee with a good crema the moment he entered his office. He was still bewildered by the events of the previous evening and had barely slept a wink all night. He could still see the image of that head rolling out of the basket and across the floor. How could he forget it? He had raised the head by its long hair and spent ten minutes staring into the gracious young face of a woman no more than twenty years old, studying her fresh beauty, her last bitter smile of astonishment and the terrified look of innocent defeat in her half open eyes. After thinking long and hard, he had come to a decision, albeit with many misgivings, and had made a space for the woman's head on the top shelf of a cupboard full of personal documents. Then, taking a pair of scissors, he had carefully cut a few strands from the braided hair, before looking at her beautiful face for one last time and locking the cupboard door.

When the Grand Vizier's manservant arrived to do the morning cleaning, he wondered what had happened to all the fruit and nuts that were in the basket he had delivered the previous evening. As he cleaned the bloodstained carpet, he puzzled over where the Grand Vizier had thrown all the shells and finally came to the conclusion that it was better if the house steward knew nothing about the basket and its contents.

On the way to his office, the Grand Vizier had made a mental list of the things that needed doing. The satisfied smile that spread over his face as he finished his coffee was the smile he wore when he achieved success. He was now in good spirits. Before moving on to matters of state, he took a few puffs on his narghile and, exactly five minutes after the exhalation of thick smoke reached the decorative mouldings on the ceiling, he summoned his bailiffs.

"All hamams used by women in the city are to be searched and all the beauticians are to be brought here," ordered the Grand Vizier.

The hamams played an important part in the renowned architectural beauty of Istanbul, referred to by visitors as the Domed City. Some were famed for their warmth or their spaciousness, others for the beauty of their marble or for their attendants. They were all over the city because whenever a sultan, grand vizier, pasha or governor had a mosque built, it was always accompanied by a hamam nearby. Over centuries, the Islamic emphasis on cleanliness had led to the building of numerous hamams, with rich foundations to ensure their functioning and perpetuation. Recently, however, some of these hamams had become notorious for the festivities held on their premises. Private pre-wedding parties for brides were particular favourites. Over time, these revelries developed into more than just eating, drinking, gossiping and listening to music, particularly at Çinili Hamam, Irgatlar Hamam, Vefa Hamam and Mahmutpaşa Hamam. The only hamam not to permit such riotous entertainment was Haseki Sultan Hamam, where they tried to offer a genuine service to ordinary people.

Having received their orders from the Grand Vizier, the bailiffs sent out women to round up all the beauticians working in the hamam cool rooms. Some were found arranging damp hair smelling of fresh soap over their knees, braiding silver thread into the tresses of rich clients, or spraying musk and ambergris on to chignons and ringlets. Others were applying kohl to sable eyelashes, painting rouge on to cheeks and lips, and drawing fine crescent eyebrows. They were made to drop everything and, grumbling and trembling, led away to the Grand Vizier's palace. The most famous and skilled among them assumed the Grand Vizier was going to offer them work. They each had their own particular method of styling hair or applying make-up and were known personally by the elite households of Istanbul. However, the Grand Vizier merely wanted to find out which of them had braided the hair of the murder victim delivered to his bedroom. That was all.

By the time the mid-day call to prayer was being chanted, nine attendants with two beauticians on each side stood waiting to be taken from the harem into an ante-room, where the Grand Vizier made the women wait. Once they started grumbling, he knew he could start interrogating them, but he soon found out that they were prepared to say anything to get away as quickly as possible. His interrogation technique was simple. The women were brought to his room one at a time and, after being interrogated, were ushered out through a side door so that none of them saw who came in next. Finally, a middle-aged Greek beautician from Sultan Hamam recognized the hair in the Grand Vizier's hand.

"Your Excellency, I braided those plaits for the wife of a toymaker living in Eyüp."

Sultan Hamam was a long way from Eyüp. However, the Grand Vizier sensed he was on to something and thought it might be a ruse to confuse him or put him off the scent. After all, who would commit a crime on home ground? He finally summoned his bailiffs and told them to invite the Greek beautician to his house that night, but on no account was she to talk to anyone nor was she to be treated as a criminal. Then he sent his spies off to search the address she had given. The toymaker was not at home. In accordance with the Grand Vizier's orders, the spies went straight to the bedroom where they filled a chest with women's clothing and accessories and took them back to the palace. Two bailiffs went to the toymaker's shop in the market to tell him that His Excellency the Grand Vizier wished to see him.

The next day, as the mid-morning sunlight poured into the Grand Vizier's office, the toymaker was brought in.

"Where is your wife?" asked Grand Vizier İbrahim Pasha.

"She went to visit her aunt in Izmir three months ago. I heard from her recently. She'll be there for another two months," replied the toymaker.

The Grand Vizier signalled to his men to bring in the chest. The toymaker was astonished to see his wife's belongings in the Grand Vizier's office.

"Let us know if any of these robes do not belong to your wife," said the Grand Vizier, as his attendants took out the dresses one by one.

The toymaker recognized all the jackets, waistcoats, robes, shalwars, veils, headscarves and shawls.

"That belongs to my wife!" he kept repeating.

Finally, he was shown an expensive garment made of velvet with silver thread running through it.

"That robe doesn't belong to my wife!" he said without a moment's hesitation.

QUESTION 9
WAS NAKŞIGÜL DISMEMBERED ALIVE?

The number of ferries, market boats, sailing dinghies, gondolas and rowing boats going to and from Eyüp dock was always greater on Tuesdays and Fridays, because it was market day at Eyüp. Families munched halva on their way to visit the tomb of Abu Ayyub al-Ansari at the mosque built in his honour and known as Eyüp Sultan Mosque, while lovers took the opportunity to pursue their loved ones and crowds came to make sacrificial offerings. At the meat market, the influx of clients, slaughterers and meat distributers, not to mention the drifters, drunkards and other hangers-on, brought a significant swell of people to Eyüp Sultan village.

The village was famous for its halva and, on that uncommonly hot autumn Friday, the halva shops were overflowing. As the last feeble rays of sunlight glinted through the poplars on to the walls of the Abu Ayyub al-Ansari Mausoleum and created sparkles on the waters of the Golden Horn, a skiff carrying Falco and two guards passed by the waterfront villas with their half-open latticed blinds. The evening call to prayer began at Dersaadet and, for the first time in his life, Falco felt the spiritual effect of the evening azan that, since time immemorial, had resounded like a chorus from both sides of the Golden Horn. His whole life had been spent by the Golden Horn, in the towns and villages that lay between Alibey Köyü and Kağıthane, Eyüp Sultan and Bahariye, Fener and Hasköy, Balat and Sütlüce, Cibali and Kasımpaşa. However, perhaps because of his wayward lifestyle and the places he frequented, the azan had never before affected him as it did on that evening. It seemed strange that it should happen now, while he was being transferred by boat from one prison to another.

Falco was still feeling wretched and miserable, but his mind was more lucid than on the previous day. He had stopped crying and was able to match his thoughts to the images that kept flashing into his mind. It was as if he had been in a drunken haze or in the grip of a terrible nightmare since the morning after his wedding. However, he seemed to be thinking more clearly now and, as well as thinking of his bride, was able to focus on where he was being taken. Whatever had happened, the cruel truth was inescapable: Nakşıgül was no longer there. His beloved had departed from this world. It was not a dream. They had indeed consummated their love and he had stroked her hair while calling her his darling, but she was no longer there and he was left alone yearning to hear her voice and see her face. The pain of Nakşıgül's absence was so strong that it mattered little to him where he was being taken. He had already decided that, since he had been unable to protect her,

it was fitting that he should die. His memories of the wedding night and the hours spent in the prison intermingled and he kept his eyes fixed on the oiled rope that bound his hands. It seemed a bit slack, but he thought nothing of it. His mind kept reverting to his recent experiences and the memories of Nakşıgül, which coursed through his veins like the water swirling past the boat that carried him.

After a while, Falco pulled himself together and started to review what had happened in a careful and rational manner. He forced himself to concentrate, just as when the Prison Custodian had left him to write his confession. On that day, he had dipped the pen into the ink, examined his heart and decided that whatever became of him was of little consequence since it was the loss of Nakşıgül that troubled him, not being a prisoner. Everywhere was a prison if Nakşıgül was not present in his life, whether he was in prison, at home, in a boat, or at liberty to roam. That was why, when he handed the Prison

Custodian a blank sheet of paper, he had paid little heed to his angry curses.

However, all this was clearly important to someone. The first blow to Falco's head had landed with the words, "We'll settle this at Galata Prison, you'll see!" This was followed by kicks and punches to his face and belly, accompanied by a plea for God's forgiveness. After blacking out for a while, Falco had opened his eyes to see the Prison Custodian rolling up his sleeves, getting ready for a second bout. The tattoo on his biceps alone was enough to instil fear of the punches to come. Falco remembered it more clearly now. It was a tattoo of a viper stretching from elbow to shoulder, where the open mouth seemed to smirk as the snake waggled its tongue. The tattoo artist had done his job well, because the snake's face was truly frightening. Falco still had a burning sensation in his temples from the Prison Custodian's first punch and felt as if his face been torn to shreds. However, the Prison Custodian stopped after the thunderous first punch and walked out saying, "Don't worry, we'll sort you out at Galata Prison!"

Orderlies, guards and policemen had then started arriving in ones and twos. Falco was not allowed to sleep or relax, whether he was standing or seated, nor was he given anything to eat or drink for a whole day. He was not only subjected to bastinado, put in a clamp, bound to stakes, beaten and had his genitals twisted, but also told that he would have to suffer the intolerable torture techniques used at Galata Prison unless he confessed to the murder of Nakşıgül. However, Falco had managed to withstand all the torture and beatings, possibly because he was wrapped up in his own thoughts of Nakşıgül. He had managed to keep his only souvenir of their night together, half of the twin tulip bulb, squeezed tightly in his hand as if it were the hand of his lover. It had given him the strength to remain silent during another night and day of brutal beatings at the prison..

Falco now had his gaze fixed on the gradually darkening water of the Golden Horn in front of Cevahirci Villa next to the Defterdar landing dock and he shuddered as he recalled how his interrogator had kept pausing the questioning so that the strongest of the prison guards could inflict more beatings.

"I'll make you confess, if I have to cut you up alive like Nakşıgül!" the guard had snarled.

"What did you say?"

"Why do you look so surprised?" the guard had asked, looking taken aback. "Don't you like me saying that Nakşıgül was cut up alive? Murderer!"

The image of Nakşıgül's dismembered body floated before Falco's eyes again. It was only two nights since they had been wrapped in each other's arms, whispering love poems to each other. Falco's head began to pound to the rhythm of the boat as it rocked on the waves. He had to recall and scrutinise absolutely everything that had happened. After what the prison guard had said, Falco knew that everything relating to the dismemberment of Nakşıgül needed investigating. The images it provoked made him so nauseous he thought he was losing his mind. One of his wife's arms was hanging from the door latch, the other swinging from a string attached to the ceiling. Her legs had been chopped off at the knees and placed in the fireplace in the shape of a cross, the flesh sliced down the muscle line to expose the bone. Her trunk was slit open from her belly to her breasts, exposing sinew and raw flesh. The bloody section of skin stretched across the window like a piece of parchment must have been excoriated from there. Scattered among the blood and sinew that was all over the room were gold coins. Was that intentional or significant? The only exception was where he and Nakşıgül had laid their heads. There was not a single drop of blood on the lavender-scented pillow where, as dawn was breaking, he had found Nakşıgül's head lying as if she were still asleep. He recalled quite clearly that, when he sensed the empty space next to him where her arm should have been, the pillow had been spotlessly clean.

Falco's mind clouded over again and, still under the effect of the torture and beatings, he lost his balance for a moment in the skiff as he pondered over a question that kept going round and round in his head: Was Nakşıgül dismembered alive?

When he managed to pull himself together, he considered a second question: Was his interrogator one of the people who had dismembered Nakşıgül?

Falco thought about this for a long time. When the prison guard had said '...like Nakşıgül', was it the truth, or a crude simile? When Falco had queried his words, the guard had looked bewildered and innocent. Yet he had said, "....if I have to cut you up alive like Nakşıgül." What did he mean?

Falco finally decided that he had to dismiss the notion that life was futile and not worth living without Nakşıgül. It would have meaning if he dedicated his life to her, because with her he had experienced not only one night of conjugal bliss, but the most significant few weeks of his life. It was the moment when he resolved to find the Nakşıgül's murderers that he noticed the looseness of the ropes binding his hands.

When the prison skiff reached Kasımpaşa, Falco saw signs of a wedding through a gateway on the quayside. On the water there must have been a hundred caiques arranged around a large galleon, all lit up with hundreds of candles and lanterns.

The groom, no doubt the captain of the ship, was being given a send-off by his naval officers and the guests in caiques. It had become fashionable in recent years to have weddings on the water like this. Illuminated summer or spring weddings by moonlight were now frequent events on the Golden Horn, just as they had been in the olden days. In the winter when the water froze over, weddings and other festivities would be held on sledges across the Golden Horn. A most attractive aspect of these occasions was the plentiful supply of alcohol, because it was impossible to impose controls. Although the ban on alcohol had been lifted ten years previously, public consumption of spirits and wine was still not permitted in the city. However, on the water, people just tossed their wine gourds and casks into the sea, because nobody was going to investigate every caique to discover the culprits.

For a moment, Falco imagined that he was not in a prison skiff, but in one of the wedding caiques. The wedding looked to be a grandiose affair, from the number of people afloat that evening. The songs and ballads, the yelling and swearing, the gunshots and pyrotechnics were all typical of such celebrations and Falco smiled sadly as he remembered the pleasurable if dissipated times he had spent at such weddings with his former friends.

As the skiff approached Kasımpaşa, one of the guards took some fisherman's netting out of a bag and put a large weight inside.

"Let's change places so that I can bind the gentleman's feet," said the guard to his colleague.

Falco realised that he was about to be thrown into the water. He felt a surge of rage and tried to loosen the rope binding his hands. The oarsmen did not challenge what was happening as the guards stood up to change places. Then, while the oarsmen were making way for the guards, a barge carrying bales of cloth came up behind and crashed into the rear of the prison skiff. The blow was so violent that the collision seemed almost deliberate, particularly since the boatman in the barge appeared to lose all control. Everyone in the skiff clutched on to something, lunging this way and that to keep their balance. One of the guards fell into the water and the others reached out to him, making the skiff tilt dramatically. Falco was still struggling to free his wrists from the ropes when one of the oarsmen hit him with an oar, hurling him into the water just seconds before the guards were going to throw him overboard. With his hands still bound, he swam and swam without looking back.

QUESTION 10
DID THEY TAKE HIM THERE TO KILL HIM OR LET HIM GO?

There were three people in the room, which was lined with shelves filled with rows of different sized bottles and gourds of medicines. The sun was shining through the window on to a bench covered with a clean cloth, while a physician sterilised his blades over a flame.

"What your name is, Lord Pasha?" he asked, in broken Turkish.

Falco almost replied that his name was Ahmet, thinking it might be a way of avoiding the people who were after him, but then remembered his mother's wishes. Ever since he was twelve years old, she had called him 'my son Falco' or 'my lord Falco', even addressing him as Prince Falco on days when she was really proud of him. She had always used that name and, one day before her death, had made him promise to use it also. Only Judge İshak knew his name was Ahmet, but even he called him Falco. As for his childhood friends in the villages along the Golden Horn, they had forgotten his old name long ago. Anyway, he liked the name Falco and enjoyed people comparing him to a falcon – it made him feel heroic. However, he now had to change his identity, but he was about to do it in another way

"Falco," he said. "My name is Falco."

"Wonderful, wonderful! You look just like falcon!"

Falco's friend had told him that the physician, a Hungarian convert to Islam, did his job well and could keep a secret. Best of all, he would be boarding a ship to Beirut in twelve days.

When the physician had finished his preparations for the operation, he spread a fresh cover over the bench and told Falco to lie down. He checked Falco's mouth to ensure that he had not spat out the opium paste given to numb the pain, and bound his hands and feet to prevent them from moving.

"Come, sit on your friend. Make sure he does not move," said the physician, signalling to the friend who had accompanied Falco.

"Very well, Efendi, but..." said the friend.

"Don't worry, doctor, I'll clench my teeth," said Falco.

The physician smiled and, despite Falco's assurance, bound his jaw with a strap, pressed padding on both sides of his head, and tightened the clamping mechanism.

"Let's see what happens!" murmured the physician.

When the bandages were removed on the second day, Falco looked warily at himself in the tarnished mirror. It was unbelievable. His eyebrows were now almost joined in the middle and their edges rose towards his temples. Possibly because the changes emphasised his aquiline nose, his face really did resemble a falcon. If his dear mother could have seen that face, she would not have recognized it. Although the physician had only altered the eyebrows, the result was extraordinary and he was looking extremely proud of his work.

"Grow a long, thick moustache and your bride will never look at another," he joked, seeing the mixture of amazement and pleasure on Falco's face.

Falco held the doctor's hand tightly as he thanked him, inwardly reflecting that his bride would never have the chance of another bridal bed.

There was of course one person to whom he would be indebted for ever. That person was Lanky Osman, the old sailor who, three days before, had leant out of his boat and caught hold of Falco when he was struggling in the water at Kasımpaşa where the wedding was taking place. When Falco had fallen into the water, he had managed to swim, but with difficulty because his hands were still bound. He had eventually come to the surface, seen what looked like a toy galliot with an old sailor sitting in it and swum alongside the oars. After thinking he was destined for the press at Galata Prison followed by a spell rotting in Dockyard Prison, fate had brought him face to face with a guardian angel in the form of Lanky Osman, something for which Falco would be eternally grateful. Lanky Osman was an itinerant who had ended up in Istanbul after leaving his home on one of the Mediterranean islands. Guessing from Falco's state of mind that he, like Lanky Osman, was a victim of love and probably on the run, Lanky Osman had taken pity on him and rushed him off to the Hungarian physician and had used his small savings to pay for the operation. Falco had frequently heard that fine men were to be found living around the dockyards, but he had never believed them. Now he had met one.

When the naval wedding was over, Falco and Lanky Osman had considered trying to drown the other men who had fallen out of the prison skiff in order to avoid being followed. But Falco felt that, while it might have been the best way of dealing with the guards, it would have been wrong to drown the oarsmen, who were merely transferring him from one prison to another. They obviously knew every inch of the Golden Horn and might have deliberately waited until Kasımpaşa before throwing him into the sea. Were they really unable to catch him? Or had they let him go intentionally? Did they take him there with the purpose of killing him or pretending to do so?

"If I am to do anything for Nakşıgül, I have to solve this riddle."

QUESTION 11
WHY SEEK REFUGE IN THE ANONYMITY OF A STOKEHOUSE?

"Children of Layhar! This is your home. Yours, not mine. You are all brothers. Those with two parents have been known to cut each other's throats, but the children of Layhar, who know neither father nor mother, see themselves as one and the same. The pain of a needle piercing the flesh of one is felt by his brother as if it were his own. Those who don this robe regard each other as equal in life until death. It is union within a duality. He is your right hand, you are his left. Two sides of one. One body, two heads. You watch out and care for each other all your life. Here, there is no 'mine' and no 'yours'. If there is little, it is made to go far; if there is plenty, it nourishes you all. There is one pot that feeds all, by the grace of God!"

Those were the words recited by Stokehouse Baba at the ceremony when they became 'brothers'. It was followed by a feast in honour of Layhar that lasted until morning. That evening, two more unfortunate souls were claimed by the notorious underworld of Istanbul and added to the list of unregistered orphans.

Layhar was a half-crazy man who lived in the tenth century in Ghazni, the town where Sultan Mahmut was born. He slept in the stokehouse of the local hamam, where he existed on dregs of wine, made prophesies like a clairvoyant and performed miracles like a saint. He castigated the famous poet Hakim Senai for eulogising Gazneli Mahmut, whom Layhar regarded as no more than a fleeting presence in this earthly world. Many who listened to his views on Hakim Senai became disciples. Later, Layhar was regarded as a sage among the alcoholics and drug addicts living in the hamam stokehouses.

The stokehouses were referred to as Hooligan Lodge and their inmates believed that Layhar had flown away one day as a glorious rooster, which was why it had become traditional to leave the stokehouse when the roosters crowed in the morning and, after a day of begging in the streets, return when the birds settled down to roost in the evening. When the two desperate youths arrived at the stokehouse, they were filled with such hope that they put up with being made to beg, chased away, pestered and even threatened with having their bodies carved up and their blood turned to wine.

The stokehouses maintained links with Bektashi lodges, but paid little attention to the janissaries. In the past, there had been a three-way link between Bektashi lodges, janissary coffee houses and stokehouses. However, most of the men who took shelter at the stokehouses had little interest in religious orders or dervish lodges, and no understanding of what it meant to be an Alevi or Bektashi. What they did know was that as long as they remained at the stokehouse, they could live their lives untrammelled by responsibilities. Many of them had come in off the streets as orphans or children of neglectful parents and found life to be comfortable there with the freedom to do as they pleased.

The two brothers gradually got to know one another and discover each other's secrets and problems. During the day they would carry out the tasks assigned to them by the Foreman, such as begging, pilfering, sweeping the square or cleaning the muddy alleyways. In the evenings, they would return to Hooligan Lodge and listen to people singing ballads, reciting a *gazel*, sometimes even playing passionate tunes on the *bağlama*. At other times, they played backgammon, knucklebones or chess before stretching out exhausted to sleep on the ashes. It was the duty of new recruits to scatter hot ashes over the stokehouse floor, heap cinders into the long trough that served as a divider in the middle of the long rectangular room, and bring in sacks to put beneath the heads of the stokers, who lay in groups of five on each side with their feet stretched out

towards the cinders in the middle. The last ritual before sleep was to go to Stokehouse Baba, who would be holding the rooster and a three-branch candelabrum, and snuff out the candles.

"In the name of Layhar, his heart and his soul!" they would call out before each puff.

The next morning, everyone rose at the sound of the sacred rooster. Stokehouse Baba lit the candles in the candelabrum with the same prayer and the stokehouse day began all over again. The men slept in a pair of thin shalwar that went up between the legs and covered their bellies, to prevent their clothes getting covered with ashes during the night. After waking, the two new brothers fetched hot water from the hamam and brought in a cauldron of hot soup and fresh bread made by Cook, while the other men brushed the ash off their bodies and shook out their shalwar.

Everybody at the stokehouse had a nickname, including Jarhead Cafer who oversaw their general needs and checked their earnings. The stokers' duties involved a rota for lighting the hamam fire, getting the flames going, dowsing the flames, reviving them, and so on. Sometimes they were given the opportunity of serving as a bath attendant, towel dispenser, keeper of the purses or shoe minder. They took care not to swear, but their language would slip into a friendly banter that was full of slang, and the older ones taught newcomers how to strut, thrust their shoulders forward and poke people with their elbows.

The latest recruits were not yet allowed to speak, but they were beginning to understand and learn the argot spoken at the stokehouse. They now knew that in stokehouse jargon, 'stokehouse' was 'mother', 'stoker' was 'father', 'feast' was 'mud', 'janissaries' were 'moustaches', 'market place' was ‘farm’, ‘loincloth’ was ‘modesty towel’, ‘female bath attendant’ was ‘clad’, ‘hamam’ was ‘rose garden’, ‘fire’ was ‘red festival’, ‘prison’ was ‘school’, ‘sultan’ was *‘tuğra’*, ‘vizier’ was ‘seal’, ‘spy’ was ‘scorpion’ and ‘rich man’ was ‘goose’.

The stokehouses had started out as a kind of guild, but over time they gained a reputation for being places that harboured people with no official identity, and as centres which organised everything from begging to robbery or from protection rackets to abductions. Nobody delved into anyone’s past or future and personal details were known only between ‘brothers’, who of course kept them secret.

Just before falling asleep one night, having completed their mandatory three days of silence, the older of the new recruits turned over to look at his young brother lying next to him.

“What’s your name?” he asked.

“Yusuf. And yours?”

“Falco.”

“Shall we choose ourselves a nickname tomorrow?”

“Fine.”

They lay back to back on the warm ashes, for the first time falling into a deep sleep with a feeling of trust in each other’s presence.

QUESTION 12
WHICH TAILOR MADE THIS ROBE?

Grand Vizier İbrahim Pasha had given orders for the toymaker to be kept in the palace detention room as if he were an overnight guest. Early the following morning, he summoned his bailiffs.

"You are to go out and round up all the tailors who make silver-threaded robes and bring them here by noon," he ordered.

İbrahim Pasha felt cheerful as he went towards the breakfast pavilion that looked out at Sultan Ahmet Mosque and across the water to the Marmara islands. The fruit baskets in there were always full and the Grand Vizier made a habit of eating an apple before taking breakfast as he gazed at the view. He ordered some milk, a stick of cinnamon, cheese and honey to be brought to the table. This pretty little breakfast pavilion with its stone patios reminiscent of old Turkish houses was occasionally used as a summer house. It was İbrahim Pasha's favourite part of the majestic palace, which his namesake İbrahim Pasha of Parga had had built on the ruins of the Roman hippodrome walls. Since the time of Sultan Süleyman I, almost every grand vizier had lived in this palace. It consisted of a tower, pavilion, treasury, hamam, council chamber, cellar and numerous kitchens. When the current İbrahim Pasha moved into the palace, he had overseen sweeping renovations to the property and was now inclined to regard it as his own. It was his preferred place for carrying out his duties and the Sultan had no objection to this. Another reason why Grand Vizier İbrahim Pasha wanted to remain at his palace that day was that he wanted no one to know about his investigation. If news of the murder were to reach the ears of anyone at the Seraglio, it would interfere with his plans.

By noon, seven master tailors had been brought to him. The Grand Vizier interrogated each of them in turn, letting them out through a side door so that they did not meet each other. Not one of them admitted to having touched the silver-threaded velvet robe. Among them was an English tailor who attached special crocheted buttons to the expensive clothes he made for foreigners in the Galata district. The Grand Vizier knew that this tailor had made robes for his wife, Fatma Sultan and two of her ladies-in-waiting to wear on the occasion of his daughter's marriage to Admiral of the Fleet Kaymak Mustafa Pasha the previous year. All the garments he made for wives of foreign diplomats were much admired by society ladies in Galata and a special courier was dispatched to tell him that the harem of His Excellency the Grand Vizier would be placing an order.

İbrahim Pasha was pleased to have this tailor involved, because whoever had ordered the murder must have been a wealthy person who appreciated modern European fashion, which had a bearing on the note in the basket of fruit and nuts, which had read, 'Honourable Grand Vizier! Let's see if you are as clever as they say!' It also added to the excitement of solving the problem. İbrahim Pasha picked up a bright red apple and, looking around to see if any servants were nearby, bit into it noisily.

QUESTION 13
HOW CAN A HOUSE DISAPPEAR, HODJA?

The Foreman had sent them out begging again, which they usually did around the Covered Bazaar. However, that day they set off in a different direction and spent three hours making their way from Gedikpaşa to the Cannon Gate, where Sultan Mehmet the Conqueror entered Istanbul in 1453. Once outside the city walls, they walked towards Takkeci İbrahim Ağa Mosque to find the house where Falco had met and fallen in love with Nakşıgül. The plan was for Stocky Yeye to act as lookout while Dusky Falco (they had now adopted these nicknames) tried to talk to the nanny. He had been fond of Nakşıgül's nanny and thought she might help him or be able to give him some information. His appearance was now quite different because, apart from having his eyebrows lifted by the Hungarian physician, his complexion had darkened from living at the stokehouse, which was why he had the nickname Dusky Falco. Still, it was possible that someone might recognize him and he did not want to arouse suspicions when he started asking questions.

"We must be careful, Stocky Yeye!" said Dusky Falco, his heart pounding.

Initially, Yusuf had found it strange to be addressed by anything other than his own name, but he trusted Falco and did not mind him using this nickname. At the asylum, they had called him Yearning Yusuf, but he thought Stocky Yeye sounded better and it also matched his stature.

"Okay, Dusky Falco!" he replied.

As Dusky Falco continued walking, he became aware of a strange sensation. He normally paid little attention to his surroundings, but now he realised that there were many more trees than he remembered on this dusty road leading from the mosque. He assumed that his memory had become confused, but felt certain that there should be a house to his right. He stopped to collect his thoughts. He had been along this road to Aslan Ağa's house three times before, but each time it had been in a horse-drawn landau and he had spoken to no one. However, he definitely remembered seeing a house there. On one occasion, he and Nakşıgül had been in the landau with her mother and nanny, who had embarrassed them into silence by discussing them. He even remembered the nanny proudly handing out iced sherbets and nibbles that had come all the way from India.

"No, no! I must have remembered it wrongly. There can't have been a house here!" he thought, once again doubting himself.

The water that ran down to the moat at the foot of the old Byzantine walls was used by Greeks living inside the city to cultivate vegetables in fields that lay outside the walls. The area, which had always been particularly good for growing cos lettuces, provided a regular supply of seasonal vegetables that were delivered through Cannon Gate to the royal kitchens. Ten years earlier, the Imperial Estate Manager had allowed parts of the cemetery outside the city walls to be turned into gardens, which was why the area was called Yenibahçe, or New Gardens. Takkeci Mosque remained in the middle of these gardens, but its congregation mostly came from within the city walls. Dusky Falco walked towards the mosque. There was nobody in the gardens except for a few labourers, whom Stocky Yeye would be able to distract if necessary. It was only mid-morning, so nobody would be in the mosque. Feeling confident, Dusky Falco walked up to the mosque, then stopped, rubbed his eyes and looked again. His legs felt like cotton wool and he thought he might collapse. Either he was going crazy or he was already completely out of his mind. He ran over to the garden walls and gates and started examining them with his hands. Anyone watching him would have thought he was a lunatic. His strange antics certainly startled Yeye, who had come up to check on their surroundings. He had never seen Dusky Falco like that before. Was there something in his character that he did not yet know about? Yeye hesitated for a moment then, remembering their vows when they donned the Layhar robe at the stokehouse, he ran up to Dusky Falco to offer his help.

"What's happened?" whispered Stocky Yeye.

"The house isn't here, Stocky Yeye!"

"Which house?"

"The house where I got married. The house where I won and lost Nakşıgül!"

Stocky Yeye followed Dusky Falco as he ran through the vegetable plots and gardens until they came across two labourers working in front of a little hut.

"Hey, Gardener, we're lost. I thought Aslan Ağa's house was around here. Can you tell us how to get to it?" asked Dusky Falco.

"Hmm, Aslan Ağa? Are you joking, my friend."

"Do I look as though I'm joking?"

"There's nothing but gardens around here. No houses, only garden sheds and I've never heard of anyone called Aslan Ağa."

Dusky Falco and Stocky Yeye asked four more gardeners and received similar replies. They were at a complete loss as to what to do and Yeye, who felt they had already spent too long there, insisted on returning immediately, otherwise the Foreman would punish them.

"You must have dreamt it," said Stocky Yeye, as they sat down next to a fence.

"Oh, Yeye, if only it had been a dream, I could have woken up from it. But Nakşıgül and the beatings I had at the prison were no dream. Nor was the oily rope they put around my neck when they arrested me. If only it had been a dream!"

They heard the noon call to prayer start at the mosque.

"What about asking the imam at Takkeci Mosque?" said Stocky Yeye.

They jumped up and ran back to the mosque, which was not big enough to have both an imam and muezzin. The man they saw coming down the steps of the minaret was a Hodja who performed marriage ceremonies. Dusky Falco was not sure if he wanted to be recognized, but the Hodja gave them a vacant look and obviously did not know him anyway. Falco put this down to the physician's good work on his eyebrows.

"Welcome. What can I do for you?" asked the Hodja as he locked the door to the minaret.

"We're looking for the house of Aslan Ağa. You recently solemnized his daughter's marriage here," said Dusky Falco.

"Who?"

"Aslan Ağa. We're looking for Aslan Ağa's big house in Yenibahçe."

"Son, this is Yenibahçe," said the Hodja. "But there's no one by that name here, nor is there a house here. What would a house be doing here? There's nothing but a few sheds used for selling vegetables. I can ask the congregation, but there's no such house around here."

"But last Friday, you performed a wedding ceremony. Don't you remember?" persisted Dusky Falco.

"Hmm. No, not I. Could it have been another imam?"

"No, it was you!"

"Me? No, no. I didn't perform any wedding ceremonies that day."

"How can that be? I was married there that day."

"Sir, you're imagining things. You must pray. Go straight to the hamam. In fact, you should have bloodletting treatment."

"Hodja, I can assure you that I'm not deranged. But if this goes on, I will be. I tell you, my wedding ceremony was performed there. Why don't you know anything about it? How can a house disappear, Hodja?"

"Son, you really should seek help. There's a European doctor in Çukurçeşme who..."

"See that gentleman there? He was a witness at our wedding," interrupted Dusky Falco, recognising a man who was entering the mosque.

"Husam Efendi, were you a witness at a wedding here last Friday?" called out the Hodja.

"Friday, you say? I think I went to see my daughter in Scutari on Friday. I wasn't here at all," replied the man, looking confused and scratching his head.

"Hodja," said Dusky Falco, raising his voice with growing irritation, "take a good look at me. Do you really not remember me?"

"Nooo..."

"How can that be? You married me in Aslan Ağa's house."

"You must be mistaken, my son. Think it over until the next prayer time."

"Hodja, on Friday night last week, did you not sit next to me and say, 'By the will of God and the word of the Prophet, do you take...' and then did you not say, 'I pronounce Nakşıgül, daughter of Aslan Ağa, and Ahmet bin Abdullah to be man and wife!'?" persisted Falco.

"I said no such thing, son. This is the first time I've seen you in my life. But that's enough. My congregation is waiting for me. Go and repent!"

Yeye believed the Hodja when he said he had not performed the marriage ceremony and he believed Husam Efendi when he said he had not been a witness. They were not the sort of men to lie and had no need to. Furthermore, nobody in the congregation had heard of Aslan Ağa or knew anything about his house. Clearly, there was something unbalanced about his stokehouse brother Dusky Falco.

On the way home, Stocky Yeye listened as Dusky Falco told him everything that was on his mind, which had left him confused and not knowing whether to believe his friend or not. Since the stokehouse twinning ceremony, Falco had confided a great deal in him, including the name of the lady he loved, which was something he should not really have done. Although Yeye was younger than Falco, he had a more refined attitude towards love and considered that everything related to love was to be treasured. In the stories he heard from his mother and the handwritten tracts left by his father, there was no mention of anyone ever sharing the name of their beloved with another person and it was not sanctioned by treatises on love, which advised that love should always be kept secret and never shared. Yeye would never, could never, confide in anyone about his love for Şehnaz. If he did, he was certain that it would diminish his love. Everything he had read advised lovers and mystics to keep such matters to themselves. "Love only grows in the heart if kept secret," his mother had said once, before telling him the story of Leyla's love which grew in secrecy. He believed that if two people broke a shared confidence then, although their friendship and loyalty would be broadcast verbally, it would in fact become devalued. Yeye vowed that he would keep his love for Şehnaz safe within his heart and never tell Falco or anyone else about it. After all, it did not help the doctors at the asylum find a remedy when he mentioned her name. He felt ashamed when he remembered speaking of Şehnaz in front of the lunatics and vowed never to make that mistake again.

Postscript: Love, a secret not to be shared

They asked Leyla:

"Did you love Kays more than he loved you?"

Leyla, with her black eyes, black hair and black beauty spot, sighed and lamented:

"Friends, what kind of question is that? How can you ask me this? Of course I loved him more than he loved me."

"But Leyla, it is because of you that he went crazy and wandered out into the desert, where he became known as Majnun the lunatic and spent his time talking to wolves and birds."

"Look, he went off and talked to everyone about his love for me, whereas I kept my love right here in my heart. I told no one, nor did I complain. So you decide. Did he love me more than I loved him?"

QUESTION 14
WHAT IS THE SECRET OF THE TULIP BULB?

Summer was over, yet the sun was still shining brightly on Kağıthane River at Sadabat. The fishermen called it *pastırma* summer, when the warmth of the late autumn sun lifted everyone's spirits before the onset of winter. Crowds from the villages along the Golden Horn gathered at Sadabat, arriving at the waterfront in skiffs, barges and gondolas, or along dusty roads by landau and ox cart – everyone wanting to steal one more day before the inevitable cold ahead.

Dusky Falco and Stocky Yeye wandered along the marble-clad Silver Canal beneath the trees that lined the water at Alibeyköy and mingled with the crowds in order to beg, plead, cry, play for sympathy, or sometimes just to watch people enjoying themselves. Their favourites were the bear and monkey impressionists. Everywhere was buzzing with life. In the pretty inlets on the Eyüp waterfront, slender caiques set out for different islands, ferrying women, men, mystics, young girls, adolescent boys, fugitives, pursuers and those who enjoyed being pursued.

Falco and Yeye entered the large garden of a modest little house a short way from the cemetery which stretched along the coast as far as the ridges of Eyüp. They held out their begging bowls, repeating over and over, "I beg you, in God's name..." Everyone in Istanbul knew that a man named Hafız Çelebi cultivated special varieties of tulips in that garden and sold them for two gold pieces each.

Hafız Çelebi was a prominent man in the Istanbul tulip trade. He was respected by all and, until the previous year, had managed the seasonal tulip stock market and chaired the commission which determined the price of tulips. However, he had now withdrawn from the bustle of the commercial world, saying that he wanted to devote all his time to tulips. It was for this reason that he had moved the garden fence so that access to the well was no longer inside his garden.

Everyone in Istanbul knew about Hafız Çelebi's domed well next to the cemetery and the people had named it the Well of Souls. If a person or item went missing, say a child or wedding ring, people would come to this well, make their ablutions and perform the *namaz* ritual twice. They would then kneel in front of the well, recite the *Fatiha*, promise a good deed in the name of the prophet Yusuf, say a prayer, and look down into the water hoping to see the location of the lost item or person. Interestingly, everyone claimed to see whatever it was they had lost and sometimes even identified the location. In fact, several thieves had confessed to crimes after being identified in its still waters. There was a constant stream of visitors and all who went there had a tale to tell. During the past year, female visitors had started coming to the well, including spinsters seeking a bridegroom and expectant mothers wanting to know if their child would be a boy or girl. Hafız Çelebi disapproved of such practices and had tried to close the well, but it proved impossible to stop people coming.

Despite all the visitors, the Well of Souls had never revealed the secret of Hafız Çelebi's tulip cultivation. Nobody noticed that, on the shore of the Golden Horn, there was a natural pool which was fed by a small channel from the well and covered with sweet sedge. Although the pool appeared to contain salt water from the Golden Horn, there was not a drop of sea water in it. In fact, the River Cendere provided a continual flow of fresh water that made its way to the pool through Kağıthane and the Well of Souls from its source three hundred metres above. In this pool, Hafız Çelebi cultivated sweet sedge for feeding to his turtles. Occasionally, the turtles would escape and enjoy a few days on the river bed, but it was also not unknown for them to be captured by turtle hunters. Turtles were regarded by many as a health remedy, which was particularly sought after by foreigners living in Galata and businessmen from Europe. Large sums of money would change hands for these turtles, which were boiled in their shells and eaten. When the hunters moved on from Cendere River and started stealing the turtles at the Well of Souls, Hafız Çelebi submitted a strong petition to the government and succeeded in getting the Imperial Estate Manager to issue a decree stating that turtle hunting was to be penalised because it was damaging the ecological balance in the area.

In fact, these turtles fed on sedge roots were the sole source of Hafız Çelebi's wealth. What no one knew was that, before planting the tulip bulbs in the autumn, he would collect the turtles into wooden cages and keep them there for two nights. During that time he would mix the sedge with mint, basil and different coloured paint powders and put the mixture in piles on the floor of the cages for the turtles to eat. He then moved the turtles into empty cages and left them to go hungry for two days before setting down his tulip bulbs before them and monitoring the hungry turtles carefully as they pounced on the tulip bulbs. As soon as the turtles had scarred the bulbs with their teeth, he would remove replace the bulbs with more. Then he laid the scarred bulbs, still covered in turtle saliva, in grease taken from the tails of well-fed sheep for one night and planted them the following morning. It had taken him thirty years of experiments to work out this procedure for achieving a desired colour of tulip. The colour of the paint powder fed to the turtles determined the colour of the bloom that emerged from the bitten bulb. Thus, from the day of planting, Hafız Çelebi was able to forecast the colour of tulip he would produce the following spring. He could keep people curious throughout the winter and amaze them when the tulips emerged in exactly the colours he had predicted.

The creation of new colours of tulips was considered hugely important, especially during the time when İbrahim Pasha was Grand Vizier. Merely replanting bulbs each year and getting the same colour tulip was of no interest. Anyone could do that in their own garden. However, until then, producing a tulip in a totally different shade from the previous year was considered impossible. The latest colour of tulip became a major topic of conversation in the wealthy neighbourhoods of Istanbul. Every spring, people would doubt the likelihood of a new shade emerging, yet Hafız Çelebi always managed to surprise his clients. His fame spread to Holland, people had become gripped by tulip mania on learning that new shades were being produced. So far, despite some success in varying the length and markings of tulip petals, nobody there had yet managed to change the colour.

It was for this reason that Hafız Çelebi's house was sometimes burgled, his belongings rifled and his tulip bulbs stolen. Occasionally, mysterious men would turn up at his house and make him tempting offers, or even creep off like thieves to search inside the Well of Souls for the mystery of his tulips. Yet still Hafız Çelebi managed to keep his work a secret from everyone. Despite all the desperate attempts to find an answer, or the fact that it was right in front of their eyes, nobody had identified the link between the tulips and the turtles feeding on sedge in the water that came from the well. The turtles were merely considered a symbol of Hafız Çelebi's love of nature, nothing more. It was rumoured that Hafız Çelebi had written his secret down on a piece of paper and entrusted it to someone who would reveal it after his death. That had led to more rumours, each more mysterious than the last, not only about the secret of the tulips, but about this unknown person. Was it a child, a woman, or a man?

Perhaps that was why Hafız Çelebi's heart seemed to miss a beat when Dusky Falco went up to him to ask, "What can you tell me about this tulip bulb?"

QUESTION 15
CAN THE GRAND VIZIER SOLVE THE RIDDLE?

Some brazen-looking men sat cross-legged on rush matting in the cool autumn shade under the yellowing vine leaves that covered the Pergola coffee house, filling their earthenware vessels with wine and talking politics. Janissary coffee houses were renowned for being home to debates about politics, the sultanate and government. This particular coffee house was a den of dissent where new ideas were propounded and even conspiracies hatched for deposing and replacing the sultan. There was a close association between the janissaries and the Bektashis, who also occasionally used the coffee house as a centre for decision-making instead of the Şahbaba Monastery. The Bektashis retained certain beliefs of the Shamanist Turks, but also took inspiration from other faiths and philosophies, including Buddhism, Brahmanism, Zoroastrianism, Bâtınism, Jaffarism and various Shiite and Alevi sects. Janissary coffee houses were also points of contact between Bektashi lodges and the stokehouses. While leaning more towards Jaffarism than the Alevi sects, these places were places of reverence for the Twelfth Imam.

There were twelve Pergola coffee houses in Istanbul, which had been established as twelve links to the Twelfth Imam. Three of them were built on platforms over water and nine were built against the Byzantine city walls. Each was run by a Baba, exactly like a Bektashi lodge. At each of the Pergola coffee houses, there were twelve posts at which a janissary officer made regular collections and twelve youths wearing twelve-point crowns who served twelve types of drink, one for each of the twelve months of the year. In the evening, everyone kissed the sacred twelve-point stone of submission and received forgiveness. Then a collection was made, a portion of which was taken as tribute and the remainder shared among those who worked there.

Over the previous fifty years, many political plots had been hatched in these coffee houses by janissaries, even clean-shaven novices and beardless new recruits. The Pergola coffee house at Eminönü was the most famous and stood majestically on a platform reaching out over the sea in front of the Yeni Mosque. The place teemed with ideas as varied as its clientele, who ranged from market traders to sailors and from porters to layabouts. People who visited the area on business from quarters such as Scutari, Galata and Kadiköy would also stop at the Pergola coffee house to take a reviving cup of coffee. That evening, Dusky Falco and Stocky Yeye were sitting on cane stools, drinking *salep*, a beverage made from orchids, to revive them after a day of begging. They had made a habit of calling in there almost every day. Beggars were tolerated at the coffee houses as long as they did not beg. In fact, Dusky Falco was now an official stokehouse messenger and went round the markets handing out and collecting payments and meeting various people with connections to the stokehouse, so his attire was slightly better than that of a mere beggar. Stocky Yeye however was still only assigned to begging and scavenging, something at which he had quickly become very adept, with his short stature, innocent face and stocky build.

Dusky Falco liked going to the coffee house because it meant they were out of the public eye and could observe others. They both thought it might be a good place to pursue their hunt for the murderers of Nakşıgül, since it was unlikely anyone would recognize a pair of stokehouse boys, especially with their dirty, stained faces. Thanks to the work of the physician, Dusky Falco now really did resemble a black falcon. As for Stocky Yeye, it seemed that he had so far managed to elude the asylum guards. However, if either of them had done anything crazy, they would have been caught immediately.

The three Pergola coffee houses on platforms over the Golden Horn were used in the summer, while those that backed on to the city walls provided a pleasant place to sit in winter. People would go to these coffee houses to smoke a pipe or narghile and discuss politics. Falco and Yeye sat quietly on their stools, sipping their drinks and eavesdropping on the conversations around them. Here, it was possible to learn about and discuss every event that had happened, was happening or was about to happen in Istanbul. However, were they ever to repeat to anyone what they overheard in these conversations, they would undoubtedly be condemned as spies of the Grand Vizier, or ‘seal’s scorpions’ in stokehouse argot, and taken off to the cemetery behind the prison and put into a deep hole.

This was an elite circle which did not use normal language in its conversation but spoke in rhyme of variable quality, sometimes surpassing what was considered worthy poetry. Dusky Falco and Stocky Yeye listened in astonishment to the conversations, which sounded like music to their ears. It was all part of the tapestry of life in Istanbul.

“Hey, Muşkara İbrahim! Confectioner’s apprentice!

“That *lala*, that *damat* is now vizier, no less.”

“What’s it to you, brother? Why should we bother? Let’s just hope our war-weary nation is spared any further degradation. He thinks opening letters is work of importance.”

“True, dear Baba, while the rich become richer and the poor lose patience.”

“And what about dignity? He bows to Europeans in conciliation.”

“Laughable, dear Baba. It’s exploitation!”

“Müteferrika set up a printing press. The scribes have become quite speechless.”

“Lies, sir, all lies. To believe that is unwise.”

“So, who raided the printing press? Did someone burn it down? Is the nation so illiberal as to do that to its own?”

“Sharia disappears from our lives without trace and the people complain it’s an absolute disgrace.”

“Sharia is based on law, not belief. It’s fair, it’s just and saves mankind much grief.”

“If only each home contained books that were read, and each town had schools where young readers were bred.”

“I think you’re on the pasha’s side. Have you seen the villa he built for his niece?”

"His pavilions are everywhere, the building does not cease."

"Hammering down stakes and digging wells."

"Laying down open sewage canals."

"He cares only for riotous entertainment."

"As if it is his main attainment."

"That profligate is heading for ruination."

"He'll be destroyed by his own dissipation."

"He dupes the nation with diversions, showers the ladies with perversions. Robs the people to fill the parks with swings that send them high as larks."

"When women are in short supply, he charges men to peek and pry."

"Then the janissaries said they'd give it a try."

"Chaste women in any district now number less than ten."

"Shame on you! Forget not that you're gentlemen."

"Which of you can truly say that one of them is yours? Before condemning others, just take a moment's pause."

"He makes men work through Ramadan, just to make Sadabat spick and span."

"In lieu of cash, he gives them whores, the treasury's empty so the bills are yours."

"That's slander, gentlemen, desist. Such spurious talk you must resist."

Dusky Falco and Stocky Yeye left this lively poetic discussion, their heads buzzing with what they had heard. Little did they know that they would encounter yet another side of Istanbul as they approached a group of four men huddled around a narghile, deep in conversation at a table shaded by some ancient plane trees. The men were talking in low voices, so Dusky Falco and Stocky Yeye had difficulty in hearing them from where they were sitting behind some hanging branches.

The four men looked as if they were just staring at each other, because any movement of their mouths was obscured by their thick moustaches, yellowed by tobacco and the narghile smoke. Dusky Falco and Stocky Yeye listened in astonishment to the conversation through the hiss of tobacco and the bubbling of the narghile.

"They say sharp wits can work miracles. Well, our man became grand vizier and good luck to him!"

"Very true, Glowering Veli. Just think, he used to be that nervous little git who sat by our fire. He didn't know how to smoke and had no backbone, yet now his scorpions are everywhere and he knows about almost everything."

"That's right, isn't it, Dockyard Beagle? Our man got the better of Köprülü, and that Bosnian Sokollu Mehmet Pasha. He gathers information out of thin air and sends his couriers out as if by smoke. He understands what's cooking and which way the wind blows."

The only objection to this nonsense came from Janissary Sergeant Bindallı Mahmut, who bore a tattoo on his shoulder of an anchor of the 46th division.

"You're talking rubbish," said Bindallı Mahmut. "He's nothing but a puppet. Our country cousin İbrahim Efendi is merely there to prop things up and keep the people sweet. Take away his trappings and then see what happens. There'd be no logic, no ideas left!"

"You're wrong, Bindallı Mahmut, my brother. His mind is as sharp as a diamond. It glitters for all to see."

"Fellow travellers, results are what count. Let's prove it and see," challenged Bindallı Mahmut.

More questions mixed with laughter followed.

"How can we prove it, brother?"

"He could be a match for you, Bindallı Mahmut."

"You've clearly overfilled his wine glass!"

"Give me two days," retorted Bindallı Mahmut, obviously offended by their words. "We'll look at the result of my test together."

The three friends pleaded with Sergeant Bindallı Mahmut to say any more about his test, but he refused.

"I pulled a little stunt last week. Just wait and see!" was all Bindallı Mahmut would say.

The hanging lamps in the Pergola coffee house were being lit as Bindallı Mahmut rose to bid his friends farewell. The five people sitting at the next table also started moving. One of them picked up his pipe, while another threw a jacket he was clutching over his shoulder, and two moved aside to make way. Behind them all scampered a dwarf trying to keep up.

Dusky Falco hung his bag around his neck, leant over towards his friend and whispered, "Time to go, Yeye."

QUESTION 16
WHOSE SCALP DID THE SULTAN WANT?

"Lala," the Sultan had said, "this is our sacred seal. Take it and be our noble Grand Vizier! Take charge of the state, for the sake of those who suffer far from home and sacrifice their lives for the country."

They had then spoken at length about the state of the nation, poverty, falling morals, foreign policy, Passarowitz, the peace with Austria, Khorasan and Afghanistan, the Uzbeks and Azerbaijan, about the ongoing rebellions in Anatolia and Rumelia, corruption within the janissaries, the urgent need for reforms, the rapid spread of westernization and the lack of educated men.

"Yes, my Sultan," İbrahim Pasha had said, "your word is my command, Your Majesty. It will be an honour and privilege to serve you."

Grand Vizier İbrahim Pasha's duties had begun with these words and lasted for eleven years. It was four days before the start of Ramadan and the markets were overflowing, yet there was anxiety among the less affluent. Over the years, all major buildings and gardens in the city had been restored and Istanbul was the envy of civilized cities throughout the world. Travel writers and diplomats from every country wrote about Grand Vizier İbrahim Pasha's achievements in Istanbul. While the city already had a natural beauty, it had been further improved to enhance its time and setting, without merely relying on natural geography. An aesthetic dimension had been created that linked people's consciousness to their hearts and was a source of endless inspiration to poets, who never tired of praising the city's neighbourhoods and architecture. However, while its citizens were elegant and well-mannered, poverty and crime were rife. Istanbul had never been so full of contradictions. Both its wealth and poverty had reached previously unknown levels, creating a treacherously dangerous imbalance.

That afternoon, guests flocked from all over Istanbul to Sadabat palace, which stood opposite the Ahmet III Fountain overlooking the Silver Canal. They came in great anticipation to attend one of the Sultan's legendary entertainments. Poetry and song, new and ancient, were significant features of these events. When men of eloquence and refinement gave impassioned renderings of poetry and music in the palace's elegant salon, the world of good taste and pleasure seemed to radiate across the phosphorescent waters of Sadabat out among the people of Istanbul.

The Sultan was always the exalted guest at these gatherings, though he did not shrink from having business discussions with acquaintances among the wine-drinking fraternity. Since the early years of his appointment, Grand Vizier İbrahim Pasha had greatly influenced the Sultan with his refined and innovative personality and, as he gained in confidence, began to assume considerable state control by arranging this sort of entertainment. "It is my duty to protect your state in your name," İbrahim Pasha would say repeatedly. The trust these words induced in the Sultan enabled the Grand Vizier to use power as a tool of oppression to achieve whatever he wanted in matters such as diplomatic relations, decisions of war, peace treaties, economic policies, civil service appointments, the assignment of offices, and even turning formal ceremonies into spectacles of entertainment. The people he brought into government were mainly friends and family, while the spies he assigned to posts in other parts of the Ottoman Empire provided him with information that he could use against the Sultan or other statesmen. The Grand Vizier's spies were present in the splendid salon at that very moment.

The guests that day included: Prince Rákóczi of Transylvania; General Stefan, a favourite of King Eugene of Austria; the

Afshar shepherd Nadir Ali, the de facto ruler of Iran known as Tahmasb's Slave Nadir Khan; Jewish Levian, head of the Russian Czar's secret service; the former Duke of Bourbon Martel Clovis, who was Chargé d'Affaires for King Louis XV of France; Bektashi Baba Sheikh Abdulhay Efendi, who was renowned for his authority over the janissaries; the famous poets Nedim Efendi and Seyyid Vehbi, and friends; the Commander of the Janissaries, some of the Sultan's viziers, the chamberlain and thirty or more other people. The guests were served with crystal glasses of white wine or silver cups of sherbet and, as the afternoon sun shone through the windows into the palace reception salon, they spent a pleasant hour or so expressing opinions on a variety of subjects while waiting for the Sultan to grace their presence.

Anyone eavesdropping that afternoon would probably have despaired of the Ottoman state. The conversations covered numerous issues: how after sixteen years of war the Ottomans had managed to eliminate any fear of Turks in the minds of Europeans by signing the Treaty of Karlowitz; how the Treaty of Passarowitz had allowed land to be taken from the Turks, making their defeat possible; how fragmented city states on the Mediterranean were being taken over by Rome and converted to Christianity; how the persistent disagreements with Iran were escalating, causing anxieties to mount within the army and Russia's influence over Iran to escalate; how Greek converts to Islam on the Mediterranean islands were being employed on active duty as Ottoman pashas; how after living in exile at Bender for three and a half years at the expense of the Ottomans, Swedish King Charles, known among Ottomans as 'Charles the fixture' had returned to his country via Russian territory and been obliged to sit at a peace table with his sworn enemy Czar Peter the Great; how measures for increasing Safavid influence over Afghan and Khorasan lands in the east had raised Nadir Ali's credibility with Tahmasb Khan and secured the defeat of Ashraf Khan; how sources of remuneration were being closed off to the Ottoman palace, which had become so accustomed to fashionable extravagances; how palace ladies were being prevented from squandering money, and how fatwas were being issued against the wearing of European fashions introduced by diplomats and foreign travellers. All these and many more topics were discussed in raised voices without any real attempt at finding a solution. The heated but pointless discussions among the small groups of nobles and diplomats were conducted in so many different languages that the gathering sounded like afternoon prayers at the Tower of Babel.

"Gentlemen, raise not your speaking voices at this gathering, but your singing voices," proclaimed the Grand Vizier, as he entered the hall, acknowledging his guests and causing a sepulchral silence to fall over the proceedings.

Occasionally, the Grand Vizier would assert himself over a gathering in this way. However, this time he was indicating that the Sultan was about to arrive and court etiquette dictated that nobody should speak until he was seated and had given his permission for others to do so. Indeed, it was not long before Sultan Ahmet entered, smiling and displaying a childish pleasure as he made his way to sit cross-legged on the high divan. Behind a curtain, some singers started performing a song in *Segah* mode:

From the lips of the beloved, secret messages do flow
Hearing words of such exquisiteness the listener is aglow
One single hint of reproach would cause suffering and woe
Piercing the heart like an arrow shot from Rustem's bow

Kemhacızade Hafız sang melodies and ballads that started in *segah* and modulated into *karcığar* to the accompaniment of Andelib Çelebi on his tamboura and zither. They then modulated through various other modes from *Hüseyn* to *Suznak*. It was a night of abundance, pleasure and beauty, during which many topics were discussed, many delicacies devoured and much wine enjoyed. The assembly lasted from afternoon until the call to prayers the following morning. Autumn breezes carried melodies across the Golden Horn to Fatih and Şehzadebaşı and, in the depths of that long night, as Nedim's song was played in praise of the approaching Ramadan and the festival to follow, indignant angels flew from the slums of Istanbul to alight on the roof of the Sadabat pavilions where they paused to flutter their wings. Everyone joined in this last song:

The magical entertainments offer a rare experience
Come to Seyr-i Sa'abad and embrace its precious radiance
Time passes by so blissfully, even in times of abstinence
Come to Seyr-i Sa'dabad and embrace its precious radiance

Here you will find the air is full of wondrous delights
Enjoyed by all as sunny days turn to endless starry nights
When more surprises there unfold, accompanied by glorious sights
Come to Seyr-i Sa'dabad and embrace its precious radiance

Suddenly, the Sultan noticed Judge İshak and his high spirits immediately evaporated. His face hardened as he swallowed and beckoned to the judge, who stooped to kiss the hem of his robe. When ordered to sit down, he made sure he was close to the Sultan. Judge İshak, who was to be the next Sheikh ul-Islam, was abstaining from drinking wine. He knew exactly what the

Sultan was going to ask him and knew the danger of speaking openly in front of people who were under the influence of alcohol, which was why he bent close to the Sultan. However, one pair of ears heard what was said between them: Grand Vizier İbrahim Pasha, who was sitting right next to the Sultan.

"You were to bring me news, İshak Efendi," said the Sultan.

"Yes, Your Majesty, but there is no news yet," replied Judge İshak.

"Is it not a punishable offence to be so late with news about my state and property?" muttered the Sultan, in a low voice that was nevertheless heard by half the people in the room, making them turn their heads and shudder.

The Sultan's next sentence, which though uttered in a whisper was audible to the whole assembly, made Judge İshak raise his bowed head.

"I want a scalp delivered to me by three o'clock!"

QUESTION 17
HOW DID THE PLAYER BECOME A PAWN IN HIS OWN GAME?

Stocky Yeye and Dusky Falco followed the unsavoury characters out of the Pergola coffee house at discreet distance. Even at the stokehouse, they had never seen such fierce-looking people and Yeye and Falco's hearts were trembling. The men went along Tahtakale road and past Sultan Bayezit Han Madrasa to the main entrance of the Covered Bazaar, where they separated. Three took the Şehzade Mosque road towards Saraçhanebaşı, and one turned off towards Sultan Ahmet accompanied by the dwarf, who was gesticulating wildly with his hands to emphasise his words as he ran alongside trying to keep up. For a moment, Dusky Falco thought about separating from Yeye so that they could follow both groups, but abandoned that idea when he remembered that stokehouse brothers should never leave each other's side and that they would be reprimanded if they arrived home separately. It was his duty to protect Stocky Yeye and he could not take the responsibility of sending him off on his own.

"Which way shall we go, Yeye?" said Falco.

"Well, we know the janissary barracks are that way, but what's in the other direction?" replied Yeye.

"Let's find out!"

Falco and Yeye followed the men as far as the entrance to the Sunken Cistern, a sixth-century Byzantine underground water cistern of a thousand pillars.

In the days that followed, they went regularly to beg or steal in the area around the Sunken Cistern. They saw the same four men and the dwarf on two consecutive days and then, at noon on the third day, they finally learned something about these characters when five state security guards appeared from nowhere and surrounded them at the Pergola coffee house.

"Sergeant Bindallı Mahmut, His Excellency the Grand Vizier wishes to speak with you," said one of the guards.

Bindallı Mahmut was a janissary sergeant with a finger in many pies. Not only did he run an extortion racket among the traders of dried fruit and nuts at the city docks, his commercial enterprises also extended to foreign exchange dealings, which enabled him to influence the price of foreign gold coinage and the financial whims of foreigners in Istanbul.

"Bloody hell. What have I done to deserve this?" swore Sergeant Bindallı Mahmut under his breath as he rose to his feet.

QUESTION 18
WHAT DID YOU DISCUSS WITH THE SULTAN?

"Can you read?" muttered Supreme Judge İshak despairingly.

"No, but you can read it out to us, Judge."

"In that case, bring me pen and paper."

The previous evening, while taking his usual route home, Judge İshak had been stopped at the corner of an isolated alley, where his head had been beaten to a pulp and covered with a sack before he was led to the evil-smelling, damp and dirty hovel where he was now lying. He had lost all sense of time and could only tell if it was night or day by the sound of rats and the varying level of humidity. At first, he had assumed he was being held inside part of the old Byzantine walls or in an unused underground reservoir, places commonly used by gangs of robbers and beggars. For the first time in his life, he had understood the meaning of desperation on seeing the walls covered with clamps, barbed wire, chains, helmets, straps and various other strange devices, and three marble slabs which, with their orderly rows of needles, cutters, pincers, curved knives, knuckledusters and bottles of chemicals, poisons and opium paste, looked like surgical tables. As Supreme Judge, it was his duty to protect the city, so he was not surprised to discover what went on in its underground world. However, he felt compassion for the desperate people who were put in such places merely because they were unable to fulfil their civic obligations. He was of course curious as to why he was being held in that centre of torture, but what really distressed him was the probability that it was on the orders of some senior government official. At his first interrogation, he had learned that the two masked men who had brought him there were not after money. They gave no indication that they wanted to know where he hid his sacks of gold or in which garden he buried his treasure. They were obviously after something else and would undoubtedly be paid handsomely if they managed to extract the right information out of him.

Judge İshak was half naked and his hands were numb from two days spent lying face down like a corpse on one of the marble slabs. His captors said he would not suffer if he told them what they wanted to know, but that they would not leave until he did. Judge İshak refused to answer any questions for a long time, but each time he resisted, they increased the level of violence, eventually making a deep dagger wound in his right calf and torturing him further by teasing out the nerve ends with tweezers. The captors proved to be unexpectedly brutal in the way they implemented their sequence of well-tried torture methods for obtaining answers to their questions. Judge İshak kept losing consciousness, but the moment he came round they would return, with only their eyes visible above their masks, to start the torture all over again,.

Images of his relatives, children and friends flashed before Judge İshak's eyes. While he was sorry about the worry his disappearance would cause them, he nurtured the hope that they would come looking for him. However, this was unlikely because he had two wives in two different households in Istanbul and the government only assembled at the palace every other day. Thus, his wives and children were accustomed to him not coming home for days at a time and had never once dared send a messenger to enquire after his whereabouts to the other house. His only hope was that a search party would be sent out for him when his absence was noticed at the Domed Stateroom. He had resolved during his first day of captivity that he would not talk until after the next divan assembly, which meant gritting his teeth and refusing to say a word for two days.

The captors clearly knew this and understood what Judge İshak was planning because, having achieved nothing by the end of the first day, one of the guards went off cursing loudly to search among the bottles of chemicals in the corner.

"Now, we'll see what happens," jeered the guard as he returned carrying a container with the remains of some diamond powder.

They stopped pulling out his nerve endings and resorted to sprinkling handfuls of diamond powder into the wound on his calf every ten minutes. Judge İshak's screams of pain echoed through the cell walls and down the long corridors, scaring even himself. With every scream, rats emerged from their nests and made strange noises, further compounding the atmosphere of terror. The judge just hoped that his screams would be audible at the Hippodrome and that someone might raise the alarm.

Judge İshak had heard about diamond powder being used as a form of torture for slaves or people who would not talk, but had always assumed the level of pain was exaggerated. However, a single particle of that dust in his wound caused his whole body to shudder with shock as if his internal organs were being displaced, which intensified the pain even more. The term torture normally refers to physical pain, but the pain to which he was being subjected was more than physical, it was taking hold of his spirit which felt as if it was being squeezed to extinction, added to which his conscience was now causing him as much pain as the diamond powder.

Judge İshak had been the first person to tell the Sultan about young Prince Ahmet, whom his family had been protecting like a sacred charge for so many years. It was the betrayal of his own conscience that now troubled him. What should he write to make up for what he had done? Could he protect the prince any longer? When news of the prince's existence, or slaughter, was made known, the good work of his ancestors would soon be forgotten but he, Judge İshak would always be remembered for this betrayal. A person was expected to live and die, leaving the honour of his family name unsullied. It was bad enough that he had not kept his knowledge of İtir Banu and her son secret as his ancestors had done, he had actually informed the Sultan of their existence. The torture he suffered on that marble slab was perhaps just reward for his betrayal of that poor woman. "The torment of Hell must be like this!" he thought as he gritted his teeth. Every time he came round after an application of the diamond dust, he vowed to protect Prince Ahmet and repeated the same answers again and again.

"What did you discuss with the Sultan?"

"State business! Nothing personal."

"What else?"

"The reform of the janissaries. The Admiral of the Fleet's wedding."

"And?"

"Repairs to the pavilions at Sadabat, price-setting during Ramadan, the astrologer's..."

But Judge İshak could hold out no longer. The diamond powder made him feel as if every cell of his body was being torn apart, his skin peeled away and his bones filed down. Finally, when asked 'Can you read?' Judge İshak had taken the piece of paper offered by his captors, who were now half delirious from smoking opium.

"You're worthless wretches!" cried Judge İshak furiously, handing back the paper on which he had written one sentence. "You have no right to this secret. Be under no illusion, this knowledge will cause you to meet an early death. Take this paper to your master, whoever he is."

QUESTION 19
ARE YOU SURE HE IS DEAD?

"Your Honour!" murmured the Prison Custodian almost inaudibly as he bowed down to the floor. "The nightingale has sung."

"Was he tricked or was he forced?" asked Grand Vizier İbrahim Pasha.

"Your Honour, it seems he ate a few berries, so there were a few difficulties."

"So, what is it?"

"It's written in this note, Your Honour."

"Who else has seen this note?" asked the Grand Vizier as he took the paper.

"No one other than I, Your Honour. The men I sent to get this information are illiterates who don't know one word from another."

“And that’s how it should be! Such details should never be neglected.”

“Of course, Your Honour.”

“So, has the bird flown the cage?”

“Yes, Your Honour, we have him perched on a branch as arranged.”

“No one has seen him, have they?”

“Don’t worry, Your Honour. No one has seen him and he has seen no one. There were a few hitches, but nothing significant.”

İbrahim Pasha had never really liked Judge İshak and was curious to know what he had discussed with the Sultan two nights ago. Had he offered a bribe? Or asked for a particular job? Perhaps he had passed on some gossip that might make the Sultan reconsider his own position as grand vizier. İbrahim Pasha had recently appointed a number of friends and relatives to important positions and had also recalled certain men who had been loyal to him during his term in Anatolia to take up administrative positions in Istanbul. He thought it better if these job allocations were not widely known and he certainly did not want to upset the Sultan.

The Sultan’s anger when he saw Judge İshak at the festivities two nights before had not escaped İbrahim Pasha, who had exhorted the Prison Custodian to find out the truth. The Prison Custodian had proceeded with this task in his usual brutal manner. İbrahim Pasha did not condone his methods and felt no sympathy for the Prison Custodian, whom he left cringing on his knees while he slowly read the paper, his expression turning from one of horror to anger. Twitching nervously, he read it again to make sure he had not misunderstood, before pacing furiously round the room, crumpling the paper in his hand and tearing it into tiny pieces. As he clenched the pieces of paper, he glared at the Prison Custodian who was still kneeling and looking at the floor.

"We need to lose this evidence. Don't you agree? Open your mouth!" roared İbrahim Pasha, striding towards the Prison Custodian and stuffing the pieces of paper into his mouth.

The Prison Custodian did not understand what was happening. What could have been on the piece of paper to anger the Grand Vizier so much that he was being made to swallow it? He regretted being foolish enough not to have read the writing before handing it over. Finally, still swallowing hard, he was allowed to rise to his feet.

"What do you make of this matter?" demanded İbrahim Pasha.

"Which matter, sir?"

"The matter on the paper."

"I don't know what was written on it, sir."

"It says here that the prisoner known as Dusky Falco who is currently being held at Galata Prison is the late Sultan Mustafa's youngest son Prince Ahmet!" proclaimed İbrahim Pasha.

The Prison Custodian almost passed out on hearing these words. Why was everything going wrong that day? If Prince Ahmet was indeed the Falco he had punched a few days ago at Eyüp Prison, it would be disastrous. It would mean he had actually sent a member of the Sultan's family to be tortured. Someone who might even become ruler one day! A person who would undoubtedly make him pay for what he had done in a most disagreeable way. He was trying to collect his thoughts together when he remembered something else. Judge İshak, whom his men had tortured the previous night, had called him over as he was leaving the assembly two nights ago and enquired about a young prisoner in Galata Prison named Ahmet. The Prison Custodian had said that he would make enquiries and reply within a few hours. However, before the few hours were up, he had been instructed by İbrahim Pasha to arrange a cross-examination of Judge İshak. Thus, hearing İbrahim Pasha mention Prince Ahmet had compounded the disaster even further. Two people had now referred to this Ahmet: the Grand Vizier and the Supreme Judge, both of whom were responsible for state security. The Prison Custodian felt himself to be between a rock and a hard place. Furthermore, he did not have the information they wanted. Silence fell over the room as he struggled to swallow the last piece of paper. The acrid taste of ink made his mouth go dry. He felt nauseous, his head was spinning, and his legs felt as if they were about to give way beneath him. Either the acerbity from the paper or the ink was burning his gullet. He tried to clear his throat in order to ask permission to leave.

"As if one Ahmet wasn't enough," muttered the Grand Vizier, referring to the current Sultan, "another one has turned up. Go to Galata Prison immediately. I want to see this Ahmet."

"Er, Your Excellency,..." mumbled the Prison Custodian.

"What?"

"Your Excellency, that prisoner was thrown into the Golden Horn the other night."

"What do you mean?"

"Sir, we interrogated him at Eyüp Sultan Prison about a murder and he was sent to be tortured at Galata Prison. But during the transfer, the skiff capsized in the Golden Horn and he fell overboard," said the Prison Custodian, trying to appear innocent of any involvement.

"Are you sure he's dead?"

"That's what we think, Your Excellency, because he had stones tied to his feet," lied the Prison Custodian, surprising even himself. "My men waited around for a long time, checking the water and the coastline there."

"They checked, did they? Huh! How can you be sure that he's dead without seeing his corpse? Get out! And don't come back without him, dead or alive!"

QUESTION 20
WHY DID ASLAN AĞA GO TO SEE THE PRISON CUSTODIAN?

Dusky Falco and Stocky Yeye left the stokehouse at daybreak. They were now allowed to go out begging separately during the day and would meet up later to return home together. They did not make much, but it was more fun that way and suited their aims. One of them always went to the courtyard of the Prince Mehmet mosque, built by Süleyman the Magnificent in memory of a son who died young, from where it was possible to keep watch on people coming out of the janissary barracks. The other would go prowling around the Sunken Cistern in the hope of meeting one or more of the men they had seen at the Pergola coffee house.

The janissary barracks were situated opposite the Prince Mehmet mosque on a cobbled street that ran from the neighbourhoods of Fatih Sultan to the Covered Bazaar and which was a major route for traders bringing their goods to market. In the mornings, the road quickly filled up with heavily laden mules and overloaded carts driven by villagers who had set off in the middle of the night in order to get there in good time with their produce which included milk, butter, honey and various types of flour. Dusky Falco and Stocky Yeye knew that it was pointless to beg from passing villagers at that hour. They were all hurrying to join the queue for the price-fixer, who obstinately closed his books at the first sound of the mid-day call to prayer, leaving any latecomers without an official price and therefore unable to sell. Nobody was allowed to set their own market price. One trader caught selling goods illegally in that way was strung up in front of his booth and his corpse left dangling for days as a warning to people. Anyway, traders never gave alms before they had made their first sale of the day, and any beggar who approached them was reprimanded and chased away with much noisy cursing. Nor was there any chance of getting anything out of the janissaries when they came out of their barracks, because they ran a protection racket that collected money from beggars.

However, the pickings could be quite good if there were any gentlemen among the early morning travellers making their way along the cobbled street towards the Sublime Porte. Most of these gentlemen were statesmen or aristocrats who believed that starting the day with a charitable act brought them good fortune. They would pass by in landaus, which had recently become popular, on horseback or in convoy with their attendants. Such ceremonial processions of Ottoman statesmen added to Istanbul's character as a capital city. People would make way for them, each hoping to be noticed by bowing from the waist, lowering their heads over their chests, or even honouring their betters with sweeping bows. The stokehouse elders maintained that it was a good opportunity to beg when everyone stopped to genuflect in this way. That morning, Dusky Falco seized the opportunity and threw himself in front of a procession of dignitaries.

"God have mercy on you! Can you spare something for your slave?" he pleaded.

When Falco raised his head, the world seemed to be spinning around him. Good God! That face! He nearly fainted. Quickly, he lowered his head again, his heart pounding so hard he thought it would explode. He remembered a voice resonating in his ears, saying, "I'll put you in Galata Prison with my own hands and you'll discover what torture is really like. I'll sort you out there!"

Falco waited, his head between his hands, expecting to hear daggers drawn from their scabbards and feel gaping wounds inflicted on his body. He expected to hear a voice shout "Get rid of that murderer!" Just when he thought that his end had come, a young woman was heard screaming a short distance away.

"Thief! Thief! Over there! Is there not a single gentleman among you?"

"Be off with you, wretch! Get out of my sight before I send you off for bastinado!" said the familiar voice and, with a sharp kick at Dusky Falco's shoulder, he was gone.

Dusky Falco remained in a heap on the ground. God had taken pity on him and engineered his escape by diverting attention to the capture of a common thief. Then he relaxed slightly, remembering that his face was no longer the same. The new eyebrows had completely altered it. He wanted to cry out,

"Thank you, my Hungarian doctor! You're a genius!" However, he just murmured to himself, "Get up and walk away, Falco! If the Prison Custodian didn't recognise you just two weeks after he punched you in the face, then you have nothing to fear!" He felt strengthened and confident that he no longer needed to worry about walking the streets.

Clenching his fists, Dusky Falco took a deep breath as if he had scored a victory and looked up to watch the receding procession. But what was going on? Two men were chasing the Prison Custodian, the man who had just kicked him, and panting out an explanation as they went. It was the huge janissary officer they had seen in the Pergola coffee house and Aslan Ağa, his father-in-law! Why on earth was Aslan Ağa masquerading as a market trader? When Dusky Falco had visited Nakşıgül's father at the house in Yenibahçe, he had been a prosperous businessman. Dusky Falco felt confused, but there was no time to lose. He took another deep breath and cursed himself for not noticing who had come out of the janissary barracks. He had been so uneasy about begging early in the morning that he had missed what he really needed to see.

Dusky Falco retreated to a quiet corner and sat down on a broken pillar. Nothing made sense. Had Aslan Ağa's business taken a downturn after Nakşıgül's death? If so, what was he involved in now? Why was he wearing those orange fisherman's trousers and that peculiar cap? Had he been reduced to working as a trawlerman? Falco felt a pang of sorrow for his father-in-law. "Poor Aslan Ağa! This happened to him because of me!" he murmured to himself. "His family must be in terrible straits now that the house in Yenibahçe is no longer there. But how did it disappear?"

Dusky Falco was extremely sad to see Aslan Ağa in that state. But what could be his connection with the janissary from the Pergola coffee house? His connection with the Prison Custodian was understandable. Aslan Ağa had every right to want his daughter's murderer found, and the Prison Custodian would be the person to ask. But what was his connection with that surly janissary?

Dusky Falco finally made a decision. He jumped up and started following Aslan Ağa, the janissary and the Prison Custodian, who were talking to each other in a familiar, light-hearted manner without the normal class etiquette, perhaps because their acquaintanceship was mutually beneficial.

"If only Yeye was with me," thought Dusky Falco. "I could have followed Aslan Ağa and Yeye could have kept an eye on the janissary. We might even have heard what they're talking about."

Falco followed the three men as far as Kazasker Gate in Bayezit Square, where he saw them enter a two-storey stone building next to the Old Palace. The Prison Custodian had an office there where he worked three days a week, spending the other three days checking on his security officers and ensuring that everything was in order at Scutari, Eyüp and Galata prisons.

Dusky Falco found a corner and started begging, having decided to wait as long necessary in order to follow Aslan Ağa. If the opportunity arose, or if he found himself alone with Aslan Ağa in a deserted street, he thought he might even summon up the courage to speak to him, but quickly abandoned that idea for fear of being recognised. Although Falco felt heavy-hearted at the thought of his father-in-law's suffering over Nakşıgül, he felt his own situation was even worse. Not only had he lost the woman he loved, he was accused of killing her. "Where are you now, Stocky Yeye?" he thought. If they had been together, he would have sent Yeye off to obtain an explanation from Aslan Ağa about the disappearing house in Yenibahçe. Perhaps the janissary knew what had happened. Should he follow him instead? No, he already knew where he lived and could always find him again at the barrack gates if necessary. But Aslan Ağa! What was he to make of him?

The noon sun had disappeared behind some clouds and a strong wind was blowing towards Bayezit Mosque when four hands seized Dusky Falco by the arms and marched him away. While waiting for Aslan Ağa, and still fearing the Prison Custodian's security officers, Falco had stumbled into a group of Judge İshak's military police. Being apprehended twice in one day was too much for him and he succumbed without resistance.

QUESTION 21
WHY DELIVER THE SEVERED HEAD TO ME?

Sergeant Bindallı Mahmut sat all through the humid afternoon heat until the cool of the evening waiting to be summoned. It was only three nights since he had covered his head with a towel and delivered a basket of dried fruits and nuts to the house. He had not expected to be summoned so soon.

Grand Vizier İbrahim Pasha had heard many accusations made against this huge fearless janissary officer. He looked intently at Bindallı Mahmut and paid no heed to the way his pipe smoke was making the man's eyes stream. İbrahim Pasha appeared to be harbouring a rage that was about to erupt and Bindallı Mahmut shivered at the thought of being sent to the cells. For a while, İbrahim Pasha said nothing. He wanted to fray the janissary's nerves and break his spirit. Gazing casually out of the window, as if he were alone in the room, he eventually spoke calmly and without any suggestion of anger, as if speaking to a colleague.

"My dear Sergeant! What have you done with the toymaker's wife?" he asked.

Bindallı Mahmut was not expecting that question. He had hoped to get away with simply denying everything he was supposed to have done. There were many questions he might have been asked, such as 'Where have you been for the last two days?' or 'I've summoned you here on suspicion of murder, are you guilty?' or even 'Is the severed head anything to do with you?' Yet here he was being asked about the toymaker's wife. The question ruined all his plans. It gave him no scope for confounding the Grand Vizier and enabling him to return to the coffee house to brag to his colleagues. He had expected people in Istanbul to be rocked by this murder and to berate the Grand Vizier for his impotence. It was meant to provide proof of the Grand Vizier's stupidity, yet here he was calmly smoking his pipe and suggesting that he knew everything.

"I sliced the head off three weeks ago and hid it in a honey bag. I washed it the day before bringing it to you," confessed Bindallı Mahmut, realising there was no point in lying

"But why?"

"She made advances towards me, but the moment I turned my back she had a child by another man. I found out and punished her with my own hands."

"Why deliver the head to me?"

"You are clever, Your Excellency. They say you make the dead speak, converse with the birds and use them as your spies. I wanted to find out if it was true."

"Very well. Do you believe it now?"

"Indeed I do, Your Excellency. Truly, you are intelligence itself. May you have a long and prosperous life! This nation needs a person such as you."

"Have you heard the saying 'Those who are intelligent are also just'?"

Bindallı Mahmut remained silent.

The Grand Vizier stood up and started pacing round the room, his fists clenched in anger and his feet making sharp sounds on the wooden floor. His unexpectedly agile movements for a man of his age intimidated those around him. The guard at the door stood to attention, knowing from experience that the Grand Vizier was about to erupt when he was in that state.

"So what do you think I should do, Bindallı Mahmut?" boomed the Grand Vizier.

Despite his huge physique, Sergeant Bindallı Mahmut cowered like a frightened child. He had faced danger and even death many times in his life but had never before felt fear in this way. The monumental grandeur of the Grand Vizier made him shudder.

"Master, I was wronged. The whore was unfaithful to me. It would have been her punishment in any case. I did what had to be done. I'm the injured party here," whined Bindallı Mahmut.

The Grand Vizier could have responded with a clip to the head, explained the futility of expecting fidelity from someone who has been untrue, or advised that Sharia law did not require its sentences to be meted out literally. Instead, he sent a request for the Sheikh ul-Islam to issue a fatwa ordering Bindallı Mahmut to spend the rest of his life in the dreaded Dockyard Prison.

"Injured party. Huh!" muttered the Grand Vizier as he watched the guards march Bindallı Mahmut out through the garden gate.

QUESTION 22
DO GRAVEYARDS ONLY CONTAIN THE DEAD?

For the first time in their lives, Dusky Falco and Stocky Yeye realised that what they had taken to be the smell of freshly dug earth meant the presence of a corpse. Starting from Cannon Gate, they had run through almost all the graveyards outside the city walls in their search for Nakşıgül, reading the names on the sticks that stood like temporary witnesses at the head of each newly dug grave. It was two weeks since Falco's arrest by the Prison Custodian and his escape from death in the Golden Horn, but his fear and memory of those times was still fresh in his mind. His subsequent arrest by the military police had made him assume that his time was up, but he soon discovered that it was part of the Grand Vizier's programme to clear beggars off the city streets and, realising that the same thing must have happened to Yeye, had set about searching for his friend among the hundreds of other beggars, who all looked much the same. Yeye had become the most important person in his life, the only person in the world who belonged to him and to whom he felt he belonged, and he could not bear to lose him.

Eventually, Falco and Yeye had managed to find each other. They were put aboard a newly-rigged galleon that set sail for the Marmara Sea with no idea what would happen to them. They did not know that, every three months, Grand Vizier İbrahim Pasha arranged for all the beggars to be rounded up, put on a ship and, after a few beatings and pledges not to return, dropped off at Mudanya or Tekirdağı, after which the beggars would take the quickest route they knew back into the city. Their numbers always increased during the three holy months leading up to the end of Ramadan. Law enforcers wanted to punish the phony beggars who poured into Istanbul, but the Sheikh ul-Islam would not issue the relevant fatwa, so the police used this method to get them out of the city. Since it was difficult to re-enter the city without official papers, and even foreigners were obliged to show travel documents, for a time at least Istanbul was rid of these vagrants.

The journey was exciting, if nerve-wracking. Dusky Falco and Stocky Yeye picked up a few trade secrets from master beggars, nearly fell into the sea while helping the deck-hands, survived on half a loaf of bread for two days and were made to hand over every cent in their possession to the sailors.

For Dusky Falco and Stocky Yeye, Grand Vizier İbrahim Pasha's desire to be rid of the influx of beggars meant two weeks of tramping around, which was both difficult and dangerous, whether on desolate hillsides or urban areas. It took them exactly ten days to reach Istanbul via the caravan route that ran through Çorlu, Kumburgaz and Küçükçekmece. The rainy season was approaching and they needed to be back at the stokehouse before the onset of winter.

As soon as the city walls were visible, they started considering which gate they would use to enter the city. Hoping to strike a deal with some passing villager taking a load into the city, they found themselves in a graveyard near Mevlana Gate. It occurred to Dusky Falco that it might be worth having another look for Nakşıgül's grave. If she was buried there, they might be able to get some information from a gravedigger or even find someone who had been present at her funeral. Yeye did not think much of that idea because he wanted to enter the city and reach the stokehouse before nightfall. Once they were back in the city, he thought, it would be easy enough to come back another day because the guards at the city gates always gave permission for graveyard visits.

"The graveyards of a city conceal its best kept secrets!" said Yeye, who had been deeply affected by spending so much time in graveyards. "These stones provide a historical record of the city's dreams and memories."

"Indeed, Yeye. It would be our good fortune indeed if there were a memory of Nakşıgül here. Come on, let's keep looking."

"How many lovers like us have come seeking the truth on these stones, I wonder? No story, no ballad, no official history or record tells a story with such rigorous honesty as these graves. The stones are like stories in themselves. See Falco, how some are sleeping, some are tired, some are broken, some are leaning on one another – all attempting to withstand time."

Dusky Falco listened to Stocky Yeye in amazement. He knew the boy was very intelligent but had never before considered him to be such a deep thinker. Yeye was a person of few words, but Falco had been particularly touched when he had said 'lovers like us'. Was this boy in love? If so, why did he never talk about it? How did he know so much?

"Yeye, can you read and write?"

"Of course, Falco. I've read lots of books."

Dusky Falco remained silent. As Yeye talked, Falco felt increasingly ashamed that he had not made the effort to know his friend better.

"For instance, the poems written on these gravestones...," continued Yeye. "Who knows which poet wrote them? And what about the craftsmen who engrave the verses on the stones? Their artistry lives on for centuries. What pride they must take in their work. How do they achieve such graceful lines with a hammer and chisel? We should never underrate a gravestone."

"Enough, Yeye! If you like graves so much, go and lie in one!"

For a moment, Yeye wondered if he was to be sacrificed for the sake of Şehnaz. He did not know which was more painful: dying and being saved from a life without Şehnaz, or living and constantly thinking about her. Of course, he welcomed the first of these and would succumb without a second thought if she requested his death. But was that really what she wanted? "If only it was!" he thought. If Leyla had requested anything from Majnun, could he have refused? He recalled a touching story that told how a lover could never refuse a request from the beloved. For Majnun, it was enough that he knew what Leyla wanted.

When Stocky Yeye fell silent, Dusky Falco was ashamed of the way he had said 'go and lie in one'. He had of course been joking, but they both knew that underneath he was reacting to his realisation that Yeye knew more about life than himself. He deeply regretted that this might have been reflected in his tone of his voice, even if unintentionally. Meanwhile Yeye was feeling sad that he must have unwittingly offended his only true friend in the world. The adage 'the older you are, the wiser you become' did not always apply. He vowed that henceforth he would never express an opinion unless asked. Still, thought Yeye, it would have been enjoyable to discuss graves and the designers who created bouquets by grouping Greek flower motifs with acanthus leaves, the poets who put the names and reputations of the deceased into epitaphs, the calligraphists who wrote out the epitaphs and the craftsmen who engraved the work of all those artists on to the tombstones of the rich and poor, young and old, mothers and brothers, lovers and spouses. What stories they could tell!

While Yeye remained silent, Falco tried to steer their conversation away from allusions to love. As they sat in the graveyard waiting for an opportunity to get through the city gates, they inevitably started thinking about death and concluded that it was painful and natural, startling and normal, and that it was to be both avoided and embraced.

The thought occurred to Yeye that if Istanbul had no graveyards, it would be deficient in some way. A city with a graveyard was like two cities. The ephemeral earthly adventures that took place in Istanbul were complemented by this second city. Life and death flowed through the two cities, like two intertwining rivers continually nourishing each other. Every day, silent corteges or grand processions passed between these two cities, which were so close, so intertwined, yet still maintained an indefinable distance between them – just like the distance or closeness between life and death.

It was only as dusk was falling that Dusky Falco realised how this distance was being increasingly emphasised. They had felt very close to death in the cemeteries with the freshly dug graves and Armenian tombstone engravers. But these graveyards, as well as being situated outside the city walls, were surrounded by high walls that further distanced death from life. It was easy to see that if people viewed a graveyard as the gateway to an afterlife, they were able to welcome death as a natural phenomenon and feel at ease with its concept. But building walls around the cemeteries created a barrier. Falco wondered who had ordered this untraditional practice. Perhaps it was someone from Grand Vizier İbrahim Pasha's urban planning organisation. He worried for anyone who now strayed from the paths that ran alongside the network of high cemetery walls, because this total concealment of death and its segregation from life would only increase the people's fear of death.

That day, as they wandered through the graveyards and meandered between life and death, they had asked anyone they encountered about the freshly-dug graves. But none of the stone masons or the tombstone engravers knew anything about the death of a young bride. So who had chopped up Nakşıgül's corpse and where could she be buried? Since the family and the house had disappeared, the grave could be anywhere. Who were her pallbearers? Which hodja had been her spirit guide? Who had stood by her to read the Koran? How could Falco put these questions to the local imam if, despite performing their marriage ceremony, he denied ever having seen him?

Dusky Falco finally had the idea of searching the death records that were kept in the city, or get someone else to look at them. While making that decision, the opportunity they had been waiting for arose. Some Jewish and Armenian stonemasons had packed up their hammers and chisels and were walking towards them on their way into the city via Mevlana Gate. Dusky Falco and Stocky Yeye simply melted in to their noisy procession of jokes, curses, complaints and squabbles, and passed through the city walls.

"Twenty-seven of the filthy mob which went out at dawn have now returned, sir!" reported one of the guards to his sergeant.

As they entered the city through Mevlana Gate, the filthy mob had no idea that their number had increased to twenty-nine.

Postscript: Leyla's request

Majnun found an opportunity to spend time alone with Leyla, who made one request of him.

"Lover! Bring me whatever you have."

"Light of my life! Since loving you, I have no water, nor a well to draw from. There is no blood left in my heart and no sleep in my eyes. I lost everything when you devastated my mind. Now all I possess is my soul, which has turned into a wounded bird. I await your command and will give you anything you request"

Leyla laughed and reproached him.

"Oh, my hero! When I want that from you, I will take it. What else do you have?"

Majnun thought for a moment and looked around him. Then, as if he had suddenly remembered, he took a needle from the frayed collar of his ragged robe and offered it to her.

"Truly, this is the only thing I own in the material world. I have no other physical possessions. You, oh stealer of my heart, you are the reason I carry this! I stumble frequently and my feet become pierced by thorns as I follow your image in the desert, over plains or in the mountains. This needle is for removing those thorns from my feet."

"That is exactly what I was looking for. Oh miserable lover, if you are truly in love, why should you even have that needle? Is it right that anyone pierced by a thorn while in pursuit of a beauty such as me should remove it? Are you truly faithful if you remove that thorn? A lover whose foot is pierced by a thorn on the way to his love should notice if a rose becomes attached to his clothes, should he not? Every year, the rose gardener puts up with thorns in order to obtain a rose. Are you so feeble that you cannot bear to have a thorn in your foot and must remove it with a needle? Is a thorn which pierces your foot with Leyla's love not more valuable than a hundred bunches of roses she might give to others?"

QUESTION 23
IS A TULIP BULB WORTH ONE HUNDRED AND FIFTY GOLD PIECES?

Dusky Falco and Stocky Yeye were sitting deep in discussion with Hafız Çelebi next to the Well of Souls.

"Two years ago, I tried out something new," said Hafız Çelebi. "I wanted to produce two bulbs from one and grow rare tulips in pairs. The first twin bulb I produced, I gave to Grand Vizier İbrahim Pasha. But I heard that he gave one half to his wife Fatma Sultan and the other half to Dilnüvaz, his favourite concubine at the time. When spring came and both bulbs produced the same flower, Fatma Sultan considered this an insult and complained to the Grand Vizier. He summoned me to provide an explanation, after which he said he was delighted with my success and, at the end of our conversation, asked if I could produce a deep purple twin bulb such as no one else had ever produced. 'If God permits, they will flower in your palace garden next spring!' I replied. His Excellency told me that they were not for planting in the gardens, but for sending to the rulers of Flanders and Austria. For this he presented me with two bags of gold. At first, everything went to plan but, unfortunately some thugs ambushed me and stole the bulbs as I was going to deliver them to the Grand Vizier. Clearly, you're not one of those criminals, yet what you hold in your hand is one of those bulbs. If you like, I'll buy it from you for one hundred and fifty gold pieces. But tell me, how did you come to have this bulb?"

Dusky Falco liked this gentleman, but was not prepared to share his secrets with him. Anyway, what could he say? That he was being sought for the crime of chopping up his wife on the morning after his wedding? That he was a condemned convict who had escaped from the prison authorities? That he had had his eyebrows surgically altered because he was considered guilty by the Ottoman state? Or that he belonged to a gang of beggars and thieves who took shelter at the Gedikpaşa Hamam stokehouse? Would Hafız Çelebi believe him if he told him any of this? Even if he wanted the thieves to be caught and punished, he would never cooperate with a stokehouse beggar. Furthermore, according to Hafız Çelebi, other people were also after the bulb. Dusky Falco realised that what he had learned only made his own situation more dangerous, because even more people were pursuing him.

Hafız Çelebi was a clean-faced man whose countenance indicated that he had a clear and honest disposition. Dusky Falco did not know how to answer the question that had been put to him. He was stretching his neck awkwardly and just about to mutter something when Stocky Yeye broke his vow of silence and attempted to save the situation.

"Is a tulip bulb worth one hundred and fifty gold pieces?" asked Yeye, quite unware what a profound effect this man was going to have on his life.

"Why not? Do you think this bulb is going to produce the commonplace flower you see everywhere, my boy?" replied Hafız Çelebi.

"Tulips certainly sprout all over the place," commented Dusky Falco, now feeling more at ease.

"Indeed, you see tulips in every garden and every patch of grass in Istanbul. But of all those gardens, only one produces a truly stunning tulip that encapsulates its history from Central Asia all the way here. And that tulip is the one our ancestors put into their saddlebags as a souvenir when they migrated from the Tien Shan mountains to warmer climes. It's the red one to which Mevlana Celaleddin-i Rumi referred with such delight in his *Mesnevi*, the one that sprouts like poppies in the grass and alongside garden fences. Like the hapless smile of the Turcoman dervish Yunus Emre with the dark fiery wound in his heart. Like the dark heart of Ebussuud Efendi producing the red ink that flowed from the pen or, in his own words, like salt to a sweet palate: *"Had not tulips in varied hues appeared / Their beauty would not be thus revered.*"

Dusky Falco was transfixed by Hafız Çelebi's excitement as he talked about tulips. He had always regarded the tulip as a simple flower with a cheerful red exterior and a dark centre, though he remembered his mother saying that the tulip as a symbol of misfortune. However, the emotion with which Hafız Çelebi spoke about the flower indicated the importance it had for him and how much love and care he put into its cultivation.

Stocky Yeye was also aware that this pleasant man was no ordinary gardener, but someone who wanted people to respect his work and who had no time for those who scorned his passion. It reminded Yeye of the story ***Majnun receives news of Leyla's death***. Then, when Hafız Çelebi spoke of the tulip reaching its pinnacle of beauty on arrival in Istanbul, he thought of Sadî of Shiraz's story in his book *Gülistan*, entitled ***Jealousy of another's love***. Yeye had always cried when his mother read that story to him.

Dusky Falco decided that if he was going to plant his tulip bulb and wait for it to flower, it should be in Hafız Çelebi's garden, because this man made him feel excited and glad to be alive when he spoke about tulips. Although he had ignored Hafız Çelebi's previous question, his eyes were now wide open with excitement and admiration.

"Sir, listening to you makes it seem as if this bulb arrived from Central Asia only yesterday. You speak about the tulip as if it had a soul," said Falco slowly, enunciating each word carefully.

"Young man, of course it has a soul," said Hafız Çelebi, looked slightly peeved. "Its spirit is the living embodiment of our Seljuk and Ottoman heritage. Just as tulips grew throughout Manisa in the fifteenth century at the time of Mehmet the Conqueror, a century later they decorated and adorned the gardens of Istanbul during the reign of Süleyman the Magnificent. Sadly, in the Flemish world these days, they resemble a brashly dressed bride who yearns and weeps for her homeland. The bulb you hold conceals a deep purple sadness which, when it flowers, will make tulips in the Flemish world remember their true identity, like kidnapped daughters snatched from their roots. And so, until they return to their humble origins in the gardens of Sadabat, this old man will do everything humanly possible to produce a special flower every spring, such as the one that will grow from the bulb in your hand. My efforts are a continuation of the work done by Ebussud Efendi, producer of the first tulip variant called 'Light of Heaven', the physician Mehmed Âşıkî Efendi who produced a corpus of works containing pages of paintings of different tulip varieties, and Mehmet Efendi, son of Imam Ahmet Ubeydi of Çerrahpaşa Mosque and author of *The Effect of Flowers*, plus hundreds of other well-known floriculturists. They toiled to ensure that our daughters may return home again and the work of successive generations was not in vain. Ever since the time of Ebussud Efendi, every Flemish ship coming from Holland to Istanbul has returned with new bulbs. We still have gardeners from Holland and Austria among our horticultural community. Grand Vizier Damat İbrahim Pasha's head gardener Sheikh Mehmet Lalezâri Efendi explains this fully in the first part of his *Harmony of Flowers*."

Dusky Falco not only found Hafız Çelebi's knowledge inspirational, he was pleasantly surprised by his willingness to talk to two beggars. After the daily curses and contempt to which they had become accustomed, Hafız Çelebi's words seemed to flow like honey and his generous manner put them at ease.

"Who kidnapped her?" asked Falco, with the earnestness of a justice fighter, forgetting for a moment about his beggar's attire, as if the person who kidnapped this 'daughter' could be found and punished.

"Wait, wait. Don't get excited," cautioned Hafız Çelebi, "All this happened two centuries ago. At the time of Süleyman the Magnificent, there was a Fleming named Busbecq who served in Istanbul as the Holy Roman Emperor's ambassador. Every year, he filled three chests with volumes that he found in the book market, put them on a ship and sent them up the Danube to Vienna, or via the Mediterranean to a friend in Holland, who was a floriculturist. On one occasion, Busbecq sent off a chest full of tulip bulbs to this friend. Was it abduction or kidnap? Decide for yourself. The ambassador's friend wrote a letter of thanks saying that he loved the flower and that it was as decorative as a bride. When Busbecq returned to his country, he took with him a huge basket of bulbs and presented them to the House of Habsburg."

"What happened then?" asked Falco.

"According to the ambassador's memoirs, the Habsburgs showed little interest in tulips, but their cultivation became fashionable in Holland and they were sent as presents to the royal palace."

Stocky Yeye had been feeling a strange emotion come over him as he listened to Hafız Çelebi. He wished that he had a father to tell him of such things and that, instead of going to the stokehouse, he could have lived with this man and listened to him every day. However, the sun had now long since slipped behind the Kağıthane peaks and he remembered that they needed to be back in the stokehouse before dark. He caught Dusky Falco's eye and they rose to their feet together.

"Don't wait too long," said Hafız Çelebi, realising that he would get no answer to his earlier question. "It should be planted very soon, at a depth of one hand span."

Dusky Falco and Stocky Yeye left feeling calm and relaxed by Hafız Çelebi's gracious demeanour. He had been particularly gentlemanly when giving his parting advice to them. On the way home, Falco told Yeye a story about such behaviour. Yeye had heard the story from his mother, but said nothing. He did not even point out that the story was about Adaletli Nuşirevan, not Caliph Ömer, because Dusky Falco's pride had been hurt in the graveyard and Yeye needed to see that it was restored.

"Two women came with an infant to Caliph Ömer," recounted Dusky Falco, "both claiming to be the mother of the child. Ömer said, 'Since you both say you are the mother, let us divide the child in two and you can each take one part away with you'. The first woman agreed to this command, but the other cried, 'No, no, don't cut up my baby! Let the other woman have him!' whereupon Ömer gave the child to the second woman. What do you think, Yeye? Did you not hear the same pleading in Hafız Çelebi's last words?"

"True, Falco, but the tulip bulb is your only evidence."

As they entered the stokehouse, they were both thinking how they would like to become labourers and grow tulips in Hafız Çelebi's garden. Yeye in particular wished he could do that job for the rest of his life. Cultivating tulips in a city like Istanbul! Was it really impossible for a stokehouse boy?

***

Postscript 1: Majnun receives news of Leyla's death

Majnun had lost his way. As he ran hither and thither, someone came up to him and said, "Leyla is dead!" At this sombre news, Majnun immediately stopped running, opened his hands in gratitude and cried, "Thank you, God!"

"See how crazy this wretch has become!" shouted the man, angrily. "If you are so passionate about her, why do you say that?"

"I was never able to do anything for that precious ray of moonlight. Now, at least no one else can either!"

* * *

Postscript 2: Jealousy of another

The poet Sadî said:

"I was still a fresh young man when I fell in love with a in Shiraz. She was not uninterested in me. We met and talked a few times, but then became separated when I travelled to foreign lands. For ten years, I brimmed with love and burned with desire for her. When finally, I returned home, my first task was to find her. As soon as she saw me, she reproached me.

"Ah Sadî! How faithless you are! So many years passed with no news of you, not even a letter."

I said to her:

"O my slender beauty who has filled my heart with love! If I was denied the fortune of seeing your face, would I grant that honour to a postman?"

QUESTION 24
WHO WILL TEND THE SULTAN'S WOUND?

Supreme Judge İshak could barely stand upright as he entered the presence of the Sultan. He had received an urgent summons and assumed the Sultan knew of his troubles and wanted to find out the details. However, the Sultan's demeanour suggested that this was not the case. He was standing at the window with his back to the door gazing across the Bosphorus at the Scutari shore and looked furious.

"Still no answer," the Sultan hissed angrily. "Is it not a sign of incompetence to seek and not find? Well? Can a nation survive with such incompetence? If you cannot track him down, then find someone who can! How does a ruler command the respect of his subjects if he cannot trace a man in Istanbul? Even his slaves would not submit to such a ruler. Tell me, Efendi, why have you not obeyed my orders?"

When the Sultan turned round, he saw that Judge İshak was black and blue all over. He looked humiliated, uncomfortable and embarrassed. Furthermore, he was leaning heavily on a stick that he clutched in his right hand.

"Your Majesty!" said Judge İshak in a trembling voice.

"What is it, sir? Are you unwell?" asked the Sultan in a softer tone.

"Yes, Your Majesty," replied the judge. "I have a festering wound in my calf. But of course, that is no excuse for not executing my duties. I am at your service, my Sultan. I would sweep your path with my eyelashes and wash it with my tears if Your Majesty so ordered. Other parties are seeking the information you want and I have had to deal with them. I sent out several search parties for them, and of course I still have men searching for the one you seek." Judge İshak lowered his voice so that no one else could hear and continued, "The Prison Custodian also sent out eight mute scorpions to search for this person."

"What happened to you? Tell me that first. What are you doing with that walking stick?" enquired the Sultan.

"Your Majesty, this atrocity was perpetrated by the men who are looking for the one you seek," replied Judge İshak. "They tried to make me speak by subjecting me to two days of torture and putting salt in the wound on my leg. Not satisfied with that, they laced it with diamond dust. It will take time to heal, my Sultan."

The Sultan turned to the footman standing at the door and signalled for him to summon the Court Physician.

"Efendi, we must have your wound tended. What you have told me has quite turned my stomach. Who knows about this? Who wants this information from you?"

"I thought that only Your Majesty, Allah and myself knew about this matter. But there are others who know."

"Who are these people? Are they insiders, or outsiders?"

Until the Sultan asked this question, it had not occurred to Judge İshak that any outsiders would be interested in Prince Ahmet. Since the signing of the 1718 Passarowitz peace treaty, little thought had been given to outsiders. Eleven years of peace had generated a general air of complacency. Judge İshak realised that the Sultan was thinking that perhaps more attention should be paid to events outside the boundaries of the Ottoman Empire. He ran his mind over the most recent foreign policies, trying to identify anyone who might have cause to make contact with Prince Ahmet.

Üveys Khan, an Afghan who had written reports on İbrahim Pasha's governorship in Damascus, had just seized Esfahan in Iran and, according to state intelligence, had been sending spies into Ottoman territory at the same time as the Druse were planning an uprising in the region. Üveys Khan had had his eye on Istanbul ever since Passarowitz on account of some secret dealings with Venice. Austria had managed to benefit from the peace treaty while Venice had suffered and the Ottoman Empire had become caught in the middle.

Meanwhile in the east, the Russian Czar, nicknamed Mad Petro by the Ottomans, was heading towards Baku and claiming the protection and support of Shah Tahmasb II of Iran. Mad Petro was proving to be very astute; he knew a great deal about political science and was obviously planning to rebuild Russia. The collapse of the Safavid state meant that the Ottoman Empire was suddenly exposed to the Russian threat on its eastern front, where it had been unable to strengthen its fortifications.

Furthermore, in Crimea, Gazi Giray had eliminated his brother Fethi Giray II and was trying to pursue his own policies, perhaps even considering independence.

As these considerations flashed through his mind, Judge İshak recognised the potential danger of 'outsiders' seizing Prince Ahmet for their own advantage. He could recall the sullen manner of his interrogators, but had no idea of their ethnicity or country of origin. They had spoken a crude form of Turkish, yet there were many such people living next to the city walls and, as for their coarseness, they were no different from the Gypsy executioners employed by the palace.

The Sultan's fury had done nothing to soothe Judge İshak's wound. His manner indicated that he was extremely irritated by the whole matter and wanted it dealt with immediately. Indeed, no sultan would wish to know that there was a prince at large, who might be involved in a conspiracy or have designs on the coffers of the sultanate.

Meanwhile, the Sultan's anxiety was increasing even further as he counted up the number of men on whom he could rely. For the first time, he realised that he had probably leant far too heavily on his Grand Vizier by entrusting him with so many matters of state. What would İbrahim Pasha do if he found out about Prince Ahmet? Would he turn against him and try to depose him? The Sultan felt deeply shaken by this notion. Could he trust his son-in-law İbrahim Pasha? After careful thought, he reluctantly decided that the answer was far from clear and that he had to keep a close check on his grand vizier and son-in-law. Was it possible to fulfil both roles simultaneously?

When the Court Physician entered, the Sultan pounded himself on the chest and roared, "Ah Doctor! I'm wounded here. Only İshak Efendi knows how to treat it. Heal his wound quickly so that he can tend mine."

As Judge İshak left, leaning on the Court Physician's arm, a thousand and one thoughts were running through his head, eating away at his brain like hornets.

QUESTION 25
WHO WILL TEND THE GRAND VIZIER'S WOUND?

While Judge İshak was with the Sultan at the Seraglio, the Prison Custodian was with İbrahim Pasha at his palace in the Hippodrome. The conversation between the Grand Vizier and his slave was almost identical to the exchange between the Sultan and Judge İshak. The Grand Vizier was just as grave and furious as the Sultan, and he too was standing with his back to the door, gazing through the window at the Marmara Islands.

"Still no answer," growled the Grand Vizier. "Is it not a sign of incompetence to seek and not find? Well? Can a nation survive with such incompetence? If you cannot track him down, then find someone who can! How does a ruler command the respect of his subjects if he cannot trace a man in Istanbul? Even his slaves would not submit to such a ruler. Tell me, Efendi, why have you not obeyed my orders?"

"Sir, I have men searching everywhere," said the Prison Custodian ingratiatingly, conscious of his slave status. "They have looked everywhere, from coffee house benches to grand sofas, from fishermen's huts to royal halva kitchens, dockyard hearths to respectable suites, and have questioned janissaries of all ranks, the literate and the illiterate. It's as if the earth has opened up and swallowed him. I cannot get his face out of my mind."

"If you cannot get his face out of your mind," interrupted İbrahim Pasha, "then why can you not find him? Or are you looking for the wrong face? Is this man a bird that he must always wear the same plumage?"

As the Grand Vizier said this, the Prison Custodian realised how foolish he had been. Of course! All the time, he had been looking for the face he knew. But what if the target had altered his appearance? What if he had changed his clothing, the shape of his face, his identifying characteristics? What if he was going around dressed as a scribe, a mullah, a cavalryman, or even a janissary and was staying in the cell adjacent to his? The Prison Custodian tried to imagine Falco with a beard, or dressed in a silver-embroidered kaftan, or even disguised as a foreign traveller. He visualised Falco slipping from one disguise to another a thousand times, and a succession of faces, each a different version of Prince Ahmet, passed before his eyes, mocking him, teasing him and poking out their tongues. The Prison Custodian shook his head to get rid of the images and slumped at the enormity of the task. Additional searches would have to be made, stretching the forces at his disposal even more.

While the Prison Custodian was pondering this, the Grand Vizier was musing on what kind of discourse he might have with Prince Ahmet if they ever came face to face. He could present the Sultan with the prince's scalp on a golden platter. Or he could lead the Sultan to think that he had disposed of the prince, but keep him hidden at one of the hunting lodges, where he could enjoy life until or unless it was necessary to reveal his existence. Depending on the prince's ambitions, he could either be groomed for the sultanate or left to rot. Whatever happened, this prince was a potential source of great wealth and power. As long as the Grand Vizier retained the Sultan's trust, there was no need for the prince, but if he fell out of favour, the prince would be a deadly weapon at his disposal. A double-edged sword. A fire-ball which, once ignited, would burn to ashes anyone or anything that got in his way. The prince had to be kept under wraps until he, the Grand Vizier, decided to unleash him.

A cool breeze blew up from the Marmara, breaking the silence between the two men. They stared at each other, one angry and powerful, the other subservient and cringing, until they were distracted from their thoughts by a knock at the door and the arrival of a team of singers and arabesque dancers. The Grand Vizier's angry expression softened at the sight of his vivacious concubines entering the room. Nodding towards the door, he dismissed the Prison Custodian.

"Sir!" said the Grand Vizier, beating his right fist on his chest. "I feel a fire burning here. If you don't bring me the water to quench it with, I swear I'll snuff out the fire in you."

The next morning, the Prison Custodian issued an order to all those under his command, which read: 'Falco, murderer of Nakşıgül Hanım has changed his appearance. He is to be brought in for interrogation and handed over to the Prison Custodian immediately!'

QUESTION 26
WHAT IS IT LIKE TO ESCAPE THE RAIN AND GET CAUGHT IN A HAILSTORM?

Dusky Falco and Stocky Yeye left the foul-smelling poultry market in Çemberlitaş and made their way towards the stokehouse, where they saw a group of security guards outside the hamam. As a precaution, they hid behind some horses to see what was going on. Something had obviously happened inside the hamam because crowds had gathered in the square outside. At first, Falco and Yeye thought it was just one of the usual fights. Or maybe there had been a wedding party at the hamam and, while everyone was enjoying themselves around the navel stone, a guest had lost a piece of jewellery, which would explain why the guards and janissaries had been summoned. It was not uncommon for the coiffeuses and beauticians who sat waiting in the cool room to rifle through their clients' belongings and help themselves to a few valuables while their clients were absorbed in the festivities. This practice, in which the stokehouse played an intermediary role, resulted in a substantial amount of jewellery changing hands or coming up for auction. The racket had recently progressed even further, when two connoisseurs at the Covered Bazaar managed to produce imitations of three legendary jewels and have them exchanged for the originals, all within the time that the owner was in the hamam. Dusky Falco had found out about this scam when Stokehouse Baba told him to deliver a box to a jeweller at the Covered Bazaar. The jeweller had looked into the box with gleeful disbelief, exchanged its contents and instructed Falco to take it back to the hamam immediately. Falco later learned that, on one occasion, this jeweller had made a fake which was returned to the hamam before the owner had even had her first wash.

On disagreeable days like that, quarrels that started inside the hamam would spill out into the street, where wedding guests would publicly accuse each other of stealing and get into fights. Husbands would then wade in, at which point the Prison Custodian, guards, the Chief of the Constabulary and even the Janissary Chief Commander might turn up and attempt to calm people down, meanwhile of course taking handsome bribes from the aggrieved families.

However, the scene that Falco and Yeye were witnessing appeared to be for a different reason.

"Yeye! Is it another robbery? What do you think?"

"I don't think so, Falco. There are no squabbling kids and no swearing husbands."

"You're right. Shall we wait a bit?"

"Okay."

"Make sure you're not seen."

They did not need to wait long. The Prison Custodian and two of his men emerged from the hamam, creating a ripple of fear through the crowd outside. They mounted the horses brought to them by their grooms and rode off shouting and swearing at the stokehouse brothers.

The Prison Custodian's visit to the stokehouse seemed ominous. Falco and Yeye looked at each other with consternation. They remained hidden, thinking it might be better to find out what had happened before entering. Then one of their friends stumbled into the street and told them that he had been thrown out for smoking hashish, but that the police were really looking for a twenty-three-year-old man. Falco silently thanked the Hungarian surgeon yet again because the description that had been issued bore no resemblance to himself. If even his stokehouse brethren did not know that he was the wanted man, then the surgeon had indeed worked a miracle. Dusky Falco relaxed and explained briefly to Yeye about the operation and how his eyebrows had been altered. He assured him that, even though he was in fact the person they were seeking, there nothing to fear. However, Falco knew that it was too dangerous for him to enter the stokehouse in case he was identified or interrogated by Stokehouse Baba. And so, Stocky Yeye went in alone and, after bundling up their few paltry personal belongings, slipped out to join Falco without anyone noticing.

The die was cast now and they had nowhere to go. Falco did not want to leave Yeye alone at the stokehouse and Yeye did not want to remain there without him. They consoled each other by trying to convince each other that their miserable and disorderly life at the stokehouse would only have led them into trouble. Falco knew that he had to find Nakşıgül's murderer before the Prison Custodian found him and Yeye was being hunted because of his own past escapades. However, neither of them had anywhere to stay and Falco had not the slightest shred of evidence to go on. Falco decided they would have to separate so that Yeye was not exposed to danger by being associated with him. But where could he leave Yeye? With whom could he entrust him? If he left Yeye to roam the streets of Istanbul on his own, he was bound to fall into the hands of predatory rogues who would introduce him to unsavoury aspects of street life.

They walked from Gedikpaşa to Bayezit. The sun had set and the streets were deserted. Soon the janissaries would start their patrols and they could be detained for questioning merely for being out without a lamp. It would be almost impossible to fabricate convincing answers, so finding somewhere to shelter was urgent. The sound of horses' hooves in the streets had stopped and the city was almost completely silent, except for the barking of dogs. Bayezit Square was deserted apart from a few people returning slowly from evening prayers, tapping the ground with their walking sticks. The garden gates of nearby houses and mansions were now firmly bolted, cutting off all contact with the outside world. Every passing minute was working against them. They needed to find a sheltered corner or creep into a private garden for the night, because it was too late to attempt going to another district. In any case, if they went to Fatih it meant passing the janissary barracks at the Hippodrome, which would be dangerous. They had heard stories of people who wandered alone in that area being taken inside the barracks and turned into slaves. In fact, there was an epic poem on the subject entitled *The Hussy with the Beauty Spot,* which was recited by Şahbaz Mecit of Diyarbekir for months and listened to with fear and dread in the mansions and pavilions of Istanbul. If they walked down towards Kumkapı, they could be pounced on by the notorious Kadırga fire-fighters so, as a last resort, they decided on the Bayezit Hamam stokehouse, which would at least be like a second home to them. They could say they needed to spend a night there because it was too late to get back to Gedikpaşa Hamam.

Until that night, they had no idea what it meant to escape the rain and get caught in a hailstorm. The moment they stepped inside Bayezit Hamam, they felt their blood freeze.

QUESTION 27
WHO IS THE SLENDER BEAUTY OF MOUNT QAF?

Four men were sprawled on the navel stone under the dome at Bayezit Hamam surrounded by slick-tongued, fearsome villains who stood in attendance next to the nearby basins. An array of semi-naked city orphans, rent boys and exotic young profligates, each wearing only a *peştamal* or waist cloth and clogs, wandered about serving the clients who came in all shapes, types and sizes – fat and skinny, giants and dwarfs, long-haired and bald, bearded and clean-shaven – and who kept their voices low out of respect for the men being pummelled on the navel stone. It seemed to Dusky Falco that all Istanbul's extremist and errant rogues were there. Out in the street, identity was defined by headgear and dress, such as style of robe or breeches, sash, waistcoat or bolero, but the state of undress in the hamam rendered everyone equal, suggesting that these men had been summoned from various strata of Istanbul society to congregate for a common purpose. When Dusky Falco and Yeye arrived at the hamam, they were castigated at the door by a man dressed in hamam cap and clogs, his long black hair and handlebar moustache entwined in his straggly uncut beard. They realised that he must be Bayezit Hamam's stokehouse foreman and that his function that evening was to greet guests and direct them towards a private room, the cool room, the middle room or the navel stone as appropriate, in addition to dealing with youngsters who had been summoned from other stokehouses.

"Hey, you bastards, what are you doing here?" he asked. "Weren't you told to come in by the back door?"

There were no further questions and no answers required. All they had to do was wash the dust off their feet. They sighed with relief as they entered the passageway that went through to the stokehouse. However, their legs were still trembling and they were in such trepidation that they were unable to speak or ask what they were meant to be doing. In the stokehouse, they found ten more boys, each unknown to one another and as fearful as themselves. The stokehouse baba cursed Dusky Falco and Yeye for being late and threw them each a white Layhar robe, mask and a pair of clogs. It was only when they followed the stokehouse baba's instructions to remove their clothes and put on the gowns that they began to grasp the situation they were in.

"Bastards of Layhar! Ensure that you make Layhar's spirit happy tonight at the stokehouse. Do not falter in your work until the cock crows. The soles of your clogs have been covered with cloth so that you are silent as you walk. Whatever you do, pay attention. Do everything the guests command and never bring dishonour on the stokehouse. Keep the trays filled with fruit and meze, and the wine glasses topped up with rooster's blood. Offer the pipes gracefully and light them with care. Do not upset anyone."

Now it was clear. An evening of *sakilik*, a Sufi term for drinking and enlightened discussion, was being held at the hamam that evening, and stokehouse brethren, mostly unknown to one another and selected from various hamams for their beauty and grace, were there to provide service.

Such hamam gatherings had become fashionable in recent years among certain clienteles, including statesmen, notables, janissary rebels and ordinary troublemakers. The navel stone at the centre of the hamam was referred to as the 'universe' and anyone who entered this universe would cover their face with a mask and slip into the anonymity of the assembly. The masks allowed people to disregard class and behave on equal terms, whether they were commoners or dignitaries. Rumours of what happened at these gatherings used to circulate for days, and these 'universes' took on a completely different meaning as places where matters of state were discussed. The central navels were places where members of the ruling class and their critics, regardless of class, could meet to discuss their secret aspirations, make plans, give instructions, incite, blackmail or bargain with each other over wine and meze. Interestingly, the Sultan and the Grand Vizier always ensured that they had at least one scorpion present at these assemblies.

The evening started with a heated discussion about Mad Petro's ambassador to Istanbul, who had been in the city for two months, yet had still not been granted an audience with the Sultan. The Grand Vizier had said that the French and Austrian governments proposed to divide the Iranian Empire and Mad Petro's Russian territories between them, and that the Sultan's delay in receiving the ambassador was because this situation was still being investigated. Word was that the Grand Vizier was pushing forward a secret policy for securing half of Iran and thought it would do more harm than good to open up a new front on the European frontier. The army's position was self-evident because of the setbacks in the north of Iran, where Moscow had captured the provinces of Mazenderan and Gilan.

Dusky Falco wandered around the hamam carrying a tray of wine, pipes, narghile tobaccos and various meze dishes. While keeping a constant check on Stocky Yeye, he had to be careful not be a nuisance or to make a blunder. He was also worried that some idiot would drink too much and reach out to molest him. The men had been drinking in the sweaty hamam environment for nearly an hour and they were becoming increasingly raucous, their voices resonating under the dome with the courage afforded by alcohol, heat and masked anonymity.

"Masters, lords and gentlemen! Did you know that İbrahim Pasha follows a secret religion?"

"Indeed, yes. I hear he's an Armenian from Cappadocia."

"They say he's not been circumcised. We should have him circumcised!"

"He has the Sultan wrapped around his little finger, despicable man!"

"Sharia law is disappearing before our eyes, gentlemen! What is to be done about the drag queens, pretty boys, harlots and prostitutes?"

Beneath the dome of the hamam, the navel had become a platform where everyone was at liberty to voice such opinions. Someone started beating time and the dome reverberated as everyone joined in the singing of a janissary chorus:

Words of heresy we chant
Established order to supplant
For our rights we all do toil
To bring the cauldron to the boil

As the masked choir sang these brave words about bringing Hajji Bektaş's cauldron to the boil, one of the men sitting by the basins called out to Falco as he passed by with his tray.

"Hey you, boy! You must be tired of strutting around with that tray. Come and rub the soles of my feet," said the man, taking a piece of ice from the silver table next to the basin and tossing into his wine, before grabbing Falco's waist cloth and stepping on his foot.

Falco recognised the voice and knew instantly that more disaster was ahead. He handed his tray to another serving boy, bowed his head and knelt down. His Layhar robe was sticking to his body with perspiration as he did as he was ordered, all the while glancing from under his eyebrows to keep an eye on Yeye. At one point, he tried to get a glimpse of the masked man whose feet he was rubbing in order to be sure that he had identified the voice correctly. It was indeed the Prison Custodian. Falco felt as if he was doomed that day, otherwise how could it be that, having managed to escape the trouble at Gedikpaşa Hamam, he was now once again at the mercy of the Prison Custodian? Falco listened carefully to make quite sure, but there was absolutely no doubt and he knew he was in danger. He scrutinised the people around him, but everyone's eyes were fixed on the Prison Custodian's biceps. The tattooist had done a good job. Whenever the Prison Custodian moved his arm, it looked as though the forked tongue of the viper was reaching out towards him. Falco recalled the beatings he had had at Eyüp Prison and felt afraid. The man next to the Prison Custodian was addressed as Stiletto because of an equally terrifying stiletto tattoo that ran from his wrist to elbow. The strong lines and frightening detail of the two designs were similar in style, suggesting that the two men were created by the same tattooist and that they were good friends. Falco kept his head down and listened as four men whispered to Stiletto, clearly trying to gain his favour.

"Master! Listen carefully to me. Who is responsible for all the martyrs' blood spilled in Iran? Is the Ottoman Empire to be run by people who engage with the Moscow infidel? There are so few honourable women and honest men in our streets. Sharia law is being eroded. You are respected among your peers. Speak to them."

"That may be, gentlemen, but we need an edict, a fatwa or royal decree for this. We need a prince who is prepared to exert his will to replace Sultan Ahmet," said Stiletto.

"Sir, you may not be able to do this, but Preacher İspirizade could issue a fatwa, Judge Zülali Hasan Efendi a decree, and you would do the rest."

"Peaky Agop and Kurdish Celo can round up the market porters and greengrocers, while Mad Mullah İbrahim and Muslu Beşe get the traders involved."

"Wildcat Recep and Dockyard Tazı can deal with the sailors and seamen."

"It's a sin for the ancient legend of İbrahim's *put-şiken* to be usurped by this İbrahim's *put-diken*."[2]

"People say the Moscow bear might be going berserk, but he's winning the hearts of the ladies of Baku. So where does that leave Islam?"

"Gentlemen, you are my guests here! Let's leave this topic for another time," said Stiletto.

"No, no. It's an important matter of state. I entreat you, for the sake of the slender beauty with the arched eyebrows and rosebud mouth of Mount Qaf!"

"Gentlemen, these are matters you should be including in your night-time prayers, not discussing while intoxicated at a hamam universe. Is this the right place to put the great Ottoman Empire to rights?" said Stiletto.

"Surely, you're not afraid!"

---

2 *put-şiken*: destruction of false idols – as called for by Abraham in the Old Testament.
put-diken: construction of false idols – of which İbrahim (or Abraham) Pasha was accused.

"Brother, why do you think I have this decoration? I live up to it, when necessary. But not here. There is a time and place for everything. All right?" said Stiletto loudly, pointing to the tattoo on his arm.

The people sitting around the basin fell into an uncomfortable silence, as if someone had just dropped a bombshell.

"Son-of-a-bitch! You're hurting my feet!" said the Prison Custodian, taking out his irritation on Falco and pushing him away.

Falco staggered and fell. As he did so, his mask almost revealed his face, causing his heart to leap.

"Excuse me, sir! I'm so sorry!" he muttered, disguising his voice as he rose to his feet.

Falco understood that he was being punished for overhearing things he was not meant to hear. He looked up to get a glimpse of the man who would punish him and came eye to eye with the Prison Custodian. They both averted their eyes quickly, fearing recognition, and Falco's gaze rested on a marble basin with a picture of a galleon and two lines of clumsily engraved verse:

For the old and infirm there will be a cure
In the expert hands of Halil the masseur

Falco hurried away, his heart still pounding with fear of the Prison Custodian, who merely gulped down another glass of iced wine and forgot about the stokehouse boy, quite unaware that he was the very person he was seeking for murder. In his mind, now befuddled with alcohol, the Prison Custodian was imagining how he would search and find Falco and sell him to two buyers, who would each present him with a bag of gold

– one from Judge İshak who wanted him alive and one from İbrahim Pasha who wanted him dead or alive. The first payment would undoubtedly be greater than the second. The Prison Custodian congratulated himself for not having been excessively rough with the Supreme Judge when interrogating him. That was something else to drink to. If only he had thought up a heroic plan for appearing to rescue Judge İshak from the captors, whom of course he had hired. Now that would have been a masterstroke!

Once everybody had left the hamam universe, Falco and Yeye lay on the ashes until dawn. Yeye fell asleep the moment his head touched the floor, but Falco lay awake for a long time, thinking about what they should do the next day. The meaning of the verse on the basin clearly meant Halil was the answer to the problems of the poor and vulnerable. The crude verse had been engraved on his basin, in the tradition of hamam attendants who had their individual stamp carved on to their basins, into which clients would place tips according to their satisfaction with their treatment. Some attendants would give special services to select clients and provide massages that were more than the usual rub down. The picture of the galleon above the basin indicated that its owner had either started out as a street boy from the dockyards or been a ship's deserter. It was no mean feat for a dockyard boy to rise to the position of having a basin at Bayezit Hamam and gain. It would provide him with a reasonable income, even if he rented his basin out to others, and earn him the respect of other hamam attendants. According to the verse on the basin, the person's name was Halil, possibly the famous Patrona Halil, whose name was legendary among the stokehouse brethren. Falco wondered if he was present that night, but the masks hid everyone's identities. Stiletto was obviously someone important and Falco knew he would hear that name again. The term *'put şiken'* which had cropped up in their discussion was presumably a reference to the denunciation of false idols by the prophet İbrahim, while *'put diken'* referred to the decadence of his namesake Grand Vizier İbrahim Pasha, who had had statues of women placed among the lions, dragons and snakes by the pools in Sadabat. But who was the slender beauty with the arched eyebrows and rosebud mouth of Mount Qaf?

QUESTION 28
CAN A TOUCH OF SORROW PIERCE THE HEART?

Hafız Çelebi bowed his head and thought long and hard. He had no family and therefore no children. Could he take on the responsibility of an adolescent boy? He longed to teach him how to grow tulips and send him to college to be educated. The boy standing opposite him was undoubtedly smart, in fact very smart. He had a good physique, pleasant character, intelligent mind, decent beliefs and a nice face, but he was only at the start of his adolescence. Would he want to spend the rest of his life in a garden?

"I'll do my best, with Allah's blessing!" said Hafız Çelebi finally, opening his arms wide.

Stocky Yeye and Hafız Çelebi embraced like father and son. Hafız Çelebi had always regretted being childless, while Stocky

Yeye had lamented never knowing a father's embrace. And when Hafız Çelebi mentioned college, Stocky Yeye felt as if all his dreams had come true.

After witnessing the party at Bayezit Hamam, Dusky Falco had started to worry that Yeye might go astray one day and get mixed up in the treacheries of city life, so he set about ensuring that this did not happen. Falco could not bear to think of his own pursuers harming Yeye, who had a brilliant mind and could achieve a great deal with the right guidance. He was a gem that required careful handling. Thus, Falco thought he had found the perfect solution when Yeye agreed to his idea of approaching Hafız Çelebi. They had rushed over to Kağıthane to see Hafız Çelebi, who was now welcoming the idea of taking in Yeye as a son to whom he could teach the secret of his tulips, while Yeye was feeling excited about all the books he would read at college.

At this point, the paths of Dusky Falco and Stocky Yeye went in different directions, but they did not lose contact. In fact, with Hafız Çelebi's consent, they made a pact that Stocky Yeye would plant Dusky Falco's tulip bulb and, when spring came, they would set out together to find the killers of Nakşıgül. They were of course obliged to tell the whole story about Dusky Falco to Hafız Çelebi, who believed them and embraced them both. Then, for the first time in his life, Stocky Yeye was given some solemn paternal advice.

"Son, you are an intelligent boy, but not everyone has your intelligence. A wise person takes only the worldly goods he needs and gives the rest to the poor. He prefers humility to eminence, never tires of learning, is never disdainful about helping others, applauds the good deeds of others while making no mention of his own, and regards all others as better than himself."

Hafız Çelebi loved Yeye, but knew that his association with Dusky Falco posed something of a risk. While he would not inform the police, he did not want to get into trouble. Falco was clearly a brave young man and, when he recounted what had happened to him, Hafız Çelebi had believed him completely. He could tell from Falco's face that his heart was pure and his words sincere. However, Hafız Çelebi knew that it was inadvisable for someone with Falco's lack of experience to be openly wandering about in Istanbul. A person sought for murder could not hide for long, even if his appearance had changed. Hafız Çelebi therefore meted out some stern advice to him as well.

"My son, listen to someone who knows best. Never disregard advice. Impatience is more wearying than patience on the path you are taking. Your enemy is a prestigious and sly man, so do not expose your identity without knowing how you will overcome the cunning of your enemies. Cheap gains are costly in the end. Ensure that you are the ultimate winner. Never assume that anything can be resolved quickly. Do not let the exuberance of youth allow you to create impossible dreams. Your personal strength will never be greater than the might of the state. Be circumspect at all times but do not despair. Too much hope can enslave one. Beware, the greatest weakness is to be foolish and the greatest treasure you can possess is intelligence. Use your intelligence wisely! Do not stray from your path, but do not pursue it to the bitter end without good reason. Pause every so often to listen to your heart and to evaluate what you are doing. Never do anything you might regret."

Hafız Çelebi spoke at length to both of them until daybreak, hoping to alleviate the pain of parting that awaited them the following day. The youths fell asleep that night listening to each other's heart beats, their hearts heavier than at any time since they had met. The next morning, their sorrowful farewells overshadowed the dawn splendour, turning it into a tragedy. Their one pleasure was the hope they shared when the tulip bulb was planted. While the sun was rising above the Çağlayan ridge, Yeye dug a hole as directed by Hafız Çelebi. Dusky Falco placed the tulip bulb into the ground and recited a prayer as he covered it with earth. In memory of that moment, they named the tulip Touch of Sorrow. With sad hearts, they looked at each other and felt at peace. All that remained was to wait until spring and to find the partner to the Touch of Sorrow. Meanwhile, it was Yeye's task to check on the bulb daily and protect it from foxes, beavers, geese and ducks. Hafız Çelebi's task was to teach him how to do this.

No one wanted to be the first to move when the little planting ceremony was over. The sky seemed to be weighing down on them and a long silence ensued as they stood with bowed heads, each waiting for someone else to speak. A tear rolled down Yeye's cheek. He could not conceal his love for Falco. Despite his stocky frame, knowledge and wisdom beyond his years, there was still a childish side to Yeye, which was evident in the way he hugged Falco, who had correctly recognised that Hafız Çelebi could give Yeye the tranquillity he needed to take stock of life. Dusky Falco now gave up trying to hide his own feelings and the two boys held each other in a long embrace. Then, something strange happened. A mass of black clouds gathered above through which, for a moment, a single quivering ray of sunshine penetrated, seeming to link the tears of emotion on the cheeks of the two young people with the Touch of Sorrow that had just been planted. Then the clouds closed over and the ray of light disappeared.

"Falco, my son! I believe your Touch of Sorrow will produce a beautiful flower," said Hafız Çelebi, embracing them both. "God willing, your fortune will be just as beautiful. However, do not regard the Touch of Sorrow as a symbol for everything. After all, it might not bloom, it might be eaten by worms, or its partner might never be found. You never know."

"Yes, Efendi. Of course I realise that. The Touch of Sorrow will not lead me to the murderers of Nakşıgül. I have to seek them out for myself."

"Good. In that case, it is now time to say farewell."

Dusky Falco had started carrying a small jack-knife tucked into his belt. He had discovered it with the pearls after his mother's death and knew it had meant a lot to her so he thought it had probably belonged to his father. A few days earlier when walking past Pearl Villa, he had remembered this knife and knocked at the door on the pretext of begging for bread. When the elderly servant went indoors, he had dashed into the garden and retrieved the knife from where he had left it under the well crank. Now, Falco wiped away Yeye's tears, placed this knife into his hands and wrapped his own hands around those of his young friend as if their four hands and two hearts would be locked together for ever. Remembering ***The tale of a young couple***, which he had read in a book entitled *Spring Garden*, Stocky Yeye felt he would never love anyone more than he loved Dusky Falco and would give his life for his friend and brother if he were to request it.

"My dear boy," said Hafız Çelebi, "our ancestors have always had an appreciation of goodness and grace that is still unsurpassed by any other civilisation. The way they tended their flowers was a manifestation of their love of everything in nature and of the care they took to prepare the ground for future generations. Turks regard flowers and gardens as an ancestral tradition and love them as a symbol of their spiritual aestheticism. You should know this."

Dusky Falco listened to Hafız Çelebi's final words and set off without glancing back, feeling satisfied that the tulip bulb and Yeye were safe in his care.

Postscript: The tale of a young couple

Once upon a time there was a man who was always sighing and weeping. When a friend asked him the reason for this, he told the following story:

I was a slave trader. I bought a slave for three hundred lira. Her face was paler than the moon and her lips sweeter than honey. I worked hard to teach her feminine graces. When I took her to market, the place reached fever pitch. As the customers increased, so did her price. I did not sell, but waited. Afternoon came and a swarthy young cavalryman appeared. When he saw my slave, he dismounted from his horse, came over, smiled at her and said, "What is your name?" I saw my slave smile at him. The young man turned to me and asked her price. "She is worth her weight in gold, which is one thousand gold coins," I replied. He said nothing and wandered around for a bit. Then he came back and secretly pressed something into the girl's palm. When evening came, I was surprised to see that it was one hundred gold coins. The next day I raised the price of my slave and kept delaying her sale. That afternoon, the young man came back and once more put one hundred gold coins into the palm of her hand. Four days passed like that. On the fifth day, I followed the young man and discovered where he lived. I made some enquiries and found that he had just sold his last horse. On the sixth day he came to the slave market yet again. However, this time he just gazed at the slave from a distance. That night, I led the girl by the hand to the young man's house. "Some urgent business has come up this evening. If I entrust this slave to you until the morning, will you watch over her?" I said. At first, he did not want to do this, but finally agreed. I returned home. In the middle of the night, I sat up in bed wondering how they were getting on and what was happening between them. Suddenly, I heard a loud knocking. I opened the door to find my slave trembling and in tears. "What happened? How did you fare with the young man?" I asked. She could not stop weeping.

"The young man died," she murmured after a while.

"How did that happen?"

"When you left, he took me inside and brought me some food. He sat watching me as I ate and brought a bowl for me to wash my hands. Then he prepared a bed for me. He sprinkled musk and rose water over me and told me to close my eyes, which I did. He put his finger on my cheek, saying over and over again, 'Oh! What beauty! What touching beauty!' Then he suddenly cried out 'We all belong to Allah and to him we will return!' and fell to the floor. When I opened my eyes, I was devastated to see that he had consigned his soul to God."

After my slave told me this, I kept repeating the young man's name and blessing his soul. Now, all my tears are for those two lovers. I wander the world in the hope that, one day I might find a couple as pure and beautiful as they. As I age, I am still searching and will die doing so.

QUESTION 29
SHEIKH EFENDI, WOULD YOU ALLOW ME TO DISROBE?

"There has always been God and nothing else like Him. That is how it is and how it always has been. Therefore, dispose of your wealth and bury your ignorance. Because nothing ends that is not buried in the soil. Meditation is the candle of your heart, without which it remains in darkness. The hearts and mysteries of the wise are the source of light. When someone gives you just praise, you should praise God who has made you that way. See God in every living creature and see every living creature in God's countenance. See God in the bloom of a rose and the uniqueness of a tulip."

Dusky Falco was astonished. These words were almost identical in meaning to those spoken by Hafız Çelebi a few nights before at Kağıthane. Yet now he was listening to Sheikh

Ahmet Dede preaching in the room of the whirling dervishes at the Mevlevi Lodge next to Çırağan Villa in Beşiktaş. The tone, emphasis and content of the two speeches were so similar, it was as if Hafız Çelebi and Sheikh Ahmet Dede had been taught by the same teacher. The only significant difference was their location. Whereas Hafız Çelebi resided in a humble shed nestling in the shadows by the River Cendere, Sheikh Ahmet Dede lived in a waterfront palace with wonderful views of the Bosphorus. One was a gardener devoted to lifting people's hearts by producing flowers, the other a sheikh devoted to making hearts bloom. One had beds of hearts in his garden, the other a garden of flowers in his heart. One surrounded himself with flowers of the season, the other experienced the flower season in his soul. Hafız Çelebi had made his love of flowers into his profession, while Sheikh Ahmet Dede executed his profession of love through flowers, even going so far as to fill numerous pots of flowers in deep mid-winter to brighten the prayer areas in front of the Mevlevi Lodge windows. Dusky Falco's tender young heart was touched to hear these similar words delivered in such different surroundings. It was as if Sheikh Ahmet Dede was continuing the role of Hafız Çelebi in his life.

"It's hard to think of a Turkish house without the sound of water, because the most select flowers are kept on the ornamental rooftops of these houses," said Sheikh Ahmet Dede. "Flowers are honoured as evidence of Almighty God's graciousness and pleasure. Every prayer is linked to the heart through a refreshing perfume of flowers. Everyone should sow flower seeds here at our Mevlevi Lodge, in front of its bay windows, on its window pediments or in front of the walls along the waterfront. Make sure there are always tulip bulbs in the garden. God willing, we will have the most beautiful tulips blooming in our garden again this year. Hopefully, statesmen and even our dear Sultan will grace us by coming to see them and joining our circle."

"You're too late, Dede. This year the most beautiful tulip has already been planted!" interrupted Dusky Falco, choking back a cough and rubbing his arms to soak up the heat from the wood burning in the hearth.

For three days, since Falco put Yeye in Hafız Çelebi's care, he had been looking for a place to stay. There was little he could do before the Touch of Sorrow bloomed, which meant lying low for a whole winter in the hope that his troubles would blow over and he would be forgotten. He had wandered the streets in the driving autumn rain seeking shelter until eventually, when his coughing and shivering turned to fever, he had ended up at the Mevlevi Lodge, saying, "I've come to disrobe!"

In Mevlevi terminology, 'disrobing' meant entering a dervish sect, giving up worldly interests and pursuits, and taking the Sufi path towards God. Falco could not say why he had suddenly announced, "I've come to disrobe'. Was it because winter was approaching and he needed somewhere to stay? A need for urgent medical treatment? Hafız Çelebi's advice to disappear for a while? To experience the dervish tranquillity? His own spiritual emptiness? The simple fact that their words soothed his soul? Actually, Falco had numerous reasons for wishing to disrobe. His words merely confirmed that he had made up his mind.

"Sheikh Efendi, would you allow me to disrobe?"

Sheikh Ahmet Dede had assumed that Falco would be like many who came in off the streets hoping to laze around at the lodge, whose decision was based on a sudden desire for a hot meal and a soft bed. His ragged attire at the start of winter had certainly suggested that his wish to enter the lodge was based on more than mere spiritual reasons. However, Sheikh Ahmet Dede showed no sign of annoyance and in fact was quietly amused when he heard Falco say, 'I've come to disrobe!'.

"Disrobing is easy, son. But first, we must dress you!" whispered Sheikh Ahmet Dede. "There is no glory in demands and wishes. True glory is found in good morality. This is a place of morality and the best garment a person can wear is made of the finest morals."

Then he clapped his hands twice. A servant who had been waiting at the door entered and fell to his knees.

"Yes, sir!"

"Go with this dear boy. Tell Boilersmith Dede to give him a set of clothing and prepare a cell. Healer Dede will look after the patient."

Sheikh Ahmet Dede had called him 'dear boy', just as his mother used to do. As Falco walked across the courtyard towards the dervish cells, he was aware that he felt no fear, for the first time in weeks. He could hide here and spend the winter in peace until spring, when his Touch of Sorrow would peep out of the soil, all being well.

Healer Dede had trained in medicine as a young man. He removed Dusky Falco's clothes, wrapped him in dry felt and lit a big fire in one of the dervish cells to make him sweat. After giving him some camomile tea, he spent the night at Falco's side, holding his hand and listening to his delirious talk. Later, Falco would associate that first night with a story. He was not sure if he had dreamt it, Healer Dede had read it to him, or someone else had told it to him. What he did know was that by the end of his first night at the lodge, he knew all about ***Majnun's love for Leyla***. In the morning, that story was on his mind when he walked past some dervishes, who were chanting 'İsm-i Celal' and fingering their prayer beads, as he made his way to see Sheikh Ahmet Dede to explain his situation.

Postscript: Majnun's love for Leyla

One day a kind-hearted man encountered Majnun and asked, "What news of Leyla? Tell me about her."

Majnun bowed his head and fell to the ground.

"Leyla," he moaned. "It's futile to keep asking me the same thing. If you're asking about Leyla, then is not merely her name sufficient as an answer?"

On hearing this, the kind-hearted man recited the following poem:

'There is one God' Majnun would say
Given a chance to see her, 'No' he'd say
His passion for Leyla was such that
Instead of Mevla, 'Leyla' he'd say

Whereupon Majnun stopped, sat down and started rummaging in the earth as if searching for something.

"You poor soul, what are you looking for?" asked the man.

Majnun sighed.

"I'm looking for Leyla of course," he replied.

"But what would Leyla be doing in the earth? Why would a rare pearl such as her be buried in a dusty path like this?"

"Of course, my sweet angel would not be in this earthly domain. But I look for her wherever I am. Maybe, one day, I will find her."

PART II

Development: Ferment in Istanbul

(May 1730)

Few pleasures should from life be drawn
So when lost, there's less to mourn

QUESTION 30
WHICH SHOULD I TAKE, SAKİ? THE ROSE, THE GLASS OR YOU?

As the late morning rays of sunlight reflected off the April geraniums, stealing their colours and scattering them in the water that sprayed out of the fountains, crowds of people made their way to Sadabat, revelling in the pleasures of spring. Animated laughter and the sound of tambourines could be heard coming from the harem garden, where Fatma Sultan and her ladies-in-waiting were enjoying themselves at a poetry gathering. They were seated at tables around the pool and being served dishes of meze and wine, while singers and dancers entertained them. Outside the garden, small groups of men and women formed on either side of a brook, youths lingered near the girls sitting on swings hanging from the trees a short distance away, and there was a medley of toy-sellers, pedlars, horses, decorated ox-carts, conjurors and fire-eaters. The mingled sounds of music and revelry that filled the air heralded tulip time at Sadabat.

Before beginning his speech, Grand Vizier İbrahim Pasha leant over to his wife Fatma Sultan and whispered that he loved her.

"My beautiful wife, my angel! I bring you special good wishes from your father, our great Sultan. I was with him today at the ambassadors' presentation ceremony. We made plans to open a school in Scutari and, as you know, our publishing house was established last month. The first ten books have been presented to your father, the Sultan. It was a very special occasion."

İbrahim Pasha saw that Fatma Sultan was not interested in what he was saying, so he tried to engage her attention by paying her compliments in rhyming couplets.

"But that's enough of matters of state, the light of my eyes I must captivate. Let this day be one of pleasure, with my lady's permission, a time we can treasure!"

"Yes, yes, of course!" replied Fatma Sultan, her face radiating youth and beauty.

"See, I've brought Nedim, a son of our city, whose verse excites all with its ingenuity."

Fatma Sultan looked around and was pleased to see that Nedim was indeed present. She had always liked reading poetry, whether in the palace library or from her personal library of divan poetry, but Nedim's poems were somehow different. His elegant, playful lines were pleasing to any woman's soul. Through her interest in poetry, Fatma Sultan had developed a poetic style of her own, which she displayed by responding to İbrahim Pasha's rhymes. It was as if a play in verse was being performed before the gathered assembly.

"Like a crazy nightingale you sing your song, may this delightful game continue all night long," warbled Fatma Sultan.

"As players caress the strings of your lute, Nedim's words will your mood suit."

"Let's steal a night of grace at Çırağan palace."

"Taste nectar from the honeycomb, juice of the pome."

"Everyone should raise a glass, for nothing can this day surpass."

At this point, Nedim joined in the battle of words, instantly filling the room with witticisms and subtle allusions. In those days, Nedim's reputation coursed through the city like a strong wind polishing the stars, illuminating every assembly and lighting up people's hearts. Some poets found his works inferior and primitive, but the people adored them and they were memorised and passed around by word of mouth. Any reference to Nedim's couplets, sonnets, songs or odes would fill the promenades of Istanbul with laughter, skittish melodies and gaiety.

İbrahim Pasha had discovered this a few years before and now summoned Nedim to all his gatherings, where he never failed to shower him with gifts. Only two months ago, after reading one of Nedim's poems at a halva party graced by the Sultan, İbrahim Pasha had felt compelled to fill Nedim's mouth with diamonds and pearls, much to the disapproval of the Sultan.

Nedim did his job well. His sexual proclivities were questionable, but he conformed to etiquette and made people happy, whatever their predilections. However, once he had hit on a rhyme, he could not wait to use it and would often speak out of turn. This was one of those moments.

"May the wine be mature, the song an overture," he interrupted when Fatma Sultan said 'Everyone should raise a glass, for nothing can this day surpass'.

"Let each take turn without interruption; enjoy the moment without disruption," reproached İbrahim Pasha, who did not want Nedim to get too cocky with his flashy rhymes.

"Since the world-famous poet Nedim is here, let him entertain us and fill us with cheer," chimed Fatma Sultan.

"But only for ears in this room forsooth, for these dreams are based on words of truth."

"Now, a test for you, oh poet of our time, you have here an audience, so show how you can rhyme."

"My lady, you have such wit and verve, a thousand rhymes you do deserve."

"Pen and paper I request."

"A glass of wine for your guest?"

"Whatever you desire, dear sir, for your inspiration!"

"Oh my gracious lady, how you stir the imagination."

"Were I a moth that flew into your light."

"I'd be your candle and melt into the night."

At that point, Nedim suddenly stopped. He had noticed a Polish concubine with a rose pinned to her dress coming towards him carrying a tray with two tulip-shaped glasses of wine. Knowing that all eyes were on her, she walked with a slow seductive swing of her hips and presented one glass to the Grand Vizier then, turning towards Nedim, she offered him the other. As she did so, the rose fell from her dress to the floor. A deep silence descended over the assembly as she bent down to pick it up. The guests watched with curiosity to see how Nedim would thank the girl.

With a glass and a rose, you made your debut
Should I take the rose, the glass, or you?

İbrahim Pasha laughed to see his concubine addressed by Nedim with these libidinous words. He decided to inspire the poet even more the next day by adding some lines before and after this couplet and turning it into a *gazel*. The music was now getting louder, the party was warming up and everyone was forecasting that the coming tulip season would be more festive than ever.

Suddenly, a man wandered into the middle of the gathering from the direction of the dragon-headed fountains. The guardsmen had tried to stop him, but they were caught unawares and were too slow. İbrahim Pasha stepped forward and invited the man to join the party and greeted him like a guest, even though he looked more like a lunatic or beggar. His legs were trembling and he was carrying a soaking wet bag which was torn and covered with mud and weeds. The man stumbled towards İbrahim Pasha and carefully placed the bag on the ground in front of him.

"I was f-fishing from my boat in the Golden Horn today," stammered the man. "A mate was f-fishing nearby and his net got caught on something big which turned out to be this b-bag. My mate was happy because he thought he'd found a bag of gold in the Golden Horn, like they did in the days of Murat Han. But his dream turned into a nightmare and he seemed to go crazy. He pulled his boat to shore, threw away the bag and legged it. S-sir, this is the bag. I brought it here because I thought you should s-see it."

A heavy stench had pervaded the garden. At first İbrahim Pasha was unsure whether or not to look inside the bag that lay before him. The smell immediately told him what it contained and he wondered why this madman should bring it to him. As he reached out for the bag, the assembled guests started holding their noses. He was about to tip out the contents but, feeling everyone's eyes on him, thought better of it and pulled the bag towards him with two fingers, lifted the flap and grimaced with revulsion and nausea.

"God damn it! Bring the Prison Custodian to the Domed Stateroom immediately. This party is over! Tell the grooms to prepare the horses. We're going to the Seraglio!"

QUESTION 31
WHAT BROUGHT THE MYSTIC OUT OF HIS SPIRITUAL WORLD?

Falco spent a wonderful winter at the Mevlevi Lodge, absorbing knowledge from wise, learned people. Had he been able to erase Nakşıgül's murder from his mind, he would have been content to remain there until the Day of Judgement. The torment in his soul had been calmed by listening to the sermons Sheikh Ahmet Dede gave at this lodge, which been founded by Ohrili Hüseyin Pasha a century before on the most beautiful stretch of the Bosphorus coastline. The torrent of events that had tossed Falco from one disaster to the next had finally settled and, like a waterfall descending into a still lake, eased into peaceful tranquillity.

When Falco entered the Mevlevi Lodge during the autumn rains, it was in order to hide somewhere safe for a while. Ahmet

Dede tended his tortured soul during that winter and within just two months instilled in him a respect for the teachings of the eleventh century Persian Sufi Abdolkadir Gilani. However, with the approach of the tulip season, the emotions which Falco had been suppressing began to re-emerge.

Beşiktaş Mevlevi Lodge had the most splendid views of any building along the Bosphorus waterfront. When Ahmet Dede's father Memiş Mehmet was the Sheikh at the lodge, İbrahim Pasha was a frequent visitor, seeking respite and peace of mind. In fact, only two years before, he had acquired and restored the adjacent Kaya Sultan Villa, built by Sultan Murat IV, and had given it to his wife, Fatma Sultan. This villa became known as Çırağan Palace, because İbrahim Pasha organised entertainments and concerts by the light of lanterns, or *çırağan*, in its waterfront gardens, later known as Kazancıoğlu Gardens.

Six months passed. Those months of serene evenings spent listening to music played on the *ney* and drum in the elegantly domed Mevlevi lodge contrasted sharply with the colourful soirées of poetry and song that took place during the winter months at the ornate Çırağan Palace, with its alcoves and oriel windows. Now, the early days of summer had arrived and the waterfront was being transformed into a paradise of unsurpassable splendour.

During those six months, Falco also spent many memorable hours listening to stories told to him by an Iranian dervish named Brother Selman. As well as sharing their intimate thoughts, they read, discussed and memorised the works of the Persian poets Hafız and Omar Khayam. Falco loved these winter evenings spent discussing and exploring the meanings of the rich Persian vocabulary and metaphors that had found their way into Turkish poetry. He was keen to improve his knowledge of Persian, which he had learned as a child, and set about memorising not only the works of Turkish poets such as Fuzuli, Baki and Nef'i, but also Hafız, Khayyam, Sa'di and Mevlana's *Mesnevi* and *Divan-i Kebir.*

Brother Selman was in his early forties and had been a guard in the Iranian army before arriving at the Lodge. He gave graphic accounts of his adventures, with a bit of customary Persian hyperbole, and spoke of the terrible suffering of Ottoman soldiers who were still fighting in Iran and of their despair at being virtually forgotten by their own rulers. He even went so far as to suggest that Grand Vizier İbrahim Pasha had intentionally provoked irresolvable disputes with Iran. Like Stocky Yeye, Brother Selman had entered Falco's life quite by coincidence, with the difference that, while Falco had always protected Stocky Yeye, Selman quickly took on the role of Falco's protector. The one thing that remained a mystery to Falco was that, even though Brother Selman had 'disrobed' in order to become a member of the Mevlevi Lodge and now dressed as a dervish, he carefully kept his Iranian garments as if he intended to discard his dervish apparel one day.

Falco developed a habit of standing alone to watch the sunset reflected in the windows across the Bosphorus in Scutari, Beylerbeyi and Çengel Köyü. It was a brief interlude that gave him a few minutes of happiness, alone with his thoughts and dreams of Nakşıgül. When this bliss turned to sorrow, he would join the other dervishes in their practice of whirling, but he could never get her completely out of his mind.

Falco abstained from conversation for eighteen days after proclaiming 'I came to disrobe' and followed the daily routine of life at the lodge, as was expected of anyone wishing to become a Mevlevi. On the eighteenth day, when asked yet again if he wished to disrobe, he answered 'yes' and was made to endure days of hard manual labour and nights without sleep. All winter, his endurance was tested to the limit as he shivered and trembled like an autumn leaf through nights of snowfalls, storms, frosts and thunderstorms. Apart from his prayer beads, his only company was Crazy Sieve-eater, who occupied the adjacent cell and ate wire mesh. Crazy Sieve-eater was an eccentric who had never stepped off dry land, never even walked from Eyüp along Kağıthane to Beşiktaş, and knew nothing of the shores on the other side of the Bosphorus at Kadıköy or Scutari. The previous winter, Crazy Sieve-eater had set a trap for a fox that had taken to feeding on the lodge's chickens and then released it with a bell attached to its tail. The poor creature was the talk of Istanbul. No hunter would ever deign to kill a fox with a bell on its tail!

After evening prayers, there was a lull until night-time prayers, then another long wait until dawn prayers, after which the dervishes would sip the comforting soup sent from the kitchens by Cook Dede. After two months, Falco started to join in the dervishes' whirling ceremonies and his duties as servant were reduced. However, despite his best efforts, thoughts of Nakşıgül kept coming back. While the other dervishes whirled and voiced their passion for God, his heart was burning with passion for Nakşıgül. Every mention of love for God in the sermons given by Sufi masters such as Sheikh Ahmet Dede, Boilerman Dede, Healer Dede and Poet Dede told him that he should clear his mind of any thoughts about Nakşıgül, yet his yearning for her continued to increase. Nevertheless, he liked listening to sermons about love, especially those of Poet Dede, because they soothed his soul.

Poet Dede's real name was Süleyman Nahifi Efendi. He was a financial adviser at the Ottoman Treasury where he was in charge of Rumelian revenues. He came to the lodge three days a week to attend dervish ceremonies, recite poetry with Sheikh Ahmet Dede, and make pronouncements about love and the state of being in love.

One day, Süleyman Nahifi Dede handed Sheikh Ahmet Dede some pages of a book he was working on, and asked for his opinion. Sheikh Ahmet Dede passed the sheets to Falco, who was rounding up coffee cups nearby, and asked him to take them to his cell. As Falco walked down the flagstoned corridor to Sheikh Ahmet Dede's cell, he started reading and was amazed to find that the poems were true literary gems.

Listen to the ney, and the tale it tells
Of separations and tragic farewells:
Since the day when I was plucked from the reeds
My cries have touched each one who heeds
This separation which broke my heart
Will now for ever pain impart

According to Poet Nahifi Dede, a heart torn apart by separation was nothing compared to the yearnings of one that has been uprooted. For months, Falco's heart had been haunted by the mournful ney keening at being plucked away from the reed beds, but the fluting sounds had not penetrated his soul as these words did. Nor had Brother Selman's exaggerated versions of the *Şahnameh* tales affected him in that way, or the tragedy of Mevlana and Shams. For the first time since Falco left the house at Yenibahçe, the pain of separation seemed to engulf his whole being with fire. The lines he was reading were Turkish translations of Mevlana's famous *Mesnevi*, a book from which Falco had frequently read excerpts when learning Persian as a child. But Poet Nahifi Dede had not only translated this work, he had retained its poetic style.

That was the day when Falco started memorising the *Mesnevi* and giving serious through to great Iranian poets like Hafız, Khayyam, Sadi and Fardowsi. Inevitably of course, whenever he came across a couplet referring to love, he would remember Nakşıgül and his heart would ache again with yearning.

However, this was a day filled with the happiness and joy of spring. Afternoon prayers were over and the dervishes were sitting in a circle around Sheikh Ahmet Dede.

"Perhaps our noble brother might say a few words to enlighten our souls," said Ahmet Dede, addressing Poet Nahifi Dede.

Falco was standing by the window, gazing out at the tulips in Çırağan Palace gardens. The peace of the Bosphorus shores seemed to blend with the tranquillity of the sea as the distant voices of fishermen in their boats between Scutari and Beylerbeyi mingled with the sound of nightingales on the lush wooded hillsides of Yahya Efendi and Ortaköy. Falco found himself thinking of tulips, particularly the Touch of Sorrow.

For some unknown reason, Poet Nahifi Dede started talking about tulips. Falco fixed his gaze on one of the tulips in Çırağan Palace garden. Its fiery red bloom was gradually closing as the sun dipped behind the mountains and the light faded. While Poet Nahifi Dede spoke of tulips, Brother Falco gazed lovingly at the petals of this tulip, almost conversing with it and embracing the wound at its centre. Falco felt as if he were elsewhere in a world of happiness and tulips, a world without time. What was happening inside the Lodge became a blur and the flow of Nahifi Dede's words seemed to pulsate through a scarlet haze, turning into a scorching fire that burned his heart and mind, the red blood of Nakşıgül, her eyes and finally her hands. Every mention of tulips touched his heart.

"Tulips are from the east of course," Nahifi Efendi was saying. "Just as Christianity, Judaism and Islam are from the east. Tulips can be as demure as a young bride or bashful as a beautiful receiving a compliment. With their six petals, they can be fickle, looking out in all directions. The tulip is planted deep in the earth in the autumn and remains there until it reawakens in the spring, thus symbolising perseverance, determination and resurrection. The history of the tulip is like that of the noble Turkish people. After all, they've made parallel journeys. Like the tulip, the Turkish people were perceived as uncultured because they inhabited the steppe. But they dominated, even owned the steppe. Their word was law on the steppe, but they could not gain acceptance when they came to this city. City dwellers regarded them as peasants and wanted them to leave. They perceived Turks to be uncivilized and unworthy of this city, just as they did not allow the wild tulip into their gardens. Whenever Europeans encountered the Turks, they wanted to send them back to the steppe. However, the Turks persevered against all odds. After settling here in Istanbul, they established a world empire spreading across three continents and created a culture and civilisation that has become the envy of the world. Thus, the noble Turkish people, who were so despised, insulted and denigrated, began to bloom, just like the tulip, and went on to rule the largest and most powerful empire in the world. The tulip is to flowers what the Turks are to nations. Just as the tulip became a symbol of Islam, so the Turks came to represent Islam. That's why, when people speak of Turks, they think of Islam and vice versa. Meanwhile, the tulip also represents love, perhaps even that love which wounds or burns the heart, like lightening striking a velvety coronet of tulip petals. Why else would the hundreds of varieties of tulips have such poetic names?"

Poet Nahifi Dede continued with his speech, but Falco was in another world. Eventually, the effect of seeing the tulip in Çırağan Palace garden diminished and he came back to normal, though still somewhat confused. He realised that he had become a completely different person since donning his dervish garb. Only a few days before, some of the brethren had told him how radiant he looked with his newly grown beard. After six months of listening to the counsel of Sheikh Ahmet Dede and Poet Nahifi Dede, Falco felt as if his soul had been massaged into a state of tranquillity and otherworldliness that was so transcendental that he felt almost transparent, like a spirit. Brother Selman was the only person to remind Falco that he had a completely different life waiting for him outside the Lodge, a life filled with plans and visions of Nakşıgül, who was the reason for the emotional turmoil he had just experienced.

Poet Nahifi Dede had recently told them the story of ***The Youth who fell in love with a Singer***. Falco felt himself to be like that youth, running for all he was worth towards that single fiery red tulip in the sunlit Çırağan Palace garden. He imagined it blooming, wilting and falling to the ground, changing from pink to indigo like a ruby and transforming into a twin bulb that ended up in the palm of Nakşıgül's hand, where it absorbed the pink of her cheek, the red of her lips and the indigo of the birth mark on her shoulder. How long was it since his mother had died? So many things had happened to him since then. If he had had a father, would he have thrown him out to live like a tramp? For years, he seemed to have been cast adrift in stormy seas and had finally found salvation in Nakşıgül's love. Anything he could do for her would be worthwhile and might make him feel as if he were alive. The love he felt for her, which had been challenged and suppressed at the Lodge, was burning his heart again. As he dropped to his knees, exhausted and feverish, he visualised the red tulip in Çırağan Palace garden turn to indigo as if covered by deep purple tulle and become lodged in his heart. With a cry, he fainted and fell to the ground.

Postscript: The youth who fell in love with a singer

Seeing a vision in a dream is perhaps the most unlikely reason for falling in love. Anyone might see their Beloved in a dream, but is it possible for a being only seen in a dream to be a Beloved? Examples of such extreme love are Hüsrev and Şirin or Vamık and Azra. A heart captivated by a non-existent being is like a person who exists on nothing but air. People assume that a person who claims to love a beauty he has never seen, nor will ever see, has probably taken leave of his senses. They find it inconceivable that the spirit might be a source of inspiration or the heart guided by wishes and desires. Yet, even if a lover cannot determine whether his Beloved is the moon, the sun, or a trick of the mind, can it not be that his love is genuine when her image appears to him? Does love require the presence of a physical being? We believe the dervish who feels love on seeing the beauty of God in a vision, so why not believe the lover who feels passion for a Beloved seen in his dreams? If we do not believe this, what is love other than the adoration of a pretty face? A person can indeed be in love without having sight of the Beloved. The lover does not need sight of the Beloved in order to worry, feel passion or suffer sleepless nights on her account. Merely hearing the sound of an invisible person singing behind a wall can be enough to capture a heart. Some might see such love as an edifice without foundation, yet love is very adept at constructing edifices. If challenged, a person preoccupied with love for an unseen being will use dreams to create form and attire, to attribute colour, smell and manner. The Beloved will be constructed within the lover's mind. Her beauty will be intensified by the fantasies and aesthetics of the lover. If a lover who has been enraptured by a voice catches sight of the singer, his love will either fade or intensify. He will be guided by his vision. But if he never sees the singer, should he be criticised for falling in love? We know Paradise only through images, do we not? A lover whose heart is captured by the singing of the Beloved will gauge her beauty by her voice. If his love intensifies when he finally sees her, he will be viewing a beauty that matches her voice. However, should the singer's appearance be more beautiful than her voice, is the lover not to be congratulated for discerning such beauty through her voice? Are not even the most beautiful images of Paradise a far cry from the real thing? Can it not be claimed that all great beauties carry a trace of divinity within them?

QUESTION 32
WHAT WAS IN THE BAG FOUND AT THE BOTTOM OF THE SEA?

Seven people stood around the table under the ornamental ceiling at the Seraglio staring at the bones of two forearms from which tendrils of flesh still hung. Judge İshak and the Prison Custodian stood on either side of Grand Vizier İbrahim Pasha, who was waiting tensely for them to answer his questions. Next to them stood the Janissary Chief Officer of the Three Crescent Society, a secret intelligence organisation, and the stuttering fisherman who had retrieved the bones from the sea.

"Well, Efendi, tell us what you found!" said the Sultan, sounding angry.

"Your Majesty, the Grand Vizier sent these arms over here in a sack," replied the Court Physician, covering his mouth and pointing to the body parts with a stick. "I and four other physicians have spent three days analysing them, after cleaning them in the dissection room and leaving them to soak in water to get rid of the smell. The arms belong to a man. They were severed and thrown into the sea about two months ago. This happens a lot around here. The arms indicate that the owner had been handcuffed for some time before his death, and the state of these tendons with the skin hanging off suggests that he was tortured. The rate of decomposition and other factors indicate that he was in his forties. It might be possible to find out his identity from the bruise markings you see here on the bones."

"Your Majesty, with your permission, I'll look at the records for the last two months and try to find out who it is," offered the Janissary Chief Officer of the Three Crescent Society.

"Actually, if you don't mind, sir," said Judge İshak, "I would like to pursue this matter myself. If the Society would send us the records, we'll work on resolving the matter in a properly judicial manner."

"Is that so, İshak Efendi? And what happened about the task you were given six months ago?" retorted the Sultan.

Judge İshak felt deeply humiliated by the Sultan's rebuke in front of other lower-ranking officials and he hung his head in shame. The Sultan thought that this matter was known only to him and Judge İshak. He had no idea that the Grand Vizier and Prison Custodian also knew of the existence of Prince Ahmet and the reason for his rebuke. The Prison Custodian affected ignorance and merely bowed his head to hide his pleasure at witnessing this humiliation of Judge İshak. However, he could not help murmuring, "Let's hope the prince's corpse ends up on this table one day."

The Grand Vizier had remained silent until then, but was no longer able to suppress his urge to get personally involved. He loved unravelling complex issues, exposing secret transactions, interrogating murderers and delving into paranormal matters, which was perhaps why the fisherman had brought the bag straight to him.

"Where exactly in the Golden Horn did the bag get caught in the net?" asked the Grand Vizier, turning to the fisherman.

"B-b-between Ayvansaray and Kasımpaşa. In the middle."

"What do you mean 'in the middle'? Either the sea is very shallow 'in the middle', or your nets needed to go down very deep," said the Grand Vizier, who then turned to the Court Physician, pointing with his little finger to one of the bones. "Doctor, look at this. Was that purple mark on the finger made by a ring, I wonder?"

"Yes, sir. It is indeed the mark of a heavy seal ring."

"Perhaps made of chrysolite?"

"Very possibly, sir. The ring would have had the seal engraved on either a gemstone or gold."

"But no ring was found, is that right?"

"That's right, sir."

"Could it have fallen off by itself in the water?"

"No sir. The flesh is swollen. If there had been a ring on the hand when it was severed, it would still be on the finger."

"Tell me, my friend," said the Grand Vizier, addressing the fisherman. "Do you know anything about this ring?"

"No, oh no, sir. P-perish the thought!"

"With your permission, I will deal with this case personally," interrupted the Grand Vizier, turning to the Sultan.

"That would be most appreciated," replied the Sultan. "Relieve me of this distress as soon as possible. How can it be that someone in my land is murdering people and dismembering their corpses while I sleep peacefully in my bed? I give you three days! Issue immediate orders for divers to comb the seabed and find the legs, trunk and head belonging to these arms so that I can have the perpetrators thrown into the sea. You may now all withdraw!"

QUESTION 33
IF HE STOOD ON TOP OF ALL THAT HE DID NOT KNOW, WOULD HIS HEAD TOUCH THE SKY?

They had been digging deep holes between the tulip beds in the lush garden and were now planting young boxwood saplings into each hole. The tulips had started sprout their fine green leaves. All winter, Hafız Çelebi had been purring, "Yusuf, my boy, the tulips this year will bring a smile to everyone's face." Yusuf had spent six happy months under the roof of this kindly, paternal man. Together they had established a comfortable domestic routine. Snowy winter evenings were spent roasting chestnuts in the hot ashes of the brazier and, while Yusuf peeled them, Hafız Çelebi would read to him, tell stories, or initiate didactic conversations about culture, new ideas, historical events, wars, syntax, and religion, not to mention numerous myths and facts about tulips. Apparently, heavy snows in winter meant that tulips would grow tall with brilliantly coloured blooms in spring. After their autumn planting, tulip bulbs worked their way deeper into the warmer earth below for protection from winter frosts, which was why tulips had to be planted at least half a metre deep. Stony terrains produced short, scraggy tulips. Planting trees around a tulip bed helped to keep the flowers free of insects, a fact Hafız Çelebi had learned just one month before from an Austrian visiting Istanbul for the Nowruz celebrations, and was the reason they had been digging holes for the boxwood saplings.

"These trees, Yusuf," said Hafız Çelebi, as he planted the first sapling, "never lose their leaves. Of course, they bear no fruit either. But the fragrance! When September comes, we'll collect the bark and boil it. It smells divine and the water it's boiled in can be used as seasoning for all kinds of savoury and dessert dishes. It's also good for certain skin complaints and contagious diseases. The fragrance is just wonderful."

"Ah! It smells like my mother," said Yeye, plucking a leaf from one of the saplings and rubbing it between his fingers to inhale the scent.

"Then your mother must have put drops of boxwood water into the tub she used for washing clothes, or maybe she placed boxwood leaves in the clothes chest."

"No, Efendi, it was neither of those. My mother had a small bottle of perfume which smelled like this."

"Did it have a golden yellow base?"

"Yes, how did you know?"

Hafız Çelebi dismissed this question with a hand gesture and smiled, as if it were of no consequence. Yeye was extremely fond of Hafız Çelebi and often wanted to call him 'Father' but he realised there were aspects to his guardian that he would never comprehend. He recalled being told, 'My boy, there's no honour to be found in bad morals' and 'A mature mind needs few words'. Hafız Çelebi's counsel was indeed always worth heeding, yet now, for the first time, Yeye felt his question was being brushed aside as if there was something unseemly about his mother. Yeye felt deeply offended, but was unable to say anything.

Hafız Çelebi returned to the subject of boxwood and explained that the first scholar to prescribe boxwood oil as an elixir was Ebussuud Efendi, a renowned sixteenth-century statesmen and Koran exegete. However, Hafız Çelebi claimed that he was also a fine cultivator of tulips and the first person to grow the Istanbul Tulip. After Ebussuud Efendi, the tulip was regarded as more than just a garden flower. It was used in designs for porcelain, cloth, carpets and kilims, and on architectural structures such as mosques, mausoleums, madrasas and fountains, just as the Seljuks in Konya had used the tulip motive to decorate artefacts made of stone, metal, wood, mother-of-pearl, leather and cloth.

After the long winter evenings of tulip tutorials, spring arrived like a glorious caravan, ablaze with beauty, colour and fragrance. From Istanbul city it spread outwards to Kağıthane, finally reaching Hafız Çelebi's garden. Hafız Çelebi and Stocky Yeye spent their days tiling the Well of Souls, tending the long cemetery, weeding the tulip garden and then, weary from their work, preparing the evening meal. All the while, Stocky Yeye would ask questions as they occurred to him.

"Efendi, with all your knowledge about tulips and how to create new colours each year, why haven't you tried to grow more than one flower from a single bulb? Or have you?"

"No, my son, I've never tried that. A tulip bulb produces just one flower on one stem, almost as if representing the uniqueness of God. A twin bulb is very rare. With special effort, it is possible to cultivate a twin bulb. However, the symbolic oneness of a tulip resembles *alef* (ا), the first letter of the alphabet, which is why, whenever I've thought of trying to produce more than one bloom from a single bulb, I've suspected myself of seeking to create a partner for God and immediately given up the idea. In the homeland of the Turks, the tulip became almost sacred in its current form. It was seen as a flower which symbolised the existence of God, and that was thought to be the secret of its loveliness. Do you not think it significant that beautiful ladies sometimes wear a tulip as decoration instead of jewellery?"

Although Stocky Yeye greatly admired Hafız Çelebi's innovative and creative ideas, he could not accept all the symbolism his mentor attributed to the tulip. However, Yeye took it to be an indication of his strong faith and did not attempt to argue. He was content to continue listening attentively to how a tulip bulb produces new bulbs every year.

"If a tulip bulb is left in the ground after flowering in spring, it produces seven or eight bulbs – a bit like a potato. Of those, only the largest two or three will flower."

"Efendi, how do you know so much?"

"Know? My boy, if I were to stand on top of all that I do not know, my head would touch the sky. Never forget, there is no condition as incurable as ignorance! Knowledge gives one more sorrow than happiness, more grief than pleasure, but we gain by learning. In time, you too will learn all this. And in doing so you will understand about life. You will get to know the Almighty Creator."

"What I really want to learn about is the Tulip of Istanbul that Ebussuud Efendi wrote about in his book *Cultivation of the Tulip of Istanbul.*"

As Yeye said this, he visualised a glowing red flower set in a green crest of sabre-like leaves with filaments extending from their tips, its stamens heavy with yellow pollen emerging from a dark interior. He took a deep breath at the exciting thought that spring had come and a Tulip of Istanbul would soon be flowering in their garden.

Hafız Çelebi was having similar thoughts as they stood in the fading daylight. Then suddenly, they heard a loud noise coming from the pool where the turtles lived and started running anxiously towards it.

QUESTION 34
WHAT COLOUR IS A TOUCH OF SORROW?

When Falco regained consciousness, Brother Selman and a few other dervishes were pressing damp cloths to his forehead and stroking his face with rose water. A physician came to feel his pulse and started asking questions in a language he did not understand. It was not unusual for foreigners to be present at the Lodge. They would obtain permission from the Sheikh to observe the dervishes whirling in their *sema* ceremony. This lodge was perched between the Occident and the Orient, and allowed people the pleasure of belonging to both simultaneously. Thus, as the dervishes whirled in the *sema* room overlooking the Bosphorus, they could be observed from behind a latticed screen by merchants, envoys, admirals, ambassadors, travellers and painters from as far away as Britain, Italy, France, Holland and Russia. These foreigners would mingle with local Jews, Armenians and Greeks, vying with each other for the best positions and talking in a multitude of languages. In the winter months they would go to the Mevlevi Lodge in Galata, but now that winter was over they came to the ceremonies at Beşiktaş.

The physician taking Falco's pulse was one of these foreign visitors. His manner and tone of voice suggested that he was trying to probe right into the soul of his patient. Falco tried to recall what had been on his mind before he passed out. What had he been dreaming of? What had he been yearning for? But he said nothing. Despite the physician's persistence, he remained silent. That night, Falco tossed and turned on his mattress, his mind filled with so many thoughts coursing through his mind that he did not know which to pursue.

Seeing the tulip in Çırağan Palace garden turn from red to purple had made him decide to draw up a new plan. He would start by visiting Hafız Çelebi and Stocky Yeye and asking to see the Touch of Sorrow they had planted the previous autumn. He would ask if it had flowered, and if so what colour it was. What colour should a touch of sorrow be? He knew that tulips had no smell, but might this one have the scent of Nakşıgül? It would be the start of an investigation that would give meaning to his life. The moment he saw that tulip, he would devote his life completely to Nakşıgül. The Touch of Sorrow might even lead him to the murderer. That tulip represented not only love, but also mysticism. It might bring the dead to life, or possibly death to the living.

For Falco, the Touch of Sorrow represented the end of a winter of Sufi philosophy and an awakening from a peaceful dream. It had helped to keep him going through that winter. Maybe he had invested too much hope in it. Perhaps, as Hafız

Çelebi had warned, it would not flower at all. If that were the case, however, he vowed he would not turn back. Even without the Touch of Sorrow, he had to find Nakşıgül's murderer if he was ever to live in peace. His life would be pointless if he did not do this for Nakşıgül.

Falco spent that night in a delirious fever. Whenever he dropped off, he was woken by nightmares and would then try to console himself with visions of Nakşıgül. To his surprise, he rose at dawn feeling refreshed and prayed earnestly until the sun rose. Voices chanting the *İsm-i Celal* in the *sema* room mingled with the creaking of the wooden building filtered down to his cell on the ground floor. Falco set about putting his thoughts in order, thoughts which he had put on hold for six months. He remembered that he needed to go to the Sheikh ul-Islam's office in Süleymaniye to search through the official death records in the hope of finding a clue to the identity of Nakşıgül's killers. With luck, the men who had been hunting him would have given up after all this time.

On his way to Süleymaniye, Falco thought about all that had happened to him and realised that nobody would understand if he tried to explain. However, he was no longer the confused person he had been when he entered the Mevlevi lodge. The deep emotional scars from living life on the run had been healed. Besides, no one was likely to bother a Mevlevi dervish!

As he made his way up the Süleymaniye slope, he looked into the rows of workshops making cauldrons, spoons, saddles and sandals. On the way, he visited the tomb of Süleyman the Magnificent, where he sat outside on the wall for a while, absorbing the magical beauty of the city below and the ever-enchanting Golden Horn. He was thinking how there was no better place on earth to live, when something totally unexpected happened. A half-crazed fireman ran past shouting, "Run, or you'll be burned alive!" over and over again before disappearing out of sight. Falco gazed after him, thinking how many crazy people there were in the city and wondering how many became that way because of love. Sometimes it was impossible to tell if they were saints or lunatics – but there were certainly plenty of them. For instance, there was Crazy Sieve-eater at the Mevlevi Lodge and a master tinsmith called Mad Seyit Mehmet who worked with his feet. There was Loony Cadi, who lost his mind after realising an error in one of his rulings and now wandered the streets in the same robe, whether it was summer or winter. There was Toady Osman, an ascetic from the Black Sea area who proclaimed miracles, and Novice Mustafa, a Bektashi *fakir* who cried out "Farewell, lover!" whenever taking his leave of anyone. There was Cadi Süleyman Efendi, who spent his days running from one end of the city to the other crying out "Clear off, you infidels and hypocrites!", not to mention Mad Stationer, Egg Maniac and so many more. Falco did not know whether to be surprised or alarmed that there were so many people known to be mad in one city and undoubtedly many more who never achieved such notoriety. He had even known a lunatic at the stokehouse who always made pertinent comments whatever the topic, as if he had some sort of spiritual guidance.

While Falco sat on the wall thinking about lunatics and lunacy, he noticed a group of fifteen or twenty men in the distance going towards Tahtakale and clearly involved in a heated dispute. One of them in particular caught his attention. He looked very much like the man who had been standing next to the Prison Custodian at Patrona Halil's basin in the hamam. Just then, Falco heard some people close by crying out, "He insults the honour of the Janissaries! We want justice!" and three constables appeared from nowhere.

"Come now, everyone has honour to protect!" said one of them, trying to calm them down.

Someone had obviously been molested and an honour fight was about to break out. As if on cue, the muezzins in the minarets of Süleymaniye started calling out, "Allahu ekber! Allahu ekber!"

⁂

When Falco left the Sheikh ul-Islam's office, he was none the wiser. Despite putting a few coins into the pocket of the elderly official who looked carefully through two volumes of records for the previous six months, they found no death or burial record for anyone by the name of Nakşıgül. Falco emerged from the office to a pungent smell of smoke and a roar of voices that disturbed the normal calm in the streets. As the smoke thickened, some of the people resigned themselves to yet another neighbourhood fire and others fled.

Falco took the crazy fireman's advice and made his way down the Tahtakale slope to the bridge, where crowds of people were running for their lives. The flames were getting bigger by the second and were now leaping out of the roofs from

Kasımpaşa to Galata and progressing steadily down towards the Golden Horn, where ships had already started moving out into the Bosphorus.

Falco walked towards the fire, watching the movement of the flames and thinking about the people whose houses were being devoured. He reflected on the ability of fire to change everything. It had the power to transform the substance of earth, water and air. Even people were changed. The ferocity of the fire was now changing life itself. By the time he reached the bridge, majestic flames were licking at the Galata walls and sending out red sparks which glinted on the blue water of the Golden Horn. The earth and sky appeared to be in joint conflagration, with everything in between reduced to crepitant waste. A spiritual force seemed to be commanding the savage power of that fire. It had appeared from nowhere and engulfed everything in no time at all, as if a knot of fate had been unravelled. Falco knew only too well that when this happened people threw caution to the wind. He crossed the bridge and raced through the smoke towards Beşiktaş. As he ran, he thought back to the fight he had witnessed, and the crazy fireman's warning, "Run or you'll burn!" On reaching the Mevlevi Lodge, he ran into Poet Nahifi Dede and started telling him about the fire, but the red warning flag was already flying on top of the Bayezit fire tower. Inside the lodge, the dervishes were praying for peace and salvation. When Falco heard the response 'Amen', he was reminded of the men who had shouted, "We want justice!" and tried to imagine him in a mask standing by the hamam basin. Falco felt sure it was the same man. He even remembered his words, "We're waiting for the slender beauty with the arched eyebrows and rosebud lips from Mount Qaf."

But who was this Beloved? Falco spent all night wondering about this until he was finally able to ask Nahifi Dede who arrived at the Lodge early the next morning.

"It's a simple code, Falco," explained Nahifi Dede. "Each element represents a letter. Qaf mountain represents the letter *qaf* written as ق and the arched eyebrows represent the letter *ye* written as ى. The slender figure, tall and upright represents the letter *alef* written as آ and the rosebud lips represent the letter *mim* written as م. Put these letters together and you get *Q(i) yam*, which translates as *Resurrection* or *Day of Judgement*, the name given to the seventy-fifth *sura* of the Koran.

Nahifi Dede thought he had merely explained a simple code. He failed to notice the look of alarm in Falco's eyes.

QUESTION 35
IS THERE A CULTURAL DIFFERENCE BETWEEN *TÜLBENT* AND *TULIPAN*?

Just before Stocky Yeye and Hafız Çelebi rushed to find out the reason for the commotion by the turtles' pool, they had been quietly commenting on the velvety texture of the Istanbul Tulip. They had taken no more than half a dozen steps before they heard voices talking in a foreign language. There was a common belief among foreign residents in Galata, and visiting Venetian seamen, that the meat of turtles bred in fresh water contained life-prolonging properties, so Hafız Çelebi thought they were about to catch some of the usual turtle thieves. Despite the new law for the protection of turtles, interest in them had increased recently and some foreign elements had gone back to stealing turtles, either for their own use or to sell at inflated prices to the seamen. It was only two weeks since Hafız

Çelebi had approached the government seeking protection for his turtles on the grounds that they helped maintain a natural ecological balance. He had explained at length to the Grand Vizier that a reduction in the number of turtles meant an increase of water snakes in the Sadabat reed beds, which caused a decrease in insect life and consequently harm to vegetation and trees. With Grand Vizier İbrahim Pasha's permission, Hafız Çelebi had helped to draw up a bill prohibiting the hunting of turtles which had recently been proclaimed throughout the Galata district by the Imperial Estate Manager. However, when Hafız Çelebi and Stocky Yeye arrived panting and angry at the pool, the three men they found were obviously not thieves. In fact, Hafız Çelebi was very pleasantly surprised.

"My friend! Welcome, my loyal brother!" he cried out to a burly, blond man with blue eyes and a long nose, and embraced him affectionately.

"I am not late, no?" replied the man in Turkish with a foreign accent.

Introductions followed and Stocky Yeye learned that one of the visitors was Seyis Efendi, who worked as a groom for the Austrian Ambassador, and another was Jean Baptiste van Mour Efendi, who had just arrived from Flanders. But who was the foreigner who had made Hafız Çelebi so extraordinarily happy? Stocky Yeye did not have to wait long to find out. When Hafız Çelebi asked for the key to their private room, which was always kept locked, Yeye immediately understood that this man was none other than Pit Jan, about whom Hafız Çelebi had spoken all winter. It was ten years since Pit Jan had first disembarked from a ship and started working as a gardener in Hafız Çelebi's garden. He would turn up every year at the end of winter and return home in June when the tulips began to fade.

During his stay, he would also spend hours doing drawings of tulips to take back to his country. Stocky Yeye had heard Hafız Çelebi praise Pit Jan's skills at propagating tulips countless times, to the extent that he had even occasionally felt a twinge of jealousy.

Jean Baptiste van Mour was an artist of about sixty, from the town of Valenciennes in Flanders. He had visited the palace of Sultan Ahmet III a few years before and produced a series of paintings showing various kinds of dress worn in Istanbul. His fame spread quickly when he started painting palace dignitaries. Van Mour had heard of Hafız Çelebi's reputation and wanted to ask him about tulips. That afternoon, Van Mour had gone to meet his former student Pit Jan and Seyis, who took them via Sadabat to watch the sunset before hurrying to get to Hafız Çelebi's garden before dark. They had taken a wrong turning at the brook in Kağıthane and, in their confusion, they tried to enter by the rear garden and tripped over some earthenware pots by the pool, which had been the cause of the commotion. Poor Hafız Çelebi had gone to a great deal of trouble to have those pots specially made and brought Kağıthane Village to replace the cracked ones in the shed. In fact, as Hafız Çelebi lit a lamp and invited his guests to sit down on an old bedstead propped up against the trunk of a walnut tree, he could not help ruing the fact that because of those broken pots it would now be another two weeks before the boxwood trees they had just planted could be watered. However, the arrival of Pit Jan was compensation enough.

"Pit Jan, my friend, how is everyone? Business going well?"

"Business not bad," replied Pit Jan, in his heavy accent.

"We very curious to meet you, Khaviz Selebi," said Seyis, in broken Turkish.

Stocky Yeye could barely contain himself. These men with their funny accents, strange dress and clumsy manners reminded him of comic Karagöz characters in the shadow puppet shows that took place near Eyüp Sultan Mosque. He went to the storeroom to fetch some walnuts and slices of dried apples and pears to offer round, as he always did when they had guests. He also collected some fresh plums and raw almonds. The men talked about tulips for almost two hours. It was clear that Pit Jan's knowledge of tulips matched his artistic ability, which reawakened that feeling of jealousy in Stocky Yeye. As he sat listening to their conversation, he noticed that van Mour kept saying the word *tülp*, which he realised must mean tulip.

After a while, Seyis and van Mour said their goodbyes and disappeared into the night with as much commotion as on their arrival. Hafız Çelebi and Pit Jan gave each other a look of despair and burst out laughing.

There were now just the three of them. Stocky Yeye did not dislike Pit Jan, but he could not help feeling that he might be a rival for Hafız Çelebi's friendship. As Hafız Çelebi and Pit Jan settled down to catch up on each other's news, Stocky Yeye withdrew to his room and went to bed. However, the sounds of their voices and animated laughter kept him awake all night and by the next morning his feelings of unease had turned into outright jealousy. As they were having their breakfast soup, he raised the matter which had intrigued him the previous evening.

"Sir, what do foreigners say for tulip?" asked Stocky Yeye, hoping to draw Hafız Çelebi's attention.

"Why do you ask that, son?"

"I kept hearing Bit-Janlı and that painter say a particular word," said Stocky Yeye, indicating his dislike of Pit Jan by deliberately pronouncing his name so that it meant 'live bug' and squeezing his fingers as if to squash it.

"Oh, I see. You heard him say *tülp*," remarked Hafız Çelebi, silently congratulating his protégé on his sharpness.

"Yes, that's the word."

"You remember when I told you that tulips were like daughters who ran away from home?"

"Yes, you told us that the second time Falco and I visited you. But you didn't say 'ran away', you said they were kidnapped," said Yeye, looking accusingly at Pit Jan as if he was the kidnapper.

Hafız Çelebi and Pit Jan laughed.

"Did I say kidnapped? Well yes, they were kidnapped. The man who kidnapped them was Busbecq, an Austrian diplomat during the time of Süleyman the Magnificent. He was also the person who coined the name for tulip that you heard. The name, just like the flower, caught on and spread far and wide. The word *tülp*, which our friends Pit Jan Efendi and van Mour Ağa keep saying, actually comes from our word *tülbent*?"

"How do you mean, sir?"

"The story goes that Busbecq Efendi was sitting in one of the coffee houses near Ayasofya and saw a young man with a tulip tucked behind his ear. It was a little velvety red bud, which the young man wore as a signal to his Beloved which said, 'my heart is yours'," explained Hafız Çelebi.

Hearing Hafız Çelebi speak of lovers in Istanbul, reminded Stocky Yeye of a story his mother had told him called ***The lovers who died of love for each other***. He thought how Istanbul seemed to have been created for love. It was a city where love was natural, even normal part of life which included people like the lover who tucked a tulip behind his ear, like his friend Falco, and indeed himself. Although Yeye never admitted to anyone how much he pined for Şehnaz, he still could not help shedding a few tears at night. He turned his attention back to Hafız Çelebi.

"Istanbul and love – the two words are almost indivisible," Hafız Çelebi was saying. "The habit of tucking a tulip behind the ear was unknown in Busbecq's country, so he'd pointed to the tulip and asked, "What's that on your head?" The youth had forgotten about the flower and thought he was referring to the *tülbent* or cloth wrapped around his head, so he replied, '*tülbent*'. The diplomat naturally took this to mean that the flower was called *tülbent*, which he spelled as *tülipent* when he wrote about it in a letter to a friend. From then on, the Flemings always referred to these flowers by that name, which passed into other European languages as *tulpan*, *tulipano*, *tulip* or *tulipe*."

Pit Jan nodded, confirming Hafız Çelebi's explanation and saluting Yeye's powers of observation.

Postscript: The lovers who died of love for each other

Once upon a time in Istanbul there lived a maiden who lost her heart to a nobleman's son. The young man had no knowledge of this. The poor maiden became melancholy and her despair was such that she became ill and took to her bed with a broken heart. Of course, she could not explain her situation to the young man if she was to retain her honour. Moreover, she feared that he would not believe her if she told him. Maybe he would not like her and would reject her! Her health deteriorated and she grew limp and pale. Her nursemaid had known her since infancy and understood what was happening. After vowing absolute confidentiality, the nursemaid said, "You should express your feelings in a poem." The maiden tried this, but the young man listened to the poem without even a thought for the person who had penned it.

The maiden was close to death from her unrequited love, but one night fate looked kindly on her and brought them together.

The girl kept her composure and dignity, even though her patience was spent and her heart was pounding. At the end of the evening, the maiden got up to leave and, with controlled grace, leant towards the young man to plant a kiss on his lips. Then, she left without a word, her hips swaying like a dove, her earrings tinkling.

The young man was of course very confused. He suddenly felt weak and overcome by feelings of anger, shame, happiness and bewilderment. Before the maiden had even passed through the garden gate, he was consumed with love. The next day, his heart was on fire, his breathing irregular and he was gasping for breath. On the fourth morning, after three sleepless nights, he set out to see the girl. But sadly, the maiden had taken her last steps on the journey towards infinite love on the previous night.

His father asked him what the matter was.

"The passion I felt for her was such that, had I approached God with the same passion, all my sins would have been forgiven," replied the young man. "Had I prayed with that devotion, even wild beasts would have shown me mercy. Had I tried to drink enough water to quash the fire that burns within me, I would have drowned. If only they had cut open my heart while she was alive, placed her inside and sewn up the wound. Then she could have remained in my heart for ever, aging as I age, until the day when I enter the deep darkness of the grave and await resurrection."

For seven days, the young man was seen wandering near her grave. After that, he was never seen again.

QUESTION 36
WERE THE FLAMES PART OF THE NOWRUZ CELEBRATION?

Whenever the Sultan went to Sadabat, he boarded one of the royal caiques at the royal landing stage on Seraglio Peninsula and his subjects would congregate along the shores of the Golden Horn to greet him on his slow approach to the district of Eyüp Sultan. There he would visit the mausoleum of Eyüp Sultan, standard bearer of the prophet Mohammad. After handing out gifts to the people, he would continue by royal carriage following the marble-clad Silver Canal along the Bahriye waterfront to Sadabat Palace.

That day the tulips were not yet in flower, so there were no entertainments at Kağıthane. However, the Sultan was going to Sadabat to inspect some new building work, attend the Nowruz celebrations and receive gifts from his son-in-law, Grand Vizier

İbrahim Pasha. He was also going to listen to some new poetic works composed especially for Nowruz. According to the almanacs, Nowruz occurred at the time in spring when the sun had radiated sufficient heat to warm the air, water and earth, and it heralded the start of the Persian New Year. It was traditional to light large fires in public spaces where people congregated for the celebrations. According to Mongolian mythology, it was the day when the Oğuz Turks, who were members of the House of Osman and the Kai tribe, were guided by a grey wolf out of their homeland of Ergenekon to begin a new life. Every ruler of the Ottoman Empire celebrated Nowruz. Sweetmeats and other delicacies were made in the palace kitchens and distributed to the people, astrologers presented their new calendars to the Sultan for his approval, poets gave recitations celebrating the occasion, and leading state dignitaries held ceremonies to exchange holiday greetings. Since Nowruz was on a Friday that year, İbrahim Pasha, who never missed an opportunity for putting on an entertainment, issued special orders to the commanders of the imperial guards and janissaries that there was to be a public banquet and the day was to be treated as if it were a holy day.

A ripple of excitement spread through the crowds as *The Swan*, the Sultan's elegant imperial caique, came into sight at Cibali, preceded by Grand Vizier İbrahim Pasha's official barge and a number of oared vessels containing imperial and janissary guards. They were followed by dainty vessels carrying the ladies of the palace, while caiques carrying and guards and boatmen brought up the rear. When the Sultan and his attendants arrived at Eyüp Sultan, they ceremoniously stepped on to the cradle stone or *beşik taşı* at the Bostan landing stage. There was absolute silence as the Sultan mounted a purebred

Arab steed adorned with a white-plumed headdress and intricately decorated saddle. Then a huge roar erupted as the Sultan slowly proceeded from the landing stage to the tomb of Eyüp Sultan, greeting people as he went, with a footman in front and flanked by imperial cavalry guards and mounted janissaries. The people who thronged all along the processional route waiting for the Sultan to pass were entertained by a medley of performers who held out tambourines for tips from onlookers and passers-by. All the masters of entertainment were there, including the renowned fire-eater Mahmut Çelebi of Scutari, the tightrope-walker Kara Şuça from Arapgir, the famous plate-spinner and juggler Kamberoğlu, the conjuror Kubadî Ağa of Bursa, and men with performing monkeys and snakes. There were also acrobats and impressionists displaying a multitude of skills. Albanian Bekri Mustafa's silent mime was particularly popular, while Blind Hasan made his audience cry with laughter at his embellishments of lewd tales taken from the Karagöz puppet theatre about what the Bosnian judge did when he found the spendthrift Civan and flirtatious Nigâr together at the hamam.

Among the audience laughing at Blind Hasan, there was a dervish in Iranian dress who was trying to contain a mixture of excitement and fear as he waited for the Sultan to arrive. This was none other than Falco, carrying a basket and wearing the Iranian dervish outfit that Brother Selman had kept folded up all winter. He blended silently into the crowd behind the street entertainers and laughed at their antics while keeping one eye fixed on the procession.

When the Sultan finally dismounted, the chants of the crowds resounded right down the Golden Horn.

"Long live the Sultan!"

"Our illustrious Sultan, long may he reign over us!"

"May Fate do you no wrong / may your life be long / to you we belong!"

"Oh Sultan, the brave and true, only Allah is superior to you!"

The janissary troops and imperial guards lining the Sultan's route waited for the crowds to quieten down. While everyone's attention was on the Sultan, Falco calmly took a wide-rimmed bowl out of his basket and threaded a cord through its handles. He filled the bowl with turpentine, ignited it with a flint and quickly put the bowl of flames on top of his head, tying the cord under his chin. As the flames rose upwards, he pushed through the crowds to find a place where he could be seen by the Sultan. His mother had told him about this practice and he had actually witnessed one such occasion as a child. It had frightened him, and now it was his turn. 'Lighting the way', as the Alevis called it, was a way of gaining the attention of the Sultan for commoners who had no other means of doing so.

After the day when his passion for Nakşıgül was reignited by the sight of the red tulip in Çırağan Palace garden, Falco had decided he had to find a way of engaging with someone much more senior than the Prison Custodian. He needed to explain to a person of real significance what had happened and to prove that he was innocent. If he could do that, perhaps the murderers would be caught and he could lay to rest the responsibility he felt for Nakşıgül's soul. His plan was to gain an audience with the Sultan, by posing as an Iranian dervish and reciting the Farsi couplets learned from Brother Selman about the Iran-Ottoman war. He then hoped to gain the Sultan's trust by telling him about the signs of rebellion he had witnessed in the city. He would speak in broken Turkish with the accent of someone from Tabriz and explain that his sheikh had sent him to Istanbul to obtain tulip bulbs. If only he could make himself noticed, he was confident the Sultan would believe him. That was why he had spent so long watching the Sultan sitting astride his heavily decorated horse, dressed in a kaftan and sporting a pearl-covered turban set off with a peacock feather. That was why he pushed through the jostling crowds and cried out, "Khoda Khuuuuuub! God is good."

Pandemonium broke out. Three of the Sultan's guards rushed over to clap their hands over his mouth. As the flames in the bowl on top of his head gained height, some people wailed "Oh, poor lunatic!" while cynics wondered what it could achieve and officials rushed about trying to contain the situation. The Sultan saw what had happened and signalled to the Grand Vizier to deal with the matter. Falco felt as if a cauldron of boiling water had been poured over him as he realised this meant he would not be meeting the Sultan. He hunched his shoulders and his mind clouded over. It could all go wrong now. All his plans were turned upside down. He might even be delivered back into the hands of the Prison Custodian. The situation could hardly be worse.

The man who grabbed him by the arm was a burly 45th Division janissary officer with a magnificent curled moustache. The strength in his fingers was such that, despite barely touching Falco's elbow, the officer was squeezing the flesh so tightly that Falco had to clench his teeth to stop himself from crying out. As the janissary maintained his grip, the smile on his face was made more formidable by the moustache, which covered his mouth and curled outwards to beneath his ears where it merged with his beard. It was enough to make any man tremble. Such beards and moustaches were fashionable in Istanbul at the time and janissaries who sported them were referred to as 'Axe-proof moustaches'. This particular janissary was certainly very full of himself and Falco dreaded to think what might happen if he was left in his hands.

Falco realised he would have to be satisfied with an audience with the Grand Vizier rather than the Sultan. The most important thing was to ensure that he was understood and believed. His heart was pounding and he remembered Hafız Çelebi's words, "When disaster falls, agitation only makes things worse." It was essential to remain calm in order to turn disaster into good fortune. The plans he had made for his audience with the Sultan would have to be implemented in the presence of the Grand Vizier. There was no other option, because the Sultan and Grand Vizier had now gone back to handing out gifts to the people in Eyüp Square. Two mounted constables escorted Falco to the Grand Vizier's house at the Hippodrome and locked him in one of the rooms in the courtyard.

QUESTION 37
WHO WILL PAY FOR THE SPILLING OF INNOCENT BLOOD?

The Sultan had received an invitation from his Grand Vizier, saying:

Always your servant, always your slave
For your sake I'm happy to serve our state
This house is your house, O ruler so brave
To you, this evening I dedicate

To which, before setting out, the Sultan replied with the following compliment:

Your insights and wit never fail to enthral
And your loyalty to me is known to all

The Sultan had been pleased to receive the invitation. It promised to be an entertaining evening of poetry and music. Yet, for some reason, he felt out of sorts. He did not have the usual sense of pleasurable anticipation as he passed by palaces, bridges and fountains inscribed with names of great poets and the pavilions of Cinan, Nevpeyda and Hayrabad, or even as he mounted the steps to Sadabat Palace. He felt no pride in the calm waters, the green plane trees, the silver brocade tents and marquees. The javelin throwing, polo games, wrestling matches and musical evenings, which he normally enjoyed so much at Sadabat, seemed somehow meaningless. When he thought back over the years, he realised that he had never felt such despondency there before. Had he known what terrible scenes he was to be faced with at this frivolous gathering, he would have remained at the Seraglio, or at any rate refused to give an audience to the Janissary Chief Officer of the Three Crescent Society on this day when he was supposed to be enjoying himself. Fortunately, he had sent his daughter Fatma Sultan and son-in-law İbrahim Pasha elsewhere, because he would not have wanted his darling daughter to witness such scenes.

At a signal from the Sultan, one of the guards removed a cloth covering a pile of things in the centre of the room which looked like a heap of sacks and the room was filled with a disgusting stench. The Sultan knew what was inside them, but had not realised there would be so many, nor that they would be in such poor condition. He shuddered with horror and anger, making the men around him quake. The sacks were laid out on a large copper tray supported by a table in the centre of the richly ornamented room. The sacks were all much alike and contained various body parts, including hands, feet, heads, legs and trunks. Some had shreds of flesh clinging to them, while others were nothing but bone. Pieces of crimson flesh, still showing bruise marks made by the teeth of fish, were stuck to the fibres of the sacks. Each had belonged to someone who had once walked, talked, listened and felt emotion.

"I apologise, Your Majesty," said the Janissary Chief Officer of the Three Crescent Society, seeing the Sultan stare furiously at the pile in front of him. "The seabed where we cast our net was very muddy. This is the best we could do to clean up the body parts and sacks, if we were to protect the evidence."

"My man, was it not your duty to protect these people when they were alive?"

"Indeed, Your Highness. We failed in our duty and should be punished."

There was a deafening silence beneath the Bohemian chandelier. Everyone stood with bowed heads, not daring to move as they listened to the Sultan pacing up and down between the door and window, each footstep resounding like a kick to the head.

"How many bodies do we have here?" asked the Sultan, suddenly drawing to a halt.

"There are the parts of three different people here, Your Majesty. We also have the corpse of a young man. We did not bring it today because it's still being examined by your physician and other doctors. According to them, the people in these sacks include two old men and one woman of about thirty. But the woman's head and one of the men's torsos have still not been found."

"How deep was the water where you found them?"

"It was at Kasımpaşa waterfront, which is about thirteen fathoms."

"And who are these dead people? Have they been identified?"

"Only one of them, Your Highness," said the Janissary Chief Officer. "I'm told that one of the old men is an Indian merchant who disappeared five months ago. He had lost part of one arm, so some of the traders recognised him from that. None of the corpses had any personal belongings on them. We think they were stripped of any clothes, jewellery or signet rings before being thrown into the water. The divers recovered some pieces of jewellery, a few bowls and a dagger, but they weren't in the sacks. They also brought up some older sacks that were disintegrating and scattering human bones. The contents had either spilled out over time or they'd been pulled out by fish as food. Your Majesty, the area is very muddy so visibility is poor and searches can only be made by touch, which then churns up the mud again. But all the fishermen and divers think it was mostly the work of flesh-eating fish on the seabed. Even the fishermen didn't recognise the fish we caught in the nets. And, Your Majesty, the way the corpses were chopped up suggests that the same axe was used for each corpse."

"Did you find the axe?"

"No, not yet, but we've traced one someone who made the sacks, which were all made of hair cloth," said the officer. "I had one of the sacks washed and sent someone with it to the market. He spent three days searching for the man who wove that sack and eventually one of the weavers recognised it. I had him brought to me and questioned him myself. He trembled when he saw the disintegrating sacks in my hands and asked where I got them from. I asked if he knew who had bought them and he said, 'Yes, a fisherman called Aslan Ağa bought them last year. I recognised them because I wove them out of goat's hair. I don't know why he bought them, but that sack is one of them.' Sir, the weaver is innocent, but I had Aslan Ağa investigated and was horrified to discover that he's an evil piece of scum who offers help to naïve people and then traps them into handing over control of their business. We think he belongs to a gang that preys on lonely rich people in order to acquire their wealth. People who know him say he has contacts all over the place, but they won't say any more. They're afraid of repercussions, which is obviously why no one has ever lodged a complaint against him. And I heard a story about him. Apparently, he was in love with a singer for many years. The singer was a beautiful slave with a heart of gold. He first tried to buy her from her master. But the master wouldn't let him anywhere near her, so Aslan Ağa set a trap and kidnapped her. Then he sold her back to the owner for three hundred gold coins and kidnapped her again. The second time he sold her back for five hundred coins before kidnapping her again. Finally, the slave's master went bankrupt. His household was dissolved, his house fell into rack and ruin and he fled Istanbul in a half crazy state. Later on, Aslan Ağa gave the slave to a toymaker in Eyüp for his harem. But all that scheming and trickery seemed to make the slave go a bit crazy. Later, a janissary called Sergeant Bindallı Mahmut started pestering her. Eventually, the slave disappeared into thin air. Neighbours said she went to Izmir and never came back. However, we believe the female corpse belongs to her. Even though the head hasn't been found, your physician says her age matches the age of the body parts we found."

At that point, the Sultan raised his right hand and interrupted him. Everyone in the room stood motionless again, waiting in silence to see what their Sultan, that great sovereign and magnificent ruler of the Ottoman Empire, would do next.

"Somebody in my lands is killing people and tearing their bodies apart, yet I know nothing about it," said the Sultan sorrowfully, in an almost child-like voice. "Will not God hold me to account for this? Will I not have to pay for the spilling of innocent blood? If such felonies are taking place right here under my nose, just think what people are doing in other parts of the empire? You, all of you, are as much involved in this as I am! Do you not all feel guilt as I do?"

The silent heads made no response and merely bowed a little lower.

"Remove all this from my sight immediately and tell the Sheikh ul-Islam to arrange a suitable burial," continued the Sultan, raising his voice. "If any of these people have heirs or family, they must be found and helped. You, officer, if you want to keep that head on your shoulders, keep me informed about the perpetrators of these and any other murders. Make sure the place where they were found is kept under guard. Keep looking and extend the search area. If necessary, search every inch of the Golden Horn seabed and pull out anything you find. The stones to which these sacks were tied must be down there. Bring up those stones and examine each and every one to find out where they come from. Go immediately and tell my Grand Vizier what you have just told me. He will take charge. And tell my physician to come and see me immediately."

The Sultan was seized by melancholy and unable to enjoy his surroundings with fountains and springs that poured water out of the mouths of lions and dragons into the Silver Canal. His physician joined him and they sat opposite each other watching the sun go down when the Sultan suddenly recalled that he had had nothing to eat or drink all day.

"Doctor Efendi, how old was the youth whose corpse was found?" asked the Sultan, hoping for some welcome news.

"Twenty-three or four, Your Majesty."

"Exactly how many months ago did he die?"

"About seven months ago, Your Majesty."

"Did he drown by throwing himself into the sea? Or was he thrown in by somebody else?"

"I believe he was thrown in by somebody else, Your Majesty, because his hands and feet were bound with rope. In fact, gauze was extracted from his mouth, which was tightly bound shut."

"So someone definitely threw him in?"

"Yes, Your Majesty, I believe that is the case."

"And when he fell in, was he still alive?"

"That is what we think, Your Majesty, because we could not see any sign of a heavy blow to the body. He'd probably had a light beating and struggled to get away before being tied to some stones and thrown into the sea."

The Sultan signalled with the back of his hand for the Court Physician to leave. He felt another pang of hunger – his appetite had definitely returned. The dead youth had to be Prince Ahmet, because what the physician had told him corresponded exactly with the manner and time of death given to him by Judge İshak.

QUESTION 38
TELL ME, WHY DID YOU LIGHT THE WAY?

İbrahim Pasha returned home early from the Sadabat pavilions and sent for Twenty-eight Mehmet Çelebi, whom İbrahim Pasha had once sent as ambassador to France and so named because he had previously served in the 28th Battalion of the Janissary Corps, and İbrahım Müteferrika, the head of the new printing house. The agenda that day included their previously published Arabic-Turkish dictionary Vankulu Lügati and Persian-Turkish dictionary Ferheng-i Şuurî, a reprinting of historical works by Naima and Râşid, and other works such as History of Egypt, History of Tamerlane, and Takvîmü't-Tevârîh, which was an account of creation up until 1648 and for which new typefaces were required from Paris. Despite opposition from certain petty intellectuals, the publishing house had been a spectacular success and the three men were convinced of the need to continue this good work. That very day, a ship was being loaded with iron at Galata docks before setting sail for Toulon and someone needed to be on it in order to obtain the typefaces. The Grand Vizier's intention that morning was to propose to İbrahim Müteferrika that he undertake this errand, to give him money for his travel expenses and wish him a safe voyage.

While the Grand Vizier was taking coffee with Twenty-eight Mehmet Çelebi, a servant whispered in his ear that the Janissary Chief Officer of the Three Crescent Society had arrived. The Grand Vizier always made sure he was alone when talking to this officer, because it was inadvisable to question such a man with so many state secrets in the presence of someone else, especially if he was working for himself. Since the identity of the man had be kept secret, he gave instructions for Twenty-eight Mehmet Çelebi to be given a pile of presents and sent on his way before the new arrival was brought in.

After kissing the hem of the Grand Vizier's robe and sitting down cross-legged on a bench, the Janissary Chief Officer started to give his account, repeating almost word for word what he had said to the Sultan at Sadabat about chopped up corpses, sacks, divers, and how he was trying to find answers. When he got to the part of his story about the missing slave, the Grand Vizier shuddered, remembering the severed woman's head that had been sent to his palace eight months before. He almost blurted out that he had buried the woman's head with his own hands in the cemetery next to Sultan Ahmet Mosque. However, what really irked the Grand Vizier was that the secret intelligence organisation knew about his dealings with Sergeant Bindallı Mahmut and the fact that he was in prison. How had they obtained this information?

The Grand Vizier had mixed feelings. On the one hand, he was angry that this had happened without his knowledge, yet he also felt secretly pleased to be the only person who knew the full facts. He barely heard the rest of what the officer had to say because he was thinking about the next stage of this exciting story, which would provide him with amusement for days as he tried to solve the riddles, find answers to questions and evaluate the clues. After all, he was the only person who knew the burial place of the severed head that the Three Crescent Society had been unable to find. Bindallı must know the secret of the corpse. That would give him a lead which would enable him to find out what had happened before the Sultan did. The Grand Vizier proudly congratulated himself on being one step ahead of the secret service. What he needed to do now was to get Bindallı out of prison, hide him somewhere inaccessible and extract information from him. Or maybe it would be better to send word to the Commander of the Janissaries that he was leaving everything to them. Why spoil these delicious days of spring with such murky dealings? Yes, tomorrow, he would reprimand the Commander of the Janissaries, demand that the Janissary Chief Officer of the Three Crescent Society be dismissed and give instructions for Bindallı to be interrogated.

However, before any of that, he had to listen to the Iranian dervish who had decided to 'light the way' while wandering the streets of Eyüp. He dismissed the man sitting before him and sent for Falco.

"Welcome, my dervish friend!" said the Grand Vizier, now feeling in good spirits.

"*Han Nöker*, thank you for receiving me."

"Ah, so you are Azeri?"

"I am Persian, my lord, but I know a little Turkish."

"Good, but why you are here? Tell me, why did you light the way?"

"*Han Nöker*, people are like sleepwalkers. They awake only when they die. And I….."

QUESTION 39
WHAT HAD HAPPENED TO YEYE?

The noisy scene in front of the market toyshops was like a disturbing dream. Runny-nosed children bawled while their mothers yelled, desperately trying to quieten them. A myriad of toys hung from the shop ceilings and doors, including reed pipes and whistles, paper toys that shot out a tongue at one end or a peacock tail at the other when you blew into them, tongued whistles, alto whistles, Arab and Hungarian whistles, flutes, fifes, Eyüp pipes, tambourines, tambours and stringed instruments. There were mice and birds carved out of wood or made of cloth stuffed with rags, Karagöz puppets, roly-poly dolls, model horse-drawn carriages and ox carts. The street was full of itinerant toy vendors declaiming about wares piled high on the backs of donkeys, on handcarts or even goats. Out of all the toys, every child wanted the same thing – a croaking frog.

It was the custom for Eyüp toymakers to create a new toy in time for spring each year and to send middlemen out into the streets to spread the word among the city's children in order to create a market for their new creations. Then for the next year, they would hang around the carousels, Ferris wheels and other fairground amusements set up on public holidays. That year, the most sought-after toy was a carved wooden frog with graduated serrations down its back. A reed brushed across these serrations produced a croaking noise. Thus, the street sounded as if it was being constantly invaded by frogs. On top of this unbearable racket, mothers were arguing with their children because they did not want to buy something that made such an ugly noise. Meanwhile, merchants and caravan traders stood around waiting to put caseloads of these frogs on to their camels before setting off for Iran, Egypt or India.

Stocky Yeye stood gazing at the market and the toys for a long time. Even though he had lived nearby with his mother, she had never once brought him to this market and no one had ever bought him a toy from there. Şehnaz used to have many toys bought for her. When she grew tired of them, he was sometimes allowed to play with them, provided the lady of the house gave her permission. Recalling those days at the mansion, he realised that he had never had a toy of his own in his whole life. Not when he was small and not now, apart from the whistle he made himself under the guidance of Hafiz Çelebi. It was made of two pieces of bone bound together with leather and was played by holding it between the palms against the left side of the mouth – it only played one *perde*, or pitch cluster, but it made a nice sound. Pit Jan had been most impressed by this whistle and said it resembled a harmonica he had seen in Flanders. He was always saying how much he liked Yeye, how he was clever and talented, and would undoubtedly develop a flair for cultivating tulips. Yeye now saw Pit Jan in quite a different light from when they had first met. With his personality and behaviour, he could have been that of a native of Istanbul, until he spoke, of course. Yeye was growing very fond of Hafiz Çelebi's Flemish friend and wanted to buy him a present.

Hafiz Çelebi had sent Yeye to the market to buy provisions and candles and had also asked him to call on Mübarek Efendi and Skinny Martolozi Kirkor. Mübarek Efendi was a Jewish book-dealer who kept any books on tulips that came his way for Hafiz Çelebi. Martolozi Kirkor was a friendly Armenian carpenter who took pleasure in adapting and enlarging Hafiz Çelebi's simple wooden house whenever it was required. Since Yeye's arrival, it had become necessary to build another room and they also needed a new cellar for storing tulip bulbs in a suitably damp environment. There was no one better for these jobs than Skinny Martolozi Kirkor.

Stocky Yeye finished his shopping, collected a book wrapped in oilskin from Mübarek Efendi and extracted a promise from Martolozi Kirkor that he would come round in two days' time. After some indecision, Yeye headed for a confectioner's shop to buy some halva for Pit Jan before going to Sadabat.

Nobody seemed to notice the bell ring when Yeye opened the door. As he gazed at the trays of sweets, he saw two people whispering in a corner behind the counter. The man with the apron, handlebar moustache and thick beard was probably the master confectioner and owner of the shop. From upstairs, Yeye could year the raucous voices of customers mingled with the croaking of frogs. While waiting for the confectioner to finish his conversation, Yeye read the decorative signs on the wall. They were unique to halva-makers and written in different styles of Arabic calligraphy. Above the counter in front of him was a sign with the couplet:

Blessings to God for the heavenly taste
Plenty for all, let there be no waste

Above the door was another sign with owner's name on it:

The revered Sheikh Şazeli, master confectioner
Is here every day to welcome each customer

Stocky Yeye was particularly taken with the sign:
Curses to delight, if the price is right

Just beneath this line was a prayer, which actually seemed more like a curse:

Let the pimps who filled my life with gloom
This lousy halva in my name consume

Eating halva was an allusion to dying. Yeye knew that because halva was eaten at funeral wakes, but why the sign *No need to be crude if the takings are good*? This sign hung on the wall of every confectioner's shop in Istanbul and had probably been invented by the owner of this shop. According to Hafiz Çelebi, the trade in curses had been started by this confectioner, and people with this particular kind of verbal talent used to come to his shop to sell their wares in the knowledge that they would get a good price, especially if their contribution was in verse. The confectioner was considered to be a respectable trader, who would only sell a curse to one person and would never sell a curse that had been used. Rumour had it that one trader had been arrested for paying people to forget their purchases so that he could resell a curse if it was a particularly good one. Apparently, a lot of janissary coffee house customers went there. While Yeye pondered all this, he decided that the man talking to the confectioner must want to buy a curse, because he was being directed to look at a sign containing a list of the very same questions that Hafiz Çelebi had quoted to Yeye.

How old is the person you want to curse?
What is his position in life?
Does he have family?
Does he have a disability?

Yeye read these questions at the same time as the customer. Obviously, every buyer was asked the same questions to ensure that they bought a curse appropriate for the person in question. Yeye thought these questions were very apt because even oaths and curses should not be squandered and to abuse an invalid with a curse that targeted his disability was not only cruel and unethical, but a waste. Yeye felt a secret admiration for the confectioner and wondered if, instead of curses, he ever sold advice about love and if it might not be even more profitable because people had just as much interest in ***Advice about love*** as they did in curses. Moreover, love was more ethical and exciting. Suddenly, a voice in his ear startled Yeye out of his reverie about human predilections for love and curses.

"A sage once said, 'A person's mind should rule his tongue, he whose tongue rules his mind is doomed!'" whispered the confectioner. "My son, we don't sell curses to beardless young men!"

"But I want to buy halva!"

"Şehnaz again and again he cries, and then he dies!" chanted Skinny Martolozi Kirkor when he brought Stocky Yeye back on the back of his mule, making Hafiz Çelebi collapse with laughter.

Martolozi Kirkor repeated this so many times that he gave Hafiz Çelebi no chance to ask the questions on his mind. What had happened to Yeye? Where and how had Kirkor Efendi found him? Who was Şehnaz ?

Postscript: Advice about love

Love has a power over people, an acute ordinance, unassailable domination and enduring influence, which creates unbearable pressure. It unleashes pent-up emotions, melts away discipline and undermines moral defences, leaving a person vulnerable to the forbidden.

Love needs no more than a glance – the rest is superfluous. After that first glance, the lover gazes continually at the Beloved, full of desire to be with her, because the eye is like a window that opens on to his dreams. It seeks to discover the secrets of the heart and reveal its innermost thoughts. The eye of the lover does not wish to rest on anyone other than the Beloved. Magnetic attraction is born of that bond between the eye and the Beloved. As the word implies, the eye is drawn to the lover and becomes attached for ever.

When a person wishes to utter words that can only be said to the Beloved, it means love is at the door. Listening with the soul to the words of the Beloved, admiring everything she professes, believing her when she speaks nonsense or even tells lies, putting her right when she goes wrong, following her whatever she says or does – these are all signs of love. Love may even prosper in inauspicious times. The pain of separation is welcomed by the lover, who finds it almost pleasurable. As love progresses, the lover may be happy to resolve the problems of the Beloved. In nature, there are extremes in everything. Just as when the wheels of the cart spin fast and appear to be going backwards, so all sadness ends in happiness, all laughter ends in tears. Extremes of pleasure and grief can kill a person. The person who laughs most heartily will end up crying.

Lovers are like shepherds who herd flocks of stars. They choose solitude and withdraw into seclusion where they spend their time weeping. During endless nights, they count the stars, shedding tears of starlight. Clouds could take lessons from the eyes of lovers. Were Ptolemy still alive, he would create a team of lovers to watch the movement of the stars. As an ancient poet of the east once said, "No astrologer or alchemist knows the longest night of the year. Only a lover addicted to sorrow knows that."

QUESTION 40
WAS IT SAFER OR MORE DANGEROUS TO BE CLOSE TO THE GRAND VIZIER?

"An important person who pursues insignificant issues is worth less than an insignificant person who pursues important issues," Hafiz Çelebi once said. Now, as Falco lay between clean sheets on lavender-scented pillows staring at the ornamental ceiling of his room, he mused over the significance of the Sultan's son-in-law İbrahim Pasha's work. Falco's life had been transformed since that Friday evening when he chose to 'light the way' and, instead of getting an audience with the Sultan, was taken to Grand Vizier İbrahim Pasha's palace. It was quite possible that the Sultan would not have believed him and turned him away or even punished him, thinking he was just one of the thousands of dervish impostors who wandered throughout Anatolia. However, the Grand Vizier had not done this. He was a gracious man who understood the meaning of the poems that Falco recited and took pleasure in responding in kind. When one of them recited in Persian, the other responded by quoting the lines in Turkish and vice versa. Falco would never have believed that his life could be so changed by four lines from the famous Shiraz poet Sheikh Sa'di's *Golistan*:

Solh ba doshman ager khahi har geh ke tu ra
Dar kafa ayb konad dar nazaresh tahsin kon
Sokhun-e akher be dahan migozarad muzi ra
Sokhunesh talekh nakhahi dahanesh shirin kon

İbrahim responded by translating these lines into Turkish:

If with the foe you seek to make peace
Flatter him till his taunts do cease
To curb his bitter altercations
Beguile the beast with sweet supplications

Falco was staggered to hear the Grand Vizier translate these four lines of Persian instantly into Turkish verse. It demonstrated an intellectual ability which made Falco understand how this Grand Vizier could hold sway over the Ottoman palace. İbrahim Pasha then surprised Falco by reciting a verse and asking him to translate it into Persian:

You keep saying that you're in love
But proof of this you must display
Would you risk all for a chance encounter
If there were simply no other way?

This was difficult. Not because the lines were hard to translate – especially for an Iranian dervish – but because if he did this, it would put them on an equal footing and Falco was not sure that the Grand Vizier would want that. He studied the Grand Vizier's face carefully, looking for signs that he was really prepared to pit his translation skills against those of a dervish. His expression seemed to be saying "Come on, I'm listening!", so Falco took a deep breath and recited his Persian translation. When he finished, he pleaded:

My failings are many, I am a mere dervish
A slave to your every wish
Should I wait at your door, beseeching forgiveness
Or accept my flaws and my life relinquish

For the next hour, Falco and Grand Vizier İbrahim Pasha continued weaving verse into their conversation. They discussed the contexts, meanings, allusions, sarcasms, jokes and quips in the poems they recited. They spoke of the war in Iran, the janissaries' desire for insurrection, the conversation overheard by the basin in Bayezit Hamam and the rumours about İbrahim Pasha's private religious beliefs. Finally, İbrahim Pasha summoned one of his men.

"This gentleman is our guest. Prepare a room for him in the palace and give him whatever he requires!" he ordered.

When Falco entered the room that had been prepared for him, he saw that a case had been placed on top of the silver brocade bedspread. Inside the case, he found a pear-shaped pearl, thirty gold coins and a note saying, "A reward for your services. Buy yourself some new clothes." He understood this to mean that he was being asked to shed his dervish garb and take his place as one of the Grand Vizier's poet companions. Naturally, it would take time to learn all the conventions, such as on which days the Grand Vizier held his gatherings and who attended, but Falco knew that it was no small matter to be summoned to these poetry gatherings. That night, he hid the pearl inside his armband – he would keep that for when times were hard – and put the gold coins beneath his pillow, knowing that he would spend them straightaway. He slept little that night, but felt happy, grateful and optimistic that İbrahim Pasha would help him to find Nakşıgül's killers, because he knew of the Grand Vizier's legendary ability to solve complex and arcane matters.

It was common knowledge that İbrahim Pasha kept a retinue of artist friends around him. However, once Falco was settled in at the palace, he also discovered that there were rooms on the ground floor which were set aside for artists arriving from other cities or countries. For instance, one of these rooms was occupied by Lütfi, a painter from Bukhara, another by a master engraver introduced to İbrahim Pasha by the Marquise de Bonnac, wife of the French ambassador, and yet another by a calligrapher from Damascus who had engraved the Fatiha verse from the Koran on to brass. The Grand Vizier lived up to his reputation of being a true patron of the arts.

QUESTION 41
WHO KIDNAPPED HIM, AND WHY?

Hafız Çelebi heard the sound of a horse neighing and looked out. He could not believe his eyes when he saw Falco, who was not only mounted on a horse but dressed in totally different clothes.

"Good gracious, Falco, my son? The last we heard of you was that you had become a Mevlevi dervish!"

"Well, until the last few days, I was indeed a Mevlevi," replied Falco, tying the horse's reins to the ring on the doorpost. "The truth is I spent a pleasant winter training under my master Sheikh Ahmet Dede and Poet Nahifi Dede, but as the tulip season approached, I started yearning for Nakşıgül again. As you see, I am no longer Falco but have become a wandering dervish called Selman Abdal."

"Selman Abdal? But why?"

"The wonderful training I received at the Mevlevi Lodge put an end to Falco, sir. The Dark Falcon who thought so much of himself, who tried to control everything, is no more. He has been replaced by this pious, repentant dervish called Selman Abdal, who thinks only of Nakşıgül."

"In that case, should you not be wearing a sinner's cloak around your shoulders?"

Falco chose to ignore this dig at him. What could he say? Hafız Çelebi was right. It was only too common to see well-dressed dervishes posing as mendicants. Fortunately for him, the gate opened and Pit Jan entered before he could reply. Pit Jan nodded at them both as he walked past towards the long cemetery and the Well of Souls. However, Falco had hoped it would be Stocky Yeye. Once Pit Jan was out of earshot, Falco looked directly at Hafız Çelebi and asked about Yeye. Hafız Çelebi's reaction was quite unlike his normal self. He seemed absent-minded and to have suddenly aged as he turned away with an agitated look.

"Ha, of course you don't know Pit Jan Efendi," said Hafız Çelebi, fumbling slightly for words. "He's from Flanders and a real treasure in our tulip garden. My loveliest tulips have been raised by the sweat of his brow. Before he leaves at the end of summer, he paints pictures of the tulips he has grown to take home with him. Sometimes, he even stays up all night watching over your tulip to see if it comes out in the correct colour. He can't wait for it to bloom so that he can paint a picture of it. Pit Jan also takes care of the turtles, carries water up for the saplings and keeps the garden tidy. But never mind all that, tell me about your life."

"Don't worry, Efendim," said Falco, sensing that Hafız Çelebi was referring to what they had been talking about before

Pit Jan arrived. "I haven't fallen into bad ways or gone back to thieving. I am a guest of my benefactor, our Grand Vizier İbrahim Pasha. I don't know how long this patronage will last, but I intend to use the time as an opportunity to explain what happened to me and to ask for his help in avenging the death of Nakşıgül. I'm sure he'll believe me if I can find a time to tell him when he's in a good mood. And if he does, I'm hoping that he will personally order a search for Nakşıgül's killers. He takes a special interest in complex matters such as this and his belief in the rule of law is well known. As long as he believes me, I know he's not the kind of vizier to overlook an injustice."

"But Falco, my son…sorry, I mean Selman Abdal, how has this come about?"

"A few days ago, I took the opportunity of lighting the way in front of the Sultan. However, instead of getting an audience with our gracious Sultan, I was received by His Excellency the Grand Vizier. And now, as you see, I've become his slave and have been given a horse. He feeds me and clothes me and I am to attend his poetry gatherings where I shall meet eminent people. These clothes I'm wearing today are for just such an event."

Falco continued chatting about what went on at the Grand Vizier's palace, all the time hoping that Yeye would appear or that Hafız Çelebi would send for him so that they could go off together to look at the Touch of Sorrow.

"There's a painter from Flanders, like your Pit Jan Efendi, staying in the room next to mine. His name is Jean Baptiste van Mour and he paints pictures of the Sultan and his family. But he's a crook because he's swindling the foreign diplomats."

"Haa! He came here recently with Pit Jan. How is he swindling the diplomats?"

"According to Lütfi, a mural painter who is also staying in a room close to mine, van Mour panders to the vanity of diplomats by painting pictures of their receptions by the Sultan, which of course they wish to take back to their countries!"

"But aren't such receptions private affairs between the Sultan and the ambassador?"

"Of course they are. But the Sultan receives them all in the same room dressed in the same clothes, so our van Mour Efendi keeps a few pictures of the background ready in his room for when an ambassador wants a picture and then simply superimposes his portrait on to one of them."

"Well, well." said Hafız Çelebi despondently.

It seemed impossible to Falco that this man who had been so full of life and wisdom could be reduced to this. Was it possible for a person to change so much in just one winter? He felt sure that Hafız Çelebi was keeping something from him. With a sigh, Falco inhaled the pure scented air of the early spring day and remembered how in the past Hafız Çelebi had always manage to put his mind at ease.

"Can I see Stocky Yeye and the Touch of Sorrow now?" asked Falco, stroking the front of his sable-collared kaftan as he rose to his feet.

"Ah yes, the Touch of Sorrow. Hopefully, it will be the most beautiful tulip of the season this year. It isn't in flower yet, but it's looking strong and beautiful. Poor Yeye has spent all winter protecting it and watching over it."

Falco was alarmed to hear Hafız Çelebi say 'poor Yeye' instead of 'my son Yeye' and did not dare ask about him again. He had heard about the incident in the Eyüp toymakers' market, but it had not occurred to him that the youth concerned might be Stocky Yeye. However, Hafız Çelebi was clearly about to give him some bad news. How Falco longed to see his friend, to embrace him and pat his head, and how happy Yeye would be to see him. But Hafız Çelebi still said nothing, as if he wanted to avoid talking about Yeye. The silence between them intensified as they made their way to where Falco and Stocky Yeye had planted the Touch of Sorrow bulb the previous autumn. Falco saw immediately that the Touch of Sorrow was strong and tall with shiny vibrant leaves. Nobody would have thought that it had grown from half a bulb. It seemed to have forgotten the meaning of its name. As it swayed gently in the breeze, its bud nodding from side to side as if greeting onlookers, it seemed to rejoice in Falco's arrival. His eyes filled with tears. This half bulb, which had once been clasped in the hand of the woman he loved, would soon display a beauty that carried traces of her nobility – a beauty touched by sorrow.

"Touch of Sorrow!" murmured Falco. "You symbolise my one true love and all the sadness in my heart."

Then he remembered he had a question to put to Hafız Çelebi.

"When van Mour Efendi returns from the palace with his pictures, he sometimes brings back gossip too," said Falco. "Next Friday, he's moving out to rented premises in Galata and he takes a boat over there almost every day. He told me something which I later heard from our Grand Vizier. Perhaps you've heard about it too. A sack of body parts was found in the Golden Horn and they say there was a woman's body. As you know, I've never managed to find Nakşıgül's grave. So I can't help wondering…Oh, God forbid!"

"Falco, I mean Selman, my son, thoughts like that will get you nowhere. You have to let this go. Remember, Nakşıgül is gone. She's not coming back. And you have to stop punishing yourself for a crime committed by others. Focus on that, rather than always thinking of Nakşıgül."

"I am being very careful, sir. You are the only person I confide in about these matters. I've found out a name – Bindallı Mahmut. Have you ever heard of him?"

"I haven't, but I'll make some discreet enquiries among my friends for you. Bindallı, you say?"

"I'd like you to find out where he is, because Yeye and I both know who he is. We saw him last autumn at the Pergola coffee house and followed him to the janissary barracks at the Hippodrome. He's rumoured to be a member of a criminal gang that instigates murders. If it's true, then Yeye and I know who the other gang members are."

"Are you certain Yeye knows about this?" said Hafız Çelebi, turning pale.

"Yes. Why?"

"Oh my God! They'll tear him to pieces, the poor boy. We must do something."

"I'll speak to Yeye and explain everything to him," said Falco looking startled.

"If only! Oh Falco, if only! Yeye's been gone for three days. I've had men searching everywhere for him. He hasn't been himself since he saw Şehnaz in the sweet-maker's shop at Eyüp Sultan."

"Who's Şehnaz?" interrupted Falco.

"Didn't you know? Apparently, the boy has a sweetheart."

"I don't believe it. He's never mentioned it to me."

"Well, you have to believe it now. Her name is Şehnaz. When he went missing, I put it down to his infatuation with Şehnaz and thought he must have gone to search for her. I've told all my friends in Eyüp that he might be frequenting the places where he used to see her and that if they see him they're to keep him busy and send word to me. But nobody has seen him. I was stupid enough to think that Şehnaz's father, Veyis Ağa, would have organised a search for him, because it was on the day that Yeye saw Şehnaz with her father that he started raving. Apparently he started accusing Yeye of being crazy and saying he should be sent back to the asylum. When Yeye started coming round, the father took the poor girl away. I told Pit Jan Efendi that Yeye was worried Veyis Ağa might have tracked him down here and I have two watchmen on guard around the house at night. But nobody saw anyone enter or leave the house when Yeye disappeared three days ago.

"Did he take any belongings with him when he left?"

"No, his room is just as it always was. Except that he always made his bed and that day it was left unmade."

"You mean he was kidnapped?"

"I hope not, because his emotions have been all over the place recently. Sometimes he's been able to keep them under control, but most of the time they've been getting the upper hand. He reached a stage when the only thing he would say was 'Şehnaz'. He hasn't attacked me, but he had a go at Pit Jan Efendi one day for pulling up calamus roots by the river to feed to the turtles."

"Why would he do that?"

Falco felt unable to continue the conversation any longer. He ran to Yeye's room, which looked completely abandoned, and threw himself on the bed where he lay for a while trying to calm down. Then, he stirred, picked up a whistle that he found by the window and sat stroking it, saying, "My brother, my dear, dear brother!"

As Falco was returning from Kağıthane to the Grand Vizier's palace at the Hippodrome, he pondered over a matter which he had been unable to mention to Hafız Çelebi. It was a task assigned to him by İbrahim Pasha, who wanted him to mingle among the people looking for any signs of unrest or popular movements in the city. He was of course very well aware from his days at the stokehouse that he would be regarded as one of the Grand Vizier's scorpions if he passed on such information. He had lied when he told Hafız Çelebi that he was dressed in expensive clothes and going around on horseback because he was going to a poetry gathering at the palace. That lie, to man whom he loved and respected more than any other in the world, was now burning away at his heart and he felt the heavy burden of hypocrisy. From now on, he would be going out every day dressed in different outfits to roam the squares and streets seeking out people with whom he could engage in private conversations so that he could report back to Grand Vizier İbrahim Pasha at the end of the week. The Grand Vizier had given him this task after Falco had told him about the conversations and what the Prison Custodian had said by Patrona Halil's basin in Bayezit Hamam six months previously. İbrahim Pasha had immediately worked out the meaning of the slender beauty with the arched eyebrows and rosebud lips from Mount Qaf. He emphasised in his most persuasive manner that, by sending Falco out into the streets to seek out the roots of this insurgence, he was placing a trust in him that on no account should be abused. Falco had of course made no mention of the references made that night to *put diken İbrahim*, who erected statues, and *put şiken İbrahim*, the Old Testament prophet who demolished statues as false idols. The Grand Vizier was an intelligent and cultured person who could be extremely generous, but no one wanted to risk being on the receiving end of his anger. The Grand Vizier trusted him enough to share confidential information, yet Falco also knew that his trust could be more than matched by his fury.

Falco wondered whether the Grand Vizier might send men out to look for Stocky Yeye if he told him what an important part of his life he was. However, that would mean revealing his true identity and he could not afford to risk being handed over to any of the prison guards again. Since he now felt as much of an obligation to trace Stocky Yeye as to find Nakşıgül's killers, Falco decided to use the powers at his disposal and what he learned from the Grand Vizier to find and punish the criminals himself without his patron's knowledge. Thus, whenever İbrahim Pasha questioned him, he would use it as an opportunity to extract information from his master, like the proverbial relationship between the fire and the scorpion. He tossed and turned all night long wondering if he was capable of all this subterfuge and whether it would turn him into someone unrecognisable.

"Don't forget, Falco my son, debasing yourself will get you nowhere," Hafız Çelebi had called out when he was leaving, as if he understood everything.

That night, it was with those words echoing in his ears that Falco finally shut his eyes as the morning call to prayer rang out.

QUESTION 42
CAN SOMEONE HELP ME?

Falco recalled how the previous autumn, when he was staying at the stokehouse and being sent out to beg, he had seen Aslan Ağa dressed as a fishermen in the company of the Prison Custodian. He decided to go to the fish market outside Unkapanı to see if anyone knew him there. This fish market consisted of a row of huts on top of a broad two-tier structure supported by stakes driven into the seabed and all types of fishermen came there. While brokers yelled out the names of their fish, wholesale and retail customers haggled loudly with each other. It was difficult to distinguish one fisherman from another because they all wore similar caps and leather waistcoats, with clogs or rawhide sandals on their feet. However, their fishing methods ranged from seine fishing, dragnet fishing and net casting to spear fishing and angling. Most of the seafood on sale was caught using nets or lines along the coastline of the Golden Horn. It included crabs, various types of mussels, horse mackerel, anchovies, scorpion fish, striped goatfish, smelt and squid. Another section sold larger fish, such as mackerel, bonito, bluefish and sea bass, which were caught from fishing boats and longboats that went from the Seraglio peninsula up the Bosphorus or out into the Marmara Sea.

Falco mingled with the noisy crowds, pretending to be a rich customer, but was careful to conceal his face as much as possible. He walked slowly through the market looking around carefully in the hope of seeing Aslan Ağa's big eyes and crooked nose beneath one of the orange caps. When he reached the large fish section, his heart started to pound. There was Aslan Ağa, standing with his back to him, busy taking fish from a basket and laying it out on a counter. Falco decided to find a position where he could see his face better to be absolutely sure. As he got nearer, he heard the man cry out, "Swordfish from Beykoz fisheries! Turbot from Karataşlar fisheries! Oarfish from Terkos! All alive and fresh today!"

Falco stopped in his tracks. That was not Aslan Ağa's voice! He had been mistaken. From behind, the man looked identical. However, there was still time and Falco was determined not to give up. He could spend all day there, since it was his job to observe what was going on among the people so that he could report back to the Grand Vizier. Falco went upstairs and found a corner café where he could sit and watch everyone who came and went on the lower floor of the market. He ordered grey mullet soup flavoured with dill, pilaf and mussels, and oysters with green salad. For a while, his attention was taken by watching fish sizzle in butter in tinned copper frying pans and he noticed that most of the cooks were Greeks, as indeed was the handsome young apprentice who brought him a plate of stuffed onions, which he called *kormidya*.

"It's a delicious mezze dish," said the boy, as he walked away. What he actually meant was that it would go well with alcohol, which he could supply from a secret store. Falco pretended not to hear. He knew that in the evening, this café, like most of the others, would turn into a tavern and would be overflowing with customers from Galata. Thinking of this reminded him of how many fishermen he had to get through in his search for Aslan Ağa. Wherever there was a tavern in Istanbul, there were fishermen and the city was rich in fish. Fish markets were to be found at Beacon Gate, Cibali, New Gate, Sand Gate, Pomegranate Gate, Piripaşa, Kasımpaşa, and Galata. He made a resolution to go to each one in his search for Aslan Ağa if necessary.

Falco was on his soup when he spied Aslan Ağa who, to his surprise, was wearing neither a fisherman's cap nor a leather waistcoat. He was bargaining with a fish merchant and about to hand him a bag of something wet. Falco could not help feeling felt a pang of sorrow for him. "Poor man," he thought. "He must have been in a dreadful state after losing his daughter. Maybe his business failed and he's been reduced to catching and selling a few fish. Falco rose from the table and hurried to catch up with Aslan Ağa. When he reached him, their eyes met, but although Aslan Ağa was looking straight at him he had difficulty identifying the face. Aslan Ağa was obviously confused and felt uneasy about the eyes that were staring at him. When he eventually recognised Falco, his face started to twitch. The two men were equally bewildered and neither knew what to say or do. As Falco politely leant forward to kiss the older man's hand, he felt heavy-hearted and sad, thinking of former days and the grief suffered by his father-in-law. However, Aslan Ağa suddenly threw his basket of fish over Falco and started running, overturning trays, counters and baskets as he went, making it difficult for Falco to keep up with him.

"Can someone help me? Murderer! Murderer! Catch that killer!" yelled Aslan Ağa as he ran.

Falco was in a quandary, not knowing whether or not to follow Aslan Ağa, who might do something crazy if he thought he was being chased by his daughter's killer. The fact that he ran away meant that he was still afraid of Falco and believed him to be his daughter's murderer. Six months had done nothing to change his mind. Yet nothing made sense to Falco. The last time he saw Aslan Ağa, he had been dressed as a fisherman and appeared to be on close terms with the Prison Custodian. However, there was no time to dwell on this now. He had to get out of there, because Aslan Ağa had pointed at him and yelled "Murderer!" He needed to disappear before he was collared by someone who believed what Aslan Ağa said. Falco headed towards a street that ran parallel to the street down which Aslan Ağa had run and kept running until he knew no one was following him. It then occurred to him that, the previous time they had met, Aslan Ağa had gone off down the very same street. Falco worked out that the two streets would eventually join up and he ran past a row of houses surrounded by low garden walls until he reached the corner where the two roads met. He was now in an ancient Byzantine forum, the like of which no longer existed anywhere else in Istanbul. It was a small paved square lined with terraced houses and it opened out into six streets. Falco reversed the kaftan he was wearing so that, instead of a blue kaftan with a tulip design, he was now to be seen in a crimson kaftan embroidered with gold thread, and he rewound his white turban so that it was green on the outside. Then, hiding behind an upright stone in the centre of the square, he waited. If he was right, Aslan Ağa would appear in a few moments. If not, it meant he had entered one of the premises along the street, which meant it was probably either where he lived or worked.

Falco was not mistaken. Aslan Ağa approached with rapid steps, constantly looking anxiously over his shoulder. Falco concealed himself behind a tree where he unfolded one layer of his green turban and covered his mouth and beard, as if to keep out the cold. Aslan Ağa would never recognise him now. Having reached the square, Aslan Ağa seemed more at ease and he set off down a street that led to Sirkeci. Falco began tailing him, maintaining a distance of about fifty yards. Although his appearance was now that of a traveller, he nevertheless kept in the shadows of the trees so as not to be noticed.

Once past the garden walls on either side of the street, Falco expected to see Aslan Ağa enter one of the wooden houses further along. He hoped this would be where Aslan Ağa lived, because it would help him feel a little closer to Nakşıgül's memory if he knew where her family lived. Perhaps he might even catch her maid or the stable boy alone one day and ask what had happened that morning at the house which disappeared so suddenly. Where had it gone? Where was Nakşıgül's grave? What was her mother doing now? Were they still grieving for their daughter? His mind was full of these and many other questions, almost as if they were questions about a story he had read. But sadly, it was a story of which he was a part, and one which made him feel miserable.

Falco watched Aslan Ağa walk past the houses without entering any of them. He was still assuming his father-in-law's innocence, but then he suddenly saw Aslan Ağa enter the janissaries' Pergola coffee house and embrace the Prison Custodian. Falco followed him inside, ordered a coffee and perched on a bench by the door, where he was half hidden by smoke from the narghiles and Persian tobacco.

The summer section of the coffee house was still closed, so the inside was teeming with casual labourers, wastrels, dissolute janissaries of indeterminate gender and infidel sailors, sitting back to back and cheek by jowl, all deep in conversation. It was a place where a man sitting alone would draw attention. In a place such as this, where people openly discussed, criticised and cursed their rulers and government, Falco knew that people were likely to take him for a scorpion working for either the Sultan or Grand Vizier, especially dressed in that crimson kaftan and green turban.

Falco was unable to get close to his targets and had to make do with studying their gestures and facial expressions. He had to do this without drawing attention to himself because the slightest slip could be fatal, and even managed to drink his coffee without slurping. Suddenly, he noticed two people approach them. He recognised the young man who sat down on the right-hand side of Aslan Ağa as the young cook's apprentice from the fish café and the other as Sergeant Bindallı Mahmut, whose fearsome face Falco had seen at Binbirdirek. The cook's apprentice sat listening in amazement while Bindallı Mahmut was laughing with Aslan Ağa as if he did not believe a word he was hearing. Falco then looked at the others who were sitting around them. Those sitting on the benches at the back were regulars, but there was also the dwarf whom he had previously seen running after the Prison Custodian.

Falco strongly suspected that some plan was being hatched. It seemed that Aslan Ağa was not the man he thought he was, and that the Prison Custodian, rather than being a keeper of public order, was in fact working for some underground group. He decided to continue following Aslan Ağa, not only to find out about Nakşıgül, but also to discover how her father was linked to these people. It was almost time for the evening call to prayer at Dersaadet, but Falco had to stick to his decision, even at the risk of being late for İbrahim Pasha at the palace. He decided to wait outside in the dark so as not to attract attention. As he paid for his coffee, he noticed four armed palace guards stride past him towards the Prison Custodian. It was definitely time to get out. There was a ripple of excitement and a roar inside the Pergola coffee house as, despite the Prison Custodian's protestations, the four guards hauled Aslan Ağa to his feet.

"Aslan Ağa, sir, His Majesty the Sultan wishes to speak with you."

Falco remembered hearing the very same tone of voice when Bindallı Mahmut was arrested. That time, it had been police constables. This time, palace guards had been sent to do the job, indicating that they were there on the orders of the Sultan himself.

"Gentlemen, you are mistaken," cautioned the Prison Custodian. "I can vouch for Aslan Ağa. Let him go!" He followed this with a threat, "Who ordered you to do this? I'll see you pay for this!"

However, the Prison Custodian was completely ignored and one of the guards silenced him, saying, "Sir, bodies have been found in the Golden Horn and this man is being held responsible. It would be in your interests not to give him your support!"

These words to the Prison Custodian made manifestly obvious the friction between the Sultan's protection team and the Grand Vizier's state security team.

"Get on with it, you vile lot. This isn't the end of Aslan Ağa!" muttered Aslan Ağa angrily as he stood up.

"Aslan Ağa? Really?" murmured Falco to himself sorrowfully.

QUESTION 43
WHO GAVE THE ORDERS TO THE FALCON HUNTERS?

"Sir, we have learned that Falco, whom we suspect to be Prince Ahmet, is alive and well. He has changed his appearance and identity," said the Prison Custodian, unaware that the words he said to Grand Vizier İbrahim Pasha as he bowed down to the floor were almost identical to those being uttered by Judge İshak to Sultan Ahmet.

"So what identity is he using now?"

"We do not know yet, sir, but we will find out as soon as possible."

"If you weren't such a loyal servant, I'd have had your head chopped off. However, you are definitely stupid, so get out of my sight!"

"I have to catch Prince Ahmet before anyone else does," thought the Sultan and the Grand Vizier simultaneously, each wondering how they could keep the matter secret, as Judge İshak and the Prison Custodian were each dismissed.

The Sultan recalled the proverb, 'The foolish man's heart is in his tongue; the wise man's tongue is in his heart,' while the Grand Vizier remembered the saying 'A wise man holds his tongue'.

Two hours later, a secret service officer assigned by the Sultan and a fireman assigned by the Grand Vizier both swore, "Falco! Oh, Dusky Falcon! Even if you were an eagle, I'd find your nest and hunt you down like a crow!" as they pocketed the bags of gold that had been pressed into their hands.

Thus, Lieutenant Osman of the Three Crescent Society emerged from the majestic gates of the Seraglio at the same time as Fireman Sandy Celep of Muskara came out through the magnificent gate of İbrahim Pasha's palace at the Hippodrome, and they both set out into the streets of Istanbul to accomplish the same task.

QUESTION 44
WHY DELAY THE HUNT FOR THE LION?

"I was talking about tulips, Hafiz Çelebi, tulips! Why don't we present the tulips in vases this year, instead of flowerpots? In elegant vases, of course!"

"That will never happen in a country of the orient, Pit Jan," replied Hafiz Çelebi after some thought, as he continued pulling out weeds from between the bulbs. "Because people want to see living tulips. That's how they like them."

"But in vases, we could create colour combinations of tulips which could be refreshed daily," insisted Pit Jan, stuffing muddy weeds into a bag.

"You're right of course, but we would never have the heart to pluck these tulips. How can one do that to a flower about which the poet said, 'The power of God is manifest in these tulips'? This flower is testament to the beauty of God. That is why pots of rare tulips are a very valuable part of an Istanbul bride's trousseau. I've heard that in other countries, they cut the stems of flowers, bind them with straw and sell them in baskets. Why, in the name of God? The way that flowers fade when plucked from their roots is comparable to the way we can never return to the past. Do you know the story about Yunus the dervish?"

Pit Jan looked at him with his usual curiosity, as if to say 'Yunus the dervish? Do I know him? Which story is that?'

"Ah, of course, I'm being stupid. How would my Flemish friend Pit Jan know about Yunus the dervish?" muttered Hafiz Çelebi.

"Very well, I'll tell it to you, so listen," continued Hafiz Çelebi. "In the time of the Seljuk sultans, there lived a dervish called Yunus. As you know, dervishes seek wisdom and maturity under the supervision of a guru. A dervish distances himself from worldly pleasures, arrogance, malice and lust in order to enrich his inner life. He may be wealthy but choose to live as a fakir. He may be a sultan, but choose to live as a slave. For forty years, Yunus carried firewood to the door of his guru Taptuk Emre and not once did he bring a crooked log to the lodge, because nothing that passed the threshold of that lodge could be anything but straight and true, not even a log of wood. For forty years, he gathered deadwood from the mountains without breaking even one branch or cutting down a single tree, yet each piece of firewood was as straight as an arrow. One day, the guru said to the dervishes, 'Go out into the countryside and gather some flowers!' All the dervishes ran off to do as he said. They gathered handfuls of daisies, narcissi, crocuses and hyacinths in a myriad of colours. Each wanted to impress the guru with the beauty of their flowers. However, Yunus returned to the lodge empty-handed as twilight was falling. The other dervishes teased him, saying, 'The poor soul couldn't find any flowers. He's not much of a dervish!" However, when the guru asked him where his flowers were, Yunus replied, 'Master, whenever I reached out to pick a flower, it reminded me of God and I could not pluck a single one.' And so, Pit Jan, flowers have rarely been picked since that time, hence the custom of using pots rather than vases."

"I'm having difficulty understanding you, Hafiz Çelebi. In Flanders, we too revere the tulip and call it one of God's creations, but we have no qualms about enhancing the beauty of God's creations."

"Oh well, that's another way of looking at it, I suppose," said Hafiz Çelebi, when they heard the garden gate squeak. It was Falco.

"Come in, Selman Abdal," said Hafiz Çelebi, looking both sad and surprised. "You look like Yunus today."

When Hafiz Çelebi commented that Falco looked like Yunus, it was his way of telling Pit Jan that Yunus would have dressed in a similar way. He introduced the two men, who already knew each other by sight, and played for time by steering the conversation on to various insignificant topics. He knew that Falco had come to ask about Stocky Yeye but he had no answers, so his sadness deepened.

"Are you ill, sir? You look very pale," asked Falco

"No, Falco, my son. I'm not ill. I'm just sad. I still have no news of Yeye. I have given a description of Yeye to a friend in the palace guards who told me not to worry and said they would soon find him."

Falco realised there was no point asking any more questions, so he talked about other things. He told Hafiz Çelebi to pay attention to his own health and stop worrying about Yeye, to focus on the important work of perfecting the tulips he had been nurturing all year for the people of Istanbul, and ended by saying that he was impatient to see the Touch of Sorrow flower in a few days. Then Falco made some tea of linden and camomile flowers, which he sat drinking with the two other men. Out of politeness and to humour Hafiz Çelebi, he laughed at the jokes told by Pit Jan in his bad Turkish and displayed an interest in how things were done in Flanders. Eventually, it was time for afternoon prayers and he made his excuses to leave. As Hafiz Çelebi escorted Falco to the garden gate, he remarked that there might be a connection between Yeye's disappearance and Falco's own situation and that Falco should take great care because the killers who had taken Yeye probably had designs on him too.

"Take care, my son. Always err on the safe side," advised Hafiz Çelebi as he closed the gate.

Falco left with a host of questions about Pit Jan running through his head. Did he have anything to do with Yeye's disappearance? Could he be taking advantage of Hafiz Çelebi's naivety? Perhaps he was wrong, but where Yeye's disappearance was concerned, Falco regarded everyone with suspicion. However, it was important to keep a clear head, he told himself. Instead of suspecting everyone, he should analyse and evaluate everything thoroughly before making a judgement, and only then devise a strategy. Engrossed in these thoughts, he suddenly heard a woman's voice as he walked along the dusty paths between the gardens. He shook his head, thinking he must be hearing things, but then he heard it again. The voice was real.

"Sir, sir! Psst!" whispered the voice close behind him.

He could see no one else around, so why was she whispering to him? Something odd was going on. It was not right for a woman to be out alone among those deserted gardens. Perhaps it was a trap and better to pretend that he did not understand.

"Who? Me?" said Falco, looking around as if he thought the woman was addressing someone else.

"You dropped this, I think."

"What?"

Falco was certain he had not dropped anything and looked at the object held out by the woman. He could scarcely believe his eyes. It was the jack-knife he had given to Stocky Yeye when they said farewell to each other seven months before, the knife he believed, or wanted to believe, to be a memento of this father.

"Where did you find this?" snapped Falco, snatching it from the woman.

"Is it yours?"

"I asked where you found it!"

"And I asked if it was yours."

The woman's voice was resolute and fearless. Falco looked closely at her face. He saw a pair of black eyes through the net of her yashmak, eyes which sparkled with the fire of youth beneath well-defined eyebrows. She looked back at him in a manner that was both assertive and reassuring.

"Yes, it's mine. How did you get hold of it?" said Falco.

"If you want to know, then follow me!"

Falco looked around again and hesitated for a moment. He wanted to make quite sure that he was not being drawn into a trap. Then, in order to appear a little more decisive, he turned as if to walk on and waved the knife at the woman.

"Even a dervish can forget his knife somewhere."

The woman swiftly grabbed the knife back and blocked his way.

"Oh no, Falco, sir. Sorry, I mean Selman Abdal. Whoever you are, you're coming with me."

"Who are you, woman? Are you a jinni? Come on, tell me," he said angrily, gripping her arms.

The woman wriggled out of his grasp, walked round him and held him tightly from behind like a prisoner.

"Aha, so our dervish isn't afraid to touch a woman!" she said. Then, pulling his ear towards her mouth, she whispered, "Stocky Yeye is waiting for you."

Hearing Yeye's name mentioned made Falco think that he might at least be able to obtain information about his young friend if he went with her. It could be dangerous, but he had to do it.

"If I find this is some sort of trap, you'll regret it. Now, walk in front of me," growled Falco threateningly.

The last rays of sunshine on the Golden Horn were disappearing and everywhere seemed deserted as Falco and the woman walked along the Bahariye road engaged in a battle of words. When they reached Eyüp Sultan village, the woman went on ahead, telling Falco to follow at a distance, and disappeared through one of the garden gates. Falco walked up to the gate and saw that there were two door knockers. One was skilfully carved as a lion's head, the other as a rose. Out of habit, his hand reached out for the lion's head, but changed his mind, thinking it would make too much noise. In those days, it was customary for garden gates to have two door knockers. If a woman came to the gate, she would use the rose door knocker, which made a gentler sound that was better suited to her sex, while a man would reach for the lion's head, which produced a deeper sound. This would tell the householder whether the person at the gate was a man or a woman, so that the appropriate servant could be sent to admit the visitor. As Falco moved his hand from the lion's head to the rose, he noticed that the gate was ajar, so he pushed it open with the palm of his hand. Immediately, a hand pulled him inside and shut the gate behind him. He could tell from her scent that it was the same woman. Instead of taking him to the house, which was what he expected, the woman led him to a hut half-hidden in the garden of the very same house where Yeye had grown up and spent such happy days with his mother, and where he had fallen in love with Şehnaz.

"I'll leave you two to catch up," said the woman, removing her burka while the two young men embraced and wept with joy. "Veyis Ağa and his wife will send for me any minute to recite the story of Leyla and Majnun. We have lots to discuss, so why not stay here tonight and we'll talk tomorrow. I'll make sure that no one sees you and I'll try to send Şehnaz across with some food. See that no light can be seen through the window. In fact, don't light any candles at all, if possible."

Falco stared in astonishment as the woman turned to leave the room. The elegance of her dress reminded him of his mother. She wore slippers embroidered with silver and a long silver-threaded robe held in by a wide belt inlaid with silver, beneath which she had a pair of silk shalwar and an embroidered white silk shirt with a diamond clasp at the neckline. Her attire was certainly nothing like that of a servant or slave. As she passed through the doorway, her veil lifted slightly and Falco caught a glimpse of her face, which was that of a young lady in her twenties.

Once she had left the room, Falco took Yeye by the shoulders and studied his face, and they embraced again as if they had returned from different worlds, rather than been separated for eight months. In the dim light, Falco could see that Yeye's face was pale and his cheeks were hollow. They spent that night telling each other everything that had happened to them and what had been on their minds, just they had done on their third night at the stokehouse. However, this time, Yeye finally told his friend about Şehnaz. He no longer had any secrets or shame after his experience at the curse-trading confectioner's shop, where his love for Şehnaz had overwhelmed him as strongly as on their first encounter.

Falco pulled Yeye's head on to his shoulder and stroked his hair as he listened to him relate, with frequent fits of coughing, how he had been unable to bear what had happened at the confectioner's and had set out the next morning for his mother's old home to look for Şehnaz. He had spent the day lingering outside her house, hoping to get a glimpse of her and taken shelter under the eaves when darkness fell, listening to the heavy spring rains and guard dog barking. Finally, as dawn was breaking and the guard dog fell silent, he had managed to sneak inside, but his strength failed him and he had passed out. When he opened his eyes, he found he was in his own room inside his old house, which still retained that special aroma he remembered from his mother.

"I thought I'd died and woken up in Heaven," said Stocky Yeye.

"All we need now is a houri," joked Falco.

"No, no, there's a houri too! The person who brought you here is called Hourikin," smile Yeye.

The door opened and Falco saw Şehnaz for the first time. She was gesturing with her hands to say welcome and express her gratitude to Falco for protecting and looking after Yeye. Falco warmed to her immediately. She did not speak, but her manner had the effect on those around her of a melody that modulated through a thousand keys. Until that day, Falco had never asked Yeye anything about his emotional life and now he cursed his own stupidity and egotism for thinking only of his own problems. He realised that Stocky Yeye had been suffering for a year, but had not wanted to bother others with his hopeless situation. Love had dealt him a heavy blow, yet he had told no one. Hafiz Çelebi always said, "Love is a private affair!" Yeye had followed this advice to the letter.

When Yeye fell sick, Şehnaz and Hourikin had taken care of him. They had found Hafiz Çelebi's garden from Yeye's description and kept Yeye informed about who had been going there recently. Again from Yeye's description, they guessed that one of those people was Falco, whom Yeye hoped would return for their reunion as the tulip season approached. Yeye missed Hafiz Çelebi greatly, but he had not gone back to his house, partly because he was sick and partly in response to the wishes of Hourıkın, who engineered the encounter with Falco in order to unite the two friends.

Hourikin had told Stocky Yeye everything about herself that he wished to know. She revealed that she was one of two female recruits in the Three Crescent Society where her late father, who was the head of the society, had groomed her for a special assignment which no one else knew about. Her colleagues refrained from asking questions, gave her a few minor tasks, and took little interest in what else she did or where she went. One of those small tasks was to monitor anyone who came to visit Şehnaz's father. However, on learning that Şehnaz's former nursemaid had called at the house, Hourikin took a job as a servant in return for a pittance and moved into the house. Şehnaz still knew nothing of all this. All she knew was that someone who professed to be her suitor had molested Stocky Yeye one day. Yeye had struck the man and consequently been banished from the house and sent to an asylum. Hourikin wanted to keep Yeye with them, because she wanted him to identify this suitor, who was apparently still pursuing Şehnaz, and she feared that he might abduct Şehnaz and put her on a slave ship to Egypt. Such crimes were not uncommon. It was also quite possible that this man was not working alone, but one of a gang who wanted to harm Veyis Ağa by splitting up his family, leaving him vulnerable to exploitation.

Falco listened to all this in astonishment. He realised another sleepless night lay ahead and, with one hand propping up his head and the other soothing Yeye's feverish brow, he started examining and re-examining all the facts. At the same time, he kept thinking, "Hafiz Çelebi must be told! The poor man thinks that Yeye's in the hands of killers!" By the next morning, Falco had come up with answers to cover everything. However, before telling Hourikin his plan, he needed to ask one more question to be sure that he had the complete picture.

"Is the person you're looking for aged about forty-five, dark with a greying beard and a slight hunch?" he asked.

Falco knew that if he received the answer he was expecting, he would be compelled to say, "There's no need to remain here any longer. The man you seek is my father-in-law Aslan Ağa and he is currently in prison."

The next morning, Stocky Yeye, who had observed the brief exchange between Falco and Hourikin, remembered the story ***Between Yusuf and Zeliha*** about a heart that was lost, which he found very apt as he watched Falco and Hourikin converse, the one adopting a patronising manner that was almost scornful while the other remained quite unperturbed, as if he had nothing new to tell her.

Postscript: Between Yusuf and Zeliha

Some worldly beauties said to Yusuf: "You have stolen Zeliha's heart and ruined her! Because of you, she has fallen into despair, but you offer no remedy. You leave her to suffer in her sickness. You stole her heart and refused to give it back. Are you not man enough to return it?"

"I did not steal her heart. Nor to my knowledge has she given me her heart. I have no business with her heart."

Then the friends asked Zeliha:

"Tell us truly, did Yusuf steal your heart? If you still have your heart and are trying to win the heart of Yusuf, then you are playing hard to get."

To which Zeliha replied:

"I know nothing whatsoever about my heart. I know not why or how it fell in love, nor where it has gone."

Then the friends said to each other:

"The heart is with neither Yusuf nor Zeliha. If neither of them has it, how was this heart lost? Where did it go? What is this, if not magic?"

QUESTION 45
WHAT GAVE THE SULTAN A HEART ATTACK?

Sunlight was filtering through the silver cypresses by the Bosphorus and pouring into one of the rooms next to the main hall at the waterfront Çırağan Palace. The mingled voices of society ladies and their attendant slave girls chatting in different languages sounded as if they were in the Tower of Babel. They wafted around in a scented haze of jasmine, frankincense and philadelphus, while Fatma Sultan sat surrounded by her servants and singers, observing everything with a dignity befitting the lady of the palace.

Next door, in the sumptuously furnished main hall, Grand Vizier İbrahim Pasha was enjoying receiving his elegantly dressed guests. For some reason, he was in a licentious mood that day and had tried to match the low necklines worn by many of the foreign guests by ordering his slaves and wine-servers to wear rosebuds at their breasts and crimson carnations behind their ears. One beautiful Georgian girl drew particular attention by wearing a garland of red tulips around her chignon. In the next room, a slave girl had got carried away by the improvisations being played on an *oud* and started singing a song by the poet Nedim, who responded proudly to the congratulatory glances with the following lines.

Spring has come, the gardens are in bloom
Light the lanterns, the tulips to illume

It was impossible not to notice the contrast between İbrahim Pasha's joyful air and the Sultan's look of sadness. However, the Sultan's melancholy soon pervaded the whole gathering and transformed the gaiety of İbrahim Pasha and the assembled dignitaries into a mood of despondency. The Sultan, wearing a maroon sable over a straw-coloured silk tunic and sitting with his magnificent head leaning to one side over his large body, looked to be absorbed in the play of light on the Bosphorus and the phosphorescence which reflected off the water and merged into the opposite shoreline. Guests who were near the windows saw him sighing and holding his breath before gasping to fill his lungs again. However, only a few of the more curious noticed his barely contained anger as he fingered the beads of his coral rosary. After all, they had come to enjoy themselves, to listen to poetry and song, to be intoxicated by Nedim's seductive words, and to fill their veins with wine. They wanted to live out their fantasies through the lines of fine poets like Seyyid Vehbi or the king of poets Osmanzade Taib Efendi. However, the party was not turning out as they had hoped.

İbrahim Pasha had thought that this occasion might be a good time to inform the Sultan that Üveys Khan's had seized Esfahan and captured the Iranian Shah, Ashraf Hotaki. However, he quickly sensed from the Sultan's sighs that he had already heard about Shah Ashraf Hotaki, probably from Judge İshak, and that a storm was about to erupt. It was quite possible that the Sultan, knowıng that İbrahim Pasha had been keeping this information from him, was irritated because he did not know how to handle the situation. The fact that Üveys Khan had seized power in Iran meant that the Turkish army in the Azerbaijan region was in danger. News from Iran was already bad and causing unease among the people. According to state intelligence, Üveys Khan was sending spies into the Ottoman Empire in an attempt to penetrate the palace, and he had succeeded in overpowering the Druses. Knowing that careful execution of state policy was essential in such critical times, İbrahim Pasha had sent his protégé Handan Ağa as a spy to intervene in the Giray dynasty's claims for a khanate in the Crimea, knowing full well that there would be a price to pay for attempting to shape Crimean policy. Perhaps the Crimean Girays were supporting Prince Ahmet, who had so far proved to be successful at evading capture.

It was the first time that Selman Abdal had been in attendance at one of these gatherings and he could not help comparing it with his life as the dervish in the Lodge next door. How had he come to be hurled from that life of profound tranquillity and serenity into this sumptuous ostentation? Life at the Lodge had been devoted to spiritual matters and a serene and contemplative life, whereas here at the palace people were constantly in pursuit of worldly pleasures. It was strange that two adjacent buildings on this shady stretch of Bosphorus coastline should house such different sets of people, one seeking philosophical fulfilment and the other material gratification. He thought about himself and wondered which place had given him most happiness. Would Nakşıgül have preferred him as Falco or as Selman? Falco was a person who ran away, got caught and pushed around, whereas Selman was more stable and spent time in contemplation and searching for his true self. Falco was created to suffer, whereas Selman could lose himself in pleasure, living each day as if it were his last. He was happy being Selman Abdal, yet his love for Nakşıgül had not diminished and had in fact led him to don his dervish habit. If his true identity were never revealed, he had no need to revert to being the old Falco. He could remain as Selman Abdal even if he had no further need of a disguise. However, the shadowy figure behind him on Divan Road a few nights before had made him suspect that he was still being followed.

"Your Majesty! All I want is for you to be happy and glad, yet today you look somewhat mournful. Pray, why is that?" said Grand Vizier İbrahim Pasha to the Sultan, hoping to jolly things up and test the sovereign's mood.

"I only wish that everything in my empire was going well, my dear Lala, but there are many things that are not as I would wish. There is no money left in the Treasury and the people are restive. Are we morally bankrupt that the people are getting so out of control?"

"What are you saying, my beloved Sultan? Your viziers think only of you and are giving these matters their full attention at the assemblies in the Dome Stateroom. You must stop fretting. The people are happy and on your side. In times of peace such as this, there is no harm in making a little time for relaxation. Thanks to your Graciousness, everything in Istanbul is running splendidly. Your forebears never knew such happy times as these in this wonderful city. Think of the Hippodrome, Bayezit and Hisar. And on the other side, Yedikule, Çubuklu, Bebek and Scutari. Istanbul is enjoying life, my dear sir, so is it not appropriate that we should have a little pleasure?"

As İbrahim Pasha spoke, the full magnificence of spring seemed to surge through the windows and fill the hall. A silence followed while everyone waited for the Sultan to reply.

"Tabriz, ah Tabriz! Has Prince Ahmet taken it from me?" wailed the Sultan, startling everyone with his cry.

All heads turned towards Sultan Ahmet as his large body fell to the floor with a loud thud.

In the commotion that followed, nothing could eclipse the fact that Sultan Ahmet had had a heart attack, not even hearing the name of Prince Ahmet mentioned twice in one day or learning of the defeat of the army at Tabriz. The Court Physician knew that his work would be more difficult from that moment.

QUESTION 46
HOW CAN THE TOUCH OF SORROW BE PROTECTED?

Hafiz Çelebi could not keep back his tears as he read aloud the following letter:

"From Osmanzade to my friend Hafiz Çelebi
Greetings and best wishes to my comrade and kindred spirit

The tulip! The word tulip sums up the elegance of Istanbul. The tulip is a creation of exquisite and legendary beauty, which graces the months of April and May with its flush of splendour.

The tulip is a source of inspiration to lovers who get carried away by the vibrant colour of its six petals which radiate light and passion in six directions across gardens and fields. The tulip produces an involuntary smile that touches the heart. The tulip can symbolise love, but also a bouquet of sorrow. The tulip turns bitter truths into sweet dreams, rusting iron into gleaming silver, stern looks into sweet laughter. My love for the tulip is undying. I worship it as my sovereign. But tulips that are not of Istanbul's soil produce sullen blooms of insipid colour. The tulip encapsulates the dreams of virgin minds, which burst into our hearts creating a passion for life. Close your eyes and listen, O Saki. Do you hear the cries of the tulip of Istanbul? A tulip raised outside Istanbul is as lost as Istanbul is without the tulip. Sorrows gather in the breeze and weep over the gardens of Istanbul while tulips shed their tears at dawn, mourning like candles by a grave.

Long may this meeting of souls continue
And may your prayers always come true

"This letter was handed to me by a caravan trader who turned up seven years ago from the Crimea. When I read it, it touched my heart with fire. Osmanzade Taib Efendi, that king of poets, had sent it from Kaffa. He loved all the tulips in the gardens of Istanbul. For him, they represented Tulip Hanım, the daughter of a surgeon named Hüseyin Molla. He would sing heartrending songs of unrequited love for Tulip Hanım in the tulip gardens at Çırağan and Sadabat. I wanted to read this letter to you now because he has been on my mind since I've been tending the Touch of Sorrow. Osmanzade left Istanbul for a while and travelled to see the tulip gardens in Flanders, Damascus, Aleppo, and Kaffa. However, because of his feelings towards Tulip Hanım, he always yearned for Istanbul, hence the heartfelt emotion in this letter."

While Hafiz Çelebi was speaking, Falco could not help marvelling how fate had determined that one twin tulip bulb should be a focus not only for his own love, but also for the love of that master poet Osmanzade Efendi, whom he had recently seen at one of the Sultan's gatherings. Falco knew that the intensity of his love for Nakşıgül matched Osman Efendi's love for Tulip Hanım. He only wished he could articulate the yearning in his heart with the same eloquence as this poet who silenced listeners with the beauty of his expressions of love. That night when Nakşıgül lay in his arms and the meaning of life seemed to crystallise in his heart, she had whispered, "Do you like tulips?" and he had felt filled with her radiance and knew that he would always love tulips. He wondered whether Ambassador Busbecq had taken the tulip from Istanbul for the same reason. And Pit Jan, who claimed to have come all the way from Flanders to Kağıthane in search of a particular shade of tulip, surely he must be secretly in love with a Tulip Hanım somewhere in Istanbul. It was a tulip that had brought Stocky Yeye and Şehnaz back together. Maybe, even that sensible Hourikin would one day have feelings associated with tulips.

"I'd expected the colour to be a shade lighter," commented Hafiz Çelebi.

"So did I," said Falco, blushing slightly as he saw everyone turn to look at him with curiosity.

"It will be the colour of my cheeks," Nakşıgül had said on their wedding night, before pressing the tulip bulb into his hand. What had she known about this tulip? How had she come to be holding that extraordinary bulb? Who had given it to her? And why? Why would a young bride be hiding a tulip bulb so special that it was sought by horticultural guilds and even tulip spies from foreign lands? Perhaps she really did just think the flower would match the colour of her cheeks. Nakşıgül's cheeks were crimson red, so maybe she thought she was clutching an ordinary red tulip. Or was the tulip meant to be red and, as Hafiz Çelebi suggested, it turned a darker shade after it was planted and named Touch of Sorrow. Perhaps the colour of its bloom deepened to match its name. People say that people and things develop according to their names, do they not? Maybe that is what happened. Anyway, the Touch of Sorrow turned out to be a tulip with a colour not seen anywhere in the world before. Had its colour been derived from the blood on Nakşıgül's hand? Or Falco's grief during the last year? Was it because of the earth which the sorrowful Stocky Yeye had so carefully blended for it? Or because its petals encircled the stem so tenderly? Or because of Hafiz Çelebi's devotion to his friend Osmanzade, or his recent grieving for Yeye?

The first rays of sunlight were shining through the April rain and forming a rainbow over the Levent Farmlands as the seven friends gazed at the Touch of Sorrow for the first time. Each knew that there would be challenges ahead. The moment Martolozi Skinny Kirkor saw its beauty he went off to unpack his fretsaw, plane and hammer and start work. Hourikin and Şehnaz were new to this story, but immediately felt totally involved. Şehnaz had started coming to Hafiz Çelebi's house with Skinny Kirkor, whom she had known since childhood when she was free to wander between their interconnecting gardens. Skinny Kirkor had felt sorry for her when he learned of her love for Yeye and the muteness that afflicted her. Not wishing to lie to her father, Skinny Kirkor said he was taking her to see Hafiz Çelebi's tulip garden. Veyis Ağa knew all about Hafiz Çelebi and his cultivation of tulips and saw no harm in his daughter taking an interest in tulips. In fact, it seemed to be doing her good because she had even begun to recover her voice. Şehnaz had tried to be honest with her father and told him that she had seen Yeye once at Hafiz Çelebi's house, but her father had said nothing. Veyis Ağa appeared to have misunderstood, because he merely cautioned her to take care when going to and from the garden. Şehnaz assumed that her father was allowing her to make these visits because he had had a change of heart since the incident at the confectioner's shop. However, she did not mention Yeye to her father again. Meanwhile, Stocky Yeye, who was still recovering from his illness, stood huddled inside layers of clothes gazing at the Touch of Sorrow, which nodded to each in turn as if acknowledging all that had happened to them that winter. As for Pit Jan, ever since seeing the Touch of Sorrow start to bud, he had spent half the day watching over it and also started getting up every night to check on it. Falco of course was expecting to find answers to his questions now that the tulip had flowered.

They all knew that the Touch of Sorrow could not remain where it was. Out of the thousands of tulips in the garden, that tulip had changed everything, even before it had bloomed. First, they had to register it at the Horticultural Guild so that the owner could be acknowledged when it came to the tulip competition. Furthermore, it either had to be guarded night and day, or potted and kept in suitable atmospheric conditions under lock and key in order to prevent it from being stolen.

"My children and dear friends!" said Hafiz Çelebi, his trembling voice sounding feebler than ever. "For years, the garden at this time of year has lit up my heart, but somehow this year it makes me sad. I think I must be getting old. But from now on, my son Yusuf will always be by my side. He will never leave me again."

"Father, dear Father!" cried Stocky Yeye, stepping forward to embrace Hafiz Çelebi with genuine emotion.

It was the first time that Stocky Yeye had ever addressed anyone as Father. He had never known his own father, but Hafiz Çelebi was everything he could have ever have wished for in a father. When it was suggested that he should continue to stay with Skinny Kirkor in order to remain close to Şehnaz, Stocky Yeye had said nothing about missing this kindly father figure. Eventually, however, he had made the excuse that he wanted to see the Touch of Sorrow in order to return to his life with Hafiz Çelebi. He did not want Şehnaz to see him only as the old Yeye who pined for his mother, but as the person he had become since his life had been transformed by his adoptive father. Stocky Yeye was determined that Hafiz Çelebi's house and garden should be like a second home for her.

"My friends! Never forget that a person's worth is equal to the sum of his true knowledge!" said Hafiz Çelebi, as everyone rose to depart after their mid-morning tea.

It was not entirely clear whom he was addressing, so each person responded as if he were speaking to them.

"Hafiz Çelebi is just jealous of my bond with Şehnaz. He keeps chiding me, saying that he loves me just as much as she does. Don't be sad, Father. I will never leave either of you!" said Stocky Yeye, remembering the story of a man living in the mountains called ***A Madman's Interpretation of Love***.

"I'm sure that's true, Hafiz Çelebi," said Şehnaz, sensing that she was now accepted and welcome there any time. "However much you love Yeye, he will love you in return just as much. And I too will love you."

"I know you so well, my old friend, and I know I can never repay what you have done for me," said Skinny Kirkor, who had taken Hafiz Çelebi's words as a compliment and an indication of their years of friendship.

"A man of honour and wisdom! Why can't our Ottoman statesmen speak in that way?" said Hourikin, trying not to show her admiration for Hafiz Çelebi's philosophy.

"May I just say," said Falco, "that knowing the beauty of both Nakşıgül and the Touch of Sorrow, I will never waver from my chosen path, even if it costs me my life. Hafiz Çelebi, you are right. A person's worth is the sum of his knowledge."

And Pit Jan? He was confused. No one would ever know what he was really feeling or how he had interpreted Hafiz Çelebi's words. Seeing this purple tulip had put him in a quandary and his mind was on the turtles!

Postscript: A Madman's Interpretation of love

There once was a madman living at the foot of a mountain. He was highly intelligent but had lost his mind. He would gaze up at the sky and say with a heavy heart: "Dear God! You understand nothing of love, yet I love you still. You have countless lovers such as me, but I have loved none other than you! Therefore, O Beloved, who created, illuminated and set the universe spinning – how may I put this? – perhaps you might learn a little about love from me!"

QUESTION 47
ARE MEN AND WOMEN EQUAL IN YOUR COUNTRY?

"Here in Istanbul, when a son reaches manhood his father says, 'All that is mine is yours. Our food is plentiful and there is space for all!' By contrast, in my country, fathers urge their sons to go out and make a life for themselves. Here, a father marries his sons off to brides of his own choosing in the hope that they will bear sons and he can have three generations living under his roof. I, however, chose my husband myself and have visited my grandfather only twice in my life. Here, it's considered insubordinate for offspring to contradict their father – even laughter in his presence is forbidden – whereas we have family debates every day and enjoy a drink together. Here, women live protected by brass railings and shuttered windows amid walls hung with beautiful carpets, while our women live in houses where the rooms are so bright behind the clear glass windows that you can see dust motes hovering in the sunbeams. There is also a stark difference in perceptions of female beauty. While women in my country go out unveiled, revealing their natural attributes and imperfections, you love to paint your lips with warm shades of red, powder your faces with soft powders, comb perfumed oils into your hair and wear gowns of the finest brocades. You do anything to make your men happy and, behind these ornamental screens with the lights turned low, you are not afraid be brazenly coquettish, even quite shameless!"

It seemed that Lady Wortley Montagu almost envied the freedoms enjoyed by the ladies around her, who were listening to her descriptions of life elsewhere with rapt attention and amazement, while at the same time deploring their own ignorance. Among this stunned audience sitting behind the harem screens at İbrahim Pasha's summer palace was Fatma Sultan.

"But is it not true that in your country, husbands are led into temptation by the sight of shameless women who go out dressed in revealing clothes?" asked Fatma Sultan.

"That is indeed true, and it can be the cause of a family crisis – just as it would be here," said Lady Montagu, fluttering her fan. "My dear lady, wives in my country expect total devotion from their husbands. A faithful husband is highly respected, so husbands and wives live as equals inside and outside the home."

"Hmm, couples occasionally live alongside each other here, but never as equals. Women here are either put on a pedestal or treated as a doormat."

"Of course, I've encountered the first type in your palaces and mansions, and the second type in the streets and slave markets. I think the first type should do something about the second, don't you agree, my dear?" challenged Lady Montagu.

Startled by this question, Fatma Sultan wanted to ask what sort of thing Lady Montagu meant, but said nothing. It was inappropriate to discuss such matters with a foreigner. However, she recognised that life was different elsewhere and not everybody lived as they did in Istanbul. Then, reflecting on the strange images of life conjured up by this foreign guest, she smiled and thought, "Perhaps our life seems strange to her." Fatma Sultan recalled how at one time palace ladies regarded westerners as primitive, barely human creatures. She particularly remembered secretly laughing at the way foreigners dressed when they came to the palace. Now it occurred to her that perhaps foreigners also laughed at the dress of their hosts. "Of course, traditions of dress go back centuries," she thought. "The social mores and civilisation that we have tried to impose on others are merely because of a wish for them to resemble us. Perhaps they want the same. Who knows? Perhaps, with the recent Ottoman defeats, the troubles at the Treasury and the breakdown of public order, there is a need to rethink the meaning of civilisation. My father and my husband have both started discussing science, and I've noticed that they no longer refer to the Franks as men of insignificance."

While Fatma Sultan was debating these matters in her mind, Lady Montagu was continuing to amaze her audience of palace ladies and guests. Her pronouncement that the world was round was greeted with disbelief by some, while others reacted as if she were a sorceress or fortune-teller. Some genuinely believed that Franks were strange people and could not accept that their great Ottoman Empire was not the centre of the universe. To them it was blasphemous to suggest that it took three months to reach the other side of the world on horseback, or that it could be daytime in some parts of the world when it was night in Istanbul.

Fatma Sultan listened intently to Lady Montagu, who was relating what sounded like clever adaptations of the magical stories found in *Tales of One Hundred and One Nights* and *Tutinama*. She needed to ask her husband if this lady was telling the truth. After all, he was the Grand Vizier and he would know. Unable to wait until evening, she decided to go and ask him immediately.

When Fatma Sultan entered the men's reception room, she saw her husband whispering urgently to Sandy Celep, a boorish-looking compatriot from Cappadocia who had just arrived. She had seen him with her husband on a few occasions before and had assumed he was used for 'special' tasks. With an uncharacteristic wariness, she moved closer in order to hear what they were saying.

"I made investigations into the bodies found in the Golden Horn, or least the severed heads and body parts that could be identified as being of a young age. Doctor Dursun checked them for me over and over again and assured me that none of them could possibly belong to Prince Ahmet," said Sandy Celep.

"I don't want to hear that you couldn't find his corpse! I want to hear that you found him alive! Find Ahmet for me or I'll make you regret it! Now get out!" whispered İbrahim Pasha hoarsely.

"Sir, I've spent the last ten days trying to get a description of how he is dressed these days," protested Sandy Celep. "People are congregating in groups all over the city, but it's difficult to get near them because they're surrounded by teams of undesirables. Ahmet is probably hiding among one of these mobs. I've searched for him in every stokehouse and coffee house, and in all the areas frequented by hoodlums. I was told that a youngster answering his description stayed at the Gedikpaşa Hamam stokehouse last autumn. They called him Falco, but nobody has seen or heard anything of him for eight months."

"Well, the earth can't have swallowed him up, Celep Efendi! Do whatever you have to do, but make it quick! If the Sultan's men find him before you do, you can count yourself dead!"

Fatma Sultan could hardly believe what she was hearing. Who was this Prince Ahmet? Why was her tender and courteous old husband being so harsh and brutal to in the way he gave orders to that man? What should she say if her father the Sultan spoke about Ahmet? And why did İbrahim Pasha want to find him first? Was there a secret conspiracy going on? She suddenly wished she had not heard any of this. There seemed to be devil's work afoot and her husband was somehow involved. Despite her uneasiness, she was reassured to see him approach the Sultan in his usual respectful manner and displaying his desire to please with verses that had been composed especially for him. But what if there was really someone claiming to be Prince Ahmet? Should she tell her father about this? Ottoman history was peppered with tales of fights between sultans and their sons or brothers. What would be the outcome if there was a fight between her father the Sultan and her husband? If that happened, whose side should she take? Which one could she trust? She knew she would be awake all night trying to decide whether or not to say anything to her father. She had heard that, while the taste for entertainment among the rich had increased, poverty in Istanbul had been getting worse and that many citizens were not earning enough to feed their families. In times such as these, any dissension between the Sultan and his Grand Vizier was unwise, and definitely bad for her. What was the saying? Spit upwards and you spit into your moustachc, spit downwards and you spit into your beard! Fatma Sultan decided she should probably speak to her father first.

Grand Vizier İbrahim Pasha dismissed Sandy Celep with a wave of his hand, and summoned a man who had been waiting at the door.

"Come over here, Selman Abdal. Come, my poet dervish!"

Unaware of each other's identity, Sandy Celep and Falco, the hunter and the prey, exchanged polite nods as one left the room while the other entered.

QUESTION 48
CAN FLORICULTURAL BOOKS REVEAL CLUES TO A MURDER?

A great deal had happened since Falco had stood gazing at the Touch of Sorrow with Stocky Yeye, Şehnaz, Hourikin, Pit Jan, Skinny Kirkor and Hafiz Çelebi. The very next day, both Pit Jan and the Touch of Sorrow had disappeared, but fortunately details of the tulip and its drawing had already been registered at the Horticultural Guild. Falco had been waiting since the previous autumn for this tulip to flower in the hope that it would lead him to Nakşıgül's killer, but then it disappeared and nobody knew who had stolen it. Whoever had it presumably also had its twin flower, or was at least searching for it. If he could find the thief, thought Falco, he might be able to find Nakşıgül's killers, at the same time acknowledging that the situation had now become more complicated. Where was the purple tulip's twin? Had a gardener taken it? If so, in which garden had it been planted? Everyone assumed that Pit Jan had snatched the Touch of Sorrow and taken it off to Flanders. Why else would he disappear before the tulips were fully open, when he normally waited until mid-June before leaving with his collection of drawings of that year's specimens? Falco put this to Hafiz Çelebi, but it was clear that the old man refused to believe that Pit Jan would do such a thing. Like Yeye, Hafiz Çelebi was sure that Pit Jan would be back.

However, the day after Pit Jan's disappearance, three Flemish ships had docked at Galata Harbour, one of which belonged to the ruler of Flanders, and had set sail the same day after taking on board a single passenger. Hafiz Çelebi looked very dejected on hearing this news and seemed to age considerably. Stocky Yeye spent so much time trying to console him that the garden became neglected and the tulips wilted before they were even taken to market. The plants needed potting, their compost changing and the bulbs fertilising. Even more importantly, it was the time of year for collecting, drying and grinding up the sweet sedge with indigo dye for the turtles.

Falco tried to think through the events of the day when they had all gazed at the emerging bud of the Touch of Sorrow. The first people to leave had been Şehnaz and Skinny Martolozi Kirkor. Then Pit Jan had withdrawn to his room to do some drawing. At about noon, Falco and Hourikin had said goodbye to Hafiz Çelebi and Yeye and taken a boat to for Cibali. The boatman had certainly been listening to their conversation, but it was unlikely that he would have stolen the tulip. "Or maybe he did!" thought Falco with a sudden feeling of despair, recalling that they had talked of nothing else but the Touch of Sorrow on the boat journey.

When they arrived at Cibali, Hourikin had subjected Falco to some pointed questioning. Falco tried to keep his replies brief and noncommittal, but soon found he was struggling to keep his answers evasive. Hourikin's manner did not surprise him. He was aware that they were both keeping things from each other, but he began to fear she was getting the upper hand in their conversations. Despite maintaining a discreet distance, it was clear that both were trying to find out more about each other and were too proud to admit it. Finally, it became impossible to conceal the fact that each was acting on behalf of another party. Still, thought Falco, when it came to the Ottoman Empire, what difference did it make whether they were working for the Three Crescent Society or Grand Vizier İbrahim Pasha? However, he had to remember that in addition to his assignment, he was looking for the twin to the Touch of Sorrow. But what was Hourikin seeking?

On their journey to Cibali, Falco had drawn up a plan to which Hourikin made no objection. It was simple. The next day, he would start making enquiries among men and she among women. They would have regular meetings to pool their information, fill in any gaps and draw up new questions, before going their separate ways again to find more answers. They would meet either in Hafiz Çelebi's tulip garden or at the Horticultural Library, which was where they were now.

The Horticultural Library had rows and rows of volumes containing illustrated information on the cultivation of flowers in general, and tulips in particular. Almost all the books that Falco had heard Hafiz Çelebi speak of were there. Many were about former tulip growers, prize-winning tulips, and the interest they had aroused in previous sultans and viziers. Half of the pages were filled with embroidered, drawn or painted illustrations of tulips. A book mentioned by Hafiz Çelebi called *Bostanü'l-Ezhâr (The Flower Garden)* was there at the front, as was a book by Von Diez, a Flemish compatriot of Pit Jan. Falco and Hourikin looked at *Mizanü'l- Ezhâr (Scale of Flowers)* containing Ebussuud's picture of a tulip named Light of Paradise. They also went through the drawings of Doctor Mehmed Aşıkî and Mehmed bin Ahmet Ubeydi, the imam of Cerrahpaşa Mosque and writer of *Netâyicü'l- Ezhâr (Maturity in Flowers)*. Collectively, these books told the story of how men had striven for hundreds of years to cultivate the most beautiful tulip, always of a single colour. It was thanks to these masters that gardeners and floriculturists from Flanders, Austria and elsewhere were coming to Istanbul and returning home on ships laden with the latest tulip bulbs.

Falco and Hourikin found these books to be a rich source of information about the two thousand or so types of tulip that had been produced in Istanbul. Some had even been translated into German or English by foreigners such as Von Diez and W.S Murray.

"Many of these tulips must have had new names created after the original ones were forgotten," whispered Falco, not wanting to disturb the tranquillity of the library.

"Or perhaps there are so many listed because some varieties were lost and then categorised with new names when they were cultivated again," replied Hourikin in an equally hushed tone.

Forgetting his dervish discipline, Falco found he was envying the intelligence of this girl. It was their second meeting at the library and neither noticed how quickly time passed while they leafed through books containing floral illustrations and pretty names that stirred their hearts with different notions of beauty. They had introduced themselves as a married couple to the wise old librarian, who already treated them as regulars. However, the tulip books were just a pretext. The real reason for going to the library was to exchange news about tulip growers and what was happening in Istanbul but, after a while, they started speaking a little more about themselves and tulips somehow seemed to become less significant.

QUESTION 49
WHAT WAS IN THE LAST FLOWER POT?

The cherries had started to ripen. It was two weeks after the *Bayram* religious festival and the season when nightingales filled Sadabat with song. Throughout Ramadan, the words "God forgive us!" had appeared in lights outside Ayasofya Mosque, a practice newly devised by İbrahim Pasha which lifted people's hearts and made the nights seem like day. However, all those candlelit nights had contributed to an increase in crime and led to public outpourings of complaint among the swelling crowds.

The spring sun was shining down on the pools of Sadabat as the Chamberlain of the Horticultural Society began summoning the tulip owners to the rostrum one by one. The specimens were presented to the Tulip Commission in beautiful ceramic pots, each covered with a cloth. When the bidding process started, the Chamberlain would lift the cover, slowly and delicately as if raising a bride's veil. After one glimpse, he would pause, keeping everyone on tenterhooks, and produce a string of compliments that gave the event a competitive flavour, before finally whipping off the cover to loud applause. Then, raising the tulip high with his right hand so that everyone could see, he would start the bidding. The Tulip Commission consisted of recognized tulip growers, and Hafız Çelebi was seated in the front row as usual. It was the task of commission members to study each tulip in turn and grade it, based on the roundness of cup, the colour and sheen, the downiness of the petals, and the proportion of flower to stem. The grades were not revealed until all the tulips were sold. However, the tulips which sold for the highest prices were usually to be seen in the front row after grading, which suggested that certain bidders, especially members of the commission, had already identified the most beautiful specimens. In those unprecedented times, the hunger for taste and quality had reached its zenith in Istanbul.

The bargaining had started at a lively pace. One buyer was prepared to pay four hundred gold coins for a tulip called Colour of Pomegranate, which had been presented by a Flemish diplomat. A tulip named Kayser's Crown submitted by an Iranian merchant was priced at three hundred and fifty, and Mehmet Lalezari's indigo tulip called Holy Magic was sold at three hundred and forty. These three tulips would proliferate in the gardens of Istanbul for many years to come, until their prices fell to merely ten silver pieces.

It was the same process every year. Merchants travelled by caravan or sea from all over the world to see the tulip exhibition and take wonderful specimens back to their homelands, while entrepreneurs from Iran, Flanders, Austria, and Crimea flooded into the city, bringing tulips of different types and colours to compete with the Istanbul tulips in the quest for buyers.

Unusually, no thefts had been reported that year. However, it was not uncommon for tulips to change hands illegally. Sometimes flowers that had been produced after months of hard toil were put up for sale by thieves who had kidnapped the owners. Or someone might claim ownership of a flower they had seen in another's hand, by producing a similar specimen as flimsy evidence that the bulb had been stolen from their garden. Istanbul's Chief of Police always paid more attention to security at tulip time, because that was when the city had the most visitors.

Falco was standing directly opposite his patron Grand Vizier İbrahim Pasha, keeping a watchful eye on the crowds of visitors gazing at the tulips. Hafız Çelebi was sitting on one of the benches reserved for commission members. Stocky Yeye, who had insisted on coming, despite not yet having fully recovered, was with a group of youths who had gathered between the men's and women's sections, and Hourikin was in the women's section.

In the days following the disappearance of the Touch of Sorrow, Falco had visited every tulip garden in Istanbul looking for its twin, even though he knew that the thief would not leave it in a garden once it had started to flower. Since he had not managed to find his beloved wife's grave, his only hope was that his search would eventually lead him to her murderers. He spent days mingling with people in coffee shops, hovering around benches, going to dervish lodges, hamams and bars – anywhere people congregated – in the hope of hearing something that would give him a clue. But he found nothing. The Touch of Sorrow and its twin had both disappeared. He wondered if he would be able to tell them apart. Hafız Çelebi had said that, even if they were grown in different soil, twin tulips would produce identical flowers if the climatic conditions were the same. Falco was now finding his task even more difficult because of the exaggerated rumours circulating about the disappearance of the Touch of Sorrow. Every crook in Istanbul was probably after this tulip now. The rumours seemed to have mythologised its beauty and spread its fame far and wide. He had even heard an Austrian visitor whisper to a compatriot that it was dark inky purple. Whereupon, the compatriot had replied that it was actually black and that he had been sent by their emperor to Istanbul specifically in order to obtain this black tulip.

This was the first time that Falco had felt resentful about having to stand impotently in attendance as one of the Grand Vizier's slaves. His Selman Abdal identity no longer felt natural and he was feeling uneasy. His daily expeditions to gather information for the Grand Vizier about what was smouldering beneath the surface in the city's streets were making him almost indifferent to wickedness. He longed to spend his time surrounded by the beauty of tulips, but he had not yet earned the right to such a life. His mission was still to find Nakşıgül's murderers without getting caught. Meanwhile, the Grand Vizier had grown fond of Selman Abdal, but Falco now played the part of an unworldly Iranian dervish so convincingly that İbrahim Pasha had stopped discussing daily events and asking his advice, which was not what Falco had intended. However, he could not afford to be exposed as an impostor, because then his patron would never believe his story and would refuse to help him.

Falco could not stop thinking about the Touch of Sorrow. The bulb that he had found in his beloved's hand seemed to have vanished into thin air. Given all that had happened and everything he had learned, it seemed improbable that Nakşıgül's killers were unaware of the tulip's uniqueness. But what was the point of growing such a special bulb if it was not to be presented at this exhibition? If Nakşıgül's killers had murdered her merely for money, they would have been hired for a pittance compared to the value of this bulb. In those times of poverty, or wealth as the case may be, the price of murder in Istanbul had fallen, yet such a flower would now fetch more than five hundred gold coins, perhaps even six hundred.

Time was passing and only four flower pots now remained on the stand awaiting auction. If the Touch of Sorrow or its twin was not in one of those four pots, it meant that Pit Jan had fled with it, and possibly its twin. If that was the case, Hafız Çelebi would not only lose a fortune, he would have been betrayed by a friend, which would be devastating. It would also mean the end of all Falco's hopes. He wondered if he had invested too much hope in the Touch of Sorrow. It had certainly helped him in his search for Nakşıgül's murderers and been the reason for his meeting Hafız Çelebi, Grand Vizier İbrahim Pasha, Pit Jan, the Prison Custodian, Sergeant Bindallı Mahmut and learning more about Aslan Ağa.

"Hmm," thought Falco, "I would definitely feel more certain about what to do next if I had the Touch of Sorrow in my hand."

The cheering increased and the excitement grew as the moment everyone had been waiting for approached – the moment when it became known whether or not the Touch of Sorrow was there. Everyone was curious about the colour of the missing tulip and the surprise Hafız Çelebi had in store for them.

However, Hafız Çelebi was feeling very uneasy. If his Touch of Sorrow was not in one of those four pots, it would be very difficult to explain its loss and Pit Jan's betrayal to his friends. Deep down, he still felt that his old friend was innocent and hoped that the Touch of Sorrow had been submitted by an agent on behalf of the thieves. The only person to dash these hopes was Falco, who believed that Pit Jan had taken the Touch of Sorrow and that any flower presented to the commission under its name would be its twin. Falco, meanwhile, was feeling excited at the thought of identifying its owner, whom he had been seeking since autumn for information about Nakşıgül.

There were now two pots remaining. The Chamberlain, who had been announcing results for the last two hours, lowered his voice. The band began playing one of İsmail Dede's songs in the Şehnaz mode, starting with the words, "The graceful tulip is now open, my heart is branded deep within".

"The horticulturalist is: Sümbülzade Gate Keeper Ko-o-oç Ömer Efendi-i-i!' called out the Chamberlain in time with the song. "The flower's name is: Gla-a-a-ass of Wine! Cultivated in: Emirgu-u-une garden! Stock: Eight pairs from thre-e-e bulbs! Colour: purple!"

A heavy silence settled over the square and all heads in Sadabat turned towards the Chamberlain as he reached out to remove the cover.

"We currently have four re-e-e-gistered buyers," called out the Chamberlain, enjoying his power to increase the tension and excitement. "It won't be sold to anyone not on the bidders' li-i-st. I'm o-o-opening the bidding! For the one and o-only! Nothing like it seen befo-ore! O-opening, o-opening! The bidding is now open!"

Suddenly the crowds on the waterfront surged forward as if being pushed by a giant wave from behind, causing the platform and tulip stands to overturn. The Grand Vizier and other dignitaries were immediately whisked away by their guards as the Chief Police Officer ordered janissary security guards into the square. Falco pushed his way towards the platform, his attention fixed on the last of the flower pots, which still remained covered.

QUESTION 50
WHAT WOULD A DERVISH DO IF HE KNEW HE WAS A PRINCE?

Muşkara Fireman Sandy Celep had started his search at the house where Prince Ahmet had lived with his mother. In the second week, he discovered that the prince was known as Falco rather than Ahmet. Then, after asking a few of the prince's playboy friends, he discovered that Falco had ended up at the Gedikpaşa Hamam stokehouse. Sandy Celep was roughly the same age as Falco, meaning he could pretend to be a friend, which made it easier to pick up information. He spent two weeks as a servant at Gedikpaşa Hamam where he learned much about life in the stokehouse but very little about Falco, except that they loved him dearly as a friend but knew nothing about him. Sandy Celep was good at his job and familiar with life in Istanbul's lawless streets, so he understood the stokehouse residents' reserve.

The next door he knocked at was that of Lanky Osman, who was much more forthcoming and told him all about the Hungarian surgeon who had performed the operation on Falco's eyebrows. Sandy Celep immediately set off to track down this surgeon, who was now living in Aleppo. When they met, he decided to take the risk of revealing his connection with the Grand Vizier and, after some threats and considerable coercion, the surgeon admitted to knowing all about Falco and agreed to perform the same operation on Sandy Celep.

"What is your name, my good sir?" asked the surgeon, as he was about to start the operation, just as he asked of all his patients

"From now on I shall be Falco," growled Sandy Celep.

"In that case, we must make you look like him!" murmured the surgeon, realising that he was being threatened.

After his return from Aleppo, Sandy Celep managed to trace Falco's movements to Beşiktaş Mevlevi Lodge. It was only when he went at there and was greeted as Brother Falco that he realised what a difference the surgeon had made by raising his eyebrows and altering the bridge of his nose. Physician Dede even told him that someone called Lieutenant Osman had been asking about Falco. Sandy Celep did not pay much attention to this because he was unaware that anyone else was out looking for Falco. His main preoccupation was ensuring that the kindly brethren did not see through his new guise and prevent him from getting back to the Grand Vizier to report on how the investigations were going. Sandy Celep even wondered whether he had done the right thing by having his appearance altered to look like Falco.

Unlike Sandy Celep, Lieutenant Osman of the Three Crescent Society began his search by finding out where Prince Ahmet had last been seen, which of course was at the Beşiktaş Mevlevi Lodge. Lieutenant Osman managed to piece together much of Falco's earlier life by engaging in long conversations with colleagues like Brother Selman and Poet Nahifi Dede. Brother Selman told him that Falco had been his cell-mate and that he had taken Selman's Iranian outfit with him as a memento when he left. Lieutenant Osman thought how smart Falco had been to have hidden in a dervish lodge and changed his identity by dressing as a wandering Iranian dervish, because Sultan Ahmet III was known for his tolerance towards the Mevlevis, who were more or less free to roam as they wished in Istanbul.

Later, when Lieutenant Osman visited Gedikpaşa Hamam stokehouse, he found that everyone seemed to know a different side of Falco, but nobody admitted to knowing where he had come from, or where he had gone. It was a stokehouse, a place where no questions were asked and nobody showed interest in the identity or status of others. The last people Lieutenant Osman went to see were the friends of Falco's youth around the Golden Horn. They merely knew him as a playboy and had nothing useful to say other than that he had disappeared.

While Lieutenant Osman and Sandy Celep were making their separate investigations, each became aware that he was not the only person searching for Prince Ahmet. Neither knew who the other one was, so they proceeded with great caution, yet were determined to succeed in the hunt before their rival.

When Lieutenant Osman finally discovered that Prince Ahmet was living at the Grand Vizier's palace, he regretted being drawn into such a dangerous business. Although it was fitting for a prince to be in a palace, there had to be a political reason for him to be hiding or sheltering in the palace of the Grand Vizier, who was not only son-in-law to the Sultan but was running the affairs of state more or less single-handedly. Was the Grand Vizier keeping the prince under house arrest out of loyalty to the Sultan? Was he concealing him as a threat to the Sultan? The Sultan was obviously unaware that the Grand Vizier was hiding him because he had asked Lieutenant Osman for the prince's scalp. Or, perhaps he did know and thought best to pretend otherwise. If that was the case, why had the Sultan not told Lieutenant Osman all this when assigning him the task? What was this prince seeking outside the palace? That was what was really bothering Lieutenant Osman. And why had the Sultan not had him beheaded by now? Who would gain from the existence of an unknown son of Sultan Mustafa II? The Grand Vizier? Was it a trap? Did the unrest in the city have anything to do with this? Lieutenant Osman had long been monitoring the janissaries' revolutionary movement. Was Prince Ahmet involved with that? If the people in the city had plans for Prince Ahmet, even though there was no such intelligence so far, should the order to kill not be reconsidered? Naturally, none of these questions could be put to the Sultan, who had commanded him to return with Prince Ahmet's scalp.

Despite all these questions, not once did Lieutenant Osman asked himself the fundamental question: "Could it be that Falco does not know he is a prince?"

Initially, Sandy Celep had adopted the appearance of Falco in order to enter his world as a means of tracing or even catching him. It had been a useful ploy because those who thought he was Falco came out with much information. However, Sandy Celep still felt uneasy. The thought that someone else out there was also hunting Falco weighed heavily on his mind. He had become involved in a dangerous game by changing his appearance and he was finding it increasingly difficult to concentrate on the job, knowing that somebody else was out to kill his double. Sandy Celep had had no intention of becoming the prey when he embarked on this hunt and seeing Falco from a distance two days before had given him real cause for concern. The Hungarian surgeon had done an excellent job. His restructured nose and eyebrows were exactly like Falco's and, without very careful scrutiny, they looked identical, because his other features were covered by a beard and moustache.

Sandy Celep had been caught unprepared when he saw his prey among the crowd walking from Divan Road to the Hippodrome. Falco was wearing a nobleman's robes yet was accompanied by a couple of drifters called Jangly Veli and Greengrocer Muslu Beşe, whom Sandy Celep knew to be stooges of Patrona Halil. What would a prince have to do with these men? The way he was chanting slogans with them suggested that he was one of those with a grudge against the Sultan and Grand Vizier. But why not? He was a prince. It was natural for him to want to be monarch.

This thought made Sandy Celep stop in his tracks and wonder exactly why İbrahim Pasha had given him this task. What was he after? Being close to the Grand Vizier when the public were in their present mood was a double-edged sword. Recent developments had shown that neither the Sultan nor his Grand Vizier were very popular. People were suffering because of the costly war in Iran, and complaining about the bad news from Tabriz. Businessmen were protesting about rising taxes and there was resentment everywhere, in the streets, coffee houses, caravanserais and hamams. Unfortunately, senior statesmen and dignitaries were oblivious to all this. Public grievances were not allowed to interfere with the entertainments at Çırağan Palace. The distress of the people was never heard above the epicene voices of boy dancers at the Sadabat gatherings. Members of the ruling elite had so little contact with ordinary people that they were unaware of the ferment brewing in the city. Meanwhile, the hungry populace was becoming ever more resentful and wanting a taste of these exclusive entertainments, while the middle classes were angered by the taxes and lack of public order in the city and the tradesmen kept pulling down their shutters and closing up shop. Nobody felt secure anywhere. Only a few days before, a gang of janissaries had raided a mansion, plundered the contents and abducted the women and girls. All honour and decency was gone. The rich started having wells dug in their gardens as hideouts for their womenfolk in case their houses were raided, statesmen seethed with envy if they were not among the Sultan's favoured few, religious scholars were reduced to living on hand-outs, and clerics became sellers of religion. With all this chaos, was it a good idea for Prince Ahmet to be killed? Perhaps he should be protected. Sandy Celep had managed to find his prey, so for him the hunt was over. What was he meant to do now?

Sandy Celep wanted to rush back to the palace to tell his patron the Grand Vizier that he had found Prince Ahmet. He was not to know that the prince would also be there that evening.

QUESTION 51
CAN THERE BE TWO OF THE SAME PERSON?

In chaos that had developed at the tulip auction, Falco noticed that, before the Chamberlain of the Horticultural Society could remove the cover on the last flowerpot, it was whipped away by the Chief of Police and handed to the Prison Custodian, who immediately passed it to a departing guard. Even though Falco had been unable to see if the tulip in that pot was the Touch of Sorrow, it gave him a new reason to follow the Prison Custodian, who was now heading in the direction of the Envoys' Caravanserai.

For four hundred years, the Envoys' Caravanserai had been a sumptuous guest house where foreign envoys stayed when they visited the capital of the Ottoman Empire. This fine stone building was situated on Divan Road, close to the Çemberlitaş

Poultry Market. It consisted of square-shaped rooms above the stables on the ground floor and its walls were covered with messages and quotes written by guests who, apart from foreign envoys, also included many tulip traders, entrepreneurs and growers.

"I think I should come back and investigate this place tomorrow," Falco muttered to himself.

The following morning, Falco rose early. He looked in on Hafız Çelebi to reassure him that the last flowerpot was in the safekeeping of the Prison Custodian before mounting his horse and riding through Hafız Çelebi's gardens, nodding to the workers spreading white muslin over the tulips to protect their colour, on his way to the Envoys' Caravanserai.

Most of the caravanserai guests were standing around a well in the central courtyard, smoking their long pipes and chatting in a multitude of different languages. Falco, who introduced himself to the group as an Iranian tulip trader, had never imagined that conversations at the Envoys' Caravanserai would be so interesting. He now understood why Istanbul's more enlightened tradesmen liked to spend time there. The adage that travel broadens the mind certainly seemed well founded here, because every utterance was more interesting than the last. A man only had to sit on a tabouret and order a coffee in a spirited fashion to find he was being gaped at in wonder, even by those who did not understand his language.

"There is an instrument in the realm of souls called the lyre," proclaimed one man, "which can make all manner of sounds. God did not want to create Adam with a soul made of mere earth, so He introduced the sound of the lyre into the Garden of Eden in order to intoxicate the soul before it entered the body of Adam. That is the reason why music now feeds the soul and gives pleasure to the living."

"Music doth entertain our hearts / to this fickle world true joy imparts," interrupted another.

"Very true, my dear poet," said the first man and, not wanting to be outdone, continued, "Let me just say that the first instruments were the tambourine and the *ney*, which were created by the philosopher Pythagoras and played on the wedding night of Bilkis, Queen of Sheba, in the time of King Solomon. The harmonica was invented later in the time of the prophet Jesus."

Everyone at this place had interesting facts or tales to relate. It had become a custom to go there to be entertained by people talking about their interesting lives. The late Evliya Çelebi had spent much time there collecting stories for his travelogues, and no doubt told a good many too. No matter what the language, there was always someone present who could translate a story, embellishing it with facial expressions and gestures so that it came to life like traditional folk theatre. For example, when a Yemeni merchant started telling a story about an event in his life, his Arabic was immediately translated word for word by the famous interpreter Satı Halife, who had been educated at the school which trained interpreters for foreign embassies. Satı Halife's facial expressions and body language gave the impression that he was relating events which had actually happened to him.

While Falco was enjoying all this, he looked up at the pillars of the colonnade on the upper floor of the caravanserai, where he saw two people were arguing. He looked again to make sure he was not mistaken. It was Pit Jan! He was holding a turtle and giving the other man a bag of coins. Obviously, he had not run off to Flanders after all. There had not been time for even the swiftest of ships to sail to Flanders and return since his disappearance. But what could he be doing in the caravanserai? The man to whom he was talking was tall and fair-skinned like himself, probably also from Flanders. Falco could not understand what they were saying because they were speaking in a foreign language, most likely their native tongue. Falco remained where he was, watching them. Before long, they were joined by another, very smartly dressed, foreigner. Pit Jan and the other man both bowed respectfully before the newcomer, who must have been a person of some significance, perhaps a spiritual leader, high-ranking officer or diplomat. Flemish merchant ships, but never slave ships or royal fleets, frequently dropped anchor in the mouth of the Golden Horn. Falco studied the horses standing in the caravanserai's central courtyard, but none of them would have been this man's mount, which meant that his horse was in a stable and therefore he was staying at the caravanserai. If so, what was Pit Jan haggling with him about? There had been no sign that Pit Jan had been taken by force from Hafız Çelebi's place. So why had he run away? Did the turtle he was holding belong to Hafız Çelebi? If so, what was Pit Jan doing with it? Surely, Pit Jan would never resort to trading in turtles. What was going on?

Just then, a strangled cry was heard from one of the stables that opened on to the courtyard. All heads turned to see a man fall to the ground as a horse that had been eating hay from the trough in the corner suddenly reared up and bolted for the door. Someone in a black burka and veil grasped the horse's neck, jumped on its back and rode off at great speed. It was impossible to tell if the rider was a man or a woman. Nobody knew what to do because everyone at the caravanserai was a foreigner and the horse and rider disappeared from sight. The guests crowded around the man who had fallen to the ground. His hand was bleeding and he was clasping an unsheathed dagger, which he must have grabbed with the intention of hurling it at someone.

As the man got to his feet, Falco caught his eye and was horrified at what he saw. The man was a mirror image of himself. The eyebrows, eyes, hair and beard were identical to his own. Was it possible to encounter oneself? Falco felt faint. He looked down at his hand to make sure that the bleeding hand did not belong to him and began to wonder if he was going crazy. He had to speak to this man face to face and find out what was going on, but before he could do so, his wounded double had mounted his horse and disappeared. Everyone was now staring at Falco and uttering expressions of amazement in their different languages. They could see that this was more than just a case of identical twins. Falco did not know what to do, but he knew he needed to get away from there. He glanced upwards, but could no longer see Pit Jan.

As he walked, Falco's legs were trembling, not with fear but because of the hundreds of questions flooding his mind. Who was the person he had just seen? Who was the person dressed in a burka who had escaped on horseback? What was Pit Jan doing? Why had the Hungarian surgeon made Falco look like the man with the bleeding hand?

That night, he went straight to his room without going to see his master. He spent the whole night tossing and turning, his head filled with a torrent of unanswerable questions.

QUESTION 52
DO TEARS OF GRIEF COME FROM THE EYES OR THE HEART?

After the flower show, Stocky Yeye's illness returned with a vengeance. A physician came and diagnosed smallpox, saying that he needed to be kept in isolation and take lots of rest. This was a very bad time for Hafız Çelebi. He seemed to lose all pleasure in life. It was as if he had become another person – exhausted, weary, miserable and resentful. For him it had been a year of heartache and loss, first because of Yeye, then Pit Jan and now the Touch of Sorrow.

The tulips in the garden were wilting because of lack of care and attention. They needed to be covered with damp white gauze during the day to protect their colour and transferred into pots the moment a merchant arrived. Some had already visited and left empty-handed to look elsewhere because either Hafız Çelebi's tulips were not ready or their colours were not sufficiently intense.

Hafız Çelebi had even begun to lose interest in his turtles. A whole year's work seemed to have been for nothing. He was upset at the disappearance of Pit Jan and thought the way he had left was unforgivable. The visitors to the Well of Souls and the cemetery always increased at that time of year and Hafız Çelebi and Pit Jan used make a little extra money by selling sherbet drinks. However, this year it did not even occur to Hafız Çelebi to order snow from Uludağ for this. Such matters had always been arranged so efficiently by Pit Jan. Where was he now?

On his sick bed, Stocky Yeye was becoming greatly distressed at being unable to do anything about the decline of the garden or Hafız Çelebi, who had started having mild seizures every so often, followed by periods of absent-mindedness and bewilderment. Seeing Hafız Çelebi turn into a silent, pensive old man was breaking Yeye's heart and slowing his recovery. One morning, he got up as dawn was breaking and started watering the tulips, almost as if he were trying to get a message across to Hafız Çelebi. However, after two hours he fainted and collapsed in the middle of the garden.

"Oh, the poor boy! Did you find him in the street, Hafız Efendi? How long has he had that fever?" cried the woman who made smallpox vaccines for the children of Eyüp Village.

"It must be twenty days now," replied Hafız Çelebi.

"When did the shivering stop?"

"It hasn't actually stopped, but it's less than it was a fortnight ago."

"Where were you then? Who was with him?"

Hafız Çelebi was about to recall the names of Veyis Ağa and his daughter Şehnaz, when Stocky Yeye stirred as if from a deep sleep and blinked. He looked up and saw the woman who was patting his brow with a damp cloth.

"Do you have pain in your lower and upper back?" she asked

"Ye-es," replied Stocky Yeye with difficulty.

"Let's hope you feel better soon, young man. Have you experienced headaches and vomiting?" she persisted.

"Uh-huh."

"Convulsions? Have you been delirious and saying things without realising it?"

"How do you know that?"

"Those are the symptoms during the incubation period of this illness. It reduces even the strongest of men to gibbering wrecks."

The woman then told him everything she knew about flowers. She also told him that there had been an epidemic in the city which the Sultan's Court Physician had been unable to prevent from spreading. She spoke more like a doctor than someone who merely administered vaccines, explaining that when the temperature dropped, the spots would emerge which, if not treated immediately, could burst and turn into boils. He had to rest until the pocks on his face had dried out, otherwise his temperature would rise again and he would develop pneumonia. He also had to be careful not to let the discharge from his eyes cause conjunctivitis. The woman removed Yeye's upper clothing, took his pulse, looked at his tongue and took some medicines from a bag she kept covered with a coarse woollen cloth. She put some lemon zest into half a walnut shell and added drops from various bottles. Taking a needle out of her bag, she seared it in a flame and used it to open a vein in the nape of Stocky Yeye's neck and scratched the surrounding area. She then soaked a piece of white gauze in the solution in the walnut shell and pressed it against his neck, making Stocky Yeye cry out every time the medication seeped into his vein. Afterwards, she sprinkled some brownish powder on to the open wound and covered it with green walnut leaves. After repeating the same process on his left arm and right thigh, she dressed Yeye and buried him beneath a pile of bedclothes.

"After four days, God willing, he'll be up and good as new!" said the woman as she departed.

When Hafız Çelebi returned from seeing the woman out, Yeye noticed that Hafız Çelebi had tears in his eyes. Tears say so much about a person, he thought sadly. When, where and with whom each drop is created is significant. Tears serve as an interpreter in so many ways. The moments when they form, appear or turn to blood each have their own special meaning. Tears are like letters that reveal the innermost feelings. His mother used to tell him a story called ***The mystic who wrote letters with his tears***, which must have been about this. Otherwise, why write a letter with tears and then with blood? Now he found himself thinking of his mother and how, when he was ill, she would give him soup or camomile tea and cover him with fresh sheets. Hafız Çelebi sat by his bed, his hand on Yeye's forehead, sighing as he recited the Koran and prayed for his young protégé's recovery.

"Efendi, tell me which tulips are flowering in the garden," said Yeye with difficulty as he held back his own tears. "I feel like the tulip that travelled the world on the back of a horse and finally settled in Istanbul. After all, I too wandered from door to door before finally finding my home with you. And the tulip has a wound in its heart, just as I do. The fiery hue of the cup that grows above its slender stem is like the fire that inflames my poor heart. The tulip is given a different name wherever it ends up, just as I do. But however many names I have, nothing compares to hearing you say, 'My dear son'. Similarly, none of the millions of tulip growers would ever appreciate the Touch of Sorrow like you. But if you lose me, don't grieve over me as you do over the Touch of Sorrow. Think of me as a wild poppy or peony that appeared outside your garden. The life of a poppy is shorter than that of a tulip. When its stem is broken and its leaves wither..."

Hafız Çelebi could bear no more. He put his hand gently over Stocky Yeye's mouth and sobbed uncontrollably – for his late mother, for his wife who had died in childbirth, for the Touch of Sorrow and, leaning over the feverish brow to keep him close, for Yeye.

Postscript: The mystic who wrote letters with his tears

I once knew a mystic who was crazy to meet his Beloved. He prepared all that he wanted to say to her beforehand. However, he forgot everything when they came face to face, so he decided to write a letter to explain himself. This mystic, who not only was unable to find an opportunity to be alone with his Beloved but when finally in her company was lost for words, wrote letters with his tears. He diluted the dried contents of his inkstand with his tears. Every time he sent his Beloved a letter, it was with fresh tears. Finally, on one occasion, he cut his finger and wrote a letter with his blood. When his Beloved read this letter, she felt that she was indeed truly loved, because she thought that the red colour of the writing looked superior to even the finest of Chinese inks.

QUESTION 53
WHO WERE THE WINNERS AND WHO THE LOSERS?

Fireman Sandy Celep had not yet managed to achieve any of the tasks assigned to him. However, he had drawn up a detailed plan and was waiting for an opportunity to execute it. This seemed to be the day.

Some of the hoodlums who had caused trouble at the flower show had been caught and others had dispersed to some of the disreputable hostels and hashish coffee houses near the city walls. The plot, led by Muslu Beşe and Patrona Halil, had been to seize İbrahim Pasha and a few foreign envoys that day, but the guards had thwarted their plan. Their failure had made the plotters realise some of the difficulties involved and look for other ways. In fact, they had now decided that, instead of capturing state dignitaries, they should seize control of the government, a plan which they were now in the process of explaining to their supporters. Instead of speaking out against the Grand Vizier or the Sultan at their secret meetings, they accused the government of being rotten to the core and state dignitaries of spending their time on frivolous entertainments while ordinary people were crippled by poverty. They spoke of the rise in immorality and prostitution – which was true – and of the need to harness popular religious fervour and gain the confidence of people other than hashish, opium and alcohol addicts. They had brought in Preacher İspirizade of Ayasofya Mosque from one of the coffee houses in Bayezit Square and were listening, stupefied, to one of his fiery sermons. Sandy Celep had heard about this meeting beforehand and was convinced that Falco would be there so, having completed his preparations and put his poisoned dagger in place, Sandy Celep had donned a cheap brown Mevlevi cassock bought in the Covered Bazaar and found a place to conceal himself.

The men listening to Preacher İspirizade came from every community in Istanbul. There were fifty or so assorted turncoats from both settled and migrant communities, which included not only Muslims, Jews and Armenians, but also Croatians and their servants, horsemeat-eating Tatars, louse-ridden Kurdish porters, thieving Circassians, Georgian thugs, vicious Abkhazians and dirty Nazarenes. While they either listened or held forth about various issues of state, nationalism, morals or religion, some drank wine from flasks hidden under their robes and others smoked hashish kept tucked into their belts. Numerous people came forward to speak, including street vendors selling goods ranging from rosaries to fermented grape juice, beggars with various limbs deformed or missing, military officers of all ranks from those who had served alongside pashas down to NCOs, plus countless other rogues and ruffians. They made up a fiendish collection of blackguards.

Sandy Celep remained hidden from view by the shadow of a plane tree, watching people join the crowd. He was not mistaken. Falco was there right at the front, sitting next to Muslu Beşe and listening attentively to the sermon. This time, he wore a stoker's outfit with a cloth wound around his head Bektashi style and a begging bowl at his waist.

"Very clever," thought Sandy Celep. "Who would suspect a Bektashi dervish in a janissary coffee house?"

It looked as if it was going to be difficult to approach Falco as Sandy Celep had planned, but he waited without stirring for half an hour. At one point, a street vendor joined the crowd crying out "Gre-e-en almonds! Gre-e-en plums!" Then, apparently drawn by what Preacher İspirizade was saying, the vendor moved forwards a few paces to a place where he could hear more clearly. He sat down on a tabouret about two yards behind Falco, put down his basket of green almonds and plums and started listening to the sermon.

Unaware that he was being watched, Falco sat listening for information to pass on to his patron the Grand Vizier and also waiting for the arrival of the Prison Custodian, who he felt certain would be somewhere close to either İspirizade or Patrona Halil. It had been a good idea to dress as a Bektashi dervish. His beard had grown long, making his face look different yet again. Perhaps, if his current guise was convincing enough, he might be able to approach the Prison Custodian and prise information out of him without any fuss, otherwise, when the chance presented itself, he would get him to talk by holding a dagger to his throat. Falco was suspicious of everything and everyone which, given his fury at the way the Prison Custodian had

tried to extract a murder confession from him during his interrogation at Eyüp Prison, was not unreasonable. Falco had been unable to find either Nakşıgül's grave or her corpse – all his investigations had been in vain. He had paid out a considerable sum of money only to learn that Eyüp Prison had no record of his interrogation. Possibly the report had never been filed. Maybe the two scribes who came to record the interview had been hired by Aslan Ağa. The records at Eyüp and Galata Prisons contained not a single reference to the death of a person named Nakşıgül or the detention and interrogation of a suspected murderer named Falco, which had convinced Falco that the people responsible for Nakşıgül's disappearance were her father Aslan Ağa and the Prison Custodian. Aslan Ağa could not be questioned because he was in the prison where Sergeant Bindallı Mahmut had been sent after his interrogation. So now, the only accessible person who knew about the murder was the Prison Custodian.

These thoughts had gone through Falco's head a thousand times. Each time he found himself thinking "Really?" and going through it all over again. For days, his head had been buzzing like a beehive as he relived everything he could recall, his mood constantly changing from sadness to remorse, or to anger at his own stupidity and naivety. He even started doubting himself and querying his recollections with Sufi questions he had been introduced to at the Mevlevi lodge, such as, "Am I certain of what I know?" or "Does what I have seen and felt accord with reality?" However, despite all this doubt, there were three people he knew to be genuine: Nakşıgül, Stocky Yeye and Hafız Çelebi; and there was one constant reality: love. He was not even genuine himself at that time.

While his mind was preoccupied with all this, Falco noticed the crowd making way for some new arrivals. Then he saw the man he was waiting for. The Prison Custodian was accompanied by the Commander of the 56th Janissary Brigade, Patrona Halil and a man named Peaky Simon who was some sort of broker at Galata Prison, where he used to juggle fistfuls of money and exchange various foreign currencies.

"Of course," thought Falco, "lots of money must be needed for the slender beauty with the arched eyebrows and rosebud lips from Mount Qaf."

From where he was sitting, he did not see Sandy Celep emerge from the shadow of the plane tree and attach himself to the group of new arrivals. Those sitting on the ground rose out of respect and parted to create a passageway to the bench where Preacher İspirizade was seated. The preacher gave a low respectful bow of the head with his hands clasped beneath his belly as the new arrivals walked past in step with each other. Then suddenly, there was a cry from someone a few steps behind them and a man fell to the ground, face down, with a dagger sticking out of his carotid artery. Blood was gushing out, creating a large red stain on his brown Mevlevi robe. Interestingly, there was also a dagger in his hand poised ready to use.

"Idiots!" shouted the Prison Custodian to the soldiers close to him, as he grabbed the arm of Preacher İspirizade to move them both away. "Is that how you guard me? That dagger was no more than two yards away! Seize that vendor and make him talk."

In the commotion, Falco decided to follow the Prison Custodian and Preacher İspirizade rather than bother about the dead man. It was more important to inform the Grand Vizier of the developing unrest in the city than to tell him about a common murder. In those days, such murders happened every day. Thus, Falco was never to know that the murder victim looked exactly like himself, or that he had been the intended victim.

Two hours later, at the same time that Falco reached İbrahim Pasha, the street vendor was being received by the Sultan in the reception room at Sadabat Pavilion.

"Your Majesty, may your life be long and your every wish fulfilled," said the vendor.

"May you be prosperous, Lieutenant Osman Efendi. You have earned your promotion. But where is he now?" said the Sultan, rising from his seat and kissing the forehead of the man opposite.

"In Bayezit Square, Your Majesty. Three of my men took away his body and tomorrow we will present Your Imperial Highness with his head in a honey bag."

When Falco entered the large salon at Ferahabad Pavilion to give İbrahim Pasha the important news, he found him playing with the water in the fountain that stood in the centre of the room.

"Selman Abdal! I think we've actually missed you," said the Grand Vizier, playfully. "How are you? Are you enjoying these lovely spring days? Tell me, what have you been doing? Where have you been?"

"Your Excellency, my patron, I'm prepared to sacrifice my blood, soul and flesh for you. I've obeyed your orders and sacrificed my comfort in order to scour the city and hear what people are saying. I've found miserable wretches of all ages posing as Bektashis and poking their tongues out at you. The people at the Pergola coffee house and Bayezit Square are no longer just aimless scum. They are directing their complaints at you, your Excellency..."

At this point, Falco broke off. He suddenly forgot what he was going to say, where he was and even who he was as his eyes lit on two flower pots standing side by side on a walnut table in the corner of the room. He could not believe what he was seeing. They were there, right in front of him in İbrahim Pasha's salon, the one place he had never thought of looking. The Touch of Sorrow and its twin. Falco felt a sense of happiness spread through him as if he had caught a glimpse of Nakşıgül. Hardly aware of what he was doing, and under the astonished gaze of the Grand Vizier, he staggered towards the table, where he leant over to stroke and kiss the soft tulip petals.

"You like them, don't you Selman Abdal?" laughed İbrahim Pasha, startling Falco. "I do too. You know, they're twins from one bulb and they're absolutely unique!"

Falco had still not recovered from the shock and did not know how to manage the situation. However, he did not make the mistake of admitting that he knew all about these tulips.

"Hmm, yes, very nice, sir. Wh-where did you get them?" he stuttered.

"That one is called Tyrian Dwarf. I bought it the other day at the tulip auction. The other one was actually grown in the harem garden and is called Touch of Grace. This evening, Dervish

Abdal, I shall fill the pots with pearls and present the flowers to my Fatma Sultan."

The Grand Vizier winked at Falco and emphasised the name Abdal when he uttered the last sentence. At that moment, the Chief Eunuch entered with a servant carrying a tray of sherbet. While the servant served the glasses of sherbet, the Chief Eunuch went over to the tulips and commented on their beauty and rare form, and how by owning these tulips the Grand Vizier had surpassed even his father-in-law the Sultan. The Chief Eunuch's arrival gave Falco time to come to his senses and he decided the best thing was to join in this conversation.

"Who produced the bulb, sir?" asked Falco.

"A horticulturalist named Hafız Çelebi produced it last year," replied İbrahim Pasha. "The bulbs were lost for a while, but our Prison Custodian managed to find one of them last autumn and I planted it in the harem garden with my own hands. I don't know where the Tyrian Dwarf was grown. But what does it matter? I have them both here now!"

Falco almost blurted out, "No sir, it's all wrong! These bulbs were not for you. Hafız Çelebi produced them especially for the Sultan, who was going to send them as gifts to the rulers of Flanders and Austria!"

However, once again the Chief Eunuch saved the situation, by saying, "Very true, sir. No one is more worthy of them than you!"

"Drink your sherbet, Abdal Dervish! Today is a day of pleasure, a day to be happy!"

For an instant Falco felt parched not only his throat, but throughout his whole body. As he sipped the sherbet, he wondered about his patron who had been giving him food and shelter for so long. Was he lying, or did he really not know the truth? He must have known. Falco felt very upset that the Grand Vizier, whom he had come to respect and revere, had turned out to be a liar. He decided he needed to be more circumspect in his presence and asked to be excused.

"Oh, by the way, sir!" said the Chief Eunuch, as Falco was leaving the room. "A Mevlevi dervish called Sandy Celep was killed at one of the coffee houses on Bayezit Square today. I'm only telling you because I thought you might want to inform the Sultan."

The Grand Vizier turned pale and all signs of his former pleasure drained away. He tried to hide this reaction, but Falco, who was making for the door, saw him stagger towards the nearest armchair and collapse into it. Once outside the room, Falco found he had even more questions and suspicions to add to those already in his mind. He feared that if things went on like this, he would go crazy and be taken off to one of the asylums that Stocky Yeye had talked about.

So, the twin tulip, Touch of Grace, had been growing just ten metres away in the harem garden and the Touch of Sorrow has been sold under the name of Tyrian Dwarf. What was the significance of that name? And a Mevlevi dervish had died just behind him in Bayezit Square. Who was this dervish? Why did his death distress the Grand Vizier so much? Would he be going to Sultan Bayezit Mosque to attend the dervish's funeral?

Falco had to find answers to all these questions and realised he was missing Hafız Çelebi and Yeye a great deal.

QUESTION 54
HAPPY SOULS OR BROKEN HEARTS?

The colourful royal carriages, with their gilded latticework, roofs inscribed with lines of poetry and windows decorated with flowers and heavily embroidered red silk curtains, passed one by one through the gate into the gardens of Sadabat Palace. Five princes, twelve princesses, five princes' wives, eight royal mothers, plus the Chief Butler, Treasury Keeper, Harem Chief Eunuch and various assistants and footmen, all arrived looking happy in their splendid attire. Sultan Ahmet III normally went back to the Seraglio after the tulip show, but that year he summoned his family to the pavilion earlier than usual in order to spend a few days enjoying the good news he had received. Spring was in full splendour and Sadabat looked radiant. The Sultan's son-in-law Grand Vizier İbrahim Pasha and his daughters, sons-in-law, relatives and servants came along too, which meant that half of the state business normally conducted at the Seraglio moved to Sadabat, where the visits of foreign ambassadors in their finery were among the highlights of the season.

At Sadabat, the Sultan particularly loved the Ferahabad Pavilion which stood beneath ancient purple wisterias and pink flowering Judas trees. The place was a paradise of flowers. Behind the artificial waterfalls were beds of the finest tulips, bleeding hearts, narcissi, violets, philadelphus and of course roses. Anyone reclining on one of the verandas at Ferahabad pavilion would smell at least eight different flower perfumes at any time of day. It was a place where people found themselves composing poems and humming airs about flowers. Furthermore, that year, his son-in-law İbrahim Pasha had added new lustre to the place by having wine glasses made like tulips, plates like narcissi, compote dishes like roses and dessert plates like violets.

In a chamber overlooking the pool and fountains of Ferahabad Pavilion, the Grand Vizier sat with foreign ambassadors and guests on his right and Sheikh ul-Islam Es'ad, Nedim the poet, a minister called İzzet Ali Pasha and the chronicler Çelebizade Asım on his left, awaiting the arrival of the Sultan.

"In my view, the tulip is the most beautiful flower in the world, Monsieur de Bonnac," proclaimed the Grand Vizier. "It makes no claim to be other than it is. Simple and without affectation, its contours are perfect, its colours always appropriate and enchanting. In fact, the features of the tulip can be found in most Turkish architecture and decoration."

The arrival of the Sultan at Ferahabad Pavilion that day heralded the first assembly at Sadabat that year. His procession was approaching in full ceremonial splendour. First, the parade leader, followed by Janissaries of the Sultan's Gate and armed security officers, four squadrons of Timariot Cavalry, soldiers from the 71st Division, the Sultan himself, officers of the Ottoman Palace Brigade, a ceremonial squadron of three hundred men and the janissary band. The bright decorative uniforms stood out against the natural beauty of the tall plane trees that lined the mall and completely screened the ostentation of the sultanate family.

Meanwhile, the poor people of Istanbul had been looking on enviously from a distance at the flamboyant scenes of the procession assembling before it started out for Sadabat and the grandiose preparations for the banquet and entertainments. Happiness for a few, broken hearts for the many. For the few, the day was an endless round of ceremonial drills, horse racing, wrestling, bear-fighting, dog-fighting, cock-fighting and gun salutes – events which the rest of the population would never enjoy. For the few, it was a day of competitions, awards, recitations, musical interludes, carousels, secret trysts, dropped handkerchiefs, flirtations, love affairs – while the rest suffered poverty, despair, and destitution. For those who rushed to enjoy Sadabat, the world was their oyster that day. For everyone else, the day was a disaster, every minute a nightmare.

PART III

Resolution: The Dark Face of Rebellion

(September 1730)
History is written by the victors

QUESTION 55
DO THOSE WHO SLEEP IN A ROSE GARDEN EVER WISH TO AWAKE?

Time was passing and the citizens of Istanbul were becoming more bewildered by the day. They were being hurled into an adventure without understanding either its cause or its probable outcome.

An autumn melancholy had descended over the city and a south-westerly wind stirred people's hearts as they continued to congregate in the public squares. For months, boatmen and janissaries had been fanning the flickering flames of rebellion and this was the day when the full force of the fire would be felt. Crowds had arrived from different parts of the city, from Samatya, Fener, Balat, Tahtakale, Balıkpazarı, Hasköy, Kumkapısı and Galata, to congregate in Sultan Bayezit Square, everyone coming for their own reasons but drawing courage from the swelling numbers. But their loyalties were fluid. Unaware that they were being manipulated, they were swayed first one way then another. Among the crowds there were treacherous scoundrels ready for any kind of mischief, decent family men, artisans, tradesmen, Muslims and non-Muslims. At that moment, they were listening with sullen faces to a fierce-looking man with an imposing moustache, whose deep, rich voice resounded right across the square, delivering a speech that had been planned as carefully as a skilled game of chess. Each word, each sentence was modulated to elicit the maximum reaction from the crowd, in the midst of which specially chosen agitators had been planted to inflame the listeners with their comments and responses. The excitement was infectious and the speech was creating an impact such as had not been seen in Istanbul's public places for many a year.

"Gentlemen! Listen to this verse! Lend an ear to these crass lines of the poet Nedim, that uncircumcised infidel from Muşkara:

Noble Muslims reign supreme
Others are safe under this regime
Artisans are greeted with esteem
All is well in this wonderful world

Gentlemen, do any of you believe this nonsense? In God's name, do any of you feel that you reign supreme? Do any of you feel safe? How many artisans out there have a shop to call their own? No? Tell me, does anyone out there attend these assemblies that Nedim Efendi enjoys so much? Yes or no? If so, live it up and make the most of it!"

The voice of Master Coffee Maker Ali rang out through the crowd, striking a chord with each of them and inflating their anger. He knew how to use his voice and gestures to whip up or subdue the masses, swaying them like ears of wheat in a field. When he cried out, "Yes or no?" someone in the crowd shrieked, "No-o!" provoking the people even more. When he asked, "Do any of you…?" they cursed, "Let them rot in hell!"

Three people were directing this event: Master Coffee Maker Ali, Muslu Beşe and Albanian Patrona Halil. Three nights previously, Patrona Halil had summoned the other two to his basin at Bayezit Hamam, where they had secretly planned what they referred to as the arrival of the beauty from Mount Qaf. They each gave assurances that they would bring three thousand men with them and meet in Bayezit Square at mid-morning that Friday. Although only a thousand or so men were in the square at this point, there was no person or force there to stop them.

Grand Vizier İbrahim Pasha, unable to bear the thought of defeat at Tabriz, had crossed over to Scutari for the mobilisation of the army prior to marching into Iran. The Sultan had gone to Scutari two weeks earlier with the aim of whipping up popular support for the army. Thus, while speeches were being delivered in Bayezit Square, crowds were also congregating in Scutari and gazing at the fleet of ships in front of the Maiden's Tower, wondering what good they would do in Iran. At his Scutari palace, the Sultan had kept postponing the army's final mobilisation for an autumn attack on Tabriz, until eventually an envoy arrived from Iran and confused everyone, including the Sultan and Grand Vizier, by requesting peace.

While the rulers were deciding whether to opt for peace or war, people on the other side of the Bosphorus were being distracted by other matters. Master Coffee Maker Ali's speech was causing uproar in Bayezit Square. Falco realised that, since the Sultan's army was stationed on the opposite shores, the city's security had been left in the hands of no more than seven hundred janissaries. Doubting their ability to accomplish this task, Falco knew that he needed to inform his patron the Grand Vizier immediately about the unrest and insurrection that had broken out. Looking around him, he saw people of every class and station yelling in response to the speaker's proclamations. The gulf of water separating Istanbul from Scutari had never seemed wider. Falco knew that it would be impossible to find a boatman to take him to Scutari, even for a thousand gold pieces. Likewise, nobody would come across to Istanbul from Scutari. Meanwhile Master Coffee Maker Ali was continuing with his speech, with careful repetition and timing to emphasise his particular points.

"Gentlemen, comrades! It's become a matter of survival. We have few options left. The Grand Vizier has launched a campaign against Iran and is now mobilising the army at Scutari. But who is to pay for all this?"

"We shall! The shopkeepers and tradesmen!"

"Our Grand Vizier claims to have installed drinking water fountains and established a printing press. A printing press is good, but there are no candles left to read by. Water fountains are good, but there is no soap to wash with. Firewood now costs ten akches a load. As for coal, there's not even enough to smear round your ladies' eyes as kohl. And forget about wheat, we can't even get barley! We have no candles to burn, yet our hearts are melting and burning, burning..."

"Burning, burning..."

"I am a coffee-maker, yet we have to make it from roasted chickpeas. Gentlemen and comrades, the ports are full of grain, are they not?"

"They're full! They're full!"

"Why then this scarcity? Who consumes it while we go hungry? The guards? The gardeners? The janissaries? Those thieves who pound on our doors every other day to collect taxes? Those who seize our bread in the name of the state?"

"To hell with them! We want sharia law! We want justice!" responded the crowd.

While Master Coffee Maker Ali continued in this vein, Falco noticed a group of people on the other side of the pool in the square and moved forward to find out who they were.

"Gentlemen! Who is the Sultan? Who actually wears the crown?" continued Master Coffee Maker Ali. "Look at the Grand Vizier, that drunken sot of Sadabat! They rob people through bribes and black markets and stuff their faces with the proceeds! A time of peace, they say. But they stint on alms and shirk their responsibilities. They prefer to put on entertainments for their own pleasure. They encourage men to be profligate and abandon their families. Who has brought this tyranny on us? Who is responsible for this lack of humanity?"

"Who? Who? Make them pay! Make them pay!"

"We want sharia! We want justice!"

Falco felt a hand grab his left wrist and turned to see who it was. Those eyes! He recognised those eyes. A shabby looking figure dressed as a customs house porter stood before him, wearing striped breeches held up with a wide belt, a jacket over a collared shirt, a kerchief around the neck and a pair of worn slippers. The dirty turban looked slightly unnatural above the grimy face, which was masked by a cloth covering the mouth as if to keep out the dust created by the south-westerly wind. No, it couldn't be, thought Falco, not here among all those awful, ignorant people.

"Is that you?" Falco whispered.

"Yes."

"What are you doing here?"

"I was looking for you."

"Get away from here immediately!"

"We'll go together!"

Falco felt his hand being gripped tightly. Someone else had now taken the stage and was speaking in a deeper voice. The two of them edged forward slowly. As they did so, they passed a man whispering to a group of ten burly firemen.

"They went towards Bayezit," he said. "Take the Aksaray road and if you see any of the Sultan's armed police or Bektashi janissaries, position yourselves together in front of them and stop their horses getting through. Then shout for all you're worth and wait. Whatever you do, don't let them get away. Keep them wondering what's happening. Don't tell them anything."

Falco thought he recognised the man giving these orders. He looked more carefully, taking note of the voice and choice of words. All the while his hand was being gripped even more tightly. Then Falco remembered seeing this person with the Prison Custodian by the basin at Bayezit Hamam. It was Stiletto. Falco still recalled him pointing to the dagger tattoo that ran from wrist to elbow, saying, "Why do you think I have this decoration, brother? I live up to it, when necessary." Falco felt the hand in his begin to sweat, but dismissed it as meaningless. They were merely two friends protecting and looking out for each other.

Stiletto was a charismatic man. He took the stage after Master Coffee Maker Ali and spoke with great sincerity. His presentation appeared honest and credible – important qualities in a leader. He gave a brief explanation, with evidence and examples, of how the Sultan and his Grand Vizier had become addicted to a life of pleasure and entertainment, how they were blind to the desperate plight of the people, how law and order had broken down, and how the janissaries were disintegrating into gangs. Falco was not sure whether his quickening heartbeat was caused by the effect of Stiletto's speech or the hand he was holding.

"Long live Halil Ağa! We place our hope in you!" shouted the crowd around the pool.

"So, Stiletto is Patrona Halil Ağa!" murmured Falco in amazement.

Falco had heard many things, good and bad, said about this man. Some he believed, others not. The things he wanted to believe were that Halil had gained the nickname Patrona because he used to work on the ship of a *patrona* or vice-admiral, that he left his job as a bath attendant at Bayezit Hamam because he disapproved of the stokehouse foreman's immorality, and that he went to work as a sales clerk at the Covered Bazaar, where he treated people honestly, gained their respect by living up to his religious principles and became respected for his rational opinions. Falco pulled the hand he was holding closer to him, as if to keep the crowds at bay. Some claimed that Patrona Halil was corrupt and cruel. However, he sounded sincere when he claimed that the sole purpose of the revolution was to put an end to the immorality and poverty that had engulfed the city. He had a naivety about him which made Falco suspect that he had been indoctrinated by certain people. Falco's hand was sweating, as if he were holding a ball of fire. Or was it just that he was unused to physical contact of any sort? Otherwise, why would it have that effect on him? He assumed that Patrona Halil had come under the influence of Ayasofya

Mosque's Preacher İspirizade, and the Islamic judge Cadi Zülali Hasan, taking their revolutionary pronouncements in good faith as beneficial to the Muslim community. The 'the beauty from Mount Qaf' seemed to be a reference to Patrona Halil, and Falco longed to get a closer look at this man whose name was held in such esteem among traders in the Covered Bazaar and his stokehouse brothers at Gedikpaşa Hamam. However, the hand in his did not allow it and pulled him back. "Obedience and submission are good qualities!" thought Falco, accepting that resistance would only bring him trouble.

"Allah! Allaaah! Oh Muslim brothers!" cried Patrona Halil, bringing his speech to a close with some well-rehearsed gestures. "We have explained everything. You cannot say, hand on heart, that you have not heard! We have made a case for the law of the Prophet Mohammed! Close down your shops! You too have a place beneath this red flag of ours!"

At this point, three men in their twenties each raised a hamam loincloth on the end of a pole as a flag. The hand in Falco's hand was perspiring and transmitting an indefinable sensation through his body.

"Allah Allaaah! Illallaaah!" cried the people in unison.

This was followed by some orchestrated cries from the plants among the crowd.

"God give you strength! We're right behind you!"

"We want the law of Mohammed!"

"Very well. The time has come!" called out Patrona Halil. "The banner has been raised. Gather beneath it!"

"We want justice!"

"Let the lechers suffer their deserved torment, let the deviants have their punishment!"

Pandemonium broke out as these slogans were met with anti-revolutionary cries of "Treason!", "The Antichrist has appeared!" and "Is the Sultan to be deposed under the banner of a loincloth?" However, they were soon suppressed by some fierce-looking men and a struggle followed between those who had stayed merely to watch the spectacle and now wanted to quietly disappear and those who were genuinely motivated. Falco felt his hand being tugged again, pulling him away from the crowd, which was now dividing into three groups under the three home-made banners. This had obviously been planned in advance. People began to go towards Divan Road, the Covered Bazaar and Ayasofya Mosque. Falco moved forward to see who was leading them, dragging the person whose hand was in his, until he came to the steps by the pool. This time he was not prevented. "Obedience and submission are good qualities!" he muttered again, smiling to himself. Then, as if understanding his wish to know the identities of the marchers, Falco's companion started listing their names.

"Just behind Patrona Halil are Foreman Emir Bey from Mahmutpaşa Hamam and Pickle-seller Ismail from Cebeci Barracks. They're followed by Gypsy Horse Thief Acrobat Musa, Tiny Muslu from the Pergola coffee house and Cretan Andon Mihandoni, a pipe-maker from the same coffee house. And you must recognise the gentleman right at the back?"

"That's Preacher İspirizade Efendi from Ayasofya Mosque. He's clearly neglecting his duties."

"Ha ha! Am I supposed to laugh?"

Falco turned to look at another crowd of two hundred or so men, who were shouting as they marched towards Süleymaniye. Again, his companion reeled out the names.

"Muslu Beşe is at the front. Just behind him is Kurdish Çelo, a porter from the customs house.

"Did you buy your clothes from him?"

"This is no time for jokes. Just behind Çelo is Hiristo's son Angeli, a companion of Patron Halil, then there is Preacher İspirizade's new devotee Callous Porça, followed by two sailors called Peaky Agop and Crazy Molla, and at the back is Freckled Mustafa, the sailor who raised the flag. The dignified man on the right is the foreman from Gedikpaşa Hamam. But you must know him of course."

"I thought you said this was no time for jokes? Carry on with their names."

"All right, all right. Don't break my fingers! At the back is Bloody Veli. He didn't get that name because he spilled blood, but because blood was spilled on his account. You must also know him from Gedikpaşa Stokehouse. He's a mine of information and a good friend of Lanky Osman, the man who took you to the Hungarian surgeon. Next to him is Sultanzade Evren Bey, who is Bloody Veli's equivalent at Bayezit Stokehouse."

Falco suddenly felt very uneasy that his companion knew so much about him. He let go of the hand and felt the blood drain from his face.

"Don't worry," said his companion. "I greased the palm of Lanky Osman with fifty gold coins to ensure that he wiped his memory of that day. He knows to deny everything."

"Fine, but you..."

"What about me?"

"What do you know?"

"Never mind that. You provide information to one person, I provide it to another. You should also know that I was raised in the Three Crescent Society. My father worked there. Don't worry about it. Look, Cadi Zülali Hasan Efendi is leading a group to the office of the Sheikh ul-Islam."

While not wanting to offend the person whose hand he had been holding, Falco felt confused by the myriad of thoughts going through his mind. He rearranged the hand in his and the two of them turned towards a group of three hundred or so urban bandits, self-styled militants and ragamuffins who were heading towards the Hippodrome and Aksaray. Many of them looked as if they would be sneaking away before long. They were led by the earlier speaker, Master Coffee Maker Ali, who was followed by a young standard-bearer whom Falco knew as Dereköylü Ali. Falco remembered how Stocky Yeye had laughed when he and Dereköylü Ali went out begging in Tahtakale one freezing cold day when icicles were hanging from the roofs.

"Never mind the people at the front Falco, I'll tell you about the people at the back. You'll soon understand why. The one right at the back is the mastermind. Do you see him? He's Janissary Commander Austrian Hasan. But he's in disguise today."

Falco could not decide which group to follow. He did not want to let go of the hand he was holding, in fact he wanted to hold on to it even more tightly, but the main reason for his being there that day was to find the Prison Custodian, who was nowhere to be seen. Falco was certain that the Prison Custodian was at least partly responsible for initiating and inflating the unsavoury rumours that had been circulating in the tulip world. Furthermore, Falco could not imagine that the Prison Custodian would remain on the sidelines while the cauldron of rebellion, which had boiled over several times in Ottoman history, was heating up again. After all, Falco had already witnessed his close association with Patrona Halil at the Bayezit Hamam.

"Have you seen the Prison Custodian?" asked Falco, tugging the hand in his.

"No. Should he be here?"

"Of course he should. If he's not here, he must be in action somewhere else, because my patron İbrahim Pasha entrusted Istanbul to him and the Janissary Chief Commander when the army left for Scutari. Since the Janissary Chief Commander is here, the Prison Custodian must be taking charge elsewhere, don't you agree?"

"Quite possibly, but maybe he overslept and is just late."

"You are joking, aren't you? How many rebellions has this empire known? They always have three elements: a leader who is fed ideas by the clerics, a statesman to put the ideas into practice, and an army man to wave the sword on their behalf."

"Well, they've certainly succeeded in confounding the public."

"The poor have nothing left to lose," mused Falco. "The people always get squeezed twice, first by clerics with their religious argument and then by the armed forces. Still, the people would fare no better if they were subjected to the joint force of ignorant clerics and janissary bullies, most of whom are foreigners."

"That's why acts of rebellion have no happy endings and do not serve the interests of the people. Rebellions have never amounted to more than urban banditry, have they?"

"No, but if an ambitious pasha and a fanatic cleric join forces and manage to enlist enough bullies to support them, you have the main ingredients for a rebellion. After that, it only needs the slightest thing to topple Sultan Ahmet, which could be the intervention of Janissary Commander Austrian Hasan or the over-friendly French Ambassador the Marquis de Bonnac. Or it might be the news from Iran, or the extravagances and debauchery of the Sultan and his Grand Vizier. It could be any of one of those factors."

"You're right! With all the talk about the Grand Vizier and the splendours of Sadabat tulip gardens, someone was inevitably going to stir up a rebellion that drew the support of rational thinkers and guardsmen."

"That's it!" exclaimed Falco, "That's what's missing in this rebellion!"

"What?"

"Guardsmen! There are no guardsmen here!"

"Don't worry. The janissaries will sort it out tomorrow."

"I don't mean them," said Falco. "This is something more important. Do you see any guardsmen opposing the rebellion?"

"You're right! Why didn't I think of that? İbrahim Pasha must have ordered them all to stay away from here."

"Or prevented them from coming here," added Falco, whereupon they both chorused, "The Seraglio! The Gate of Felicity!"

Falco dropped the hand he was holding and turned to hold his companion by both arms.

"Hourikin, I'll go to the Gate of Felicity. You go to Süleymaniye!" he ordered.

"No, I'll go to the Gate of Felicity because you'll be killed if anyone from İbrahim Pasha's household finds you there. You go to Süleymaniye – you won't be seen if you go round the other way."

"All right, I won't argue. But you must warn Stocky Yeye and Hafız Çelebi about all this as soon as possible. If the rebellion proliferates, it won't take long for the hoodlums to reach Sadabat. If it all goes wrong, we'll meet at eleven o'clock in two days' time at my room in Süleymaniye. Otherwise, I'll come to

Hafız Çelebi's tomorrow evening. I've nowhere else to go, anyway!" said Falco, disappearing into the crowd that was surging towards Ayasofya.

"We want the head of infidel Grand Vizier! Forward, O people of Islam!" yelled someone in the crowd.

A few people, realising the potentially dire consequences of such a violent call for action, responded feebly with calls of, "O people of Mohammed, the sword should never be used among Muslims!" and "No! Do not say such things!"

However, it was too late, and impossible to predict what would happen next. With the Sultan, his Grand Vizier and the army all in Scutari, Istanbul was left defenceless, so it was just a question of time before the plundering began. There was confusion in front of the Covered Bazaar, where noisy quarrels were going on between innocent passers-by wanting to return home and rebels trying to force them to join the protesters under the loincloth flag. It was Friday, so the bazaar was teeming with customers. The traders had already started bringing down their shutters and locking up. They knew their lives and property were at stake and wanted the bazaar vacated immediately. Chaos was erupting and the locusts about to descend. The mob of five hundred outside swelled as people emerged from the Covered Bazaar.

Falco rubbed his palms together. He was missing the warmth of the hand he had been holding. Yet again, he repeated the words "Obedience is good!" with a blissful smile on his face. He walked along Divan Road and was wandering around near Ayasofya when he saw the person he was seeking by a fountain the Sultan had had built two years previously. The Prison Custodian was standing with his guards next to the palace gate, preventing anyone from leaving. Falco did not venture too close, but found a quiet spot in the shadow of the mosque's hamam where he waited behind some shuffling horses to see what would happen. He now had time to think about his companion in Bayezit Square and why she had grabbed his hand. If only Nakşıgül were alive, he thought yet again, at the same time regretting that her death did not give him the right to hold Hourikin's hand. He repeated Nakşıgül's name to himself hundreds of times, trying to atone for his error. Love did not die with the death of a beloved. With this thought in mind, he found himself looking at things differently. Was the rebellion an external factor or was it within him? Was he dying or in recovery? His mind became filled with a totally different blend of dreams, hopes and despair. Why had holding Hourikin's hand disturbed him so much?

Those who sleep in a rose garden like to awake early. But those who sleep in a prison want to remain asleep, because they know that to wake up is to be thrown into prison all over again.

QUESTION 56
WHO ARE THE WRETCHES WHO PLAY WITH BLOOD AND FIRE?

The muezzins of Dersaadet were just waking up for their morning calls to prayer when the Grand Vizier led Falco rapidly up the steps into Scutari palace. Both men were very nervous. It was impossible not to be, because the Sultan was definitely going to be displeased with what they were about to tell him.

When Falco was waiting near Ayasofya Hamam and saw that the city was about to be plundered by the very people who were meant to protect it, he had decided that he had to go to the Sultan. Instead of just dawdling about in Ayasofya, he had to tell his patron and the Sultan exactly what was going on without wasting any time. That was why, once darkness fell, he untied one of the horses in the square and made his way down to Sirkeci unnoticed. He needed to find a boatman, but a south-westerly wind was blowing out at sea and the caiques were all tied up in the boatyard. Furthermore, all the boatmen had either left of their own accord or been marched off to Bayezit Square. Falco knew that the rebels had done their best to sever all contact between Istanbul and Scutari, so the south-westerly was in their favour because it made Istanbul inaccessible to not only the army, but also to the Sultan and Grand Vizier.

It was easy enough to untie one of the boats in the boatyard and set out to sea, but controlling a boat in that weather required real skill. Falco checked that the pearl which the Grand Vizier had presented to him on their first meeting was still in place inside his armband, in case he needed it to pay a boatman. However, the boatyard was deserted, which was only to be expected, but Falco was surprised that not even one person had stayed behind to watch over the boats and make sure that all vessels were kept in place, in order to block all means of reaching Scutari.

"Perhaps they felt no need to guard them once the south-westerly started," thought Falco. "Or maybe all the boatmen just left of their own accord."

However, Falco realised he was mistaken when he was suddenly forced out of the harbour at gunpoint. His only recourse now was the boathouses by the Waterfront Palace at Seraglio Point. He reached the Basket-makers' Kiosk, where the Sultan's splendid navy had once celebrated its Mediterranean victories, only to find it completely empty and the dilapidated jetties deserted. In fact, it was always hard to find anyone there at the end of summer. Falco eventually came across a swarthy gardener dunking bread into a plate of aubergine, totally oblivious to what was happening in the city, but a gardener was no use to Falco. It was getting dark and he knew he was likely to get into difficulties if he waited any longer. Controlling a boat in the Bosphorus was one thing, but he would not stand a chance if he was blown into the open waters of the Marmara Sea by the south-westerly.

God seemed to be on his side. Heavy rain started as Falco pulled away from the shore, which meant the wind was abating. Within half an hour the waves had subsided. However, it was pitch black on the water because of the rain and the fact that the feeble lamps of Scutari were being extinguished as the households went to bed. When he finally reached the shore at Şemsipaşa after skirting the dangerous rocks beneath the Maiden's Tower, Falco was not only energised by feeling he had done his bit for the Ottoman Empire, he was more determined than ever to reach either the Grand Vizier or Sultan, whatever the obstacles. Falco was not very familiar with Scutari. He had been there a few times as a child with his mother, but all he remembered was riding towards Çamlıca in a decorated wagon drawn by oxen with ribbons around their necks and red apples on their horns.

Falco tied the boat up to a jetty near a newly constructed public fountain. Everywhere was in total darkness and the rain was pouring down even more heavily. Drenched to the skin, he started walking past Valide Sultan Mosque towards Scutari Waterfront Palace, on the assumption that his patron would have a pavilion somewhere nearby. Falco knew he had found it when he was stopped by some guards.

"What miserable wretch has come here at this time of night?" asked the Grand Vizier furiously on being woken up by a servant.

"Your slave, Selman Abdal, sir," replied the servant.

"Tell him to go away before I have him beheaded! What's he doing here at this hour?"

However, after hearing Falco pleading insistently with the servant and swearing his allegiance, the Grand Vizier finally jumped out of bed to see what was happening.

"You must wake the Sultan immediately!" said Falco, before the Grand Vizier had even finished dressing.

Once at the palace, Falco observed that the Sultan did not look nearly so imposing in a nightgown as when mounted on a horse. For the first time in his life, Falco was actually close enough to get a good look at the Sultan. However, he was prevented from doing so because the Sultan kept giving him incredulous stares. There was a long silence, during which the Sultan turned his head this way and that a few times, and then turned to look at Falco again. İbrahim Pasha also became perturbed by the way the Sultan was staring at Falco, whose legs had begun to tremble.

"Your Majesty," said the Grand Vizier, bowing his head, "Selman Abdal is like one of your household servants. He is the poet dervish who ignited the flames when you visited Eyüp Sultan. He wishes to inform you of what he saw in Istanbul today."

Falco's patron bowed down to kiss the hem of the Sultan's gown. Falco felt he should behave like a dervish and one of his patron's poets but, not wanting his wet clothes to drip on to the carpet nor wishing to make any movement that might provoke the Sultan's anger, he remained upright. Nevertheless, the Sultan's gaze made him feel weak at the knees and his head started to swim. He waited, his eyes fixed on the Sultan's gem-encrusted Moroccan leather slippers, fully aware that the Sultan was still studying his face.

"So, speak, brother!" barked the Sultan eventually, as if issuing a command.

"My sovereign, my Sultan, Your Majesty," started Falco in a Persian accent and poetic style. "Your city's streets and skies resound, the people's hearts with fear do pound. Your subjects, your servants and even your slaves, my Sultan, together they rise in waves. Around the banners they cluster and swarm, as if trapped in a ship in the midst of a storm, as if trying to break down the windows and doors, they fill the air with their screams and roars."

"Who are these people, brother? Who are these wretches who play with blood and fire? How many are there and what do they want?"

"They're vagabonds, ruffians, Halil Ağa's vulgarians. Your people are bewitched by him, they pander to his every whim. Support for him is found with ease, they call him the victor of Tabriz. In disarray and dressed in rags, they congregate around three flags. The Mahdi or Twelfth Imam some say, others the Antichrist do bray."

The Sultan made a gesture telling Falco to stop. He was confused and irritated by the mumblings of this dervish whom he did not know whether or not to believe. He was also wondering why a Persian was bringing him this news. Were there were none of his own citizens left in the Ottoman Empire? At the same time, the Sultan was still trying to figure out why the dervish's face was familiar.

"Lala! Is the dervish telling the truth? What is the cause of this rebellion?" asked the Sultan, turning to his Grand Vizier.

İbrahim Pasha winced, realising that the furious Sultan was accusing him of withholding information.

"My Master, this is no more than an outcry from a few ignorant wretches who will do anything for a few coins," replied İbrahim Pasha, hoping to appease the Sultan. "Such things can happen at any time or place. It will all soon be smoothed over. Do not concern yourself with this. There is nothing to worry about as long as the clerics and armed forces are not involved."

"Your Majesty," interrupted Falco, "I saw your subjects Cadi Zülali Hasan Ağa and Preacher İspirizade in disguise among the crowds. I also saw the Prison Custodian and Janissary Commander Austrian Hasan."

The Sultan could not believe what he was hearing. The last two men mentioned were responsible for the security of the city. On the way to Scutari, the Janissary Chief Commander had assured him that everything was safe in his hands. The Sultan felt a sudden need to sit down and made for the nearest divan.

"Who else did you see, brother? Stop mumbling and tell me straight!" said the Sultan.

Falco realised he now had to speak more directly, without resorting to any more rhymes. The Sultan, of course, was unaware that Falco had been using rhyming speech as a distraction in the hope that he would not be recognised.

"The rest are just rabble, Your Majesty," said Falco, now speaking as plainly as possible. "Patrona Halil Ağa is a good man, but he is carried away with honour and patriotism and has been persuaded to hoist a banner. The insurgency is actually being directed by men like Master Coffee Maker Ali, Muslu Beşe and Freckled Mustafa. Those three are behaving like dragons that have broken free of their chains."

"How many people are involved?"

"You're Majesty, there were about a thousand people in Bayezit Square. By evening, half of them had gone to the Hippodrome. Of the rest, most went via Aksaray to the Meat Market and a few to the courtyard in front of Süleymaniye Mosque."

"Lala!" said the Sultan. "The men you put in charge of guarding the state are involved in this! What's happened to the law enforcers? What about the other viziers, the Supreme Judge and Chief Executioner? They assured us that everything would be in order. See that they're all replaced tomorrow!"

"But Your Majesty," continued Falco. "Relieving them of their duties might actually be more of a blessing than a punishment to these unidentified rebels. Those men are the very people we need right now. Let's summon them, reprimand them individually and send them off to rein in their men."

"Do whatever needs to be done without delay, Lala! Find out what these men think they stand to gain from this."

"But Your Majesty!" persisted Falco. "They have no real following among the people yet, they just need bringing under control. If we'd been able to bring rabble like this together in Iran, we could have armed all the bondsmen and Azeris and had them killed on the spot. A thousand soldiers for a thousand people is sufficient, Your Majesty."

"Shame on you, brother! Who asked you? Get out!" retorted the Sultan.

The muezzins of Scutari began reciting morning prayers and the Sultan listened for any sound coming across the water from Istanbul, but heard nothing. The rain had abated and everything was still as dawn broke, so he should be hearing the fine voices of the muezzins at the mosques of Ayasofya and Sultan Ahmet, but not a single eulogy or call to prayer was to be heard from there. The Sultan turned to look across the Bosphorus and saw the clouds behind his palace on Seraglio Point flicker with red, reflecting the leaping flames of the fires lit by rebels at the Hippodrome.

“They’re probably singing songs of freedom over there,” thought the Sultan sadly, his hands held out ready to pray. Then he suddenly slapped his knee. “Of course! That dervish’s face resembled the slain Prince Ahmet whose severed head was thrust before me. I saw the same sharp lines when Lieutenant Osman held it up by the hair. Is this some sort of nightmare, or is it a bad joke? Are people created in pairs?”

The Sultan’s first impulse was to send some guards to find the dervish and bring him back, but he thought better of it. After all, he was just a Persian mystic who spoke in silly rhymes, one of many poor bondsmen or Azeris who had ended up in Istanbul. Had he been Prince Ahmet, he would have been leading the rebels in Istanbul, not crossing the Bosphorus alone on a freezing cold night to bring him news of the rebellion. This man was just a wandering dervish hoping for a hand-out. Nevertheless, an Iranian who took such risks deserved to be rewarded for his trouble. He had performed a great service. The Sultan removed an emerald ring from his finger and summoned one of the doormen.

“Run after that dervish and give him this!”

The doorman found Falco walking with the Grand Vizier in Scutari Square.

“So you’d have had them all killed on the spot?” the Grand Vizier was asking with a smile.

“Yes Pasha! You too should cut down brigands wherever and in whatever guise they appear!” replied Falco seriously.

When they reached the doorway of the Grand Vizier’s pavilion, it was time to say goodbye. The Grand Vizier was looking thoughtful and anxious, obviously much worried by what he had just learned and aware that he would have to find a quick solution to this disastrous situation. However, it was now time to send Selman Abdal on his way. The Grand Vizier instructed him to exchange his wet clothes for the dry garments of a servant standing by the door. Before handing over the emerald ring sent by the Sultan, he toyed with it between his fingers and gazed into space.

"Selman Abdal," murmured the Grand Vizier. "I recall that Sultan Mustafa used to wear this ring. It's very valuable. If you ever sell it, don't let it go for less than three hundred gold coins. The Sultan very much appreciated your bringing him that news."

"I will never sell it, sir. The Sultan called it a reward, but I will keep it as a father's keepsake," said Falco, happily.

Falco was looking at the Grand Vizier with the expression of a devoted slave, at the same time thinking of all the questions he should have asked by now. How had the Grand Vizier come into possession of the Touch of Grace and Touch of Sorrow? What did he really think of the Prison Custodian? How had he developed the skill of unravelling mysteries? Why had Lieutenant Bindallı Mahmut not been interrogated about the corpses that were dragged out of the Golden Horn? And his most urgent question: would you help me find my wife's killers? However, Falco remained silent.

As a new day began over the seven hills of Istanbul on the other side of the Bosphorus, the Grand Vizier and Falco gazed at one another, each searching for answers to the hundreds of questions in their minds. Then they smiled, thanked one another and gave each other their blessings. It was a sombre scene.

"Be on your way, Selman Abdal, my friend. For goodness' sake, keep out of trouble!" said the Grand Vizier sadly, pressing a purse full of gold coins into the young man's hand.

"Your Excellency, I wish you well whatever happens. May God protect you."

Life was starting up again in Scutari Square as they parted.

"Good luck, Selman Abdal," muttered the Grand Vizier, and then wondered why he had said that, but could find no reason.

QUESTION 57
DOES THE OLD FRIEND HAVE ANY NEW SECRETS?

"Pit Jan, my friend, why have you not shown us any of your pictures this year? Yeye wants to see them," asked Hafız Çelebi.

Pit Jan rose eagerly and returned a few moments later with an armful of scrolls, which he put down in the middle of the room. They were watercolours on vellum, mostly the same size and ready for framing and selling in Flanders. The pictures were of different tulips in Hafız Çelebi's garden, each with the name and identifying features written beneath. Pit Jan had also made smaller versions of these pictures, which he kept to give to Hafız Çelebi, saying that one day they would be as valuable as the horticultural catalogues. He brought in a few from earlier collections, perhaps wanting to remind Hafız Çelebi of better days.

They were all doing their best to keep busy in order to block out the sound of distant gunfire. "Istanbul, my beautiful city!" murmured Hafız Çelebi wearily, beckoning to Yeye to kneel at his side while he leafed through the pictures. Hafız Çelebi seemed to be forcing himself to keep cheerful as he studied each picture and told Yeye exactly how and when each tulip had been grown, for what price and to whom it had been sold, plus any anecdotes he could remember, and turning to Pit Jan for confirmation.

They moved on to the larger watercolours, which were intended for hanging on walls, and Yeye lifted up a picture which, instead of a tulip, showed a seller of animal parts who was pursuing a feral cat and a beautiful woman coming towards him. Hafız Çelebi and Yeye stared in astonishment at Pit Jan, whose cheerfulness was suddenly replaced by acute embarrassment. Hafız Çelebi noted that the picture appeared to be set in the Envoys' Caravanserai courtyard, because the Column of Constantine at Çemberlitaş could be seen in the background.

"So, while we're sweating our guts out in the tulip garden, you're mixing with sellers of animal parts. Is that right, Pit Jan my friend?"

Pit Jan hurriedly tried to roll up his pictures, but Hafız Çelebi had already seen the next one and was stunned. It was a picture of a semi-naked woman in an enticing pose, wearing a sheer yashmak and diaphanous nightgown.

"Pit Jan?" exclaimed Hafız Çelebi sharply.

Pit Jan bowed his head at this rebuke, not knowing what to say. Hafız Çelebi and Stocky Yeye were very curious, but they sat in silence musing over the fact that Pit Jan's disappearance had coincided with the disappearance of the Touch of Sorrow and that the return of three turtles to the pool had coincided with his reappearance. Neither Hafız Çelebi nor Stocky Yeye had asked him what he had been doing during his absence. They had just waited, expecting that he would tell them everything one day.

Now, after some hesitation and at the bidding of Hafız Çelebi, Pit Jan sheepishly started to explain. It turned out that the woman in the picture was the reason he had been staying at the Envoys' Caravanserai until ten days ago. They had met through a mutual friend and the woman had wanted to learn about Hafız Çelebi's method of cultivating tulips. It was at this point that Pit Jan had become bewitched by her. The so-called friends had offered him a large fortune in return for spiriting away the Touch of Sorrow. When he did not accept their offer, they had kept him at the Envoys' Caravanserai for two months hoping to change his mind. During that time, the woman had repeatedly visited his room and asked him to paint her portrait, hoping that sight of her semi-naked would make him change his mind.

"But they got it anyway!" exclaimed Pit Jan. "Some men smuggled the Touch of Sorrow out of the auction house while she was keeping me distracted. In desperation, I told them that it had come from a twin bulb in the hope that they would go looking for the other one and give me a chance to somehow retrieve the Touch of Sorrow. I was terrified that you would regard me as the thief. I tried to delay their departure by adding a few finishing touches each day to the painting you see here. However, one day, I found both the man and woman had simply disappeared. The same day, I saw Count Aragon, whom I had encountered in the ballrooms of Austria, at the Envoys' Caravanserai holding one of our turtles. As I grabbed the turtle back, there was a commotion below in the central courtyard and I saw someone dressed in a black burka escape on horseback and another person who had been knocked to the ground. The strange thing is that the one on the ground was holding a dagger."

"Perhaps that's because he was about to kill someone important."

All heads turned simultaneously towards the voice in the doorway where they saw Hourikin. Yeye and Pit Jan rose to their feet. Hourikin kissed Hafız Çelebi's hand and ruffled Yeye's hair. She was relieved that she had said, '...to kill someone important' and had not mentioned the name of Prince Ahmet, or even Falco.

Everyone was pleased to have resolved the mystery of Pit Jan's disappearance. In the excitement, nobody thought to ask Hourikin what she had been doing at the Envoys' Caravanserai that day or who the important person was. Yeye was about to ask her if Falco had also been there, but thought better of it and they all sat down and continued discussing Pit Jan's pictures. Eventually, Hourikin explained that she had come to tell them that she had been with Falco the day before in Bayezit Square where a rebellion was brewing and that they needed to keep a watch out in case the rebels got as far as Kağıthane, adding that if Falco did not turn up there that evening, she would be going to Süleymaniye to meet him the following day. They listened to her in amazement and then discussed what precautions they should take. Yeye commented that they needed to check whether Şehnaz and her family were safe.

"The rebellion might have been quashed by now. After all, the Ottoman state isn't totally incapable," said Hafız Çelebi, trying to calm him down.

Once the sun had set, it started to rain and a sense of melancholy descended over them. Nobody said anything, but they were all wondering about Falco. Where was he? Had something happened to him? Had he done something crazy and tried to follow the Prison Custodian? Only Pit Jan, who still resented Falco for accusing him of being a tulip thief, showed little concern.

Stocky Yeye was torn between worrying about Falco and Şehnaz. Pit Jan was torn between a fantasy of taking the lady in his paintings away to tulip gardens in Flanders and remaining in his beloved Istanbul. Hourikin was torn between keeping her promise about Prince Ahmet and her impatience to see Falco the next day. Hafız Çelebi was torn between rejoicing that at least he was alive and mourning the fact that death could not be far away.

"Pit Jan, do another tulip picture for us. Since you stopped painting tulips, this house has lost its sense of peace and fecundity," said Hafız Çelebi, trying to dispel the silence with a little humour.

"But I'm not allowed to paint anything to do with peace and fecundity in this house, Hafız Çelebi. In fact, it's because your religion forbids such pictures that I continue to follow the path of Jesus Christ," replied Pit Jan, thinking Hafız Çelebi had been making some sort of oriental joke and responding in a typically western manner.

Hafız Çelebi interpreted this outburst as a reaction by Pit Jan to all the talk of rebellion.

"Pit Jan, my friend, are you under the belief that Islam forbids all pictures?" said Hafız Çelebi in an attempt to calm him down and restore harmony.

"But it's true, isn't it? Why do you have no pictures, Hafız Çelebi?"

"We have painters! What about all the illustrations and portraits in the pages of our books?"

"But they're stylised illustrations, not real portraits. You have no *paysages* or *naturemorts*."

Hafız Çelebi did not really understand these terms, but commented that they were merely different genres. He had learned during previous discussions with Pit Jan about the different techniques required to produce watercolours, murals and miniatures.

"But Pit Jan, is it true art to convey the exact likeness of a God-created object or person on paper or canvas?" persisted Hafız Çelebi. "An artist can never create anything that surpasses the beauty of God's own creations! Yet a muralist may depict a horse however he wishes, say with a strong body and spindly legs, or he might make a tulip black or cobalt blue. That surely

allows him more artistic freedom. The pictures you produce in the west are like imitations of God, while a muralist's work consists of images seen within his own heart. Am I not right? Tell me, which art requires more creativity and skill, that of the west or the east?"

"My dear Hafız Çelebi, you would never worship in a room containing imagery, would you?"

"Of course not. But that is not because we are against paintings. It's to prevent our shrines becoming like your churches. What do you call those pictures?"

"The icons? Or the landscapes?"

"It doesn't matter. My friend, wherever there are Bibles in the world there are churches, all with different images of Mary and Jesus. How can you worship in such places?"

"But Hafız Çelebi, we do not worship those images when we pray," insisted Pit Jan.

"I know, I know, Pit Jan. But we in the east are more sensitive about this. However, it doesn't give you the right to perceive this as a prohibition on images."

"My dear Hafız Çelebi, do you recall the picture of the woman you saw just now? I loved that woman, and I still do. But if she said to me, 'Pit Jan, if you love me, then you should worship me', do you think I would?"

"Perish the thought!"

"Then how can you think I would worship an icon?"

"Exactly! In our places of worship, we make sure there's no chance of that happening. We don't want people to become obsessed with faces and figures, like those fanatical clerics who claim to see visions."

"Just a minute," interrupted a voice. "Faces and figures are very important! Especially at the moment!"

Everyone in the room jumped up at the sound of Falco's cheerful voice. He looked a picture of happiness. While Istanbul was seething, he brought a note of relief and joy into the room. Hafız Çelebi had not felt so happy for a long time. He now had all the people he loved around him and he wanted to celebrate. He sent Yeye to fetch a chicken from the henhouse and told Hourikin to prepare some pilaf rice. That evening, they lit a fire by the Well of Souls and sat up late, laughing, joking, sharing their dreams and listening to each other's stories – making the most of each other's company before whatever sufferings and separations awaited them the following day. It was the kind of happiness that could never be repeated and everyone wanted to last for ever.

The rain subsided for a while and the moon appeared through the clouds to shine down on the still waters of the Golden Horn. It was a night when one wanted to embrace someone dear. Hourikin stood by the Well of Souls gazing at the gardens on the other side of the Golden Horn, musing on the fact that she had no one with whom to share such an embrace. The other five people each had their own lives to lead. When the walls of her beloved Istanbul began to tremble the following day, they would blend into the city and follow their separate paths. However, there was someone who needed her, someone whom she would have to help the next day. On his deathbed, Hourikin's father had said, "You will do this, even if it costs you your life!" He had dedicated her life to this task. After her mother's death, he had placed his infant daughter in the care of the only female member of the Three Crescent Society and Hourikin had spent her whole life gathering and assessing intelligence, telling people what they needed to know and keeping herself undercover like other members. However, none of the others were aware of her father's instructions, which had started with the words 'I'm about to tell you something no one knows except me' and ended with 'No one other than you must ever know about this'. Nor did they know that when her father said "You have to ensure his survival even if it costs you your life", he had been referring to Prince Ahmet.

Hourikin was deep in these sombre thoughts when she was startled by the sound of gravel being thrown into the Well of Souls to make ripples and create an image. She became aware of some hands placing a jacket over her shoulders.

"The wind is getting up. You'll catch a chill."

Hourikin thanked Falco and hoped he had not seen her wiping a tear from her cheek.

Meanwhile, Yeye was watching them from a distance and wishing he could be with Şehnaz. "People need a special friend at difficult times like this," he thought. "Anyone can be a friend when times are easy." It helped to have a friend with whom to share one's troubles on a night pregnant with the unknown. From boyhood, he recalled a story called ***The Lovers of Scutari***.

Postscript: The Lovers of Scutari

Once upon a time, there were two young people living in Istanbul named Abdullah and Aslıhan who loved each other. They would have been happy if only fate had given them an opportunity to meet secretly, to look at each other's faces, to sip the wine of love and let their breath mingle. They had never once kissed each other and had kept their love a secret. But it was a love that three hundred curtains could not conceal and it soon became evident. The girl's father did not think the youth sufficiently noble for his daughter and forced her to marry a pasha. The pasha took her far away to live in a house among the vineyards that lined the dusty road running from Scutari to Çamlıca. However, despite becoming his bride, Aslıhan kept avoiding her husband and refused to allow him into her room.

Meanwhile, Abdullah was at his wits' end. He tried to find out where Aslıhan was living and finally encountered a slave from the pasha's household. The slave knew all about Abdullah's love for Aslıhan and, out of pity, told him the way to her house. Abdullah sought out a friend and asked, "Come with me to find Aslıhan. My love for her is suffocating me, making all my days seem like night." His young friend replied, "I hear you and I accept your proposal. I will do anything you ask of me."

Without wasting time, they crossed over to Scutari in a caique, hired two horses and set off to look for the house in the vineyards where Aslıhan was living. It was autumn, the vines had been harvested and many of the owners had returned to Istanbul. Therefore, apart from a few houses with smoke emerging from their chimneys, it was not clear which were occupied and which were empty. They waited until evening when the lamps were lit. Then, they searched in silence until, just as dawn was breaking, they finally found the house they were seeking. When Aslıhan's husband left the house, Abdullah's friend muttered, "Go and knock at the door! If anyone else comes to the door ask for Aslıhan and say that you'll be waiting in the vineyard opposite." A stable boy opened the gate for Abdullah, who said he was bringing a message to the young lady of the house from the pasha and gave details of where they should meet.

After two hours, Aslıhan came to the meeting place. Abdullah was feeling very nervous and did not know what to do. His friend wanted to leave them alone, but Abdullah objected saying, "No, stay with us. Nothing untoward will happen between us." The young friend stayed and sat down some distance away, but near enough that he could hear what they were saying. Abdullah held Aslıhan's hand and they looked into each other's eyes. Tearfully, they told each other how hard their separation was to bear. Then they spoke of the depth of their love for each other and shared childhood memories. After a few blissful hours, Aslıhan said she must return home before anyone discovered that she was missing. Filled with longing, Abdullah asked her to stay a little longer. Just then, Aslıhan asked about the young friend who was still sitting at a distance.

"Do you think your friend would do something for me if I asked him?" she said.

"Anything you want!"

"Even if it were dangerous?"

"Even if it's dangerous," called out the friend. "Even if it costs me my life!"

"In that case, come over here. We will exchange clothes and you will go back to the house in my place. My room is the third on the right. Stay there without saying a word to anyone until evening, when my husband will pass a bowl of soup to you through the door. Make sure you keep your face covered and act demurely when you take the bowl. Then close the door. I will be back at dawn."

The young man did as he was bidden. He entered the house, found the room and shut the door. It was dusk when he heard a tap at the door. In his nervousness, he was slow to take the bowl of soup and it spilled on the floor. "Why are you still being so obstinate with me?" demanded the pasha angrily, grabbing a whip made of a single piece of deer hide cut from horn to haunch. Thinking it was Aslıhan, he peeled the shirt off the young man's back and started brandishing the whip. Despite the darkness, the young man kept his face covered and refrained from crying out lest his voice give him away. After several whippings, the household slaves and servants could bear it no more and begged the pasha to stop. The pasha was tired by now in any case. The nursemaid sent everyone away and admonished the victim of the beating, saying, "My lady, are you still in love with Abdullah? Do you feel no pity for your husband? If you would only give him a chance, perhaps..." The young man listened to this advice, suffering in silence and feeling sorry for Aslıhan. When she returned the next morning, he summoned up all his strength and left, without telling her anything. Whatever had happened that night would remain secret. Abdullah never spoke of it to anyone till his dying day.

Everyone should have someone to share their sorrows with at times like that.

QUESTION 58
WHAT DID YOU SAY?

The Sultan stood gazing out from Scutari Palace at the smoke enveloping his beloved Istanbul. Never before had he felt such sadness. The city, which for a quarter of a century he had striven to adorn with waterfront pavilions, fountains, drinking water founts and elegant government buildings, was burning down. Every dark thought of his life seemed to be caught up in the smoke being blown by the north-easterly wind from the waters of the Golden Horn to the Seraglio, where he had been born and raised. It was only four months since smoke like this had been smothering the districts of Galata and Kasımpaşa. Why did these fires keep happening? Was there a curse on the city? Could it be a divine warning? If so, how much was he to blame? If he had to repent, what was it for? What crimes did the people know about that he was unaware of?

His great-grandfather Süleyman the Magnificent had written in one of his poems, "The sultanate is a symbol of universal war." However, what he was now witnessing was not universal war, but the hideous outcome of degeneracy and putrefaction.

The flags flying from the firemen's tower in the garden of the Old Palace indicated that the fire was continuing to escalate. It had started at Balat and advanced into Cibali, Yavur Selim and Fatih. Preventing the spread of fire and extinguishing it was the duty of the janissaries and the fire brigade. They were meant to erect firebreaks to hold back the fire that was devouring the city's beautiful wooden houses like kindling. Once it took hold of one building, sparks quickly flew from its rooftop to ignite another, so homes had to be evacuated and the surrounding trees felled immediately. Normally, the firemen ran around doing their utmost to hold back the fire, but this time they were rushing into the burning buildings to retrieve anything of value which, instead of returning to their owners, they dispatched to their own depots. The term 'fire looting' was a new expression that had recently become all too commonly heard in Istanbul. Even the janissaries and firemen could not be trusted in this rebellion. It was each man for himself.

The Sultan thought sadly about the aftermath of the fire. Many victims would need help with timber and masonry, while others would have to rebuild their homes completely. It was always the same. Whenever Istanbul burned or suffered the destruction of an earthquake, the Sultan would have to use treasury coffers to pay for the rebuilding of the city. But this time, the treasury was empty and there were no reserves for disasters, whether caused by rebellion or fire. Istanbul, the envy of Asia and Europe and destination of choice for travellers from east and west, was disappearing in flames, while marauding gangs exploited the situation to destroy and plunder its picturesque mansions, villas, pavilions and residential streets.

The news delivered by Selman Abdal the previous night had left the Sultan unable to sleep. Many other people, on both sides of the Bosphorus, did not sleep that night – people such as the rebels at the Meat Market and the Hippodrome, the members of the palace household who had been left without protection, the gardeners and Halberdiers, and the youths at the palace school. And janissaries of all ranks had spent the whole night with eyes wide open, waiting to see what happened.

⁂

Meanwhile, a number of dignitaries were waiting anxiously for the Sultan in the bay-windowed reception room next door, tense and uneasy at the thought of being questioned. The Grand Vizier was fuming and looked damningly at the men around him. If only the Janissary Chief Commander had silenced the rebellious janissaries who were chanting, "That wily heathen infidel / who sees all life as just a riddle…" the previous day at Şehzadebaşı barracks, none of this would have been happening today. Admiral Abdi Pasha, who was standing with head bowed as if hoping to remain unseen, had also been too cowardly to execute his duty. If, on hearing news of the uprising, he had immediately taken one of his ships to the Golden Horn and lined his men up at the Dockyard, the rebels would have dispersed. As for the Istanbul Governor Mustafa Pasha, he had been a total failure. If he had sent a message to the clerics, pacified the scholars in the madrasas and addressed the public with a few inspirational words, they would not have dared to side with the mob. Chamberlain Mehmet Pasha had of course been with the Grand Vizier in Scutari the previous day, but if he had issued proper orders to the Prison Custodian on leaving Istanbul, nobody would have dared to disobey.

"So, you are the men on whom the security of the Ottoman Empire depends!" hissed the Grand Vizier, angrily. "You are the men to whom we entrusted our state. Where is the might of the army? What about the navy? Where is your show of strength? My city is running riot with vipers, centipedes, scorpions, mongrels, wild horses, wolves and ravens! My blood curdles and my flesh is torn apart, yet you remain with your heads down, unable to look me in the eye!"

They all remained with their heads down and mouths tightly shut.

"Sir," mumbled Istanbul Governor Mustafa Pasha eventually. "Bringing the brigands under control is no problem, but the people are crying out for sharia law. Yet sharia law forbids any raising of the sword without the Sultan's consent. It is regarded as a great sin!"

"Had the Sheikh ul-Islam said this, I would have understood. But you? You failed in your duty and now you threaten me with a fatwa!"

"God forbid, no! Perish the thought, sir! I'll cut off their heads and throw them at your feet!"

"Only pledge what you can achieve! We all know your capabilities."

"My artillery is at the ready in the Golden Horn, sir!" said Admiral Abdi Pasha.

"Do you propose to bombard the city, you idiot?" retorted the Grand Vizier angrily. "Would you slaughter the innocent to suppress a rebellion? Is that what we do in our country? Is that what we call justice?" Then, turning to the Chief Janissary Commander, he continued, "You spent yesterday attending meeting after meeting, at which we heard you were fed all sorts of rubbish. But was it not your duty to protect the city? You will pay for this!"

"Gentlemen," intervened Governor Mustafa Pasha. "This is no time for talk of punishment, what we need is a solution. Let's not quarrel."

"Pasha, order will never be restored by such contemptible men. If you trust them, you'll have brigands turning up and raising their flag under your nose tomorrow. Take him away!"

"But sir!"

"Pasha! Don't interrupt again!" ordered the Grand Vizier. "Haven't you said enough? People are dying in our smoking city, blood is being shed and bodies are probably filling up the dungeons. Enough is enough! Are we supposed to work with this man who yesterday was bellowing 'Down with the Sultan!'? Pasha, if our Sultan were to hear of this, he'd have us both executed, which would do no good at all. Take him away immediately! There's no more to be said. Is there no justice or law in this country? Do you think I, Grand Vizier of the Ottoman Empire, am so feeble that I am prepared to accept such nonsense?"

Hearing the Grand Vizier utter these words, Governor Mustafa Pasha summoned one of the guards waiting by the door and pointed to the Janissary Chief Commander.

"Take the gentleman away! Look after him. He's being exiled to another city tomorrow," whispered Governor Mustafa Pasha.

Just then, a messenger rushed in.

"Your Honour, there's a problem," he panted.

"Get up, man. What is it, pray?"

"Preacher İspirizade Efendi and your slave Janissary Commander Austrian Hasan Ağa ..."

"What's happened? Are they dead? Have they been killed?"

"Worse, sir. Much worse!"

"Spit it out then!"

"They have joined the rebels and raised the banner, Your Honour! And now they're at the door demanding an audience with the Sultan."

"Ah, this is bad news, gentlemen. The people will follow these idiots. They're like rabid dogs with friendly faces!" growled the Grand Vizier, before continuing in a softer voice. "Gentlemen, you must pledge your lives in the name of the Ottoman Empire and Istanbul, both of which are now in danger. The flames taking hold of the streets are spreading anarchy. We must extinguish these flames of unrest before chaos sets in among the timariots, cavalrymen, youths, men, women and children! We wasted time yesterday – today we must find a solution. Gentlemen, before we let them in, do you have any sensible proposals to make? What do these brigands want, anyway?"

"Sir," said Admiral Abdi Pasha. "All is lost if the people become corrupted by these men We have to act immediately!"

"Yes, the people are claiming that the rulers are blind to everything but their own pursuit of pleasure."

"Let's face it gentlemen, we are all guilty of this. However, we must focus on a solution instead of just pointing the finger of blame."

At this point, movement could be heard outside the door of the salon and Sultan Ahmet III entered, wiping tears from his eyes and looking severely at each person in the room. These powerful men, most of whom were in some way accountable for the rebellion and fires, stood with trembling knees, wishing the floor would swallow them up. Never before had they seen the Sultan looking so angry.

"Lala!" began the Sultan. "What's going on? We hear the janissaries have taken up arms and are threatening to wreak havoc on the Ottoman throne and raze Istanbul to the ground. Have you seen the black smoke engulfing our city? What are you doing about it? Where are our janissary slaves? Those ungrateful wretches whom we've nurtured with the blessing of Hajji Bektash. What are they going to do next? Where is the army that conquered Rhodes and marched on Belgrade? Where are the soldiers who brought glory to our ancestors Yıldırım and Yavuz in Kosova, Varna and Niğbolu? If they no longer exist, then tell me, Lala, what are you going to do?"

The Grand Vizier turned crimson, bowed his head and squirmed at being spoken to in this way in front of his own officials. The Sultan's words hit the men gathered in the room like a cannonball.

"Your Illustrious Majesty..." started the Grand Vizier softly, using this form of address for the first time in his life. "Preacher İspirizade and your slave Austrian Hasan Ağa have come to Scutari to seek an audience with you. They may know how to extinguish the fire in the city. If you wish to hear what they have to say, I will have them brought in. Perhaps we should see what they have in mind."

The Sultan indicated with his hand that they should be brought in and there was a long silence. No one dared to raise their head. Finally, Preacher İspirizade and Janissary Commander Austrian Hasan entered the room and flung themselves at the Sultan's feet to kiss the hem of his robe.

"There's no need for hypocrisy!" snapped the Sultan, pulling away his robe. "Contempt and panegyrics don't mix! All this resentment and rampaging will never restore order! What do you want to say to me?"

"Your Majesty, we see that you are sad and in distress. But this was never our intention. Your poor subjects have no complaints against you. They will be loyal to you until the day they die. We too are loyal."

"Very good! So what is your intention?"

"Our intention is to put an end to the profligacy and decadence of your statesmen. They have created a cesspool which is an offence to anyone with a clean conscience. Your impoverished subjects have suffered for too long. They have reached the end of their tether and their loyalty is lost. It is no surprise that they are now crying out for revenge. Your Grand Vizier is a spendthrift, shameless rascal."

"Do you know what you're saying, man?"

"I do, indeed, Your Majesty. Your son-in-law surrounds himself with buffoons. He cares nothing about the problems of the people."

"You audacious wretch!"

"I may be audacious and I may be a wretch, Your Majesty. But, whether you know it or not, your statesmen are responsible for this. The people are miserable, hungry, living in squalor and forced to pay impossible bribes. While the rich eat fillet steak, the poor live on barley water. What's more, there's the news from Iran. It was our very own leaders who sank the ship carrying veterans in the Black Sea, but they conceal their sins beneath an array of tulips in the gardens of Sadabat."

"Enough, if you value your head! Tell me, what do the people out there want?"

"Your Majesty, they want your Grand Vizier!"

The Sultan paced up and down between the door and the window as if he had not heard those last words and the Grand Vizier became so anxious that he fell to the floor, delirious with palpitations.

After a moment's thought, the Sultan announced, "Go and tell those brigands that I shall dismiss my Grand Vizier and I shall increase all service pay by a few gold coins. But they must stop this fracas. My city is on fire, which is even worse than the fire of rebellion. It's burning my heart."

"They also want your Chamberlain and Governor, Your Majesty."

Those who had been singled out began to tremble. The rest breathed a sigh of relief.

"Your Majesty, if you do not give them what they demand," said Preacher İspirizade boldly, "the people will not disperse and even I will be unable to stop them. The brigands are claiming to hold the poker that can make your government go up in smoke."

"Very well, my man, I will dismiss them too. As long as this rebellion is stopped."

"It's not dismissal that they want. They want the men themselves!"

"What did you say?" cried the Sultan, reeling at the realisation that the rebels were demanding the scalps of the men they had named. "My Grand Vizier is also my son-in-law, the husband of my daughter! How can you ask for his scalp? How can I possibly grant you that? My vizier is wise and cautious, knowledgeable and chivalrous. One in a million. And the Governor of Istanbul is my oldest servant. How can I sacrifice him?"

"Your Majesty, you refer to us as brigands, but the true brigands are here in your palace. While they have one hand in the butter and the other in the honey, your people outside go hungry. The Ottoman Empire is run by your son-in-law, who is feared by every provincial governor outside Istanbul. Were you to exile him or throw him into prison, it would be like entrusting liver to a cat. The insurgents are not mere rabble, they are the people who will govern your country. Your janissary slaves have forsaken Hajji Bektash and are in revolt, with the backing of both the guardsmen and the clerics. Nothing can save your Vizier and these other dignitaries."

As Preacher İspirizade said these words, an enormous roar could be heard outside. It was like a portent, as if someone there knew what was being said inside the palace and was directing the rebels accordingly.

"Down with the Vizier! Down with the Chamberlain! Down with the Governor!" they chanted.

"So my subjects really are consumed with fury," murmured the Sultan, pensively.

"Your Majesty, the people who want to be rid of the Vizier are your heartsick subjects," said Preacher İspirizade. "If you do not sacrifice these men, your daughter will be fatherless and your concubines bereft. It is no longer possible to suppress the masses. Sacrifice your slave the Grand Vizier and let the fires be quenched."

"This defeat has not been brought on by you. No, not at all," muttered the Sultan sorrowfully. "This is destiny. I saw it in a dream. You must both now swear on the Koran that you will make no further demands. Otherwise, I will see that your heads roll. No harm must come to my household or family. And anyone with designs on my throne will have their eyes put out!"

"Of course, Your Majesty. That is understood."

"In that case, convey this to the people and tell them to extinguish the fires. If I see or hear any more of this, I will not stop until your heads have been crushed to pulp. Do not fail, or you will have me to answer to!"

QUESTION 59
WHO IS THAT?

"That wily heathen infidel / who sees all life as just a riddle / to stop his pagan tarratiddle / we boiled the cauldron on the griddle! Saying this, I took my sword and then without another word, I swore to God I'd do the deed, nothing would my will impede," chanted a janissary proudly to Patrona Halil. "Sir, we reached the main cage and the keeper gave us four keys for the four cages. I opened them one by one and set the jailbirds free –gentlemen birds, chief birds, elder birds... The fourth one was especially secure and I needed the help of seven comrades to get the door open. Inside we found daredevils with blood-stained hands, glowering heroes, and wrestlers strong enough to lift a ton of cannonballs and snap chains weighing forty *okka*. We opened the cages and let those birds breathe."

This janissary was Binbereket of the 56th Brigade, who had travelled to Istanbul with Muslu Beşe. The cauldron he referred to was the cauldron of the renowned dervish Hajji Bektash, the four cages were the prisons at Ağakapısı, Rumelihisarı, Yedikule and Babacafer, and the birds were their inmates.

"But brother, the birds in those cages had teeth like handsaws and hands capable of ripping a man apart," replied Patrona Halil, humouring the janissary and waving away the firemen who looked ready to pounce him. "Each of them broke free of his chains and tumbled into this world from Mount Qaf. Any maiden they touch is scarred as if bitten by a mongrel dog and any they kiss is sullied as if by a leper. My brother, did you have no fear of these brutes?"

"They're waiting at the gate, sir. They wish to set eyes on their angel of deliverance, to bow down before him and kiss the hem of his robe, said Binbereket. "There is just one cage left, so with your permission, I shall go there immediately, sir."

"You have my permission, my brave man. Bring the prisoners here! There should be no sea between us," said Patrona Halil.

Everyone listening knew that Patrona Halil's reference to the sea meant that he was talking about Dockyard Prison and its traitorous inmates, like Kalender Baba, Daft Osman and Pockface Çomar.

On hearing Patrona Halil's last words, Falco, Stocky Yeye and Hourikin each had the same thought: Dockyard Prison also contained Aslan Ağa and Sergeant Bindallı Mahmut, the people they were seeking.

"Sir, at your service," volunteered Falco. "We would like to act as guards for Binbereket Ağa. I have fresh scars on my wrists from the chains at Dockyard Prison. I know every inch of that cage. I know where all the padlocks, chains, bolts and keys are kept. I know who to ask and who can be of use to you. Please sir, enlist us as guards. If you wish, I can bring along some other strong men."

"Young men, go and drink your milk," laughed Patrona Halil, noting that the three young faces showed no indication of ever having spent time in prison. "What are you doing here with this rabble? They'll devour you and spit you out! Then you'll be sorry!"

"Sir, my name is Falco. The strong men I speak of are Misty Doğan and Eagle Recep. We have no fear of the vultures you speak of."

Hourikin winced slightly at the thought of having to live up to the name Eagle Recep, while Stocky Yeye nervously twisted the moustache on his perspiring upper lip. Falco had spoken boldly, like a stoker, yet his heart was pounding as if it was about to burst. He was not sure if he should have given his own name, but feared that someone in the crowd at Ağakapısı Square might recognise him and wonder why he was concealing his identity if he invented another one. Patrona Halil scrutinised each of them as if he thought he recognised them from somewhere, but could find nothing remarkable about either Stocky Yeye in his felt waistcoat with its hawk motif or Hourikin in her shabby men's clothing.

"Sir," intervened Binbereket cheerfully. "Grant me these fine young men. I could use some falcons at Dockyard Prison. Let them prove themselves!"

Patrona Halil looked hard at the three volunteers for a few more seconds before waving his hand to indicate that Binbereket's wish was granted.

The group of eighteen riders raced towards Galata Bridge, where they were held up by a crowd. Time was against them, because the city was burning all around. Binbereket had insisted that the prison could be evacuated before nightfall, but they kept running into obstructions. Some non-Muslim Galata residents had gathered on the bridge and were refusing to let anyone pass into Galata from Istanbul. They were joined by firemen and boatmen from the dockyards who supported the non-Muslims by throwing people into the sea or beating them up and leaving them helpless on the ground. Those who did manage to cross the bridge were stopped in front of Kasımpaşa Wheelhouse. The Admiral there was responsible for protecting Galata and he usually managed to maintain good public order on that side of the Golden Horn even if there was unrest elsewhere in Istanbul. However, this time was different. A fight broke out between some dockyard thugs and sailors, which ended with the sailors manning control points and charging people to cross the bridge. Then suddenly, everyone was engulfed in darkness caused by the smoke from the subsiding fires mingling with the clouds hanging over the city. This sudden change from bright daylight to gloomy darkness frightened the people, who thought it must be an omen.

Binbereket was obviously pleased with the way things were going. He and his men paid no heed to religion, conscience or morals and wanted the turbulence prolonged rather than suppressed, so long as it was going their way. When they arrived at Dockyard Prison, Hourikin and Falco looked at each other despairingly, wondering how they were ever going to achieve anything with these men. Stocky Yeye was the only one to have any kind of rational plan. He told Falco to keep chatting and giving evasive replies to Binbereket, while Yeye and Hourikin pretended to be dumb and stupid. It was clear that Binbereket and his men were suspicious of them and checking their every movement, but they had to reach Aslan Ağa and Bindallı Mahmut, whatever happened. Meanwhile, the rebels were glad to have three extra people to help with the task of emptying the prison. They knew that many of the prisoners would be only too willing to join their ranks out of gratitude for being saved from the gallows. Even if they preferred to go their own way, they would contribute to the chaos in the city, which would also serve the rebels' purpose. Realistically of course, it was unlikely that any of the prisoners would be disciplined enough to be of much use, but they could be allocated minor tasks and disposed of after their work was done. The rebels could also exploit any skills such as horsemanship possessed by these prisoners, who could also be used as scapegoats if the rebellion proved unsuccessful.

Dockyard Prison was a magnificent stone building which stood on the Golden Horn between the Kasımpaşa ridge and Kulaksız. It contained hoodlums who had not seen the light of day for many years, including brutal Galata bandits, sea pirates and slaves who had turned to violent crime. Every Istanbul citizen knew that once inside that prison, a person was forgotten for ever. The Admiral's severity allowed no respite for its inmates, who were worked every day to the limit no matter what pain they suffered, so that they fell asleep completely exhausted in the evening. The intention was to prevent them digging escape tunnels, for which, if discovered, they were made to swing on the gallows that stood in front of the prison. Falco reflected how difficult everything had become, and how the fragile, delicate beauty of Nakşıgül and the Touch of Sorrow contrasted with this barbarous, brutalising prison he was about to enter.

Stocky Yeye pulled Falco aside to whisper his plan. Hourikin should not go inside because she was a woman and all their heads would roll if she failed to play her role convincingly. Falco should offer Yeye to Binbereket to use as he saw fit until Falco brought out and delivered twenty fit prisoners to him. That way, while Binbereket was under the belief that he was exercising control over Falco and his companions, Yeye would be able to monitor Binbereket in addition to looking out for Aslan Ağa and Bindallı Mahmut. When they were found, Yeye would offer to stay with them and try to ensure that Binbereket did not kill them.

"Binbereket Ağa, this is Eagle Recep," said Falco, pointing to Hourikin as they approached the prison gates. "He doesn't talk but has the eyes of an eagle. Put him on look-out and he'll give us a signal if anything happens in the Admiral's office."

"Very well, my one-winged Falco," replied Binbereket patronisingly, wanting Falco to appreciate that he had managed to empty the other prisons without the help of these youngsters. "In fact, you can remain here too, if you like. Don't worry about being on your own, all you have to do is guard the horses."

"But sir, no one would feel afraid under your command! Give me the chance to show what I can do. If I don't bring out at least twenty fine white falcons, then you can tell me to fly off."

"Ah! See how our falcon is sharpening his talons."

"Sir, don't scorn me. I never promise anything I cannot deliver and I always do what I say. Here, take my friend Misty Doğan as hostage," said Falco, indicating Yeye, "and don't give him back until I bring you twenty fit men. The lad's used to it, he's made of iron."

"Very well, tell the mute to hide in that tree and watch over the horses. He mustn't get caught up with the lions who are about to be freed from their chains."

While everyone was dismounting, Falco and Hourikin stayed behind. Falco pretended to be relaying what had just been said, but was in fact saying, "Don't forget, Bindallı is mine and Aslan Ağa is yours!"

It was six months since Hourikin had seen the man she was waiting for. As she climbed into the tree, she tried to picture him. His hair and beard were probably long and tangled like that of a mad lion by now. Meanwhile, Binbereket, Falco and the others kicked down the large wooden gate and entered the prison compound. The guard made no attempt to resist, but merely said, "The chief guard is in the first courtyard. Sort it out with him, and you can give him one from me!"

It was clear from Binbereket's loud swearing and the corpses left strewn on the ground behind him as he progressed though the series of gates into the prison that the head guard did not hand over his keys willingly. For two days, the smell of smoke had infiltrated the cells, and the bewildered prisoners had wondered what was going on. They had been praying for the prison roof to catch fire to give them a chance of escape, yet now the gates were being opened and they were being greeted with cries of "Fly away white falcons. Run brave men! Seek your redemption beneath the flag of Patrona Halil Ağa."

What a strange turn of events, thought Falco, that this unruly lot should be rushing out to seek redemption. Then, pressing his dagger against the face of one of the wounded guards, he offered to spare his life in return for directions to the cells of Sergeant Bindallı Mahmut and Aslan Ağa. He was told that Bindallı's cell was at the far end, but there was no one called

Aslan Ağa on that corridor. Rushing to the last cell, Falco looked through the hole in the door:

"I'm here, Bindallı Ağa! I bring you special greetings from the Prison Custodian," called Falco. "Wait there and don't make a sound."

Then, starting with the padlock on the adjacent cell, he began opening each of the heavy, creaking doors on that corridor, calling out, "Fly away white falcons. Run brave men! Seek your redemption beneath the flag of Patrona Halil Ağa."

When Falco had released all the other prisoners on that corridor, he made sure that the cell doors were left wide open before returning to Bindallı, who was squirming about and holding out his hand for the key to the padlock that kept his ankles chained to the wall. Falco signalled for him to keep quiet and pretended to search in the key bag he was carrying. After a moment, their eyes met and Falco swung the key bag and chain hard against Bindallı's face until he collapsed to the floor. Falco bound his hands behind him with a piece of cord and slashed a piece of cloth from his dirty breeches to stuff in his mouth. Then he fetched some manacles attached by a chain to a cogwheel from the torture room, put the manacles around Bindallı's wrists and turned the arm of the cogwheel. Once his prisoner could neither move nor shout, Falco opened the cell door as wide as it would go so that it appeared as if no prisoners remained on that corridor.

"Sergeant Bindallı, you are in my hands now," whispered Falco in his victim's ear. "You'll be all right if you behave yourself! But I'm setting this wheel so that the more you struggle, the tighter the manacles will be. So it's up to you. I'm going now. I have to see a friend!"

It took an hour to evacuate the prison. Meanwhile, Hourikin remained in the tree, watching the prisoners emerge and congregate outside the gates. Some brandished knives to settle old scores and eight murders took place within half an hour. Some prisoners came out yelling and screaming, reluctant to leave. Some exchanged small valuables, such as diamonds, emeralds, watches or jewelled cases, making Hourikin wonder how they managed to hide such things inside a prison. There was no sound from the stables opposite, which meant they must have been locked up, otherwise the prisoners would have gone straight in there to steal the horses. After all, no one needed a horse more than a prisoner on the run. Hourikin kept her hand firmly clasped round her pistol and reflected what a cruel and bitter world it was for those who thought they had a better chance of survival inside a prison than outside.

The gates were now wide open and the flow of escapees had dwindled to a trickle of sick and disabled prisoners. Only one had looked remotely like Aslan Ağa, but after careful scrutiny Hourikin decided it was not him. Finally, much to Hourikin's relief, Falco appeared at the gate with a line of prisoners chained together. He walked past the tree where she was hiding without even a glance at her. She just had to wait. Perhaps he wanted to find Stocky Yeye first. She waited.

⁂

While opening up the prison cells, Falco had talked continuously to the occupants. He had little difficulty selecting twenty men, all Istanbul residents, to whom he promised jobs as senior civil servants once the revolution was over, advising them to say as little as possible until they were with Patrona Halil. Falco marched his line of men up to Binbereket, who was standing with Patrona Halil's companions Kalender Baba, Daft Osman and Pockface Çomar. They were scrutinising the prisoners as they came out, cutting the chains of any they knew and telling the remainder to proceed towards the sea. But Stocky Yeye was nowhere to be seen

"So, Binbereket Ağa, twenty bushy-maned lions, as promised. Brave young men who would be proud to serve under Patrona Halil Ağa. Put them in smart uniforms and they'll look as handsome as any janissary officer."

"Well done Falco! Your power of persuasion matches the force of your talons," said Binbereket dismissively, pursing his lips.

"Indeed sir. These talons always deliver."

"Do they now? Hmm!" said Binbereket, looking around him. "Where's that young boy?"

Everyone looked alarmed, dreading to think what might have happened to a youngster in that mêlée.

"Wait," said Binbereket, trying to reassure Falco. "He's in there somewhere. He'll turn up any moment."

Falco hoped he was right. Binbereket assured him that Stocky Yeye had stayed inside the prison to act as watchdog and would soon appear.

Binbereket and his men started putting the remaining prisoners aboard a ship, unfastening their handcuffs but not the leg chains, saying "This ship will take you to Tekirdağ where you will be released from your leg chains and set free." Those who grumbled or refused to board were beaten and forced on to the ship anyway, and anyone who looked as if he might get out of control was not released from his handcuffs. The loading process was clearly going to take a long time.

Falco suddenly noticed a familiar pair of eyes among the prisoners boarding the ship. The eyes were staring at him and Falco racked his brains trying to remember who it could be. The man's tangled hair and beard covered most of his face, but those eyes! He knew those eyes. Falco needed to recall the man's identity quickly, before he disappeared inside the ship. He had definitely seen him before, but where? At the Pergola coffee house? At the janissary barracks? Or at Binbirdirek? No, none of those. Falco ran his hands through his hair, narrowed his eyes and bit his lip in an effort to recall who the eyes belonged to, but he simply could not remember.

It took half an hour to get all the prisoners on board, where they were then pushed down through a hatch into the bilge. As the familiar-looking prisoner was about to enter, he bent down to pick up the ball chained to his feet and looked for one last time at Falco, who suddenly realised with amazement who it was.

"No, no! Not him. Don't take him. He's mine!" cried Falco.

Everyone turned to look at Falco.

"What is it, my young pasha?" laughed Binbereket coldly. "If that's the youth you handed over to me, he's certainly aged a lot since entering that prison!"

"Binbereket Ağa, he's a relative of mine. I beg you, leave him with me. He has an aged mother who needs him. Please, do me this favour!"

"Very well, brother, we have a good collection of brigands. One is as good as another! But it means there is one short on the ship. What will you give me in return?"

"Apart from my life, all I have is three gold coins, Ağa!"

"Done!"

While the prisoners were being locked inside the bilge, Falco and Lanky Osman were embracing on the shore. Falco had just saved the man who had rescued him from the sea one year before. Then, he had paid three gold coins to this friend to whom he owed his life, but had promised him thirty. Falco knew that Lanky Osman would have died if he had boarded the ship, because putting prisoners into the bilge was like loading it with stones. It was a practice inherited from Italian ships and the knights of Rhodes, whereby when the ship reached open waters, in this case the Marmara Sea, the captain and his men would puncture the hull in the dark of night, having set a barrel of gunpowder to explode with a half hour time delay. They would then jump into the only dinghy on the ship and row back to Istanbul. In no time at all, the prisoners would end up at the bottom of the sea, still in leg chains. Who was going to enquire about one missing ship while the city was burning and the janissaries were staging a revolution? Falco could not help wondering whether the crimes of the brigands on the ship were against the state or the revolutionaries.

"I left your young friend Misty Doğan in the wing for prisoners sentenced by the Chief Judge and Grand Vizier," snapped Binbereket. "I haven't seen him since, so he must still be in there. Go quickly and look, before he falls into the hands of thugs. He's much too young and fresh to be left with them!"

Falco was angry, both at Binbereket's offhand manner and the implications of his last words. But he could do nothing about that now.

"Binbereket Ağa, if I don't have Misty Doğan with me when I come out, you'll be sorry!" yelled Falco as he ran back towards the prison gate.

⁂

The prison compound was deserted apart from one of Binbereket's men who was retrieving horses from among the dead and wounded. At the gates, Falco released Lanky Osman from his leg chains and handcuffs.

"My friend, Lanky Osman Ağa! Stay! I still owe you twenty-seven gold pieces!"

Lanky Osman embraced Falco, removed his prison shirt and replaced it with one from a guard lying dead on the ground, and started walking away

"You owe me nothing! Someone else has already paid me the thirty gold pieces!" he called out, disappearing into the darkness.

Falco ran after him wanting to know what he meant, but was suddenly confronted by Hourikin.

"Where's Stocky Yeye?" she demanded.

"I should be asking you that. You were on lookout weren't you?"

"I haven't seen Aslan Ağa or Yeye. But I've seen plenty of violence."

"I was told Yeye might still be inside."

"Hmm, we must be careful. There may be others in there."

For a second time, Falco went in through the prison gates, this time with Hourikin. They spared the lives of the few wounded guards who still lingered there, advising them to go home if at all possible, but they had to maintain the appearance of being rebels so, once inside, they called out to ask if anyone was there. Some of the torches that hung on the walls had gone out and others were about to, but they managed to find a couple that were still alight and started searching the building. The only sounds to be heard were the echoes of their own voices. Falco locked the door to one of the corridors and whispered to Hourikin that Bindallı was in one of the cells there. Eventually, they decided there was no one else left inside.

"Yusuuuuf! Yearning Yusuf!" shouted Falco.

Hourikin looked at him as if to say, "Who is that?"

"Don't you know who that is?"

"No, I don't."

Falco called out Yusuf's name again.

"Who-o-o is calling?" came a playful response and Yeye suddenly appeared in front of them.

They all embraced one another.

"You woke me from my daydreams," laughed Stocky Yeye.

"Dreams? In a prison?" asked Hourikin.

"Yes, I was dreaming of my mother. She used to tell me a tale called ***When Zeliha had Yusuf thrown into prison***. She'd say, 'My son, if hundreds of people are weeping in a house of mourning, the most moving cries will be from the one who is most grief-stricken.'".

"This is no time to grieve over a story, Yeye. Where have you been? We were worried."

Yeye laughed.

"How did you know the rest of my plan?" he asked.

"What plan?"

"On the way here, we planned how we'd separate to carry out our individual tasks, but we didn't decide how we'd meet up."

"Yes, so..."

"Well, we've met up just as I planned, except that you were later than I expected."

Yeye's plan had indeed been designed so that they would meet inside the prison after Binbereket and his men had left. Falco gritted his teeth, shook his head in exasperation and muttered, "I always did envy that intelligence of yours!"

"Never mind the flattery. Let's get out of here," said Hourikin.

"Wait, wait. We have company," said Stocky Yeye, holding his torch over a man lying face downwards with his hands tied behind his back. Helping the man to his feet, Stocky Yeye continued, "This is the bastard who told Veyis Ağa that I was an unsuitable match for his daughter Şehnaz. He's the reason I was beaten, separated from my mother and thrown into the lunatic asylum. Now at last, he's getting his just reward!"

When the man was pulled to his feet and Falco and Hourikin saw his face, they both cried out, "Aslan Ağa!"

Postscript: When Zeliha had Yusuf thrown into prison

It is said that, when Zeliha had Yusuf thrown into prison, she started to bemoan their separation. She would visit the prison from time to time, ostensibly to check that her judgement had been correct, but in fact to relieve her suffering. If she found Yusuf asleep, she would wait by his cell, watching him; if she found him awake, she would give him a reproachful look and reprimand him. One day, she realised she was pining for the sound of his voice, so she summoned a slave, saying, "Go to Yusuf and knock him to the ground. Then, whip him so hard that his cries are audible from here." The slave set off to fulfil these orders, but on seeing Yusuf's handsome face was unable to do so. There was a fleece in the cell, which the slave spread on the floor and started beating. With every stroke, Yusuf let out a scream and Zeliha cried out:

"Beat him faster, beat him harder!"

Finally, the slave pleaded with Yusuf, "Master, if Zeliha finds no whip marks on your back, she will undoubtedly kill me. Bare your shoulders, grit your teeth and allow me to inflict just one stroke!"

Yusuf removed his shirt and the slave whipped him so hard that he fell to the floor. That time, the moment Zeliha heard Yusuf's cry, she called out, "Enou-u-ugh!"

QUESTION 60
WHAT DID THE VOICE OF COMPASSION SAY?

"This rain will get rid of the smell of burning that hangs over the city," thought Hafız Çelebi. He had removed the zinc covering from the turtles' pool, opened the gate to the Well of Souls and was cleaning around the graves. He did this every autumn so that visitors could benefit from the first rainfall of the season. However, this year, he worried that the rain might spread the smell of death, rather than wash it away. Wishes, however strong, could never sway the course of fate, which he believed to be an essential part of life. He was also convinced that humans were slaves to hope and only set free when that hope was gone. Over the past few days, Hafız Çelebi had retreated into a fatalistic state of mind and started making serious demands of God, whereas previously, he had always paid more heed to what he thought God demanded of him.

The reason for Hafız Çelebi's melancholy was that Stocky Yeye had still not returned home. He was not so worried about Falco and Hourikin, but Yeye was still young and he was witnessing a rebellion for the first time in his life. Hafız Çelebi just hoped that his young charge had not been led astray and corrupted by any wealthy gentlemen or rich playboys.

"Don't torture yourself like that, Hafız Çelebi!" said Pit Jan. "He's no fragile mother's boy! Although, of course, he is young and single!"

"Are my feelings about Yeye so obvious?" Hafız Çelebi wondered to himself, nodding gratefully at Pit Jan. His heart filled with happiness at the thought that feelings are only outwardly manifest if based on genuine love. He now rejoiced and felt proud that he loved Yeye so much. It had been many years since he had felt emotion like this. His feelings for Yeye were different from those he had for Pit Jan, with whom he had enjoyed friendship and mutual respect for many years. Yeye treated Hafız Çelebi as a father, who had unfortunately been unable to protect him in the midst of this rebellion. Şehnaz was undoubtedly worrying about him too. She seemed a good girl and, even though she barely uttered a word, she entered the hearts of everyone who met her.

For two hours, Hafız Çelebi remained motionless, his eyes fixed on the approach to the house. When Yeye finally arrived, he looked shattered and scared. This was not, as Hafız Çelebi supposed, because of the rebellion, but because of what he had witnessed when he walked past the Haseki Insane Asylum.

Whenever Istanbul caught fire, the buildings least damaged were those built of stone. When Yeye had passed by the asylum, he noticed that the flames had been whipped up by the wind and were scattering sparks on to the wooden roofs of nearby houses. People were standing in the street, watching hopelessly as their homes burned down and praying that the fire would not spread to Haseki Asylum. They tried in vain to create a corridor through the flames to get to the Asylum, but the flames blocked their way as effectively as a military defence line. Hundreds of people had now congregated, praying and weeping. Inside the asylum, lunatics rattled their chains and cried out for help, but those on the outside were unable to get in to help them. At one point, half-naked patients were seen leaping over flames trying to escape, some with their hair on fire, some with their garments in flames, and others so confused that they did not even attempt to quench the flames on their burning clothes. It was a heart-rending scene. Some patients laughed hysterically, some shouted themselves hoarse and others attacked each other. Onlookers tried to douse them with buckets of water as they emerged from the building, but in their confusion the lunatics tried to avoid getting wet. Chaos erupted as people started chasing after them to put out the flames. It had then occurred to Yeye that, if people could get out of the building, then it must be possible to get in. He was about to hurl himself forward in an attempt to enter, but was stopped by some physicians and nurses who told him that it was too late, because the flames had set the vestibule alight and the lead on the domed roof had begun to melt. The cells had been unlocked, but there had been no time to unchain the patients. The nurses said that some patients were afraid of the flames and were attacking anyone who came near them. At this point, Yeye knew he had to get inside. He had edged forward, but it was impossible to get past the flames and he retreated with singed eyebrows and eyelashes. When he tried again, people held him back and prevented him from trying again.

Seeing Yeye's blackened figure and singed eyebrows, Hafız Çelebi immediately fetched a damp cloth to wipe his face, hands and arms. Yeye was still haunted by the sound of screaming voices echoing in his ears. For two hours, he had listened to the shrieks change in tone as helpless patients were consumed by the fire, some struggling to break free of their chains, some silently submitting to the flames or even playing with them, unaware of what was happening. Yeye imagined them talking to the flames, hugging them, embracing them, and welcoming them with open arms like a lover. Perhaps the fire that burned their bodies felt less painful than the fires that had raged in their hearts for so many years. Perhaps the fire had not even touched them. Perhaps, instead of burning them, the fire had melted away their chains. Who knew what had happened inside? Only the fire knew the answers. Perhaps the fire had witnessed ***Leyla sitting next to Majnun*** in there.

"I want to weep," was all Yeye could say as he fell into Hafız Çelebi's arms, emotionally and physically drained.

Postscript: Leyla sitting next to Majnun

One day, Majnun was seen sitting on a wall, his legs dangling. He looked very happy and cheerful on the mud wall. He was talking to himself, sometimes laughing, sometimes crying. Seeing him in this condition, passers-by made fun of him. Finally, a man of compassion walked past and noticed Leyla sitting next to Majnun. He realised that he had witnessed a rare secret and counted his blessings, saying:

"I've lived a very long time and I'm very tired. But I have finally seen this couple happy together! Thank you, God!"

QUESTION 61
FOR WHOM WAS THE TRAP INTENDED?

As soon as the Prison Custodian saw the corpse of Grand Vizier İbrahim Pasha, he knew that matters were going to get worse. Janissary Commander Austrian Hasan and Patrona Halil were waving a flag from one of the minarets of Sultan Ahmet Mosque, doing their best to encourage new arrivals to join in with the roars of the masses that had congregated in Bayezit Square. The hamam loincloth flags had now been exchanged for janissary and cavalry banners. A quarter of Istanbul's citizens seemed to be there in the square to see the practically naked and now barely recognisable corpse of İbrahim Pasha being dragged along the ground by ferocious janissaries, accompanied by cries of "Uncircumcised!", "Infidel" and "See, he kept a secret faith!" It was a brutal scene that caused some observers to mutter despairingly, while others were secretly pleased.

Falco and Hourikin waited to see what the Prison Custodian would do next because, although he gave the appearance of being on the government's side, Falco knew of his secret dealings with the janissaries and assumed that his next stop would be either at Binbirdirek or Şehzadebaşı janissary barracks. Judge İshak had instructed the Prison Custodian, the Janissary Chief Commander and the Chief Executioner to restore law and order, and had arranged for police outposts to be set up around the edges of the city. Anyone close to İbrahim Pasha, or the other men seized by the janissaries and hanged from the plane trees in Sultan Ahmet Square, was either in hiding or had escaped, and the squares had filled up with their antagonists.

Falco was monitoring the Prison Custodian's every move. When he saw him turn into Divan Road, he leant towards Hourikin, whispering, "Yes! The time's come. Let's go!" and they started running towards Bayezit via the Poultry Market and Çemberlitaş. Hourikin slipped into a community garden built by Sultan Bayezit Khan, opened a bundle she had been carrying and donned a long coat, shalwar and yashmak. Meanwhile, Falco continued running towards a house in Laleli, where Stocky Yeye and Pit Jan had arranged to wait for him.

This was their last chance. They would never find out the truth unless they discovered what the Prison Custodian, Sergeant Bindallı Mahmut and Aslan Ağa had been up to.

"Sir! Heed the advice of a poor slave and you will benefit," said Hourikin, using all her feminine guile as she sidled up to the Prison Custodian, who was accompanied by two colleagues and followed by a small group of looters.

"What do you want, my dear lady?" he asked gently, clearly taken in by her manner.

"It's confidential," whispered Hourikin, leaning so close that he could feel her warm scented breath.

The Prison Custodian gave a signal for his companions to walk on ahead, whereupon Hourikin took hold of his hand and squeezed a pear-shaped diamond into his palm.

"It's treasure, sir. But I can't take it on my own," she whispered.

"This is the Ottoman state, girl! Who is taking whose treasure?"

"Sir, I used to paint faces in the private rooms at Bayezit Hamam. There are certain things I know about. I have lived in poverty since I was brought from Wallachia ten years ago. I swear, this is my first piece of luck and I want to do business with you, because I know you are skilled in these matters. If you're not interested, there are many dealers at the Covered Bazaar who would be."

The Prison Custodian understood correctly what she was intimating. This girl was in possession of jewels that belonged to some rich lady and, if this diamond was anything to go by, it was probably a valuable collection. He assumed that the diamond came from a collection which the girl had exchanged for fakes made by dealers in the Covered Bazaar. Seeing him hesitate, Hourikin looked around her with an air of impatience.

"Sir! What are you waiting for?" she said, with feigned indifference.

"Whose is it and where did you get it?"

"It came from Zerefşan Mansion in Laleli. But this is just between the two of us."

The Prison Custodian took Hourikin's hand, returned the diamond and gave her a stern look to mask his satisfaction. Hourikin's flirtatious smile had given him the impression that he had in fact acquired two jewels rather than one. Sometimes, revolutions yielded such opportunities and they needed to be appreciated. After all, it would be easy enough to dispose of her once he had his hands on the treasure. Who would look for a Wallachian slave? Especially during a revolution. Patrona Halil would be very pleased, because his greatest need at that time was for gold and treasure, and the Prison Custodian knew full well that he needed to curry favour with Patrona Halil now if he was to secure a senior position after the revolution.

"Let's go, lady," he said, squeezing Hourikin's hand.

"Keep it," said Hourikin, refusing to take back the diamond. "There are others where that came from and I'll take some of those."

The Prison Custodian dismissed his men with a nod of the head. Hourikin now felt more at ease, because wandering in areas patrolled by rebels when dressed in women's clothing was most uncomfortable. Still, she thought, Falco had waited a whole year for this day, the anniversary of the undeserved blows to his face, and he was about to get his own back.

As they walked towards Zerefşan Mansion, Hourikin spun the Prison Custodian a tale about the occupants being an elderly, semi-invalid couple whose son had fled the city at the start of the revolution, leaving them and the household valuables in the custody of herself and the butler, Hüsmen Ağa. As soon as the son left, Hüsmen Ağa had tried to molest her and make off with all the valuables so, the previous evening, after pretending to go to bed, she had got up and killed him with a dagger. Hourikin told this story in order to gain the Prison Custodian's sympathy and to convince him that she needed protection. However, Hourikin knew that at least ten men would be waiting outside the mansion gate, ready to break in if she did not come out safely. They had made their plans very carefully and were implementing them accordingly. Zerefşan Mansion backed on to Kalfakadın Mansion, and Hafız Çelebi's old friend Dukakinzade Cemaleddin Molla had given them the keys to these houses for three days. The plan was that they would enter one house and come out through the other. Thus, while the Prison Custodian's men were waiting outside Zerefşan Mansion, they would be heading down a back street towards the bridge. The owner of one of the houses was still at his summer home between Kuzguncuk and Beylerbeyi on the other side of the Bosphorus. The other owner had set off with his wife two months previously to sail round the Black Sea coast. Falco and Hourikin not only had the keys to the houses, they also had notes from Hafız Çelebi to the respective butlers inviting them to Kağıthane, where Hafız Çelebi was to entertain them for two days while Pit Jan, Hourikin and Falco captured the Prison Custodian.

"Sir! I am a poor destitute slave!" pleaded Hourikin, clutching the Prison Custodian's arm as they entered the garden of Zerefşan Mansion. "I was only nine years old when I was snatched from Wallachia and brought here. I have nobody. For ten years, I've led a terrible life, being passed from one awful household to another. I just want to lead my own life. You can take me, as well as the jewels. If you do not want me for yourself, then at least give me to a decent master and save me from this life."

"It would be foolish person who let a fresh young girl like you slip through their fingers. But first, let's have a look at these jewels."

"You will see them very soon, sir."

Within two minutes, they had opened the door into a tastefully furnished salon and the Prison Custodian was rolling on the carpet, having been bludgeoned on the head by Pit Jan, and further stupefied by the chemical Falco was pressing to his nose. After that, it was a question of binding his hands and feet and stuffing him into a strong sack. The Prison Custodian was still struggling when he was carried on Pit Jan's back from Zerefşan Mansion into Kalfakadın Mansion, but he was completely unconscious when they came out on to the street at the back. Falco and Hourikin laughed to think of the men waiting at the front of Zerefşan Mansion, wondering what had happened to their master.

Pit Jan then climbed on to a hay cart attached to a grey nag, which he drove towards Dockyard Prison. He was pleased to have been included in the plan, because it had dispelled the coolness between himself and Falco. Meanwhile, Hourikin changed her clothes yet again and Falco prepared some horses. The city was still reverberating with the roars of the rebels, while traders at Tahtakale were closing up and lowering their shutters. People milled around on street corners, in squares and alleys, desperate to get away and venting their anger on either the Sultan or Patrona Halil's gang. Crowds were massing in front of the bakeries and banging on the doors of food shops and depots, and the sound of animals bleating behind the butchers' shops was whetting the appetites of those preparing to plunder. The guards on Galata Bridge were scrupulously implementing their strict orders, but paid scant attention to the passing of a hay cart followed by two uniformed janissaries.

Stocky Yeye was still waiting in one of the cells at Dockyard Prison. Hearing the sound of footsteps in the dark corridors, he extinguished his torch and went to the door to listen for a particular sound. When he heard the sound of an owl, he was to respond with the high-pitched squeak of a bat. To ensure that Aslan Ağa and Sergeant Bindallı Mahmut made no noise, he had retied their gags and tightened their clamps another cog. The footsteps were getting closer. Stocky Yeye clasped his dagger, aware that they could belong to prisoners returning for shelter or to men seeking Bindallı and Aslan Ağa. He had to be careful. Suddenly, Stocky Yeye heard the sound of something slithering along the floor. He clasped the fingers of his left hand in the palm of his right hand, put his thumbs together and raised them to his lips.

Everything fell silent in the corridor. Hearing the sound of a dove at the other end of the corridor made them all shudder. Pit Jan knew that doves were afraid of snakes, so he responded with a hissing sound and waited to hear the flapping of wings. The ensuing silence meant it had not been a real dove, in which case, it was fine to wait. Meanwhile, Yeye was still waiting to hear the sound of an owl. They were each beginning to appreciate the reality of being in a prison. Prisons were assumed to be places that resounded with shouts and screams, whereas it was the silence that was unbearable. Within those damp walls, endless, desolate nights of waiting broken only by the occasional cry of an innocent prisoner were followed by long days of darkness, during which inmates dreamt of life in the outside world where people went to work in the morning, closed their shops in the evening, lit their lamps when it grew dark, tended their gardens and inhaled the scent of flowers.

Pit Jan felt movement inside the sack on his back. Opening it, he pressed his dagger to the man's throat signalling him to be still. The Prison Custodian blinked, trying to work out what was happening and who was standing over him. As he struggled to recognise his surroundings, he tried to loosen the cloth covering his mouth. Hourikin decided it might be best to let him cry out and untied it. The Prison Custodian's scream echoed round the prison walls, reverberating into the cell where Yeye was waiting. It was not a voice that Yeye recognised, so he knew he still had to be cautious. However, he was fairly certain that the cry was intended for his ears.

"Who's there?" called Yeye, walking warily down the corridor.

"You nearly frightened me to death!" replied a familiar voice.

After concealing the cart and giving some hay to the horses, Pit Jan's task was to observe the interrogations. Falco, Hourikin and Yeye started questioning their three prisoners, the Prison Custodian, Aslan Ağa and Sergeant Bindallı Mahmut, in three adjacent cells.

QUESTION 62
WHICH WAY WILL THE WINDS OF DESTINY BLOW?

The Sultan gazed sorrowfully across the Bosphorus at the misty Scutari horizon as the first pink rays of sunlight began to sparkle on the water surrounding Seraglio Point. Glancing down, he could see his courtiers and halberdiers wandering anxiously beneath the tall poplars and ancient plane trees in the palace gardens. Was he right to return from Scutari? He had spent three sleepless nights with Supreme Judge İshak Efendi and three guards considering what to do. That morning, on the way back from Scutari, he had been forced to listen to the escalating shouts of the people mingle with the creaking of the cart carrying the ghastly corpses of Grand Vizier İbrahim Pasha, Admiral of the Fleet Kaymak Mustafa Pasha and his much loved Chamberlain, each with black and blue marks on their necks. The Sultan was filled with remorse, having just received news that their remaining bits of flesh and bone had been put into a sack and secretly buried without even a prayer, such was the savagery of the rebels.

Government dignitaries had already gathered in the Domed Stateroom. As the Sultan emerged from his office, he noticed men moving on top of the minarets of Ayasofya Mosque. They were obviously spying on the palace, which suggest that the rebels had not yet finished. From now on, he vowed to himself, he would dictate how far they went. However, when he arrived at the Stateroom, it became clear that the plans drawn up in the sanctuary of his office were not feasible. Some of Patrona Halil's men and Muslu Beşe had already arrived and were arguing with ministers. Preacher İspirizade was also with them, acting as mediator. Absolute silence descended when the Sultan entered. Everyone stood motionless, their hands clasped in front of them.

"Your Majesty, our great and holy Sovereign! Your janissaries and your people are very displeased with you," pronounced Freckled Mustafa, as the Sultan moved towards his throne.

"Why is that, sir?"

"Instead of sacrificing your Grand Vizier, you sent us the corpse of Chief Furrier Manol, Your Majesty!"

The Sultan clenched his fists and scowled. His lower lip began to twitch. Freckled Mustafa took a timid step backwards and everyone bowed their heads. Like the Sultan, they all knew that the strangled corpse left outside the palace the previous day had indeed been that of Grand Vizier İbrahim Pasha. The Sultan had personally caused his daughter to become a widow, yet now the rebels were now claiming that the deceased was a furrier named Manol. İbrahim Pasha had a red beard, whereas

Manol had a blond moustache, blue eyes and no beard. If they did not believe him to be the Grand Vizier, why tie his corpse to the tail of a horse to be torn to shreds by being dragged along the ground to the Imperial Gate? Something was afoot. The Sultan glared at the men around him, each of whom was staring at the floor.

"What ungrateful bastards you are. What base, degenerate wretches!" cried the Sultan, his anger intensifying. "How can you be so insolent as to call me a liar when I am grieving for my Vizier whom I delivered into your hands? Where is your conscience? Have you no dignity or decency? What is this nonsense?"

"Your Majesty!" said Preacher İspirizade in a conciliatory tone. "Your subjects say they no longer want you!"

"Really? Well, you're clearly just the monkey! You can tell them I said so!"

At this point, Chief Judge İshak Efendi and the guards reached for their daggers, but the Sultan placed his hand on the judge's wrist as a sign of restraint.

"Your Majesty," ventured Janissary Commander Pallid Hasan, "We're just a few slaves who would give our lives for you. But Patrona Halil Ağa and his colleagues are united in this matter. If we tried to change their minds...."

"Enough grovelling, man. If it is me they are rejecting, why take away my beloved Grand Vizier yesterday? Because he was trying to raise an army to steal your thunder? Is that your problem? Do you expect the might of the Ottoman Empire to remain in your hands forever? Is that what you crave? If so, why not tell the Sheikh ul-Islam to issue a fatwa against me instead of my vizier?"

"Your Majesty! He could not issue a fatwa for your removal yesterday. It was only today that your lie became known, which is why your Sheikh ul-Islam has issued a fatwa."

Only then did the Sultan realise that they had come to depose him, to remove him from the throne. It was a Turkish custom originating in Central Asia that a person proved to be a liar could not be a legitimate ruler.

"Indeed? And what was my lie?"

"You delivered Manol's corpse in place of the Grand Vizier's!"

"Ah, I see! You had everything very well planned!" said the Sultan. "Well, well! This is in revenge for the soldiers who died in Tabriz, of course. Otherwise, even you vile and despicable men would not have stooped to this."

The Sultan remained silent for a while, his eyes fixed on a single point as he thought about his next move.

"I will surrender my throne on condition that no harm is inflicted on my children and family," said the Sultan gently, almost conversationally. "I will swear to this on the Koran before you all. Then, you must bring out my successor, whoever he is, from the princes' quarters!"

"Your life is our life. Your honour is our honour," said Commander Pallid Hasan. "You and your family will be welcome at Çırağan Palace. May your nephew Prince Mahmut Efendi be consecrated to the sacred throne of Osman. Today is Friday, our holy day, and our new Sultan must be enthroned and presented with the Imperial sword in the presence of our late Eyüp Sultan. A power vacuum is inadvisable because of the unrest in the city."

The Sultan signalled his intention to leave and Judge İshak prepared to accompany him. However, the Sultan whispered, "You've done enough! Stay here. You have my blessing."

Just then, the Sultan saw his Chief Eunuch and Chief Executioner walking arm in arm with his nephew Prince Mahmut. The men on either side of the prince could not bring themselves to look at their former master and stopped in the doorway. The prince was trembling. He obviously had no notion that he was to become sultan and probably thought he was about to enter a trap and be killed. What a strange turn of events, thought the Sultan, remembering how he too had entered the Domed Stateroom frightened and trembling when Mahmut's father was toppled from the throne. The poor young prince displayed a tragic mix of fear and hope. Having lived a quiet life as a composer, calligrapher and poet in the confines of the princes' quarters, he could not have known that he had been brought to the Domed Stateroom to be enthroned as the twenty-fourth Sultan of the great Ottoman Empire. Otherwise, would he have allowed himself to be sacrificed to the will of these vultures? Forgetting his own situation for a moment, Sultan Ahmet felt pity for him. At the same time, he recalled the name of Prince Ahmet and felt pleased that at least he had lived and died far from all this treachery. It would be a matter for debate which of the two brothers had been more fortunate. The Sultan had no way of knowing whether Prince Ahmet, whom he thought to be dead, had had designs on the sultanate. It was now the other brother, who had never shown any such inclination, who was to become sultan. Had Prince Ahmet been saved from a fate worse than death? Would Prince Mahmut suffer by living? With a heavy heart, the Sultan kissed the forehead of the young prince before him and put a hand on his shoulder.

"Young man, your late father Mustafa Khan was, like me, delivered into the hands of despicable government officials such as these. We were both deposed from the throne to which you are about to ascend because we entrusted matters to them. Learn from our example. Do not submit to anyone. Be strong, but just. Be fair to those in need. Respect the situation of the poor. Take money from no one and do not do as I did. I entrust my princes to your care. May the glory of the sultanate protect them! May the sultanate continue for ever! Long live its power and glory!"

Trying to conceal his tears, Sultan Ahmet turned to go down the dark corridors that led to the simple cobbled area in front of the princes' quarters. Observers in the harem quarters who saw the Sultan turn to leave the Stateroom alone finally understood the reality of the situation. Meanwhile, members of the Ottoman household waited in despair as Commander Pallid Hasan began reassigning their positions to the wretches on a list he was holding.

Any shops not yet plundered remained closed and people were still breaking into premises wherever possible in order to steal bread and food. Muslu Beşe was nagging Preacher İspirizade to start imposing some sort of order.

"Wait, sir," insisted Preacher İspirizade. "The word of a sultan not yet sworn in cannot pass for a decree. Nobody would obey his commands. Wait until Friday. One of his first decrees will concern the Sadabat pavilions, you'll see!"

QUESTION 63
DO YOU REMEMBER?

"Well, sir! You do know that I am holding kindling wood and you are sitting on a keg of gunpowder, don't you?"

No response.

"In that case, answer the questions I put to you and it will save us both a lot of time and effort. All right?"

Similar questions were being asked in three separate cells. In the middle of each was a wheeled wooden stretcher with small kegs of gunpowder placed beneath and a person holding a torch standing next to it. A man was laid out on each stretcher, his hands and feet bound by chains. The prison contained a surprising number of torture devices, divided into interrogation aids and torture implements. Falco wondered if the perpetrators of torture actually enjoyed using these devices. Racks for stretching prisoners until they could barely move were attached to the walls at the entrance to each corridor. It was much easier to control unruly inmates if they were in a perpetual state of weakness and, to keep order within the prison, it was deemed necessary for every prisoner to be fastened to the wall by their hands and feet and racked at least once a week. This requirement could of course be waived if the guards felt disinclined to listen to the subsequent howls of the prisoners.

In Falco's opinion, the men currently lying on the stretchers were three of the worst. So bad that, even had the prison guards still been in charge, they would have been kept in chains. Thus, there was no need to have all the torture devices in each cell. The plan was simple. The three men were to be questioned simultaneously. Every so often, an implement would be used to pull out nails or nerves causing the victim to scream, at which point the interrogation would be halted in the other cells to allow the other two victims to identify the scream. Then the torturers would change places with each other and let their new victim know what had been learned from the screaming prisoner. That way, they would gradually find out everything. Two of the cells were identical, but the Prison Custodian's cell was slightly larger and had additional devices, including stocks. It had been extremely difficult to move this contraption down from another corridor, but Falco was determined that this cruel man should go through the pain he had inflicted on him at Eyüp Prison. He was curious to see what this man would do when the stocks were clamped around his own legs, after a lifetime of torturing prisoners in this way,.

The torches on the prison walls shed little light on the captives, who had now been given a handful of bread and a sip of water. Their food may have been wanting, but time was plentiful. In fact, time lost all meaning in the dark prison, where the silence was broken only by the occasional sounds of voices interspersed with scuttling rats.

"Shall we begin with the prisoners who were thrown into the Golden Horn while being transferred from the Eyüp Sultan Prison to Galata?" said Falco. "What do you say, my illustrious Custodian?"

Life had been turned upside down for the Prison Custodian. The interrogator was now being interrogated. The hunter had become the prey. He had no idea what his interrogator knew about him, nor what he was being accused of. The tone of questioning suggested that his interrogator was seeking a murderer rather than a government official.

"Who are you? Scoundrel! I don't know you! And you don't know me. Look, why don't we come to a nice little understanding? You untie my hands and I'll forget this ever happened. My men will be here shortly and when they get here..." said the Prison Custodian, trying to undermine his interrogator.

"Every time you refuse to answer my question," whispered Falco softly in his ear as he turned the lever another notch, "the chains will tighten a little more! What's more, we have these stocks here, which might not be the same as yours. Better for you if you answer my questions!"

"When my men get here..." protested the Prison Custodian.

"Your men? Huh!" laughed Falco. "They're busy plundering the city instead of protecting it. They have no thought for you. Anyway, this is the last place anyone would look for you. That you can be as sure of! Now, let's start again. What were you trying to achieve by tipping people into the sea between Eyüp and Galata? Were you following orders, or giving them?"

"I don't know what you're talking about!"

"In that case, I'll help you remember!" said Falco, turning the lever another notch and making the Prison Custodian grimace with pain.

In the next cell, Bindallı Mahmut was beyond grimacing and already wailing at another turn of the lever. He was beginning to think his female interrogator might be from the Three Crescent Society, because of her impressive knowledge of torture and interrogation techniques.

"I'm asking you for the last time, you vile creature!" she cried angrily, while he writhed as his nerves were stretched even more. "Who are the members of the death squad that operates at the Pergola coffee house and Binbirdirek Cistern?"

"I don't know! I can't remember!"

"See here, you son of a bitch, if you don't answer my questions," persisted Hourikin, "I won't actually kill you, but I'll have dogs tear your flesh apart and then have you brought back for more. Now, let's start from the beginning. Do you remember Drafter Remzi Beşe? Janissary Corporeal Abduh? Or the Prison Custodian?"

"I don't remember! I don't know them!"

As Hourikin turned the lever to tighten the chains again, Stocky Yeye was being even more ruthless towards Aslan Ağa. Yeye felt a savage fury whenever he thought of the part this abominable creature had played in his life and was tightening the chains two notches at a time. His method was certainly having the desired effect because, once he stopped moaning, Aslan Ağa was starting to talk.

"I didn't know Veyis Ağa very well," protested Aslan Ağa. "People said his daughter was beautiful and I remember going to see her on some business pretext."

"What did you intend to do when you saw her?"

"I was going to request her hand for the son of a relative of mine."

"Every time you lie, I'll brand you with this knife!" threatened Stocky Yeye tightening the wheel another notch with his curved knife. "I'll start on your legs and make my way up to your hairline until you look like map. Now, tell me, what did you intend to do when you saw her?"

"Istanbul slaves were fetching good money in Egypt and Iran, and a caravan was preparing to leave. But the girl turned out to be a mute."

Stocky Yeye remembered that this man had indeed come to the house a few days after the snake had fallen into Şehnaz's lap. How fortunate, he thought, that the incident had left her mute that day.

"You mean that, if she hadn't been mute, you'd have abducted her?"

"Oh no! Others would have done the abducting!"

"Sergeant Bindallı Mahmut, for instance?"

"Men like that are easy to find around Binbirdirek or the Pergola coffee house, not to mention the guards at Eyüp Sultan Prison."

"Were any of the bosses there involved?"

"I know nothing about them."

"Don't worry! One of them knows you. He's in the very next cell!"

While Aslan Ağa was allowed a little relief, the questioning was continuing in the Prison Custodian's cell.

"Who brought you the men that were thrown into the sea? Was it Aslan Ağa?" asked Falco.

"Who's Aslan Ağa? I don't know him," replied the Prison Custodian.

"Is that so? Well, he knows you and he's in the cell next door. What's more, he knows other things as well."

"Such as?"

"He knows all about the gold paid out to interrogate innocent people brought to you as criminals at the prison. He knows about innocent men 'accidentally' falling overboard into the Golden Horn."

The Prison Custodian said nothing as he listened to the screams of Aslan Ağa in the next cell, but looked intently at the face of his interrogator in the flickering torchlight.

"It's you! Yes, you!" he murmured, shaking his head. "Damn the day I had you thrown overboard! We were meant to kill you first, but I felt sorry for you! When the men said you were to be killed, I looked at your youth and said, 'Spare him, but make sure you give him a good fright!'"

"What crime was I supposed to have committed? Tell me!"

"There was no crime. You were alone in the world and spending your way through a large inheritance. We couldn't let you use up a fortune like that all on your own. After all, you not only owned Pearl Mansion, but thirty magnificent pearls as well!"

Falco let the Prison Custodian finish and for a moment seemed ready to relent, remembering Hafız Çelebi's words

'When your enemy is overcome, be grateful for the victory and forgive him!' However, the moment passed and Falco decided it was necessary to do to the Prison Custodian one more time what he had done to so many of his victims. He tightened the chains another notch and walked out of the cell, leaving the Prison Custodian yelling and swearing in pain.

When Falco entered Aslan Ağa's cell, he was pleased to see that yet again Stocky Yeye was doing an excellent job. He sent Yeye to Bindallı's cell and said that Hourikin should go to question the Prison Custodian. On seeing Falco, Aslan Ağa forgot all about his pain.

"You!" he shouted in amazement.

"Yes, it's me, dear Father! My dear father-in-law who killed his very own daughter! Who had his own son-in-law arrested as a murderer! I could ask you countless questions and spend days and nights listening to your confessions. That is, of course, if you managed to endure it and stay alive, Aslan Ağa, my dear Father. Tell me, I'm curious, how did you kill your own daughter?"

"I'm saying nothing!"

While Falco was trying to persuade Aslan Ağa to talk, Hourikin was quietly pursuing quite a different line of questioning with the Prison Custodian.

"You must whisper your answers to the questions I put to you now," said Hourikin in a low voice, "otherwise I'll make you yell till the roof flies off. What did you do to Prince Ahmet?"

"Who?"

"Come on, don't be obstinate. You know what I'm asking."

"I sent a man out to bring him, back dead or alive. But he was found already dead one day."

"Who ordered you to do this?"

"The illustrious Grand Vizier İbrahim Pasha!"

"The same İbrahim Pasha that you tortured and handed over to the rebels?"

"I had nothing to do with his torture!"

"Oh yes, and I suppose you had nothing to do with Patrona Halil Ağa either."

"I couldn't prevent what was happening. I was just making the best of the situation."

"And what was the purpose of capturing this prince?"

"If he had been caught alive, İbrahim Pasha would have kept him under his protection. If he had been found dead, his death would have been kept secret and used as a threat against Sultan Ahmet."

"So which of these happened?"

"As you are well aware, the hands that were tightening these chains just now belong to him! He was never found, dead or alive!"

"Very well. What about the information you obtained from Supreme Judge İshak?"

"I passed the document on to the Grand Vizier."

"What did it say?"

"I didn't read it. I was afraid to read it. Sometimes knowledge brings disaster and that letter was an example. I even made sure that Judge İshak was questioned in front of executioners who were deaf mutes to ensure that the information went no further."

"So who knows about it now?"

"Only you and me. I know I'll die because of this. And you would do well to take precautions, because everyone else who's known has ended up dead."

"Keep this to yourself and there may be reason to keep you alive. But if you talk, I'll rip your heart out with my own hands!"

In Aslan Ağa's cell, Falco examined the taut chain and the row of torture implements that had been laid out on top of a dirty, mildewed box.

"I don't know much about different methods of torture," said Falco conversationally, as he wandered round the cell. "However, I certainly know how to use these pincers. I once extracted a nail from my horse's foot and made it bleed. But perhaps you'd prefer me to press your little finger back into your hand like a spike. Would that be too much to bear? Shall we start with the nail or go straight for the finger? What do you say, fisherman Aslan Ağa?"

Aslan Ağa looked startled.

"If you don't like the pincers, there's a spiked chain here. As an expert fisherman, you'd be good at reeling it in, just like a fishing line. Perhaps you feel disposed to swallow it! But no! Pulling it out would rip your insides and spoil your lovely voice, making your words unintelligible."

Meanwhile, a scream was heard in the next cell, indicating that Stocky Yeye had greeted Sergeant Bindallı. Falco saw Aslan Ağa wince.

"Why did you give me Nakşıgül's hand in marriage and then take her away?" asked Falco.

Aslan Ağa said nothing.

"Does this mean you're going to be obstinate? Very well, I have time. I'll make you tell me, even if it takes until the Day of Judgment."

"I'm saying nothing, even if this does go on until the Day of Judgement," said Aslan Ağa.

"Perhaps you would like me to stick this spike into your ear and roast your head in the flames of my torch until it turns red as a pomegranate. That is, if I have any appetite for brain stew."

"Son, take pity on this old man!"

"Like you took pity on me, you mean? When you ate your way through the eight hundred sovereigns you obtained for Pearl Mansion, not to mention my dear late mother's pearls? Tell me honestly, how much of it did you spend yourself and how much did you distribute to others?"

"I'll repay all that money."

"Do you have that much?"

"I'll get it."

"From whom? From Sergeant Bindallı Mahmut?

"How do you know Bindallı?"

"He's your neighbour here, in the next cell. We can call him if you like. Sergeant Mahmuuut!"

Hearing Sergeant Bindallı's groan made Aslan Ağa realise that all was lost.

"Son, don't do as I did! You're a decent person. Take pity on this old man!" pleaded Aslan Ağa feebly.

"Like you took pity on Nakşıgül? You're pathetic, begging for mercy after showing none to your own daughter."

"That poor girl wasn't my daughter."

"No?"

"There's more. Ask Bindallı."

Falco ran to the next cell where he found Bindallı in a completely broken state.

"Tell me all about Nakşıgül!"

"Who's Nakşıgül?" gasped Bindallı.

"Aslan Ağa says you know."

"I took a woman to him, just the once. She's the woman whose dismembered body was in the sack."

"Never mind the toymaker's wife. I'm talking about Nakşıgül."

"Who's Nakşıgül? I don't know her."

Falco was confused. He could not work out whether this man had killed Nakşıgül without knowing her identity, or whether he was talking about another dead woman. He realised that it was time to bring the captives together and let them speak in front of each other so that the different strands of the story could be pieced together. Bindallı Mahmut and Aslan Ağa were wheeled into the Prison Custodian's cell, which was slightly larger and had walls were covered with torture implements. Throughout the interrogations, Hourikin had proved to be very robust and Stocky Yeye had been skilful as always, while Falco still looked as if he could not believe what he was doing. However, they had all managed to set aside any feelings of mercy for the sake of poor Nakşıgül and also in order to spare the people of Istanbul from these despicable men.

"One of your guards at Eyüp Prison said something to me, which is ingrained on my memory as if I heard it yesterday," said Falco. "When trying to get me to confess to a crime that I did not commit, he said, 'I'll get you to talk, even if it means dismembering you alive like Nakşıgül'. So tell me now, who dismembered my wife? Was it you, Bindallı?"

"I've dismembered many men, but only attempted it once with a woman. I found it impossible and gave up."

"In that case, was it you Aslan Ağa? Did you get a savage pleasure from dismembering your own daughter?"

"Good God, no! I would never allow my daughter to be dismembered."

"You're trying my patience. Shall we stretch you all another notch?"

"All right, all right! I'll explain," yelled the Prison Custodian, as Hourikin and Stocky Yeye reached for the wheels. "We considered killing you after seizing the mansion and the pearls. It would have been very easy to kill you in some remote corner of Yenibahçe fields and toss your body into the Golden Horn, but we felt sorry for you and put you in prison, which was at least better than being killed. We wanted to make sure you didn't talk and thought that you'd keep quiet and abandon any thought of retrieving your mansion and pearls if you were the prime suspect for your wife's murder. Around that time, Bindallı confessed that he'd strangled his lover for some reason and wanted to send her severed head in a basket of dried fruit as a gift to the Grand Vizier. We told him to wait one more day and sent a prison guard to dismember the body. The guard was an expert at such things. He was always killing people and putting them into sacks for us to have dumped in the Golden Horn."

"Like the corpses that got caught up in the fisherman's nets?" asked Falco.

"There are three deep sections of the Golden Horn," explained the Prison Custodian, "where even the dredgers do not reach the seabed. The water where we had you thrown overboard at Kasımpaşa is one of those places."

"And the other two places?" asked Stocky Yeye, reaching for the lever to tighten his chain.

"One is at Hasköy and the other at Ayvansaray. Actually, there are even deeper areas of the Golden Horn, but they couldn't be used in case the men were caught by the dockyard or naval police."

"Did you murder all these people for gold?"

"Mostly."

"And doing the government's dirty work, of course!" thought Hourikin, remembering a scene at the Three Crescent Society when the Chief had ordered a prisoner to be 'taken away'. His corpse was probably still in the Golden Horn, just like all the others that had disappeared without trace.

"Who got the gold?"

"Lots of people, from the Janissary Chief Commander to Tea-maker Ali at the Pergola coffee house or the Foreman of Gedikpaşa Hamam stokehouse. Sometimes it went right up to the Grand Vizier."

"Who organised this gang?"

"Someone at the Treasury."

"Who?"

"They'll kill me if I told you."

"I'll kill you if you don't tell us."

The Prison Custodian looked at Hourikin meaningfully to indicate that he would have to divulge their secret unless she came to his rescue.

"Okay, Falco! That's enough," interrupted Hourikin. "Let's get back to Nakşıgül's death. How was the corpse made to look like Nakşıgül?"

"It wasn't difficult. The prison guard was skilled at such things. He had his own methods, which sometimes even involved replacing the corpse's skin. He did a bit of work on the face using beeswax to make it look younger. Then, while Falco was asleep, the guard led Nakşıgül out of the bedchamber and returned to place body parts of the other woman around the room. He also spread blood everywhere, even smearing some in Falco's eyes so that, if he stirred, he would think he was dreaming. That's right, isn't, Falco?"

Falco tried to remember. He had certainly woken up with a heavy head.

"Yes, that's right," said Falco, feeling unsteady at the recollection of that morning.

"In fact, to make it even more credible," said the Prison Custodian, "we told the guard to put half of the twin tulip bulb, which had been hidden in the room the previous night, into one of Nakşıgül's hands."

"The Touch of Sorrow!"

"No, it was called the Tyrian Dwarf. It had been stolen from a gardener in Kağıthane, who was growing it for İbrahim Pasha and expecting to make five hundred sovereigns when the season arrived. Judge İshak had sent out some special constables to search for the tulip that night and a bridal chamber was the safest hiding place we could think of."

"Did you steal the tulip at the auction too?" asked Falco.

"What do you think?" said the Prison Custodian. "We had to get back our property. We then hid it in a foreigner's cell at the Envoys' Caravanserai. But how it disappeared from the room after the wedding remained a mystery. We didn't know who'd removed the bulb, who it was given to or where it was planted. Then, even more curiously, the man we'd stolen it from in the first place put it up for sale at the auction. What was his name? Hafız Çelebi, I think. But he called it Touch of Sorrow, didn't he? Yes, that was it. Our Tyrian Dwarf had become the Touch of Sorrow."

"Fine, let's get back to the morning after the wedding," said Falco. "What did you do next?"

"You reacted just as we intended," resumed the Prison Custodian. "The plan was for you to be arrested as the murderer and subsequently escape during the transfer between Eyüp and Galata Prisons. A stone was to be tied to your feet and you were to be tipped overboard into the sea. We knew you could swim. It was a good plan..."

The Prison Custodian appeared to be expecting praise at this point, but instead there was a long stunned silence. His captors felt as if they were revisiting a nightmare in which the culprits were gaining the upper hand. To change the atmosphere, and in the hope of finding out the rest of the story, Falco released the three prisoners from their chains, locked their legs into the stocks and sat them down on gunpowder kegs. They each moaned with pain at having their limbs, still raw from the stretching, clamped into the stocks.

"While you were deciding whether or not to kill Falco," asked Hourikin after a while, resting a foot against the stocks ready to push if no reply was forthcoming, "did you have any idea of his true identity?"

The Prison Custodian understood the meaning of her question and, hoping the others would not notice, turned to Hourikin and shook his head, indicating that he did not know.

Falco was now perspiring feverishly and his head spinning. He was unable to ask the most important question of all.

"Where is Nakşıgül now?" asked Stocky Yeye, finding the words for his friend.

There was a long silence, during which no onc even breathed. Just as Aslan Ağa was swallowing in preparation to speak, Pit Jan's voice was heard in the distance.

"Falcoooo!"

QUESTION 64
HOW COULD YOU DO IT?

The evening rays of sun had not yet disappeared behind the slopes of Sadabat, yet a full moon was already visible above the ridges of Sütlüce. The sound of nine cannon shots echoing in the skies above Istanbul heralded the enthronement of a new sultan. Order would return to Istanbul at last, thought Hafız Çelebi, aware that he was humming a favourite song from childhood: 'Jasmine clings to the heart of a rose / what ill-fated love does there repose'. Previously, he would have been relishing his beautiful surroundings, but now that beauty was gone. All morning, the cries of pillagers could be heard from the ravaged pavilions of Sadabat, where waves of rebels were still arriving with horses, donkeys, mules and even oxcarts. While one carried off a slave, another left with a silver brazier on his shoulders, and yet another cradled a crystal chandelier. The greedier ones – those who came with carts – loaded up anything they found. They even took doors, shutters and brass railings, reducing the beautiful pavilions to ruins. Hafız Çelebi would never forget how a bunch of swearing yobs had trampled on the tulip bulbs that had been put into sacks ready for planting. These ignorant morons seemed to blame the tulip for everything. Some had tried to break into his garden at dawn and steal his turtles from the pool, but on noticing that the Well of Souls was next to the cemetery, they had thought better of it, fearing 'evil spirits'. Nevertheless, Hafız Çelebi was worried that they might return. Wandering through his flowerbeds, which he was doing everything possible to protect, he wanted to check whether the water lily seeds and tulip bulbs were safe or had been stolen. Seeing the jasmine begin to fade reminded him that autumn was coming to a close and it was time to plant the tulip bulbs.

Pit Jan had told him that he wanted to return to his country earlier than usual. The revolution had affected him deeply and Hafız Çelebi could think of no reason to urge him to stay. Pit Jan had been deeply angered that the new Sultan was allowing gangs to enter Sadabat in the full knowledge that they would plunder it. He could understand why shops and businesses were still closed and the city gripped by fear, but he found the rebels' desire to torch the beautiful Sadabat pavilions incomprehensible. Why, Pit Jan had asked, had the new Sultan obtained a fatwa from the Istanbul Cadi to prevent the burning down of these places, yet allowed them to be pillaged? Reducing them to ashes would have been insane, but the alternative was also disastrous. Town criers were now actually instructing owners of the pavilions to burn them down within three days to avoid having them destroyed by Patrona Halil. But with that crazy mob out there, who would dare to burn down his pavilion? And so, by noon on the second day, Sadabat, that splendid example of perfection, was gone. Its one hundred and sixty pavilions, a unique distillation of beauty born of nature and intellect, had been ruined. What was the point of wrecking gardens, uprooting trees, defiling waterfronts and trampling over tulip gardens? If the perpetrators called themselves Muslims, then Hafız Çelebi was an angel by comparison. The Islam recognised by Hafız Çelebi would never condone violence. Patrona Halil, with his ability to listen and behave with constraint, may have earned public respect, but he was surrounded by thugs who behaved like packs of wolves. They knew no limits and had no thought for the repercussions of their actions. Like blind, starving dogs, they could see no further than finding a bone to chew on. They were the dark face of the honourable band of janissaries making Ottoman history, a shameless, desecrating mob with no concept of self-respect, honour, patriotism, government or country. Pit Jan found it all deplorably tragic and wanted to leave.

"What's the point of remaining here at Kağıthane," Pit Jan had said, "if there are no royal caiques or gondolas carrying beautiful ladies, no flamboyant landaus, no oxcarts and horses decorated with ribbons and bells going up and down the shores of the Bosphorus, no courtiers, pashas and ministers dressed in silver-brocaded silken robes, no freshwater springs gushing down to the shores, no fountains or pools, no tulip displays, no scented philadelphus or stocks in the gardens, no Grand Vizier with his elegant entourage, no days and nights of musical and poetic entertainments?"

Why was he thinking about all this, Hafız Çelebi asked himself. He should continue with the song. He wanted – needed – his dream to last a little longer. 'Did I not tell you to depart, o my heart / damn this heart / oh my heart, damn this heart'. No, it was not working. Hafız Çelebi had lived long enough to know that merely repeating the word 'heart' over and over again would never make it happy. He could not bear to lose Yeye again and would never have allowed him to go if Pit Jan not gone with them.

"The tulips need to be buried deep. The tiles of the pool need covering," he muttered to himself. "I wonder if the turtles have eaten their black powder paint. We must have a black tulip this year. We'll call it Stocky Yeye! I must ask Şehnaz's father for her hand in marriage. According to Skinny Kirkor, this rebellion has made Veyis Ağa very edgy and he's started beating Şehnaz and her mother. If he carries on that way, he'll end up in the very place he had Yusuf sent to. I must rescue his daughter before he gets any worse. Anyway, it would be good to have a woman in the house for my dear boy. Skinny Kirkor can build us another room, and..."

Hafız Çelebi sat by the brook, immersed in his reverie, every second of which was like a thousand years of happiness. Unaware that it had started to rain, he continued singing, "O heart, damn this heart..." until he was eventually roused by Pit Jan's voice calling out, "Haaafiz!"

"How could you do it?"

"If they had lived, our own lives would have been in danger."

"But to kill people! I don't understand. A lady like you..."

"I couldn't allow Stocky Yeye and you to be sacrificed."

"You sacrificed Nakşıgül!"

Falco and Hourikin were arguing as they changed out of their wet clothes in adjacent rooms of the house. When they had heard Pit Jan's voice in the prison, they had not known what to do. Falco had instructed Stocky Yeye and Hourikin to leave immediately while he put a sack over the Prison Custodian's head and started questioning him about Nakşıgül. However, the Prison Custodian had confused him by offering to tell the rest of the story if he was released from the stocks. Pit Jan had told them that a group of sailors had rounded up some hooligans and were marching them in chains towards the prison in an attempt to establish order outside, and that it was essential to leave immediately. Hourikin had shouted, "Let's go!" and Falco had tried to release the Prison Custodian, but the key would not turn. Their intention had been to get him out and lock up the other two, but there was no time. In the end, Hourikin picked up an axe and struck one of the gunpowder kegs. Taking a handful of the spilled gunpowder, she sprinkled a line across the floor towards the door and lit it with one of the torches on the wall.

"Falco! Run for it!"

They had left the prison by the back gate and mounted their horses just as the sailors were shoving the hooligans through the front gates. The last three of the nine cannons honouring Sultan Mahmut's ascent to the throne were being fired when they heard three shots resound from inside the prison.

"That's the end of Aslan Ağa, Sergeant Bindallı and the Prison Custodian!" commented Stocky Yeye.

The argument that followed had started at Hasköy and continued over the Sütlüce hills and Okmeydan ridge until Kağıthane, where they found Hafız Çelebi soaking wet and shivering all over.

"Father! What's happened to you?"

"Yeye, come here my son and hold me. Please, don't leave me alone again!"

"Houri, quick! Go and make some *tarhana* soup," said Pit Jan, his eyes filling with tears. "Falco, go and draw some water from the Well of Souls, then go to the room where Hafiz keeps his grafted tulip bulbs. On the shelf there, you'll find some paste wrapped in finger-sized twists of oilskin. Bring them here."

Hourikin piled some dry wood on to the dying embers of the fire and reflected on Pit Jan calling her Houri, the name given to her by her mother. After her mother's death, her father had added 'kin' to her name, thinking it more appropriate while she was growing up in the all-male Three Crescent Society. The name Houri made her feel like a woman, whereas Hourikin made her feel bold.

"Yeye, my dear boy! You know the blue stream that ripples into the Golden Horn?" rambled Hafız Çelebi. "Well, a short while ago, I saw some elegant boats disappearing down there, like crescent moons reflected from the skies. You were a prince dressed in a satin kaftan , carrying a dagger inlaid with chrysolite and wearing emerald rings on your fingers. You were going to meet a woman who was sitting at a window of the white marble pavilion with the thirty columns and decorative oriel windows on the hillside opposite. In your hands was a bunch of white tulips, one of which radiated light and illuminated her face. Yeye, the woman was extremely beautiful and she was called Şehnaz. The poet Nedim Efendi came up to her and read out eulogies in your praise to the accompaniment of the sound of fragrant fountains, while palace servants sprinkled your feet with oil from the lilac trees growing on the hillside. I saw our late Head Florist, Sarı Abdullah Efendi, inviting you to take up a senior position on the Tulip Commission. The two of you walked through the assembled gathering, giving names to the new tulips, such as Heartbreaker, Grenadine, Golden Yellow, Rosetta, Chef's Pink, Red Moustache, Talon, Tissue of Love and Star of Fortune."

Stocky Yeye sobbed while Hafız Çelebi spoke, not knowing whether it was fiction or fantasy. What he did know was that Hafız Çelebi must not be left alone again. Meanwhile, Pit Jan was thinking, "If I don't board that ship tomorrow, I'll be here for ever."

That night, Hafız Çelebi's fever eventually broke, his delirium passed and he regained his lucidity, even asking, "Did you manage to sort out your business?" That simple question was a sign that his health was restored.

Everyone's faces relaxed into smiles of pleasure and before long they were all earnestly engaged in congenial conversation. Hafız Çelebi looked much better and drifted into a calm, deep sleep after about an hour and the others resumed their conversation about Nakşıgül, the interrogation and what they had learned at the prison. It was a chilly autumn evening, so they huddled around the stove, reviewing everything and trying to find answers to their innumerable questions.

How had Nakşıgül died? Where was her grave? How had the house in Yenibahçe and everyone in it disappeared? Whose were the corpses found in the Golden Horn? They knew the government needed to be told about these things, but whom should they approach? What should they tell him? They knew that they were on dangerous ground, because some of the people involved were Patrona Halil's men. How should they go about it? Were the Binbirdirek Cistern and the Pergola coffee house really dens of vice? These mysteries needed to be solved.

"Perhaps we should go back to begging so that we can keep watch on these places," suggested Stocky Yeye.

"You're not leaving this garden," said Falco sternly. "Is that understood?"

Yeye looked at him in surprise.

"Why are you looking at me like that? You're not going anywhere!" insisted Falco. "Have you given no thought to Hafız Çelebi? Moreover, all three men we questioned today made reference to this place, so one of us has to keep watch over Hafız Çelebi. And you, Pit Jan, must see to the tulips."

"The inoculated tulips need planting out tomorrow. But that's not my job any more. Yeye should be doing that," replied Pit Jan.

"Very well, Pit Jan Ağa," responded Stocky Yeye.

Everyone was glad that Yeye had agreed to this and they went back to discussing the murders and interrogations. Stocky Yeye felt happy that his friends now regarded him as the owner of the garden. He and Şehnaz would cultivate the most beautiful tulips in Istanbul, putting everything they had learned from Hafız Çelebi into enhancing and perfecting blooms that would carry his expertise for ever. Maybe, thought Stocky Yeye, his own name might even one day be remembered in association with Hafız Çelebi. He recalled a tale about ***The Moon's jealousy of the Sun*** from a section about love in a book he had read as a boy, though of course there had never been the slightest hint of jealousy between Hafız Çelebi and himself.

Yeye was eventually roused from his daydreaming when the conversation of the other three turned to inoculated bulbs and turtles.

"Yeye, Hafız Çelebi wanted you to name the new bulb," said Pit Jan.

"Oh, really?" said Hourikin. "What will you name it? If it were me, I'd call it Touch of Life in memory of the Touch of Sorrow."

"Maybe. It definitely won't be Tyrian Dwarf," replied Yeye.

As Stocky Yeye said those words, he and Falco looked at each other in a moment of simultaneous realisation. Hourikin and Pit Jan were totally confused.

"God damn it! Why didn't we think of that before?" cried Stocky Yeye.

"Of course, the dwarf was the colour of Tyrian purple!" exclaimed Falco.

"Which dwarf, Falco?" asked Hourikin.

"The dwarf at the Pergola coffee house and Binbirdirek Cistern!"

Postscript: When the moon was jealous of the sun

One day the Moon was asked to reveal his greatest wish. "I would love to keep the Sun's face covered by the clouds for ever, because even looking at her makes me jealous," he replied. "I could light up the whole world with my love for the Sun!"

"If what you say is true, then you should run after her day and night to reach her. As soon as you do, you will disappear, of course. You will no longer be visible. Her light will eradicate your existence. Should you ever manage to attract even one glimpse in her presence, people will point at you and ask, "How does the Moon manage to radiate light next to the Sun?"

QUESTION 65
IS NOT ONE BLISSFUL NIGHT OF LOVE WORTH THIRTY GLEAMING PEARLS?

One faint beam of light shone down through a small hole in the ceiling. As their eyes grew accustomed to the dimness, it became clear that they had entered a place unlike anything they had ever seen before. The floor was bare and there appeared to be no furnishings, only iron levers, ropes dangling from the ceiling and a few low benches attached to the walls. They tried to make sense of their surroundings and, just when it seemed there was no one there, they saw a pair of eyes whirling round and round in the far corner. How strange he looked without his turban and kaftan – more like a fluted, beardless pumpkin than a human being. His forehead was as flat as a board and his complexion was like a mottled melon. Ears shaped like a child's shoe stuck out on either side of his head and his hairy nose resembled a purple aubergine with ringlets of leek dangling from it. Beneath his limp moustache, he had lips like a camel and a mouth filled with pitted teeth, which was big enough to hold a whole loaf of bread. Although he had seen the dwarf before, Falco was alarmed to see what a freak of nature he actually was.

"Good God! Tiny Çaker!" muttered Falco, pulling Hourikin behind him.

The dwarf seemed unperturbed by their presence, presumably thinking he had sent for them, and sat waiting for them to approach him. Hourikin had met kind and friendly dwarfs before, but this man looked thoroughly evil, an absolute fiend. He put his turban on his large head, making his hunchbacked figure weirdly top heavy. When he spoke, he looked even more monstrous as he snarled and dribbled, almost as if he were vomiting. Was his evil nature a result of his ugliness or vice versa? Falco and Hourikin were now used to the darkness and could see that the walls were covered with carpets, except for one corner where they were covered with shelves of various bottles, containers and glass tubes. The dwarf was sitting on a bench that had been covered with carpet to resemble a throne. It had strings, ropes and chains attached to it, each obviously for a particular purpose. What was this place? A den of vice? A torture chamber? Presumably, this was where wealthy abductees were brought and forced to disclose information about their assets.

“There’s no point making a fuss. The others can’t come,” said Falco in a steady voice.

“Huh! Who sent you? Who are you?”

“Let’s just say we’re two people in need of help.”

“I can’t be bothered with kids. Get out!” said the dwarf, pulling one of the dangling ropes, which opened the door through which they had entered. “Go on! I said get out, you snivelling wretches!”

Falco took a few steps forward and stood firm.

“I have a few questions to ask you first.”

The room was suddenly flooded with a brilliant, blinding light. Then smoke started billowing over them from behind a pillar in the corner. Hourikin ran to one side, covering her eyes. She tried to inch forward by feeling her way along the wall, making the dwarf screech with laughter that reverberated among the pillars. It was a hideous laugh, which he seemed to relish. Falco thought carefully. If the dwarf was able to laugh like that, then the smoke must be harmless. Falco opened his eyes. He was right. His eyes stopped burning within thirty seconds. Looking around again, Falco saw the dwarf laughing and beckoning him with his forefinger. Moving cautiously forward, Falco saw Hourikin pressed against the wall.

“Open your eyes, Hourikin! Don’t worry about the smoke!”

The dwarf cupped his hands, blew through them and thrust them forward, making out that he had released the sparrowhawks which were now flying around attacking Falco and Hourikin on their eyes and ears. The laughter resumed, and Falco and Hourikin realised they might have made a mistake by coming there. Indeed, only the previous day, Harrier Cafer had told them that Cotton Chief Tiny Çaker could never be caught unless physically pinned down by the wrists.

They had been seeking Tiny Çaker for three days. During that time, the Sultan had been removed from the throne and some sort of order restored in Istanbul. Patrona Halil and his men were in the process of making appointments to senior government positions. Newly-crowned Sultan Mahmut I had not refused many of Patrona Halil's proposals, but both sides were being very cautious. For instance, when the Sultan proposed a position for Patrona Halil, he had replied, "I do not know what life holds in store for me. Never before has a person who deposed a sultan died peacefully in his own bed, so why should I expect anything different?" He claimed that all he had wanted was to bring an end to the nation's suffering.

The bakeries and shops were now open and much of life had returned to normal. Had this not been the case, it would have been very difficult to monitor Binbirdirek twenty-four hours a day. Binbirdirek Cistern, which dated back to Byzantine times, was right in the heart of the city and had been converted into a guild hall for traders in cotton and wool. It was a gloomy place where the shops were constantly covered in white dust. The cotton-fluffers had chosen it because the humidity helped to settle the wool and cotton dust, but the fifty or so shops on the ground floor still had to be washed down several times a day. One part of the cistern had two storeys. The upper floor was reached by a grand stairway and used as an office by Cotton Chief Tiny Çaker. Nobody other than his personal attendants had ever seen inside this room.

When Hourikin and Falco had mounted their horses on the morning after the night of Hafız Çelebi's fever, Pit Jan left with them. They assumed he wanted to board his ship, but he had insisted that he would not leave Istanbul while Hafız Çelebi was so ill.

The three of them planned that Pit Jan would pretend to be a foreign cotton trader and Falco his interpreter. It was best for Hourikin not to be seen at Binbirdirek, so they had sent her to find Judge İshak, one of the few honest people not dismissed from his post by the rebels. Hourikin was to talk to him about the corpses in the Golden Horn and encourage him to investigate what had been going on, which would suit some of the rebels but expose any who had been involved.

On the first day, they had found out some interesting information about Cotton Chief Tiny Çaker. He was regarded by some as a saint and by others as a dwarf devil incarnate. People said he had magical powers and was able to perform miracles, like making people disappear. It was said that his palatial, richly furnished office was a place of magic from which he could fly away and disappear. Evil spirits were ready to strike down anyone who attempted to enter without permission. Tiny Çaker's close friends included the Istanbul Cadi and the Prison Custodian, but he also listened to the traders' problems, gave alms to the cotton-fluffers once a year and found dowries for local brides. It was said that the slave girls at his Akbıyık pavilion surpassed even the palace concubines' beauty.

On the second day, all these stories were contradicted. They had managed to catch Harrier Cafer and take him to the Sunken Cistern, which was Istanbul's oldest reservoir and still in use. There were rumours that it was inhabited by evil spirits who held meetings there in the dead of night, and that brigands had taken traders there during the rebellion to make them talk and then disposed of their bodies outside. Nobody wanted to be seen anywhere near the Sunken Cistern, and the two people who witnessed Falco and burly Pit Jan marching Harrier Cafer into the cistern made haste to get away, assuming that they were rebels who had abducted yet another man.

When they entered the Sunken Cistern, it had certainly felt like a playground for evil spirits. The silence was broken only by the sound of dripping water. They bolted the doors and listened to be sure that no one else was there. Taking the Chief Water-taster's boat, they rowed between the columns until they reached one that stood on top of a Medusa head. They tied their prisoner upside down to the column, so that his mouth was level with the surface of the water and he was forced to keep his neck arched to prevent his mouth filling up – a position which soon became torture. Harrier Cafer had resisted when they first started questioning him but, by pushing his head into the water until he reached drowning point, his neck quickly ached so much that he was prepared to start talking.

"Tiny Çaker is a master alchemist," said Harrier Cafer. "He works in a cave beneath his office. He's passionate about precious stones and there isn't a gem in Istanbul that he doesn't know about or hasn't acquired at some point if he so wishes. He organises most of the jewel robberies in Istanbul. If he can't steal them, he has fakes made which are exchanged for the originals by people working in the hamam stokehouses."

Harrier Cafer could no longer hold his head up. He was letting it fall in the water and only managing to raise it to talk in short gasps. Soon he was begging them to stop the torture and promised to tell them all he knew. Pit Jan was reluctant to show any mercy. However, Harrier Cafer's face had turned purple from the blood flowing into his brain and he looked as if he was about to pass out, so they untied him and let him sit in the boat. Once he had recovered, Harrier Cafer told them the rest.

"He adores precious stones and should really be called Jewel Chief instead of Cotton Chief. He's also a very skilled magician and can make a person's appearance change so that he becomes someone else from one sunrise to the next. There's a tunnel leading from his cave to a shop in Sultan Ahmet bazaar. We run that shop. It sells cloth, but has few customers because we're so rude when anyone comes in that they never come back."

"Is that the secret of the disappearing trick?"

"Yes. When a person goes through the tunnel into the shop, the cotton-fluffers are led to believe that he has vanished into thin air."

Harrier Cafer was still suffering from having been held upside down and was about to pass out. However, he managed to tell them one more thing.

"That enormous head of his is filled with brains. If you intend to capture him, take great care. No one will ever catch him without physically pinning him down!"

In Tiny Çaker's domain, the brilliance of that brain was evident even through the smoke. However, the dwarf could not escape. If he ran into the tunnel, Pit Jan was waiting for him at the other end in the shop at Sultan Ahmet bazaar. Falco took a step towards Tiny Çaker, who pulled a rope that hung from the ceiling, causing flames to leap out at Falco. They were real, burning flames with nothing magical about them. While it was not uncommon for an alchemist to be able to control sulphur and fire, Falco realised that they were up against someone formidable. He tried to work his way around the fire, but found that whichever way he went the flames veered in his direction, driving him towards the door.

Meanwhile, Hourikin was still edging forward along the wall. Her hands touched a carpet with a landscape design in the middle of which was a doe with a pair of antlers attached to complete the picture. Feeling movement beneath her feet, she steadied herself by grabbing the antlers. Instantly, the floor gave way beneath her and she fell through a hole into another room. The antlers must have been some sort of key. When her eyes became accustomed to the darkness, she saw some cauldrons on the floor. This had to be the cave that Harrier Cafer had spoken of. If it was an alchemist's den, she thought, it must contain chemicals and distilling equipment. Then she saw them, lined up neatly on a shelf. Feeling certain that someone would come in before long, she took the precaution of grabbing a few bottles and filling them from the cauldrons before looking round for the door.

Meanwhile, Falco was making his way towards the door on the floor above. He saw a few water bottles on the wall and emptied them over his head to douse the flames.

"Come here, my little lamb," cried Tiny Çaker, looking both amused and amazed. "I believe I've seen you somewhere before!" he said, flying across the ceiling.

"Of course you know me! You murdered my wife!" retorted Falco.

"You're wrong there, son. As a rule, I create rather than kill," said Tiny Çaker, who was now whirling round and round the room.

Falco tried to keep his eyes on the dwarf, but he became dizzy and began to feel sick. Tiny Çaker pulled another rope and the floor slipped away from beneath Falco's feet.

Hourikin heard the trapdoor rumble open and rushed to throw the contents of the container she was holding over whoever was entering. Just in time, she realised that it was Falco. Her last memory was of an acrid smell that pervaded the room.

"Yeees! Now it's my turn to ask questions. Who sent you?"

"No one!"

"So what are you after?"

"You killed my wife and I want to know why."

"You think I killed your wife? At my age? With this body of mine?"

As he taunted them, the dwarf was breathing out a vapour that burned their nostrils, eyes and ears. Falco needed to scratch, but he was hanging from the ceiling with his hands bound together. The winch used for the alchemy cauldrons was set so that their feet barely touched the floor. Their fingers were numb and their bodies tingling. The strange taste in his mouth made Falco think that Tiny Çaker must have given him some kind of drug while he was unconscious.

"Yes, you! You, the Prison Custodian and Aslan Ağa!"

"Those two are indeed killers! Yes, they killed her. But was it really your wife?"

"Yes! It was Aslan Ağa's girl, Nakşıgül!"

"My dear sir, they're all Aslan Ağa's girls. Tell me more. Where, when and how did it happen?"

"It happened last year at the house in Yenibahçe."

"Ah, I understand. But you should be thanking these hands of mine for turning a Yenibahçe garden shed into a mansion!"

"What do you mean?"

"Sir, who would want to spend their wedding night in a garden shed? Who would fork out eight hundred gold pieces to their father-in-law for that?"

"Oh no! What a fool I've been!" cried Falco. "I had no idea. I just couldn't understand why I was unable to find the house, or why none of the locals believed that I'd been married there. Tell me, is Nakşıgül alive?"

"Didn't I tell you that I'm no killer?"

"Is she alive? If so, where is she?"

"Is she alive and if so where is she?" chanted Tiny Çaker. "The answers to those two questions are very special pieces of information, each worth thirty beautiful white pearls!"

The end of that sentence was drowned by Falco's groan, because Tiny Çaker had sat down and pulled another rope, causing an arm with a fist on the end made of cloth-covered quinces to come down and strike him in the face.

"I like my quinces semi-crushed!" laughed Tiny Çaker, turning to Hourikin. "Now what is your name? Houri, is it? Would you like one too?"

He pulled another rope and released something like a cannon ball on a pendulum, which swung out and hit Hourikin in the stomach making her retch and gasp for breath.

"I'm so sorry, my lady. It was a pumpkin. Next time, it'll be a leek. So, back to you Falco! In a few moments, some of the people I have created and had killed will visit you and you'll tell me which of them was your wife. All right, Falco? Ha ha!"

Before long, Falco began to see faces of men and women pass in front of him. Gradually, their figures also became apparent. The women were exquisite specimens, fabulously decked out with gilded headdresses decorating their voluptuous hair. They passed by him, laughing and squealing, some even teasing him, in garments of colourful taffeta and diaphanous silk, or completely nude. As the number of images increased, some of the women were seen to quarrel, while others embraced each other. Falco bent this way and that, trying to find his bride. Eventually, he cried out, "Nakşıgül, Nakşıgü-ü-l!" and Tiny Çaker pulled another rope, causing a bucket of water to empty over him.

"Did you see her?" shrieked Tiny Çaker.

Tiny Çaker's shrill laughter was more infuriating to Hourikin than the blow she had received to her stomach. Despite having no idea what was happening to Falco, the fact that he was unable to regain consciousness despite the bucket of water indicated to Hourikin that he must have been given a very strong potion of some sort and that she had to do something to save him from this terrible man. After all, she had given her word that she would protect Prince Ahmet from danger.

"That's not magic, is it? No, I don't believe it," said Hourikin, playing for time.

"Magic, like alchemy, is a science, my lady. But fantasies seen with the help of magic are not without foundation. Quite the contrary! See here, for instance, we have the tent of Esfahan Khan. In a moment, I will set up the Sultan of Lahore's dinner table and surround it with servants. Spells and dreams make people believe in their imagination. The girl whom your man thought he had married was, in reality, the wife of our marriage-broker. And only two years before, he had seen her in the guise of a Georgian slave who was later presented by Sultan Ahmet to the Mameluke Commander."

"So he passed out when you said that Nakşıgül is alive. Is that what you're saying?"

"Of course. But let him die happy, without knowing that his wife was sold as a slave."

Hearing Tiny Çaker say 'let him die happy' made Hourikin think that Falco had been poisoned. She had to act immediately, first to save herself and then Falco. Her anxiety fuelled her anger, making her determined to provoke this terrible man until he slipped up.

"You mad dog, have you poisoned him?" she said accusingly.

"Ha, ha!"

"What a damned shithole you are! Tell me, you pock-marked stunted hunchback! Have you poisoned him?"

"Oh dear, you don't like me at all, do you? But I would hardly call poisoning a happy way to die!"

"Look here, you bag of bile! He talks about his wife being murdered on their wedding night!"

"Do I look like a murderer, my lovely? Shame on you! I didn't murder anyone that night. All it needed was some beeswax on the face of Bindallı's dead lover and a little Jabil syrup in the groom's drink on his wedding night. In that state, he would have embraced anyone he encountered believing she was Nakşıgül. If we hadn't added the right medicine to his water at Eyüp Prison the following day, he would have died of grief. But today, nobody is here to administer that treatment! However, I have done him one more favour. Be patient. He will believe you to be his beautiful wife, which will make him so happy that he will start laughing. Those who weep deserve to laugh occasionally, don't they?"

"You'll pay for poisoning him like that, you godforsaken piss-faced dwarf."

"Come on! We're discussing how this man can die happily with his lover beside him."

"Shut up, you sordid creature! The magical wedding night you created has given him a lifetime of suffering."

“Is not one night of blissful love worth thirty gleaming pearls?”

“No, you worthless…”

Tiny Çaker must have pulled another rope, because Hourikin suddenly contorted with pain as an arrow pierced the skin between her breasts. Attached to the arrow was a silken fuse which had been set alight and her body was engulfed with flames. Now, neither of them could stand. All they could do was wait with hands bound, held up by a cable hanging from the ceiling. However, unbeknownst to any of them, a pair of eyes had seen everything.

Soon after Pit Jan arrived at the shop in Sultan Ahmet bazaar, the scrawny old shop-keeper had become suspicious and started asking questions, so he had thought it best to leave. As he rose to go, he pinned the shop-keeper to the floor and tied him up. Then he wrapped the old man in a bale of cloth to stifle his cries and stuffed him under the counter. Pit Jan squeezed through the cupboard door that led to the tunnel, which he immediately realised had been built for a dwarf. It became so narrow at one point that he got stuck and found he was being attacked by squealing rats. Pit Jan knew that unless he managed to free himself quickly, the sound of squealing would be heard at the other end of the tunnel, which would be like sending an invitation to his own death. For someone who had come from Flanders to live among the splendours of Istanbul, it was most distressing to think of dying in a rat-infested tunnel. Pit Jan wriggled about until his clothes were torn to shreds. He eventually managed to get through the narrow section, now wearing only his flower-print shalwar, and prayed the tunnel would not narrow like that again. Before long, he came to a door with a light behind it. Beyond the sound of scurrying rats and moles, he could hear a shrill voice say, "Is not one night of blissful love worth thirty gleaming pearls?" Pit Jan peered through a crack in the door and what he saw filled him with horror. Falco and Hourikin were where the dwarf should have been. It looked as though several people had been involved for them to be tied up like that, but the only person he could see was Tiny Çaker, who got up to hang some ropes on the wall before disappearing into the darkest corner of the room. Pit Jan waited for a long time. There was no sound except for that of Falco regaining consciousness and weeping. For Falco to be in that state, he must have learned something awful. Pit Jan had never seen him cry like that before. Then Falco looked at Hourikin, who was unconscious, and murmured happily, "Nakşıgül, my sweetheart!" At this, Tiny Çaker reappeared holding some gold ingots. If he knows how to produce gold, thought Pit Jan, he is indeed an alchemist. Then it occurred to him that the gold might belong to Falco and the other men who had been killed. Tiny Çaker put the case of ingots on the counter and disappeared again. Pit Jan sensed that something very strange was going on, but still could not see anyone else. Suddenly, Falco broke out into loud laughter, giving Pit Jan the opportunity to heave his burly frame at the door. But it seemed to be bolted. He felt all over for a latch, certain that there had to be a device for opening the door from outside. Eventually, his hand touched a loop next to the doorframe. That must be it, he thought, and looked through the crack in the door again. Tiny Çaker had returned with more gold ingots and was reaching for a rope. Pit Jan's only hope was that the dwarf would go out again to fetch more gold. However, he carried on arranging the ingots and threading a chain through the metal rings on either side of the case. Then he turned the arm of a mechanism attached to the chain, causing the case of ingots to slide along the counter and rise six inches into the air. "If he's going to hoist it upstairs, he must be preparing to escape," thought Pit Jan. But Tiny Çaker left the case where it was and sat down on his bench, where he pulled another of the dangling ropes, causing Falco to glow as if struck by lightning. After a minute or so of flailing about like a fish caught in a net, Falco fainted. Tiny Çaker disappeared again and there was total silence. Pit Jan knew he had to keep quiet, yet act quickly. Very carefully, he pulled the loop. Although not afraid of the dwarf, Pit Jan knew he might be in difficulty if there were guards hiding in one of the corners because he was not carrying a weapon. One creak of the door could ruin everything. However, he managed to enter the room and gently shut the door behind him before looking around for a place to hide. The dwarf's bench was perfect. Pit Jan concealed himself behind it and waited. Before long, Tiny Çaker returned and arranged more ingots in the case. Then he stopped, listened and sniffed the air.

"Hmm! I think we have a visitor!" roared Tiny Çaker cheerfully.

Pit Jan felt his heart miss a beat. The dwarf's bellowing voice had startled him. Nobody would have believed that a dwarf could produce such a sound. Pit Jan waited while Tiny Çaker turned slowly and moved with cautious steps towards the glass cylinders lined up on the shelf. Pit Jan considered creeping up behind and pouncing on him, but thought better of it. He clutched the legs of the bench so that he could pick it up if necessary to strike the dwarf. Tiny Çaker took a star-shaped iron nail head from the shelf, then suddenly turned and hurled it upwards like a miniature discus, whereupon a rat fell down from the ceiling and landed with a squeal in one of the cauldrons.

"Didn't I tell you to keep away from my chemicals?"

Pit Jan was stunned, amazed by the skill of the dwarf. How could he hit a rat on the forehead with a tiny nail head like that in the dark? He remained motionless, listening carefully for the sound of footsteps. Once he was sure that Tiny Çaker was not there, he raised his head and looked around. Luck was on his side! Beneath the bench, he found a sack. With this, he made his way towards the hole in the wall and waited for the dwarf to return.

Now it was Pit Jan's turn to ask the questions, while Tiny Çaker provided answers from inside the sack in which he had been strung up to the ceiling. Whenever he told a lie, Pit Jan threw another squealing laboratory rat into the sack. That way, he managed to find out from Tiny Çaker the location of the gold, the jewels, the killers and the corpses. Meanwhile, Hourikin had started to regain consciousness and Falco was embracing her, laughing hysterically.

"What on earth are you wearing, Pit Jan? Ha ha ha!" laughed Falco at the sight of Pit Jan in his underwear. "Oh my darling Nakşıgül, light of my life!"

QUESTION 66
WHAT IF HE KNEW?

After all the violence of the rebellion, the wise words of Ahmet Dede were as welcome to Falco's soul as the compassion of a loving mother and made him understand how much he had missed the Mevlevi Lodge. He felt fortunate to be seeing Pharmacist Dede, Boilermaker Dede and the other brothers again after four months. Perhaps he should come back and renew his vow to disrobe, because there were friends here that he loved. So many of the people he cared about in Istanbul had been beaten up and taken away during that autumn of fire, pillage, conflict and violence but, mercifully, the tranquillity of life at the Mevlevi Lodge had not changed. However, he was unable to see Süleyman Nahifi Efendi, because he was attending the funeral of Poet Nedim. What a sensitive, free-living and unconventional poet Nedim had been. Falco recalled how he would create lines that warbled like girlish laughter, inspired by colours and smells, melodies and witticisms, entertainments and games, or conversations over halva on winter evenings at Çırağan and Sadabat. That man, who had never found anyone in whom he could confide the sorrows that filled his generous soul, left behind not only gazels and songs, but delicious memories of libidinous laughter, rosebud lips and pink tulips. According to the rumours circulating at the Mevlevi Lodge, when the rebels broke down his door in Beşiktaşı, he had climbed up to the roof of his house in an inebriated state and thrown himself off. Falco recalled the last couplet of the gazel that had been on everyone's tongue the previous year:

O Nedim, wild nightingale, why now in hiding?
What follies and scandal for us you did sing.

On his way out of Mevlevi Lodge, while the brethren were preparing for the noon invocation, Falco went into Poet Nahifi's room and left a small, grubby pouch on the pillow. It was one of three pouches that had been unearthed from the Lodge burial ground that morning and it contained a pear-shaped emerald. Falco knew that Poet Nahifi would ask no questions but use it to help pay for the expenses of the Lodge.

Just that morning, Pit Jan had said he could find Falco's pearls if he was taken to the burial ground because, by the time the third rat was tossed into his sack, Tiny Çaker had started to talk. He had told Pit Jan that twenty paces after entering the burial ground he would find the grave of a sea captain in the corner on the left.

"It's a sarcophagus," Tiny Çaker had said, "On top is an engraving of a broken galleon mask with a sail attached."

Despite Falco's doubts, the grave was exactly as described and underneath it he had found the pearls and two other pouches. Reading the epitaph on the tomb, which certainly belonged to a seaman, Falco remembered his mother. He had not been to her grave for a long time. She too had had her life cut off in her prime, just like this seaman. Perhaps that was why he had decided to visit the Mevlevi Lodge and leave behind the emerald. As he left the lodge, he checked that the other two pouches were safe and, feeling pleased to have done the right thing, urged his horse into a trot and then a gallop.

Falco wanted to reach the Galata jetty before Hourikin. If everything was going to plan, she should have left Judge İshak, having entrusted him with ensuring that the treasure retrieved from Binbirdirek Cistern was in safe hands. Judge İshak would not only believe her, he would be discreet. There was no way of knowing which Istanbul merchants and wealthy citizens, many of whom had long since disappeared in the depths of the Golden Horn, were the rightful owners of the hoard of ingots accumulated by Tiny Çaker. The only place for it was in the treasury of the Ottoman Empire and Hourikin would see to that.

Falco rode cheerfully through the streets of Istanbul, greeting everyone he encountered. Now that life had returned to normal, riding a horse in the city was once again a privilege reserved only for senior dignitaries. Even riding on the bridge could lead to arrest. Falco decided to leave his horse at Azapkapısı, from where he ran to the jetty.

Hafız Çelebi and Stocky Yeye were standing at the entrance to the bridge. Hafız Çelebi was looking pale and fragile, and leaning heavily on Yeye. Pit Jan was there to say his goodbyes, but there was still half an hour before the anchor was raised. As Falco approached them, they looked at him with raised eyebrows, looking for a sign that he had found the pearls. Falco responded with a nod and a smile. Now they were just waiting for Hourikin to come across the bridge from Istanbul.

"She should be here by now."

"Yes, let's hope everything went to plan."

"Of course it did!"

Within a few minutes, they saw her. She was demurely dressed in a long street overcoat. Falco stepped forward and was about to embrace her, but suddenly hesitated and averted his gaze as Hourikin bowed her head. Yeye and Hafız Çelebi smiled in amusement, understanding the reason for their embarrassment.

"Oh, come on! Let's talk one last time before we part," said Pit Jan, coming to the rescue.

They withdrew to a corner behind some bales bound up with netting ready for loading on to ships.

"I'm getting old," said Pit Jan, with the wistfulness of a man saying his last goodbye. "I doubt if I'll be able to come and see the Touch of Life flower next spring. If I had two lives, I would love to spend one of them in Istanbul. Despite everything, there are still good reasons to live in this city. Yeye, the tulips are now in your hands! When you create a new tulip, send a bulb to me on this ship so that I never forget you. This pouch contains a down payment for all the bulbs you're going to send me. And this one is for Şehnaz's dowry."

To everyone's astonishment, Pit Jan produced one small and one large pouch from his pocket and quickly put them into Stocky Yeye's hands.

"My dear Yeye," continued Pit Jan, before anyone could object, "this is a small recompense for your lost youth and all that Aslan Ağa stole from you. Please, take it. Don't be embarrassed. As for you, Houri, if I had had a son, I would have let him take no bride other than you. If you wish to board this ship with me, I will marry you to a fine nobleman. However, if you wish to remain here, take these earrings and buttons to remember me by."

"Pit Jan Efendi! Have you been plundering Tiny Çaker's treasure?" joked Hourikin, looking in amazement at the large diamond earrings and chrysolite buttons in her hands. "We'll have to inform Judge İshak Efendi about this!"

"I must go, otherwise the ship will sail without me again!" said Pit Jan.

They all laughed.

"And of course, I managed to retrieve your house," said Pit Jan to Falco with a meaningful look, as if to say that any objection was out of the question. "Count it as a souvenir of your mother and hold your wedding there!"

Hourikin turned away to look at the ship. With all this talk of weddings, she did not want to meet the gaze of Falco, who had not been told whether Nakşıgül was alive. Perhaps he should never be told. If she were alive, who knew in which palace she would be living or how many children she had? And there were other things he had not been told. Would he want to know that he was a prince? What if he knew that her purpose in life had been to ensure his survival? What if he knew that, before her death his mother had given Hourikin's father thirty large pearls and made him vow to protect her son and never disclose to him that he was a prince. What if Falco found out that her father had indeed protected him, but never touched the pearls? What if she now handed him the pearls that her father had entrusted to her on his deathbed two years ago? What if he knew that she had arranged for an oarsman to ram his boat into the skiff carrying Falco in the Golden Horn and had paid thirty gold pieces to Lanky Osman for his help? What if he knew that she had been the woman who screamed and distracted the Prison Custodian just as he was about to arrest Falco in the market? What if he knew that she was the unidentified person who had knocked out the man holding a dagger at the Envoys' Caravanserai, not to mention countless other things he knew nothing about? She wondered if he had heard the proverb "If we cannot have the one we love, we have to settle for the one we have". Would he ever want to be known as Prince Ahmet or Sultan Ahmet IV? If so, would he even like the name Ahmet given to him by his mother? What if…? What if…?

Hourikin realised that, other than Judge İshak and herself, no one else remained who knew that Falco was Prince Ahmet and, after what had happened to him, she was certain that Judge İshak would never tell the new sultan and grand vizier anything about this prince. Patrona Halil had not only deposed Sultan Ahmet, but unwittingly had also precluded any claims by Prince Ahmet. With these thoughts running through her head, Hourikin did not see Falco's quizzical expression, nor did she hear his response to the mention of a wedding or his account of what he had done with the gold.

"You'll miss your ship, Pit Jan Efendi," was all Hourikin could say as she turned back towards the others.

"I hope he does!" said Hafız Çelebi.

"My dear Hafız Çelebi, as you know I missed it four days ago, but another one came. If I miss this one, yet another will come. But from now on, I want to be monitoring ships that are sailing to Istanbul, not from Istanbul, so that I can send you one of my twin tulips. My dearest friend, you Muslims say 'Go with my blessing!' Well, I want you to say this to me. If ever they accept me in your paradise, I shall come and visit you there. Otherwise, you must come and visit me, because I shall miss you deeply."

Pit Jan leant on the rails of the ship flying the Flemish flag and bound for Amsterdam. Its sails billowed as the ship turned towards Seraglio Point. He gazed at Istanbul for the last time, already yearning for it, and tears flowed from his eyes on to the precious pearl and emerald necklace in his large hands, where the moisture was absorbed by with the warmth of the emeralds and the translucency of the pearls. Meanwhile, on the quayside, his friends were gazing at him with damp eyes, knowing that they would never meet again. No one saw Falco take a pearl from his armband and press it into Hourikin's palm, and no one noticed the translucent tears in Hourikin's eyes.

EPILOLGUE

That is the end of the narrative entitled *One Murder, Sixty-six Questions* which I bought at the auction and, with some editing, have been sharing with you. I said at the beginning that I had never managed to find a copy of this book in any library. However, my curiosity about what happened to Hafız Çelebi led me to some Ottoman archives. Although I have still not found anything that relates to this story, I found some information about our heroes that was written by Suphi Efendi, a historian of the time. I present it here, in case it is of interest to you:

Fasihi was a poet of this era who wrote many verses about the rebellion. There were also numerous judicial cases in the Cadi records. In particular, there was a story in verse by an anonymous poet about Sultan Ahmet III and others who were brought down during the rebellion. The story circulated for years. It was recited to large, emotional audiences in Istanbul, Anatolia and Rumelia, and was published by Muteferrika İbrahim Efendi, who had to reprint the book within two months. The names of Hafız Çelebi and Yearning Yusuf appeared frequently in later horticultural circulars and tulip journals, but according to the records, the Tyrian Dwarf was not grown again for another twenty-five years.

After Sultan Ahmet III was deposed, he spent the last six years of his life trying to forget his fate by writing gazels and verses under the pseudonym Necib. He always regretted the day he made his daughter a widow.

Sultan Mahmut I ruled the Ottoman Empire for twenty-five years. It was said that on certain spring nights, the breezes carried the strains of his violin across to the shores of Scutari. He also wrote poetry and took an interest in fine calligraphy.

Supreme Judge İshak remained in his post for three years after the rebellion. He instructed divers to comb the seabed of the three deep sections of the Golden Horn and solved all the murders that had been perpetrated before the rebellion. Later, he was made Sheikh ul-Islam. No one ever discovered the origin of the gold bullion used to put Sultan Mahmut I on the throne.

Although Patrona Halil was indeed an upright man, his colleagues were disreputable. Sultan Mahmut I invited him and his men to the palace for a sham robing ceremony, at the end of which Patrona Halil was taken to Revan Pavilion, while his colleagues, including Muslu Beşe and Master Coffee Maker Ali, were taken to Aslanhane, where they were hacked to pieces and their corpses thrown out in front of the Imperial Gate. After that, the Sultan had the traitorous Preacher İspirizade, Admiral of the Fleet Abdi Pasha and Cadi İbrahim Efendi drowned.

Pit Jan sold two of the necklaces he took from Tiny Çaker's hoard and used the money to buy extensive tracts of land in

Flanders, where he planted the bulbs he took with him from Istanbul to cultivate tulips in memory of Hafız Çelebi. His brilliant tulip specimens sparked off the craze for tulips in Holland. Pit Jan continued sending a double tulip bulb to Istanbul every year until his death. His albums of tulip drawings were later regarded as among the most valuable collections in the Flemish royal library.

Şehnaz was still very young, as was Stocky Yeye, but they married and had their first child within a year.

Apart from wanting Yeye to have a good education, Hafız Çelebi had longed for a grandchild and, on the evening that he cradled Yeye's daughter for the first time, he passed away. He left everything to Yeye, including the secret of the turtles.

Veyis Ağa was ruined as a result of the pillaging that took place during the revolution. Stocky Yeye did not send him to Haseki Asylum, but took care of him and Şehnaz's mother for many years, although he was never able to address them as mother and father. He studied the hadith at Ayasofya Madrasa for three years and produced five generations of Touch of Life. Ten years later, he was made Chairman of the Tulip Commission and became well known among horticulturalists as Yearning Yusuf Ağa. Every year, he sent a letter and two tulip bulbs to Pit Jan. The only times that he annoyed Şehnaz was when he sat up all night by the pool talking about the old days with Falco. When he was alone, he would remember Hafız Çelebi saying "It's time to plant the tulips, my son! Let's hope we can produce the Touch of Life next spring!"

As for Hourikin, there was no mention of her in the Three Crescent Society records.

And Falco...?